Blades

of Grass

00701

Fiction from Modern China

This series is intended to showcase new and exciting works by China's finest contemporary novelists in fresh, authoritative translations. It represents innovative recent fiction by some of the boldest new voices in China today as well as classic works of this century by internationally acclaimed novelists. Bringing together writers from several geographical areas and from a range of cultural and political milieus, the series opens new doors to twentieth-century China.

Howard Goldblatt

General Editor

General Editor, Howard Goldblatt

BLADES OF GRASS

GRASS

The Stories of Lao She

Translated from the Chinese
by William A. Lyell
and Sarah Wei-ming Chen

University of Hawai'i Press

Honolulu

Publication information for individual stories is provided on pp. 309–310.

Library of Congress Cataloging-in-Publication Data

Lao, She, 1899–1966.
[Short stories. English. Selections]
Blades of grass : the stories of Lao She / translated from the Chinese
by William A. Lyell and Sarah Wei-ming Chen :
general editor, Howard Goldblatt.
p.   cm.
Includes bibliographical references.
ISBN 0–8248–1506–8 (alk. paper). —
ISBN 0–8248–1803–2 (paper : alk. paper)
1. Lao, She, 1899–1966—Translations into English. I. Lyell, William A.
II. Chen, Sarah Wei-ming, 1952– III. Goldblatt, Howard, 1939–
IV. Title. V. Title: Stories of Lao She.
PL2804.C5A26   1999
895.1'351—dc21   99–11832
CIP

This book has been published with the aid of a grant from the
Center for East Asian Studies, Stanford University.

Designed by Barbara Pope Book Design
based on the series design by Richard Hendel

Printed by Maple-Vail Book Manufacturing Group

Even though what we possessed didn't relieve us from our poverty, it did provide us that stability that made each blade of grass and each tree come alive in our hearts. At the very least, it made me a small blade of grass always securely rooted to its own turf. All that I am began here. My character was molded and cast here.

Autobiography of a Minor Character

Contents

The Grand Opening

Wang, Qiu,[1] and I scraped up some money and opened a small hospital. Wang's wife—a woman who had, through marriage, promoted herself from ordinary nurse to doctor's wife—was to be our head nurse. Qiu's father-in-law would serve as combination accountant and business manager. Wang and I had it all worked out: if Qiu's father-in-law falsified the accounts or absconded with the funds, then Wang and I would give the son-in-law a good working over. In other words Qiu would serve as a living bond for his father-in-law. Wang and I formed a solid pair. After all, the hospital had been our idea in the first place and it was only later that we invited Qiu into the deal. We'd have to keep an eye on him.

No matter what kind of business you undertake and no matter how few people are involved, you just have to split up into cliques and factions—otherwise it won't look as though you're taking the whole thing very seriously, right? At any rate we had the sides all figured out in advance, and if it ever got to the point where we had to work Qiu over, then—including Wang's wife on our side—we'd have the advantage on him by three to one. His father-in-law, of course, would probably help him, but he was so old that Mrs. Wang could probably clean his clock all by herself.

Translated by William A. Lyell

To give the devil his due, Qiu was quite talented in his specialty—piles. It was an absolute pleasure to see that man turned loose with a knife. That's why we invited him into the deal in the first place, but if he started acting up, we'd just have to forget his surgical skills and give him a good trouncing.

I would be in charge of Internal Medicine; Wang would take care of Venereal Diseases; Qiu would do piles and run Surgery on the side; and Mrs. Wang would take care of Obstetrics as well as serve as our head nurse. Altogether, we'd have four departments. I can, in all honesty, state that we planned to run the department of Internal Medicine as an open and aboveboard affair (a penny's worth of medicine for every penny a patient spent) and, consequently, we didn't plan to make anything on it. It was on piles that we expected to rake it in. In other words, all our hopes were pinned on Wang and Qiu. They were the real stars; Wang's wife and I were only members of the supporting cast. She was no doctor to begin with, but she *did* have some experience in obstetrics—after all, she'd had two kids. However, when it came to actual obstetrical skills—well, at any rate, if *I* had a wife, Wang's wife would never lay a hand on her. But no matter what her qualifications were, we just had to have a department of Obstetrics. Babies are too much of a moneymaking racket to pass up. Even when a birth goes smoothly, a woman is likely to stay ten to fifteen days. You can get away with feeding them some broth and a bit of rice, and then every day they stay, you pocket a day's profit. And if the birth doesn't go smoothly—well, you can always cross that bridge when you come to it. When he's got to, a man will do what a man's got to do—never heard of anyone drowning in his own piss, did you?

The day finally arrived and we were in business! The words *Hospital of the Masses* had already been appearing in various newspapers around the city for over half a month. The name was well chosen, too. No matter what kind of moneymaking deal you're involved in these days, it just won't do to forget the masses. If you're not going to rake in *their* money, whose money are you going to take in? Isn't that the truth? Of course in the text of the ad itself we didn't put it *quite* that way: the masses are not particularly fond of hearing the truth. The way we phrased was

**SACRIFICING FOR THE MASSES;
STRIVING FOR THEIR HEALTH**

**TECHNIQUES UP TO THE LEVEL OF SCIENCE;
FEES DOWN TO THE LEVEL OF THE MASSES**

CONVERSANT WITH THE MEDICAL ARTS OF EAST AND WEST

CLASS PREJUDICES CAST ASIDE IN ALL OUR MEDICAL ARTS

All in all, our advertising expenses were pretty high and took quite a bite out of our capital. But we knew it was money well spent; for once we had succeeded in luring the masses through the door, we could fleece them at our leisure.

Judging solely on the basis of our ad, no one could have possibly guessed the actual size of our hospital. It *seemed* to be a large, three-story building. But if the truth were known, we only occupied six rooms on the first floor. The rest of it belonged to a freight company, but we included the whole complex in the photograph.

At last we got under way. During the first week, we saw quite a few patients in the outpatient clinic—honest-to-god representatives of the masses, every last one of them. We singled out those who looked as though they might have a little more money than the others and then, no matter what they were suffering from, gave them different kinds of soda water that we passed off as medicine. We dawdled on for about a week like this, without ripping anyone one off *too* much—you can't bleed a stone. As for those representatives of the masses who looked *hopelessly* poor, well, we didn't even give them soda water. I'd usually tell them that they were too dirty to take medicine. What good will medicine do you if you don't have a clean face? I'd tell them to go back home, wash up, and come back again—someday.

One evening, after a full day of being up to our ears in the masses, we held an emergency meeting. We decided we'd never make it big doing a volume business with the great unwashed masses. We'd have to think of some way of luring in the not-*quite*-so-mass masses. We were sorry that we'd called the place Hospital of the Masses in the first place. We were getting the masses, all right, but the unwashed clods were scaring off all the rich people! Now, how can you make any money like that? A hospital is not a kerosene company: everybody uses kerosene, but how many people go to the hospital? Had we been aware of this important truth sooner, we'd have called our place Hospital of the Aristocrats. I'd lost count of how many times I'd seen Qiu sterilize his knife in happy anticipation, but still no one came to have piles removed. After all, it's the rich who get piles, and a rich piles-sufferer is not about to come to a Hospital of the Masses to have them hacked off.

Wang finally came up with a plan. First thing in the morning we'd rent a car. We'd take turns and make a whole bunch of trips. He'd bring over a grandmother and I'd bring in an aunt. As soon as we drove up to the front door in that car, a couple of nurses would pop right out and help with whatever relative we happened to drag along. After thirty or forty trips like that, people were *bound* to be impressed. Neighbors, cops, passersby, whoever—they'd all be bowled over. We really started to admire old Wang.

"We'll rent a few cars that aren't even fit to drive, too," Wang added.

"What for?" I couldn't quite figure that one out.

"Well, I've worked it out with the garage, and they'll let us rent a few real cheap that are in for repairs. We'll park them outside and then every so often we'll set them to honking. All that racket's bound to attract a lot of attention. Every time they sound off, our patients are going to think that another batch of fellow sufferers has just arrived by car. And when passers-by see all those cars out there, will they be snowed or won't they? Think about it."

We proceeded according to plan and started hauling over relatives the very next day. We'd keep them for a cup of tea and then drive them home again. We stationed two nurses outside and they helped the "patients" in as fast as they arrived. We kept a steady stream of bodies flowing back and forth through that front door all day. At the crack of dawn, the garage hauled over the dead heaps and parked them outside. We had them do a round of honking about once every five minutes. Someone got a camera, and we had to chase off the neighborhood kids who had been attracted by the hubbub so that we could get a good shot of the cars. We managed to get the picture put in the evening paper over a blurb done by Qiu's father-in-law. The old man really outdid himself with a formal and elegant old-fashioned essay, in which he described the magnificent pageantry of the automobile traffic in front of our hospital. That night none of us was able to eat a bite. A solid day of honking had been a bit much—most of us felt like throwing up.

You really had to give Wang credit, for the very next morning as soon as we opened our doors, a car appeared and an army officer stepped out. Poor Wang was in such a hurry to get out to greet him that he forgot how low our front door was. It was quite a lump he raised, but he didn't seem to mind a bit. He was so happy at the prospect of a V.D. patient that he probably wouldn't have noticed had someone taken a club and raised six or seven more.

After exchanging a few words with the officer, Wang prepared a shot of 606.² Our two pretty nurses opened up his uniform and before long, four, soft, warm, feminine hands supported and comforted the wounded warrior. Wang's wife came over and tapped the place where the needle was to go in with her chubby little index finger. Wang shoved the needle in. Oblivious to everything but the two nurses, the officer eyed them and observed, "Out of this world! Wild!"

"Give him another for good measure," I opined from the sidelines. But Qiu had apparently arrived at that idea long before I did. I saw the dollar signs dancing in his eyes as he approached with a second shot. I could tell by the color of the liquid in the syringe that Qiu was probably preparing to do his bit for the cause with a mixture of jasmine tea and salt. Wang also noticed Qiu zeroing in and told the nurses to hold the officer's arm. Wang's wife came over right on cue and pressed down on the spot where the needle was to go in with her chubby little index finger. *Zap!* Just like that and he had a shot of jasmine in him.

The officer just stared at the nurses and kept saying, "Wild!" Wang was now really caught up in the tempo of things and, bursting with enthusiasm, gave him still *another* shot as if by reflex. Judging from the looks of it, I think that that one was probably Dragon Well. At our hospital we were very fussy about our tea, you know, and always had two kinds steeping. We took twenty-five dollars for the double shot of tea and single shot of 606. Actually, at ten dollars a pop, we should have charged him thirty, but since he'd bought three shots at a clip, we gave him a five-dollar break. We told him to come back in a few days and guaranteed that we'd have him completely cured after ten visits. "No matter how it goes," I thought to myself, "we've got the tea to cover it."

After forking over his money, it seemed the officer couldn't tear himself away. Wang and I started to chat with him. I praised his courage in not trying to keep his V.D. a secret. I rambled on about how when you've got it, you ought to get help right away just as he had. Since he'd come to *our* place to treat it, I guaranteed there would be no complications. I even assured him that V.D. was an affliction common to great men, something to be proud of. When you get it, make sure to treat it, that's all—a few shots of 606 and that's that. Everything's all right as long as you don't act like those store clerks or high school students who get a touch of it and then try to keep it a secret. They'll go to any old quack as long as he keeps his mouth shut. You'll see them around the city every now and then skulking down dark alleys to buy black-market drugs. Ads for quack treatments are pasted up in all the public latrines, too. It's all designed to fleece people. I told him that suckers who go to quacks are bound to come to a sorry end.

The officer agreed with everything I said. He told me he had been to V.D. clinics over twenty times already, and none of his past experiences had been as agreeable as this one. When I didn't respond, Wang picked up the conversation. He went even farther overboard than I had. Said that as long as a man remembered to pump in a little 606, V.D. ought not be counted a disease at all. The officer seemed to be in total agreement with Wang's position as well. Even brought forth some anecdotal evidence of his own in corroboration. Said that was exactly the reason he himself never bothered to wait until completely cured before going back for another round at the houses. After all, it was just a question of a few more shots of 606.

Wang, who was not about to pass up the chance of pulling in a steady customer, saw nothing wrong with this. He told the officer that if he wanted to come on a long-term basis, he'd give him half off on the 606. Bring the price down to five bucks a shot. Or if he'd rather do it by the month, then Wang was prepared to take him on for a hundred a month no matter *how* many shots he took. Just as Wang was about to close the deal, the officer came up with a condition: we'd have to provide the same pretty nurses to support him under the arms while he was given his shots. Neither of us was foolish enough to promise him that outright; we just smiled and nodded our heads. He seemed to take that as our pledge.

The officer's car had no more than pulled away when another pulled up. Four personal maids helped an old matron out. As soon as they were all clear of the car, five mouths asked with a single voice, "Do you have any *special* rooms?" I pushed one of the maids aside, took the old dear gently by the wrist, and helped her into our little hospital. I pointed in the direction of the freight company, and said, "The special rooms are all filled, but you're still in luck. Right back here"—I pointed toward the few rooms we occupied on the first floor—"we still have two first-class rooms that are vacant. For the time being, why don't you take both of them? Actually they're even more comfortable than the ones upstairs. Besides, it will spare you the trouble of running up and down all those steps. Isn't that right, granny?"

The old lady's first words blossomed like a flower in my heart. "Ah, now *you* sound like a doctor. If a patient wasn't interested in comfort, why would she go to the hospital in the first place? Those idiots over at the Eastern Life just don't realize that."

"Why you poor dear! Do you mean to say you actually went to the Eastern Life ?" You should have caught the astonishment I was able to load into my voice.

"Just came from there. Bastards!"

Taking advantage of the head of steam she was building up in cursing out the doctors at the Eastern Life, I supported the old dear into a small room. To tell the truth, the Eastern Life is one of the biggest and best hospitals around, but I could tell that unless I enthusiastically joined her in her attack on it,

I'd never get her to stay in such a tiny room. "How long were you there?"

"Only two days, but it nearly cost me my life." The old girl sat down on the tiny bed. I propped up the edge of it with my leg. Our beds are all in good shape—don't get me wrong—but you have to admit that they are getting along in years and sometimes collapse if you don't keep an eye on them. "How in the world did you come to go there?" I didn't dare let my tongue lie down for a rest, otherwise the old girl would be certain to notice my leg.

"Let's not even talk about it. The mere mention of it is enough to make me chew nails! Just think, doctor! There I was, suffering from a stomach ailment, and they wouldn't give me anything to eat!" She was on the verge of tears.

"Didn't give you anything to eat!" I popped my eyes out in amazement. "There you were, poor dear, suffering from a stomach ailment, and *they* wouldn't even give you a bite to eat! Quacks! Charlatans! Why, just on the basis of your age alone—you must be eighty or so, aren't you?"

Any trace of tears immediately disappeared. Smiling coyly, she said, "I'm still young. I've just turned fifty-eight."

"Ah, just my own mother's age. Sometimes her stomach bothers her, too." I rubbed my eyes. "Why don't you stay here with me, granny? I guarantee that I'll cure you of your little indisposition in no time. And since the secret to curing this kind of illness depends entirely on good nourishment, you can eat whenever you want. When you've had a good meal, you *feel* better, and that in itself does you a lot of good. Am I right, granny?"

The old woman's tears had returned to her eyes now, but this time they were tears of gratitude. "Just think of the situation I was in, doctor. I just had to get something solid into my stomach, but those clowns over at Eastern Life insisted that I have nothing but rice gruel. They seemed to go out of their way to provoke me."

"You've got a good set of teeth; they should have given you something solid to sink them into." My voice was solemn.

"I kept getting hungry every little bit, but they simply refused to feed me until the regular mealtime."

"Idiots!"

"In the middle of the night when I'd just gotten to sleep, they'd shove a glass stick under my tongue and then start running off at the mouth about wanting to see how many degrees of something or other I had."

"They've lost all sense of proportion over there!"

"I'd ask for the bedpan and the nurses would tell me to wait. They'd say the doctor was coming and I couldn't have it until he'd made his rounds."

"Hanging's too good for them!"

"I'd struggle my way to a sitting position and the nurse would come and tell me to lie down."

"Bitch!"

As we continued to chat, the old lady and I hit it off better and better all the time. Even if the room had been the size of a matchbox, she still wouldn't have left. "What the hell?" I thought to myself as I took my leg out from under the edge of the bed. "Even if the bed does collapse now, she'll forgive us."

"Do you have nurses here, too?" the old dear asked.

"Yes, but don't you let that worry you one little bit." I put on my best smile and leaned closer. "Didn't you bring four maids with you? Well, we'll just let them stay in the hospital, too. It's only natural that your own people would know how to take care of you better than our nurses. We'll just forget any talk about nurses if that's all right with you."

"Nothing could please me more, but are you sure you have room for all my maids?" The old girl seemed slightly embarrassed at putting us to so much inconvenience.

"Oh, I'm sure we'll be able to come up with something. Why don't you just reserve this whole wing of our little hospital for yourself? Then you'll have room to bring your own cook in, too. He's bound to know your favorite dishes better than we do. Tell you what. I'll only charge for your room. The maids and cook can stay free. Let's see . . . all in all we can arrange the whole thing for . . . let's say fifty dollars a day."

The old girl heaved a sigh of relief. "The money doesn't matter, doctor. We'll do just as you suggest. Spring Fragrance, you go back and fetch the cook. Tell him to bring two ducks while you're at it."

I could have kicked myself. Why, oh why, had I only asked for fifty? I felt like giving myself a good crack across the mouth. Fortunately I hadn't said that the fifty included medicine. OK then, we'd make it up on the medicine. At any rate, judging from the way the old bat came across, she was pretty rich. Might even have a son who was a divisional commander in the army. Besides, if her own cook came and she started wolfing down Peking roast duck every day, she'd be with us quite a while. To get along in this world, you have to take the long view of things.

Now our hospital was really beginning to look like something. Four maids were constantly shuttling back and forth through the door and the cook was out in the courtyard piling bricks into a stove at the foot of the wall, as though preparing for a wedding feast in the house of some fat cat. Our hospital staff didn't stand on ceremony, either. We really enjoyed the exotic fruits that the old girl bought and her ducks were pretty good, too. Somehow or other in all the excitement, none of us remembered to give her an examination. Our meager powers of attention were taken up with guessing what delicacy the old dear would buy next.

No matter how you looked at it, Wang and I were in business, but poor old Qiu didn't seem to know what to do with himself. Since he always had a scalpel in hand, I avoided him as much as possible. Not going to practice on me! He was in such a high state of tension that Wang kept trying to calm him down. But it was to no avail, for Qiu was a very competitive sort of guy. Wouldn't be content until he, too, had made fifty bucks or so for our hospital. I admired his spirit!

After lunch someone—fat, fortyish, with quite a potbelly— came to see about piles. At first Mrs. Wang thought it was somebody for the baby ward. On closer inspection, however, she discovered that this patient was of the male persuasion. She yielded the poor unfortunate to Qiu, whose eyes had turned red at the prospect of a profit. Before many words were wasted on either side, his scalpel flashed through the air. Fat-and-forty screamed with pain and begged for some anesthetic, but our old Qiu was not born yesterday. "Anesthetic? We didn't say anything about anesthetic when you came in. I've got some, but it'll cost you another ten dollars. Well, do you want it or not? Make up your mind!" Fatty was too stunned by the pain to react.

Qiu gave him a quick shot and, in less time than it takes to tell, his scalpel was flashing through the air again. Suddenly he stopped. "Hey, wait a minute. You've got them on the inside, too. When you came in just now we didn't say anything about inside ones. Do you want me to remove them, too? It'll cost you an extra thirty. If you don't want to spend the money, we'll call it a day right here."

I was watching from the sidelines and when I caught old Qiu's eyes, I held up my thumb. He was really something else. Fleecing a man when you had his back to the wall—does it get any better than that?! Little fatso didn't put up an argument. Probably in no condition to. It was a real joy to see Qiu's blade in action. He wasn't doing too badly with his tongue, either, for all the while he was cutting, he was advertising our hospital as well. "Let me tell you right now, this little operation that I'm performing on you is easily worth two hundred dollars, but we won't charge you that because we don't like to take advantage of people. All that we ask is that when you leave, you pass around the good word about our little establishment. We're sanitary, too. Even if you looked at this scalpel of mine with a forty-five thousand power microscope, you wouldn't be able to find any microbes on it. By the way, you ought to drop in again tomorrow to let me check on the healing." Fatso didn't let out a peep. I figured he was probably in shock.

So Qiu had brought us in a little bundle of cash, too! That evening we bought some wine to celebrate and got the old woman's cook to prepare a few delectables to go along with it. For the most part we had him use her stuff in preparing the dishes. And while we feasted, we discussed the future of our little enterprise. We decided that, first of all, we'd add an abortion clinic and a wing for helping opium smokers kick the habit. Wang suggested we let the word get around that we'd give physicals without being overly strict. If a student wanted to take an entrance exam or a man wanted to take out life insurance, then we'd provide a clean bill of health even if the guy had already bought his burial clothes and casket. All we'd insist on is that he fork over the five-dollar fee. Wang's proposal carried without opposition.

Toward the end of the celebration Qiu's father-in-law came forward with a suggestion: he wanted us all to chip in a few dollars and buy one of those old-fashioned business plaques with our name on it. Old people always come up with the same old ideas, but since his heart was in the right place, none of us felt like disputing him. He had already decided on the four characters that he wanted on the plaque: KIND HEART; KIND HANDS—a bit corny perhaps, but appropriate.

We decided to let him go to the early market the next morning and look for a sign. Wang's wife suggested that once we had the sign painted, we could wait until a wedding procession passed by to hang it out. While the band at the head of the procession was playing, we'd hang out our sign with borrowed pomp and thus avoid the cost of having to organize any kind of ceremony ourselves. When you think about it, you've got to admit women are sometimes a lot sharper than men. Beaming at his wife, Wang looked proud as a peacock.

Notes

1. Say the *"chee"* in *cheer* and the *"oe"* in *toe* together: *chee-oe*. Say it so fast that you collapse it into a single syllable and you will have something very close to *"Qiu."*

2. Arsphenamine, or "606," was widely used in the treatment of venereal disease before the discovery of penicillin.

An Old and Established Name

After Manager Qian left, Xin Dezhi—the senior apprentice who now had quite a hand in the operation of the Fortune Silk Store—went for several days without eating a decent meal.[1] Manager Qian had been universally recognized as an old and skilled hand in the silk business, just as the Fortune Silk Store was universally recognized as an old and established name. Xin Dezhi had been trained for the business under the hands of Manager Qian. However, it wasn't solely personal feeling that made him take it so hard when Manager Qian left, nor was his agitation due to any personal ambition that might have been stimulated by the vague possibility that he himself might become the new manager. He really couldn't put his finger on the reason for all the anxiety that he felt. But it was as though Manager Qian had taken away with him something that could never be recovered.

When Manager Zhou[2] arrived to take things over, Xin Dezhi realized that his anxiety had not been unfounded. Previously he had only felt sorrow at the departure of the old manager, but now he felt downright fury at the arrival of the new one. Manager Zhou was a hustler. The Fortune—that old and established name of years standing!—now demeaned itself by employing every trick in the trade to rope customers in. Xin Dezhi's mouth hung so far open in dismay that you might have taken his face for a dumpling that had split apart while boiling. *An old and skilled hand in the silk business . . . an old and established name . . . old rules*—all had vanished with Manager Qian, perhaps never to return. Manager Qian had been honest and gentlemanly, so much so, in fact, that the Fortune lost money. The owners, for their part, found such uprightness less than impressive. Their only concern was having dividends to split up at the end of the year. Hence, they had let him go.

For as long as anyone could remember, the Fortune Silk Store had maintained an air of cultured elegance. On the outside there was a simple sign with the name of the store in black characters against a gold background; and inside the shop itself there were simple green fixtures, a black counter covered with blue cotton cloth, large square stools sheathed in blue wool, and fresh flowers always set out on the tea table. For as long as anyone could remember, except for hanging out four lanterns with big red tassels on the occasion of the Lantern Festival, the Fortune Silk Store had never exhibited the least trace of that vulgar ostentation so prevalent among ordinary merchants. For as long as anyone could remember, the Fortune had never engaged in such base practices as haggling with customers or letting them pay to the nearest dollar, or pasting advertisements all over town, or running two-week sales. What the Fortune sold was its old and established name. For as long as anyone could remember, the Fortune had never set free cigarettes out on the counter as a customer come-on; nor had any of the shop's apprentices ever spoken in loud tones; the only sound ever to be heard in the store was the gentle gurgle of the manager's water pipe intermingled with his occasional coughing.

As soon as Manager Zhou walked through the door, Xin Dezhi saw only too clearly that these precedents, as well as many other old and valuable customs, were all going to come to an end. There was something improper about the new manager's eyes. He never lowered the lids, but rather swept the whole world with his gaze as if searching out a thief. Manager Qian, on the other hand, had always sat on a stool with his eyes closed, and yet if any of the apprentices made the slightest misstep, he was instantly aware of it.

Just as Xin Dezhi had feared, within a few days Manager Zhou had transformed the Fortune into something akin to a carnival sideshow. In front of the main entrance the new manager set up a garish sign proclaiming GIANT SALE. Each word was five feet high. Then he installed two bright gaslights, whose flames lit up faces in such a way as to turn them green. As if all this weren't enough, right there by the main entrance he stationed a drummer and a bugler, whose cacophonous racket began at dawn and didn't cease until the third watch at night. Four apprentices in red hats roamed up and down the sidewalk passing out handbills to anyone who came within their reach.

But for Manager Zhou that still wasn't enough; he appointed two clerks to the specific task of providing customers with cigarettes and tea. Even someone buying as little as a half foot of plain cloth would be dragged to the back counter and invited to light up. Soldiers, street cleaners, and waitresses stood about firing up their tobacco until the Fortune was so filled with smoke that one might have taken it for a Buddhist temple immersed in a cloud of burning incense. Manager Zhou went a step farther: if a customer bought so little as a single foot of material, he'd throw in an extra one free, along with a foreign doll to take home for the kids. And now all the apprentices were expected to joke and make small talk with the customers. If a customer wanted something the store didn't have, then the apprentice wasn't to tell him right out that the store didn't stock it, but rather was expected to drag out something else and force the customer to take a look at that. Any order over ten dollars would be personally delivered by one of the apprentices. Manager Zhou bought two broken-down bicycles for that.

Xin Dezhi longed to find someplace where he could have a good cry. In fifteen or sixteen years of faithful service he had never even imagined, much less expected to see, the Fortune come to such a pass. How could he look people in the eye? In the past who on the whole street had not held the Fortune in high regard? When an apprentice hung out the lantern that served as the store's sign at night, even the policemen on the beat would treat him with special consideration. And remember that year when the soldiers came? To be sure, during the pillaging, the Fortune had been cleaned out just like the other stores, but the shop doors and the signs saying "We Never Go Back on Our Prices" had not been torn away as had been the case with some of the neighboring shops. Yes, that golden plaque bearing the inscription Fortune Silk Store was invested with a certain awe-inspiring dignity.

Xin Dezhi had already lived in the city now for twenty-odd years and fifteen or sixteen of them had been spent in the Fortune. In fact, it was his second home. His way of speaking, his very cough, as well as the style of his long blue gown had all been given to him by the Fortune. The store had given him his personal pride and he, in turn, was proud of the store. Whenever he went out to collect bills, people would always invite him in for a cup of tea. For although, to be sure, the store *was* a business, it treated its steady customers as old friends, even to the extent that Manager Qian would participate in the weddings and funerals of his regulars. The Fortune was a business conducted with "gentlemanly style." The most prestigious people in the neighborhood could often be found sitting and chatting on the bench in front of the main entrance. Whenever there were parades or any lively goings-on in the streets, the women in his customers' families would contact Manager Qian and he would arrange good seats in front of his store from which they could observe all the excitement. This past glorious history of the shop was ever in Xin Dezhi's heart. And now?

It wasn't that he didn't know that business was changing with the times. For instance, a number of old and established shops on both sides of the Fortune had already tossed their old rules to the winds (the newer shops were not worth worrying about because they had never had any traditions to begin with). Yes, he knew all that. But it was precisely *because* the Fortune had remained doggedly faithful to its traditions that he loved it all the more and was all the more proud of it. It was as though the Fortune were the only bolt of *real* silk in a pile of synthetics. If ever the Fortune hit the skids, then the world would surely come to an end. Damn! He had to admit it—now the Fortune was just like all the others, if not worse.

In the past, his favorite object of contempt had been the Village Silk Store across the street. The manager over there was always shuffling around in down-at-the-heel shoes with a cigarette dangling from lips that occasionally opened wide enough to reveal gold-capped front teeth. The manager's wife was forever carrying little children on her back, in her arms, and seemingly even in her pockets. She scurried in and out of the shop all day clucking and cackling in a southern dialect that Xin Dezhi couldn't make out. When the couple had a good spat, they always picked the shop to have it in; when they beat the children or breast-fed a baby, they always picked the shop to do it in. You couldn't tell whether they were doing business or putting on a circus over there. However, one thing was certain: the manager's wife had her breasts forever on display in the shop with a baby or two hanging from them. Xin Dezhi had no idea as to where in the world they had dug up the clerks that worked there. Although they all wore shoddy shoes, for the most part they were dressed in silk; some had headache salve plastered conspicuously on their temples; some had their hair so slicked down that the tops of their heads looked like the bottoms of large lacquerware spoons; and some of them sported flashy gold-rimmed glasses.

Besides all these specifics, the Village had a generally contemptible air about it: they had GIANT SALES from one end of the year to the other; they always had gaudy gaslights hung out in front of the store; and they were forever playing a phonograph full blast in order to attract business. Whenever a customer bought two dollars worth of goods, the manager would, with his own hands, offer him a sweet sesame cake; if the customer refused it, he might even shove it right down his throat. Nothing in the shop had a fixed price and the rate of exchange given for foreign currency often fluctuated. Xin Dezhi had never deigned to look directly at the three words on the shop's sign; moreover, he had never gone over there to buy anything. He had never imagined that such a business firm could even exist on this earth, much less have the gall to be located right across the street from the Fortune! But strange to say, the Village had prospered, while the Fortune had gone downhill day after day. But why? He couldn't figure it out. It certainly couldn't be that there was an inexorable law at work that *required* a business be run completely divorced from any code of ethics before it could make money. If this were really the case, then why should stores even bother to train apprentices? Couldn't any old oaf off the street do business just as long as he was alive and kicking? No! Things *couldn't* be like that! Just couldn't! At least he had always been sure that his Fortune would never be like that.

How could he have possibly foreseen that after Manager Zhou's arrival, his beloved Fortune would also hang out gaslights that would combine with those of the Village to light up more than half the block! Yes, now they were birds of a feather! The Fortune and the Village a pair? He must be dreaming! But it wasn't a dream and even Xin Dezhi had to learn to do things Manager Zhou's way. He had to chitchat with the customers, offer them cigarettes, and then inveigle them into going to the back counter for a cup of tea. He was forced to haul out ersatz goods and pass them off as genuine; he had to learn to wait until a customer became insistent before giving him an honest length of material. He had to learn tricks to be employed in measuring the cloth—he was even expected to use his finger on the sly to pinch back a bit of the cloth before cutting it! How much more could he take?

Yet most of the apprentices seemed content to go along with doing things the new way. If a woman came in, it was all they could do to keep themselves from completely surrounding her; they just itched to haul out every piece of goods in the store for her inspection. Even if she bought only two feet of cloth for dusting, it was all they could do to keep themselves from escorting her all the way home. Manager Zhou *loved* this kind of thing. He wanted to see his clerks turn somersaults and perform acrobatics whenever a customer came in. He would have liked it even better if they had been able to levitate and hover around the customers in midair.

Manager Zhou and the boss of the Village became fast friends. Sometimes the two of them would make up a foursome with the people from the Heaven Silk Store and play a round of mah-jongg. The Heaven was on the same street and had been in business now for four or five years. In times gone by, Manager Qian had always ignored the Heaven. The Heaven returned the compliment by making a point of going into direct competition with the Fortune and even boasted that they wouldn't be satisfied until they had put it out of business. Manager Qian had never picked up the gauntlet, but would occasionally observe, "*We* do business on our old and established name." The Heaven was the kind of store that had a Giant Anniversary Sale three hundred and sixty-five days a year. And now even the people from the Heaven were coming over to play mah-jongg! Xin Dezhi, of course, utterly ignored them.

Whenever he had a little spare time, he would sit behind the counter and stare vacantly at the racks of materials. Originally all the goods on the racks had been covered with plain cloth. Now, ceiling to floor, all the rolls of material were starkly exposed to full view in all their varied colors so that they might serve as an attraction to passersby. It was such a dazzling sight that it made one's eyes blur just to look at it. In his heart, Xin Dezhi knew that the Fortune Silk Store had already ceased to exist. And yet, after the first business third had passed, he could not help but admire Manager Zhou.[3] Because when it came time to balance the books, although Zhou hadn't made a great deal of money, he hadn't lost any, either. He had pulled the Fortune out of the red.

Manager Zhou smiled at everyone, and explained, "You have to bear in mind that this is only my *first* third. I still have a lot of tricks up my sleeve that I haven't even tried yet. Furthermore, think of my initial outlay in advertising displays and gaslights. All of that took money, you know. So—" Whenever he felt full of himself in conversation, he'd take a *so* and tack it on the end of whatever he was saying. "Later on we won't even have to use those advertising displays. We'll have newer and more economical ways of making ourselves known. Then there'll be some real profit to show. So—" Xin Dezhi could plainly see that with Manager Zhou there was no turning back. The world *had* really changed. After all, Manager Zhou was on very good terms with people from the Heaven and the Village, and both those businesses had prospered.

Just after the books were balanced, there was a great deal of commotion in town about searching out and boycotting

Japanese goods. But Manager Zhou, as if possessed, started laying in all the Japanese goods he could get his hands on. Though student-investigating teams were already on the streets, he displayed Japanese goods right out in the open. Then he issued an injunction to the staff. "When a customer comes in, show him the Japanese goods first. None of the other places *dares* to sell them, so we might as well make hay while the sun shines. If a peasant comes in, tell him straight out that it's Japanese cloth. They'll buy it anyway. But if someone from the city comes in, then say it's German material."

When the investigating students arrived, Manager Zhou's face butterflied into smiles as he offered them cigarettes and tea. "The Fortune Silk Store swears by its good name that it will never sell Japanese goods. Look over there, gentlemen. Those goods by the door are German materials, along with some local products. Inside the store we have nothing but Chinese silks and satins. Our branch store in the south sends them up to us."

The students began to eye some of the printed materials with suspicion. Manager Zhou smiled, and shouted, "Bring me that piece of leftover Japanese material that we have in back." When the cloth had been brought to him, he grabbed the leader of the investigating students by the sleeve, and said, "Sir, I swear that this is the only piece of Japanese goods we have left. It's the same material that the shirt you're wearing is made from. So—" He turned his head around, and ordered, "All right, let's throw this piece of Japanese material out into the street." The leader of the investigating students looked at his own shirt and, not daring to raise his head, led the rest of the students out the door.

Manager Zhou made quite a bit of money from those Japanese materials which could turn into German, Chinese, or English goods at the drop of a hat. If a customer who knew his materials threw a piece of goods right down on the floor at

Manager Zhou's feet, the latter would issue an order to one of the apprentices. "Bring out the *real* Western goods. Can't you tell we have an intelligent man here who knows his materials?" Then he'd say to the customer, "You know what you want. You wouldn't take that even if I *gave* it to you! So—" Thus he'd tie up another sale. By the time that the transaction was completed, it would be all the customer could do to tear himself away from the congenial company of Manager Zhou. Xin Dezhi came to the realization that if you plan to make money in business, you have to be a combination magician and burlesque comedian. Manager Zhou was really something else. And yet, Xin Dezhi didn't feel like working at the Fortune anymore. For the more he came to admire Manager Zhou, the worse he felt. Lately even his food all seemed to go down the wrong way. If he were ever again to enjoy a good night's sleep, he would have to leave his beloved Fortune Silk Store.

But before he had found a good position someplace else, Manager Zhou left. The Heaven Silk Store had need of just such talents, and Manager Zhou himself was anxious to make the change: he felt that the stick-in-the-mud traditions of the Fortune were so deeply rooted that he would never really be able to display his talents fully here.

When Xin Dezhi saw Manager Zhou off, it was as though he were lifting off a great burden that had been pressing on his heart. On the basis of his fifteen or sixteen years of service, he felt that he had the right to put in a word with the owners of the store, although he could not be sure that what he said would carry any real weight. However, he *did* know which of them were basically conservative and had a good idea as to how to influence them. He began to propagandize for Manager Qian's return and even got Qian's old friends to help out. He didn't say that everything that Manager Qian had done was right, but would merely observe that each of the two managers had his good points and that these points ought to be combined harmoniously. One could not rigidly stick to old customs, but neither would it do to change *too* radically. An old and established name was worth preserving, but new business methods ought also to be studied and applied. One ought to lay equal emphasis on preserving the Fortune's good name *and* on making a profit—he knew that this line of argument would be a potent one.

But in his heart of hearts, he really had something quite different in mind. He hoped that when Manager Qian returned, everything that had been lost would come back with him and the Fortune Silk Store would once again be the old Fortune; otherwise, as far as he was concerned, it would be nothing. He had it all worked out: they would get rid of the gaslights, the drum and bugle, the advertisements, handbills, and cigarettes; and they would cut back as much as they could on personnel. Thus they would significantly reduce their operating expenses. Moreover, without advertising the fact, they would sell low, use a long foot in measuring, and stock honest-to-goodness materials. Could the customers all be so blind that they wouldn't see the advantages of doing business at the Fortune?

And in the end, Manager Qian actually did return. Now the only gaslights left on the street belonged to the Village. The Fortune recovered its former air of austere simplicity— although, in order to welcome Manager Qian back, they had gone so far as to hang out four lanterns decorated with tassels.

The day that the Fortune put out its lanterns of welcome, a pair of camels appeared before the door of the Heaven. The camels' bodies were completely draped in satin sash, and flashing, colored electric lights were installed on their humps. On both sides of the animals, stands were set up to sell chances at ten cents each. Whenever at least ten people had bought tickets, a drawing would be held. If lucky, one had hopes of winning a fashionable piece of silk. With this sort of thing going on, the area around the Heaven soon became something of a country fair, so crowded you could scarcely budge in the press of customers. Because, you see, it *was* undeniably true that every once in a while somebody really did emerge from the crowd, all smiles, with a piece of fashionable silk tucked under his arm.

Once again the bench in front of the Fortune was covered with a piece of blue woolen cloth; once again Manager Qian sat within the shop, eyelids drooping; once again the clerks sat quietly behind the counters. Some of them toyed quietly with the beads of an abacus; others yawned leisurely. Xin Dezhi didn't say anything, but in his heart of hearts he was really worried. Sometimes it would seem ages and ages before a single customer appeared. Occasionally someone would glance in from the outside as if he were about to enter, but then he would glance at the small golden plaque and head over in the direction of the Heaven. And sometimes a customer actually would come in to look at materials, but upon discovering that one couldn't bargain over the price, would walk out again empty-handed. There were still a few of the old reliables who came regularly to buy a little something or other, but sometimes they merely stopped by to have a chat with Manager Qian. They'd usually sigh a bit over the poverty of the times, have a few cups of tea, and then leave without buying anything. Xin Dezhi loved to listen to them talk, for it would remind him of the good times the store had once known in the past. But even he knew that the past could not be easily recovered The Heaven Silk Store was the only one on the whole street that was really doing any business.

At the end of the season, the Fortune had to cut back again on personnel. With tears in his eyes, Xin Dezhi told Manager Qian, "I can do five clerks' work all by myself. What's there to worry about!" Manager Qian took courage and chimed in, "What do we have to be afraid of!" And that night Xin Dezhi slept a very sweet sleep, fully prepared to do the work of five clerks the next day.

And yet, when a year had passed, the Fortune Silk Store was bought out by the Heaven.

Notes

1. The pronunciation of Manager Qian's last name may be approximated by saying together the English word *yen* with a *"ch"* sound in front of it, so as to make the resultant one-syllable word rhyme with the English name "Ken." Xin Dezhi is a bit more difficult. Try to put an *"h"* before the English word *sin* for his family name (always given first in Chinese); for his given name, try the *"duh!"* (sound) one uses to express the idea that "Any idiot would know that!" for the *"De";* the *"zhi"* part may be roughly approximated by the sound, *"jer,"* which rhymes with the English word *her*. If you cannot be bothered with all that, just do the best you can.

2. Manager Zhou's last name is pronounced like the English given name "Joe."

3. "Third" because books were balanced three times a year: at the Dragon Boat Festival (fifth day of the fifth lunar month); at the Mid-Autumn Festival (fifteenth day of the eighth lunar month); and at New Year's.

No Distance Too Far,
No Sacrifice Too Great

When he heard that Shanhaiguan had fallen to the Japanese, Mr. Wang decided it was high time to get married.[1] But where, pray tell, was he to hold the ceremony? Neither Tianjin nor Peiping[2] was up to snuff as a "lucky place" since both were at risk to the advancing enemy, and Hong Kong was simply too far. Besides, he hadn't found a bride yet. Better take care of that before anything else.

But place was a consideration there, too, for where was poor Mr. Wang to look for a bride? Picking up a woman in some war-torn area might be simple enough, but marriage isn't the kind of thing where you just snap your fingers, and say, "Gimme that one!" No, he'd really better go someplace where the locals were still singing the joys of peace and prosperity. Upon turning this corner in his reasoning, he effectively convinced himself that his departure from Peiping had absolutely nothing to do with any fear he might have of the Japanese devils.

Couldn't get a train ticket! And how about those clerks at the East and West Stations! So high and mighty you'd have thought that God had created that little world of theirs from scratch and installed them right there in it, that beyond that sacred realm of platforms and trains, there *was* no other world!

Since he had no idea as to where he was going anyway, Mr. Wang couldn't care less whether he left from the East Station or the West one. Didn't matter *where* he left from as long as he got out of Peiping.

Now it wasn't that he was afraid of the Japanese, mind you. Only a horse's ass would be frightened by them. It was just that on the off chance he did fall into their hands, who would be left to go get married? Be it East Station or West Station, he had to get out of Peiping; ticket or no ticket, he had to get out of Peiping. *Get out of Peiping*—that was the name of the game!

In the midst of his quandary, Mr. Wang was seized with an inspiration. Why not go to the baggage room, slap a tag on himself, and travel as luggage. Wouldn't need a ticket. Trouble was, the jackasses in the baggage room refused to take luggage that came with legs attached, so poor Mr. Wang had to content himself with calling them a bunch of shit-for-brains.

But where there's a will, there's a way, and Mr. Wang was no feckless clod. He boarded a trolley at the Zhengyang Gate and went to the Xizhi Gate. There he discovered they had a train that went from Peiping to Suiyuan.[3] Mr. Wang congratulated himself on this considerable increase in his stock of worldly knowledge and reflected on the truism that it is circumstances that create great men. After all, if he hadn't placed himself in the right circumstances by taking the trolley to Xizhi Gate, he would never have unearthed the fact that trains travel over definite routes rather than traipsing hither and yon across the countryside wherever they feel like going. Be that as it may, however, he immediately ruled out the Peiping-Suiyuan route as "unlucky." It lay to the north and that's where the Japanese were. Could Mr. Wang help but feel depressed?

Where was he to go? No, it was not so much a question of where as it was a question of going at all. And where was he to get a train to go *on* in the first place? Well, it still looked as though it would have to be either East Station or West Station, one or the other. But what if not a single solitary train ever left either station? Well . . . then that would have to be that. But if a train *did* leave one of them, you certainly couldn't say there wouldn't be at least a *chance* of Mr. Wang's managing to get on it. He bought fruit, some other snacks, and a bottle of brandy: he had decided that he would just go to a station and wait for however long it took. And so it came to pass that Mr. Wang swore a solemn oath to all traindom, "OK, little friends, it's between you and me! Old Wang *is* going and he's going to ride one of you! Ride in your damned smokestack, if he has to!"

He went back to East Station—it was a tad more respectable looking than the West one. After all, a man getting set to be a bridegroom has to keep an eye on appearances. After hanging around for five hours, however, he hadn't even managed to so much as squeeze through the station gate! He couldn't help but be a bit anxious, but his head remained clear as ever. "As long as I keep waiting, something's bound to turn up. And if the Japanese do attack, I'm better off at a train station than anywhere else. After all, the people closest to the exit always have the best chance of getting out. Look at it this way: suppose the Japanese *do* start shooting, do you mean to say the engineer won't stoke up the engine and let her rip? And when he does, then all Old Wang's gotta do is hop aboard. At that point I won't even *need* a ticket! Off I'll go, off to Tianjin! The engineer will drive that sucker right up in front of a hotel in the English concession. I'll hop down, go inside, have a cup of coffee, wash up a bit, and get back on. Off I'll go again, all the way to Nanking, or maybe even Shanghai. Before the night's out, I'll be in a nice bright banquet room and—" At this point, in happy anticipation of his good fortune, Mr. Wang cranked up his voice and started singing snatches of opera.

After three more hours of waiting, Mr. Wang had sung every last bit of opera he knew, but could readily see that he still had no hopes of crowding onto that railroad platform. More and more people were arriving all the time. In fact it got so crowded that one of the apples he'd brought along was applesauced by the press of flesh around him. And yet, the more people that arrived, the more comfortable he felt. In the first place, the bigger the crowd you're with, the less there is to be afraid of. Let the night get as deep and dark as it can possibly get, and you still don't have to be afraid of ghosts! And in the second place, if a Japanese bomb did fall, Mr. Wang couldn't possibly be the only one it would kill. A nice big crowd would be blasted to smithereens right along with him, and there would be no need to worry about being lonely on his journey to the next world. And in the third place, the more people there were stacked up behind him, the less he had to worry about getting on the train. After all, if *he* had to worry about getting on, think of what the people behind him must be going through! And so it was that when he looked behind him, the more heads he saw bobbing about, the more reassured he felt.

On the other hand, he didn't want to lose the advantage he had gained, either, and thus when anyone tried to crowd ahead of him, Mr. Wang didn't bother to be polite. His elbows were never at rest, and anyone who tried to squeeze in in front of him got a good sampling of what those elbows could do. Early in the game, he determined that a side-shot to the ribs was the best strategy, while an elbow rammed into the pit of the stomach was less desirable, because if you hit somebody *too* hard that way, you ran the danger of having them upchuck blood all over you. Our dear Mr. Wang wasn't prepared to play as dirty as all that. After all, in "these times of national crisis," it would be just a bit embarrassing to cause one of your compatriots to hawk up a stomach full of the red stuff. No, a side-shot to the ribs was definitely his best bet. Thus, Mr. Wang's elbows were employed in a manner that was at once appropriate and seemly.

Wonder of wonders, a train actually pulled out of the station! Mr. Wang's spirits rose: after all, if *one* train left, then he had that much more hope of being on the next one. And if he didn't get on the next one, then he'd have an even better chance of getting on the one after that. Patience is a virtue, one that Mr. Wang felt he abundantly embodied and faithfully practiced. So what if he did have to sleep over in the station for two or three nights—no big deal.

From the depths of his throat, the man next to Mr. Wang hawked up a goober of phlegm and let fly—it landed smackdab on Mr. Wang's shoe. Mr. Wang didn't take offense for he realized that the crowded conditions he found himself in rendered that response inappropriate, for even if he *wanted* to clobber the man, he had no room to work up a good swing. Instead, he took careful aim at his neighbor's lapel, hawked up a good one himself, and returned the compliment.

It was dark now. People said there wouldn't be any trains leaving at night. But it occurred to our hero that if he didn't wait for the trains that *would* leave when daytime rolled around again, he'd have wasted all the merit he'd accumulated thus far. Since there was a comfortable-sized crowd there that obviously intended to stay, Mr. Wang decided to save a night's hotel expenses by waiting there with them. Besides, lots of female types weren't leaving, and if they saw a man leave because he couldn't stand the wait, they'd be sure to make fun of him. With courage above and beyond the call of duty, our Mr. Wang, resolved to Be Ready for Any Sacrifice! and to Fight On No Matter What the Price! In triumphant tones, he recited the two wartime slogans—to himself.

Throughout the night, however, there wasn't so much as a peep out of him—he was half-frozen to death. Mr. Wang really did shoulder his share of wartime hardship that night. Yet, for his own sake as well as that of the entire Chinese nation, what was a little suffering? Granted, there were some people—those with a bit more social clout—who didn't have to experience this kind of misery in the first place, but people's fates *do* differ. If somebody rides a rickshaw, there's gotta be someone to pull it, right? If everybody pulled and nobody rode, then who would be left for the pullers to pull? Mr. Wang congratulated himself on his own perspicacity.

Whenever the Japanese occupied a place, the social-clout set were the first to hightail it out before the enemy arrived. People with money followed close behind them. People with neither clout nor money had no way of escaping and had to content themselves with waiting around to die. Since Mr. Wang had the good fortune not to belong to the wait-around-to-die group, it would have been ungrateful to complain. Why should he whine about a small dose of suffering? After all, he reasoned, trains are divided into first, second, and third classes—so why not people? As long as the Japanese didn't make off with him bodily, Mr. Wang felt that he'd be all right. If they did get hold of him, he might well end up by *pulling* the train, and that would be a mite more than Old Wang could take! Though he didn't open his mouth to say anything all that night, his brain was busy as ever. What's more, with the help of a bottle of brandy, he was even subject to a fair share of poetic inspiration.

The next morning, according to the reports of those immediately around him, it was entirely possible that there would *be* no more trains. Mr. Wang rolled that one around in his head for awhile and then made up his mind once and for all: train or no train, Old Wang wasn't going to budge. Besides, how could you be sure that it wasn't just a rumor passed around by some people as a ploy in order to get others out of the station? Mr. Wang was not about to let anyone pull the wool over *his* eyes. No siree, you were not about to see Old Wang move so much as an inch! But if the truth were known, at least part of his not budging was due to a tingling sensation in his legs that proclaimed them too numb to move in the first place.

He ran out of food. Served him right, then, that the man selling steamed buns should rip him off—two buns for ten cents! Expensive? Sure, but he had to wrap his teeth around something. Looked as though the man selling buns was fated to make money and *he* was fated to lose it. But what could you do? A man has to eat. No point in beating your head against a stone wall.

The man selling the steamed buns had to make his way across a table formed by the heads of the tightly packed crowd to get to Mr. Wang. Not that easy! Nor was it all that easy for the people whose heads made up the table and weren't buying buns. It wasn't all that comfortable for anyone, but as the slogan has it: Shoulder to Shoulder; Hardships Make Us Bolder.

The bun seller made a tiny fortune that day, one that the Japanese would confiscate as soon as they arrived—poetic justice, no matter how you cut it. "And what if *I* were selling the buns?" Mr. Wang mused. "I might charge a dime for a single one of them. Everything depends on your point of view. Even the Japanese aren't all that bad when you come to think of it—forced to come over here, they've got no choice but to bully the Chinese. They say Japanese whores are willing to turn Chinese tricks—no imperialism there. Less V.D. among them than the local stuff, too."

He waited until four in the afternoon. It turned out that the Peiping-Shanghai Express would be running after all. Strange to tell, this bit of intelligence made Mr. Wang very uneasy—now things were going *too* smoothly. After all, he had only waited one day and a night. But since it was, in fact, possible to leave now, he saw no point in tarrying any longer.

Yet where would he get off?

Certainly he wouldn't go all the way to Shanghai, for that destination fell far short of being ideal. Wasn't that the very place where the Nineteenth Route Army had taken on the Japanese devils?[4] To be sure, the Japanese had been so thoroughly defeated that they had fallen to their knees and begged their Chinese daddies for mercy, but in the end, Japanese airplanes had flown over, dropped bombs, and killed so many waiters at the Fragrant Fields Restaurant that human guts and pork sausages had soared skyward intertwined. If Shanghai wasn't all that safe, there was no point in even thinking about Nanking, which didn't even *have* foreign concessions. And down in Jiangxi Province they've got Communists all over the place. Who wants to run around down there ducking swords and dodging bullets? Not worth it.

The man in front of him bought a second-class ticket for Jinan. Jinan? Why not? OK then, Jinan it will be. Wonder if that Jinan Massacre is still going on?[5] Well, I'll have to check that one out when I get there. If things are too bad, I can always keep heading south. Good idea.

He bought a second-class ticket, but had to ride third. That's because in these times of "national crisis," every ticket class drops down a notch. That's not entirely true, either. It goes more like this: people who just don't bother to buy tickets in the first place—bigwigs with real clout—all ride first class; that means first-class tickets have to go second; second-class tickets, third; and third-class tickets . . . well, provided they are not totally adverse to exercise, third-class folk take their tickets in hand and hoof it. And if exercise doesn't turn them on, they can always hole up in their hotels for a few days, and then try it all over again. As things worked out, Mr. Wang got lucky and was able to lay hold of a second-class ticket, which meant he could ride—a hell of a lot better than hoofing it.

Not long before this, two people holding second-class tickets had actually managed to find seats but had subsequently died in the press of the crowd. Nobody wanted to risk sitting down anymore. Too dangerous. And once you were down, you might as well just forget about getting back up. You'd have to sit there like some old monk in meditation waiting to enter nirvana. Two of his fellow passengers had already gone to the promised land in that lotus position, and Mr. Wang had no burning itch to follow them.

Besides, the position he had standing wasn't all that shabby: he was right in the middle of the coach. When it rocked a bit, people in the window seats got their heads knocked against the windows, while Mr. Wang's noggin only got banged against the passenger next to him—a much softer deal. And the passengers fore and aft of him couldn't have been better arranged if they'd tried. The Old Man in the Sky must have been keeping an eye out for Old Wang today! The man in front of him was so short that Wang was able to use the top of his head as a personal headrest, and the guy behind him was so fat he provided a pretty good easy chair. Furthermore, it was a position that gave Wang real firepower. For instance, let's say he wanted to clear his nose. In a flesh-press like that, there was no way he could raise his hands to his nose, but by using the little man in front of him as a gun carriage, he could simply aim his twin cannons, blow hard, and let go with a double barrel. Granted, it wouldn't travel very far, but far enough to blast somebody in the back. No matter how you looked at it, Mr. Wang couldn't help being pleased with his place in the coach.

The train pulled into Main Station at Tianjin, but not a single passenger got off to do any leg stretching on the platform. A myriad of different mouths harmonized in expressing the same sentiment, "What the hell are we stopped here for? Let's go! Get this damned train *outta* here!" *Tianjin!* Why the very sound of the *word* was enough to send shivers down your spine, much less actually *being* there. Although the train stopped there for over an hour, during that entire time no one dared to leave the coach. For that matter, no one even dared to sneak a look outside for fear they might end up in eye-to-eye contact with one of those Japanese devils. If a look from one of those little monsters didn't out-and-out kill you, at the very least it would make you come down good and sick.

At long last, they left Main Station and then stopped again at Tianjin's Old Station—and then they actually went *back* to Main Station again! Would there be no end to it? What were they trying to do—see if they could get struck by lightning? The passengers never got to see the station master, of course, but if they had, they would have given him such a piece of their minds that he would have shriveled up and died in the onslaught of their curses.

"*Dagong Times!* . . . Latest novels!" Peddling their wares in a place like this! People like that certainly don't value their own lives very much. Stick around long enough and sooner or later bombs will blow them to smithereens. The idiots are asking for it!

The train finally left Main Station again. Not a single passenger even dared to breathe until the lights of Tianjin lay far behind. It was a though they had just pulled out of the gates of hell and the next stop was heaven. By the time they reached Cangzhou, everyone's legs had turned into wooden clubs. Their hearts, however, were much lighter, and Mr. Wang's arias were to be heard once more. They arrived in Dezhou before daybreak and everyone got off to buy roast chicken, ham, eggs, and boiled water for drinking. After all, now that their lives were securely in their own hands again, could they go without nourishing them?

Mr. Wang was not a man to be left out in the cold. Combining the techniques of hand-to-hand combat, American football, and Chinese boxing, he cut a swath through the crowd to the stand where Dezhou roast chicken was being sold. So many others followed in his wake that the man selling the chicken couldn't have kept up with their orders even if he'd grown another pair of hands. Rising apace with the crowd's lust for Dezhou chicken, the sound of chickens being slaughtered rose to a deafening pitch. After all, if you didn't eat some of the roast chicken for which Dezhou is so justly famous, how could you any longer lay claim to being human?

Mr. Wang wrenched a chicken out of someone's hands and wouldn't let go for dear life; after all, if you didn't snatch one, you'd never get one. Having laid hold of his bird, Mr. Wang opened his mouth and stuffed it in. *Aiya!* Now that was a flavor and a half!

There really was a certain barbaric charm about eating Dezhou roast chicken, especially just before daybreak. If the country were always at peace, how would you ever get to savor that little smack of barbarism. The police and soldiers guarding the station were beside themselves, because a kid selling griddle cakes had just been torn limb from limb by the same crowd. Buying a griddle cake and having the seller's hand or ear thrown in for free—a bit cruel one must admit; but if you want to look on the bright side of things, the enthusiasm the crowd evinced for those griddle cakes shows that the nation is not entirely lacking in wartime morale.

The police, now worked into a frenzy, brandished barbed whips and lit into the crowd with real zest. Every man of them was so pleased with his own diligence in wielding one of those whips that he felt his blood beginning to rise and smiled at the carnage. After all, if the police didn't beat people up, what point would there be in even *having* policemen in the first place? And who else was there for our Chinese police to beat up if not their fellow citizens? You don't think the Japanese were about to offer themselves up for a working over, do you?

And yet all those whips didn't seem to faze the crowd in the least. Whips or no whips, those passengers who hadn't gotten their roast chicken yet were determined not to shrink back until they had. Mr. Wang, having already obtained his bird, saw no reason to join them. Granted, the single lash he'd received hadn't been enough to really satisfy his masochistic lust for punishment; but fair is fair, and if there was to be a general whipping, it should be a case of share and share alike. Wouldn't do for Mr. Wang to monopolize *all* the blows. He returned to the train—victoriously.

He couldn't get back on the train! Must have been fifty or more jammed at the door. Getting off, it had been a case of going from the inside out—fairly easy—but now he had to go from the outside in. Even if he did manage to push the people in front of him toward the train, he'd only succeed in making the bottleneck at the coach door worse than ever. Be worse than trying to get into a fortress guarded by the proverbial brass wall and steel barricade. How was he ever to crowd his way through—especially with half a roast chicken still in hand. He tried thrusting his hands between two people in front of him. *Plop!* Lost a chunk of the bird. Not even into the coach yet and part of his chicken already gone! Certainly wouldn't pay to continue trying to crowd his way on in a situation like this. Mr. Wang began to wax a bit nervous.

But just at this juncture that seething mass of passengers on the platform demonstrated once again the stuff that *real* Chinese are made of. True descendants of the Yellow Emperor will always come up with some way of dealing with any problem. Why, just listen! Someone's making an announcement even now. "Come one, come all! Who wants a shove through a window? Dollar a head!"

The announcement was no sooner made than, quick-witted as ever, Mr. Wang responded, "How about sixty cents?"

"Eighty, and not a penny less."

"Deal!"

With a *zip* and a *zap*, Mr. Wang and half a roast chicken went through a window. Fascinating! While his head was inside and his feet still dangling on the *out*, he decided that the best strategy would be to make himself firm and light as a spring swallow and *float* into the coach, and that's exactly what he did. Once inside, however, finding a place to stand was near impossible; undaunted, Mr. Wang now made himself straight and slick as a carp and slithered down among all those passengers crammed into the coach. *Clunk*—his head hit the floor. With a smile on his face and a lump on his noggin, Mr. Wang managed to right himself, forked over his eighty cents, and silently waited for the train to pull out. There were more than forty people on that platform who didn't make it onto the train. It occurred to Mr. Wang that though those forty souls might stuff themselves with roast chicken as they stood on the platform, they were a far, far cry from himself, a passenger who had managed to accomplish *two* goals: stuffed himself with chicken *and* managed to get back on the train to boot! As for those people still on the platform—idiots, all forty of them!

When the sun came up, Jinan lay just ahead of them. Mr. Wang could not have been happier. When the train crossed the famed Iron Bridge to the other side of the Yellow River, Mr. Wang, perspicacious as ever, determined that the Iron Bridge really *was* made of iron after all. A blink of the eye and the train was in Jinan Station. He was in a hurry to get off the train, but the more he crowded forward, the less progress he seemed to make. In order to keep in the spirit of things, he determined to maintain an even disposition as he worked his way to the outside.

He finally squeezed his way out of the car and onto the platform. He looked around: it really was Jinan. A white sign with large black characters stood in mute testimony to that fact. But Mr. Wang was not born yesterday. No, he was not one to be tricked into making a positive identification on the basis of one sign alone. It was only after determining that several white signs around the station all said exactly the same thing that he put his mind to rest. Slowly he climbed some steps and crossed over the pedestrian bridge to the other platform. Since it was not crowded now, he moved with a dignified and stately pace until he heard the ticket taker yell: "Hurry up, you jackass, and give me your ticket!" Only then did it occur to him to rummage through his pockets for the ticket he needed to show in order to leave the station.

Once outside the station, he began to think of his wedding plans again. Since he still had one old lady at home, however, he thought it might be a good idea to write a letter to her before going out in search of his new love. As he walked along, he asked himself, "Where, oh where, can my new love be?" He even put a tune of sorts to the question.

After he had found a hotel, written a letter home, and eaten a bowl of noodles, Mr. Wang started to read the paper. Peiping *still* hadn't been bombed. He was thoroughly disappointed. After a good night's sleep, he set out in search of his new love.

Notes

The Chinese title for this story, "Doesn't Consider a Thousand Miles Too Far to Come" (Buyuan qianli er lai), is based on the opening passage of the Confucian classic that records the words of the philosopher Mencius (372–289 B.C.). "Mencius had an audience with King Hui of Liang. The King said, 'Since you haven't thought a thousand miles too far to come, I assume you have something which will be of benefit to my country.'" Used as the title of Lao

She's story, the phrase carries a strong satirical note, for standing in stark contrast to the early philosopher, Mr. Wang, the protagonist of Lao She's story, cares not one whit for anything beyond himself at a time (1933) when Japanese aggression threatened the existence of the Chinese state. Yet, curiously, what we have here appears to be not so much a vitriolic attack against Mr. Wang and his ilk as an extended humorous anecdote, albeit written against a deadly serious background. This, in some part at least, may be explained by the fact that the story was written for Lin Yutang's humor magazine, *Analects*. That notwithstanding, one will find that Lao She's humor tugs gently at its leash most of the time, and there are occasions—this story and "The Grand Opening," which was written in the same year, are good examples—when his humor slips its leash entirely and goes off on a wild and unbridled romp. Readers interested in a complete and somewhat more literal rendering of the quotation may consult D. C. Lau, trans., *Mencius* (Harmondsworth: Penguin Classics, 1970).

1. Shanhaiguan refers to the pass *(guan)* between the mountains *(shan)* and sea *(hai)* located in northern Hebei province at the point where the Great Wall meets the sea. This was a traditional invasion route from the north. In 1644 the Manchus poured through the pass, overthrew the Ming, and established their own dynasty, the Qing, which lasted until the Republican Revolution of 1911. Thus the fall of Shanhaiguan to the Japanese is an omen of the imminent loss of all north China.

2. "Peiping" refers to modern day "Beijing." It's like this: When Lao She wrote this story in 1933, Nanking (literally "southern capital"; in the modern pinyin spelling it is "Nanjing") was the official capital, hence Peking (that's the way "Beijing" was spelled back then), which means "northern capital," was renamed "Peiping," meaning "northern peace." By way of final complication, "Peiping" would be spelled "Beiping" in the pinyin romanization used today.

3. Suiyuan is presently known by the Mongolian name, Hohot (green city); since 1952 it has been the capital of Inner Mongolia.

4. When the Japanese moved into Shanghai in January of 1932, the Chinese Nineteenth Route Army fought them to a standstill.

5. In the course of a campaign against the warlord Zhang Zuolin, Chiang Kaishek occupied Jinan on 1 May 1928. Under the pretext of protecting their own nationals, the Japanese also moved into the city. The fighting, rape, and pillaging that ensued led to the death of five thousand Chinese and was known as the Jinan Massacre. After prolonged negotiations, the Japanese finally withdrew in 1929.

Black Li and White Li

Love wasn't at the heart of that business between the brothers, but that's where I've got to begin.

Black Li was the older of the two; White Li, the kid, was five years younger. You *could* say the three of us were in high school together, though Black Li and I graduated the year White Li came in. Since Black Li and I were pretty tight, I used to hang out a lot over at their house. And that's how I got to know a thing or two about White Li, too.

In times like these,[1] five years makes a big difference, and those brothers were different—different as their nicknames, Black and White. Black Li was old-fashioned, but White Li was as up-to-date as you can get. That didn't make them fight or anything, but you could always be sure that whatever came up, you'd find them on opposite sides of the fence.

Black Li wasn't even dark, but he did have a black mole over his left eyebrow, and that was enough to make him Black Li. His kid brother didn't have a mark like that, and so he was White Li. In the eyes of us high school kids who gave them the nicknames, the whole thing made perfect sense. But truth be known, they were both light complected. Looked a lot alike, too.

They both had a thing for *her*—you'll excuse me for not

giving her name. Trouble was, she was never able to come right out and say which one of them she preferred, or if she liked either of them for that matter. And that's why their friends—me included—got so worked up over the whole deal. We knew they wouldn't be willing to fight over it, but love—the little rascal—isn't one to start acting nice just to preserve a relationship. In the end, though, it was Black Li who stood aside.

I remember it like it was yesterday. It was an early summer's night and a light drizzle was coming down. I went over to Black Li's to chew the fat. I found him alone in his room. He had four tea bowls set out in front of him. They were porcelain and decorated with goldfish. We never stood on ceremony, so I just plopped down and took out a cigarette. He was fiddling with those damned bowls. First he gave one a turn, and then another, until he had all the goldfish lined up so they faced him at exactly the same angle; he leaned back and looked down the bridge of his nose at them, the way an artist might look at a painting after adding a masterful stroke. And then he switched them all around until he had the goldfish on the *other* side lined up in the same way. He leaned back again, gave them another once-over, and then turned to me.

He was grinning just like a kid—a very young one at that. Black Li loved to tinker around with piddling little stuff like that. He took up every hobby you can think of but never got good at any of them. He didn't pretend to be an expert, either. He went in for all those different hobbies because he thought he could use them to make himself a better person. He probably had something there, for over the years, he really had cultivated a mellow, easygoing disposition. Whenever Black Li had even the slightest thing to occupy him—patching up old books or the like—he'd be happy shooting most of the day on it. He greeted me and then gave me another kiddish grin.

"I've let Number Four have her." Though there were only the two of them, whenever they talked about guys in their own generation, they always included cousins as well, and if you counted like that, White Li was the fourth born. "It wouldn't do to let a woman do damage to the feelings brothers have for each other."

"Shows you're not a very up-to-date guy," I said, trying to make light of the whole thing.

"It's not that exactly. It's just that you can't teach an old dog new tricks. Triangular love affair? Not for me. I told her right up front that from here on out I wasn't going to have anything to do with her no matter which one of us she liked. I could tell I'd done the right thing by how good I felt afterward."

"Never heard of handling *love* like that before."

"Never heard of it? Well, you got it here just now, right? To hell with it. No matter how you cut it, I'm not going to break up with Number Four over—over a *female*. If you and I ever get into a fix like this, I hope that you'll be smart enough to pull back your troops, or that I'll have the good sense to sound the retreat for mine."

"And peace, sweet peace, shall reign throughout the world once again," I countered, and we broke the tension with a laugh.

It must have been about, say, ten days later that Black Li came over to my place. I could tell right off that something was eating him. His brows were all dark, the way they always got when things weren't going right. Whenever that happened, the two of us would always down a good half catty of White Lotus. I hauled out the liquor right away because those brows certainly weren't the brightest I'd ever seen.

By the time we were on our second cup, his hands had begun to tremble. Whenever anything was wrong with Black Li on the inside, it would show up right off on the outside. He had never been able to hide his feelings. And when anything *did* go wrong, the harder he tried to stay calm, the more that face of his would give away the whole show. He was just too honest, that's all.

"I've just come from *her* place." He smiled. It was a real nothing smile, but he meant it all the same because he was happy at the prospect of unburdening himself to a good friend. Black Li was the kind of guy who couldn't make it through a single day without a close friend.

I didn't press him. Between friends like us there was no need to rush things. Besides, our feelings often poured out through those quiet little spaces between our words. At times like that, we'd just sit, stare at each other, and smile. Like the understanding that lay wrapped inside our silences, the expressions we wore were far more expressive than mere words. Whenever White Li saw us sitting quietly and drinking like that, he, of course, would dismiss us as a matched pair of imbeciles.

"Old Four and I got into a good one."

I knew exactly what he meant by "got into a good one." First off, he didn't want to come straight out and say they'd had a fight. And then, too, he didn't want to lay the whole thing on his kid brother, either, even if it *was* White Li who was in the wrong. "Got into a good one" was also a handy way of avoiding saying something that really ought to be said, but he didn't want to say.

"It was all because of her. It was my fault, though, for not knowing how women's minds work. Remember the day I told you I'd decided to let Old Four have her? I had nothing but the best of intentions. But then *she* had to go and put her own spin on it. Said I was deliberately insulting her! You're right, I'm not an up-to-date sort of guy. I see love the way I see any-thing else: you see what ought to be done and then you go ahead and do it. Who would've thought that she *wanted* to have both of us chasing after her? Well the upshot is that she got ticked off and decided to pay me back. How? Simple. Since I wasn't going to have anything more to do with *her, she* wouldn't have anything more to do with Number Four. When he found out, of course, Number Four and I *really* got into a good one.

"So today I went to see her again. I was going to ask her to forgive me. I knew she might curse me up one side and then down the other to work off some of that steam she'd built up. But if I worked it just right, she also just might get back together with Number Four. That's what I hoped. But guess what? She didn't curse me out at all! Said she wanted me and Number Four to *both* be her friends. No way! I didn't tell her that straight out, of course. I came over here to talk it over with you first. You see, if I *don't* agree to be her friend, she won't have any more to do with Number Four, and then we're sure to get into *another* good one."

"A no-win situation." I put it in a nutshell. Then after a bit, I suggested, "I'm supposed to go and explain the whole thing to Number Four, right?"

"Wouldn't do any harm." Wine cup in hand, he paused, and then said, "It might not do any good, either. But come what may, I'm not going to have anything more to do with her. And if Number Four *does* start in with me again, I'll just play it like a clam."

We turned to other things. He told me he'd recently started looking into religion. Since I knew his interests were spur-of-the-moment whims, I didn't think he was going otherworldly on me just because he was "looking into religion," or even that he'd changed his way of thinking all that much.

No sooner had the elder brother left than the younger one arrived. White Li rarely came to my place, so I knew something must be up. Though he still hadn't graduated from college, he looked a lot more sharp and worldly-wise than his elder brother. As soon as you set eyes on him, you'd think that here's a guy who was cut out to be a leader wherever he goes. Everything he said had a purpose—either to lead you down the path he'd just pointed out, or to put you up on the guillotine. The exact opposite of his elder brother, he was always straightforward and came right to the point. I reminded myself that it wouldn't be a good idea for *me* to beat around the bush when talking to him, either—didn't want him calling me an imbecile.

"Number Two's already been here, of course," he said. As I've explained, Black Li was Number Two when you counted the cousins in. "And of course he's already talked to you about us."

I thought I'd better not be in a hurry to answer because there were two "of course's" out there staring me in the face, and sure enough, he went right on without waiting for a reply. "You know, of course, that I have an ulterior motive in doing the jealous suitor bit."

I hadn't known that.

"You think I really *want* that female?" He smiled. Looked exactly like his elder brother when he smiled, except that Black Li's smile never carried that little touch of condescension with it. "Only went after her in the first place to give Number Two a hard time. Otherwise, why waste my time? After all, when you come right down to it, the male-female relationship is nothing but animal desire. And if I want to satisfy *that,* why insist on this *particular* female? Number Two thinks that there's something holy about that desire, and so he throws himself at her feet. And what's he got to show for it? Face full of dirt. He thinks I ought to do the same thing. Sorry folks, but I'll have to take a pass on that one!" He had a good laugh.

I didn't laugh. Didn't dare butt in, either. But I did pay close attention to everything he said and even closer attention to his face. Every little part of that face was exactly like his elder brother's, but the *expression* on it—that was totally different. The result was that for a second or two I'd think I was talking to a good friend, and then, just like that, I'd think I was sitting across from a total stranger. It was unnerving to say the least—sitting there looking at a face I knew so well, yet unable to find any trace of the expression that I also knew so well.

"Well I'm not about to throw myself at her feet. Get the chance and I'll show her what *real* kissing is all about. That's what she'd really like, anyway—a lot more enjoyable than having someone throw himself at her feet. But that's not what I came about. What I really came about is this. You think I ought to keep on living with my elder brother?"

I couldn't think of what to say.

He smiled again. He was probably thinking of what an imbecile I was. "I have my own future ahead of me, my own plans. He has his. The best thing would be to let each of us go his own way, right?"

"Right. But what plans?" I found it hard to come up with even this much to say, but if I didn't say something, the tension would be unbearable.

"Can't tell you right now. We've got to make a clean break first. You'll find out about it soon enough, anyway."

"It's because you wanted to make a clean break with *him* that you started up with *her* in the first place. That's why you're doing the jealous suitor bit now, right?" I was kind of proud of myself for tying it all together like that.

He nodded and smiled but didn't say anything. It was as though he was certain that I had something to add. And I did. "Why not just tell him straight out that you want to leave home and strike out on your own? Why this bit with the girl?"

"You think he'd understand? Sure, you can talk about anything you want with him. I can't. Soon as I'd even mention breaking away to live on my own, he'd start to cry. And then he'd rake up all *that* stuff again. 'Remember what Mom said when she was about to leave us? Didn't she say she wanted the two of us to always live in harmony?' You can bet your bottom dollar he'd go through all that stuff again—as though the living should be governed by the dead.

"There's still another angle I've gotta worry about. If he ever *did* agree to it, he'd insist on giving everything to me, and I certainly don't want to take advantage of him that way. He always thinks he's gotta look out for his 'kid brother.' Tries to dictate my activity on the basis of *his* feelings. Truth be known, *he's* the one who needs looking after. He's hopelessly behind the times. This age belongs to *me,* and I certainly don't need him to tell *me* what to do." His face suddenly turned very serious.

As I studied that face, my thoughts gradually took another tack. White Li wasn't simply an arrogant youngster who looked down on a couple of "imbeciles" like Black Li and me. No, he really did want to establish himself on his own, independent of his elder brother. I began to see it all quite clearly now. If White Li entered into drawn-out negotiations, he'd end up having to say things that would hurt his brother's feelings. In fact, he'd have to talk about quite a few things that would touch on the ties between them, for even if *he* didn't bring up such stuff, Black Li would for sure.

White Li had obviously decided that rather than go through all that, it would be better to start a fight and make a clean break to begin with. That way he and his brother would each be able to take his own road into the future. If White Li went the negotiation route, Black Li would never let him make a clean break. If, on the other hand, he managed to get a good fight going first, *then* if Black Li wasn't willing to let him go, everybody would think it was because Black Li was trying to do White Li out of his rightful share of the family estate. Having guessed my way this far, it suddenly dawned on me exactly why White Li had come to see me. "You want me to go and talk to Number Two, right?"

"You got it. Might be able to avoid another fight that way. Don't want to give Number Two *too* hard a time. After all, we are—brothers." The word seemed to stick in his throat as though he found it really hard to say.

I said I'd do it.

"For the next twenty years, we two just can't be—brothers— so the firmer and blunter you are about it when you tell him, the better." He paused. A smile crowded its way out from the corners of his mouth.

"I've got it all worked out for my elder brother, too. Best thing for him to do is get married right away quick and crank out a fat little guy to help him forget me. And if I'm still alive twenty years down the road, I can come back home and play the doting uncle. By then I'll probably be behind the times, too. But in the meantime, you'd better tell him that when he's in love, it'll go a lot better if he does more kissing and less throwing himself at the girl's feet. Tell him to go for it with all he's got—the wooing that is, not the kneeling." He stood up, thought a bit, and added, "Thanks." He said it in such a way as to announce that he really didn't have to say thanks, but did so as a special favor to me.

So as to keep my promise, I went over to Black Li's almost every day. He always had the White Lotus set out, but when the drinking, eating, and talking were done, we'd always break up without having decided a single thing. I must have spent the better part of a month like that. He understood all I had to say. He even seemed to want White Li to strike out and make something of himself on his own hook. But then the last thing he'd always say before we parted was, "Can't give up Number Four!"

One day I found him pacing back and forth, mumbling to himself, "Number Four's plans? What plans?" Partly concealed by the wrinkles in his brow, the black mole above his eyebrow seemed to have shrunk to a fraction of its usual size. "Why don't you ask him *what* plans, because I won't put my mind at rest until I know exactly what he has in mind."

"Won't tell me." I'd already told him that fifty times or more.

"If he won't tell you, that means it's something dangerous! He's the only brother I have. OK, so he does fight with me all the time. I can live with that. He didn't used to fight with me before. It's probably over that darned female! And you say he wants me to get *married?* If we've gotten into a mess like this while I'm still single, what's the point in getting married? But what plans? Really wants to split up? He can take anything he wants. I must have offended him somehow. I don't argue with him, but it is true that I do have my own way of looking at things. *What* plans? He can go ahead and do anything he wants to, for all I care, but why does he have to break up the family to do it?" Black Li would often ramble on like that for an hour at a clip.

He began to go in for more and more weird little stuff— especially finding ways of telling what was going to happen in the future: telling the future by tossing coins, telling the future by interpreting hexagrams, telling the future by analyzing individual words—did some religion, too. But none of it was able to help him figure out what Number Four was up to. All of it simply added to his pain. Now I don't mean to say that he *looked* particularly worried on the outside. Far from it, he was still as slow and deliberate as ever. It was as though his bodily motion wasn't able to keep pace with his feelings: no matter how excited he was on the inside, he kept on moving with that same kind of measured deliberation he'd exhibit when tinkering with some antique held in the palm of his hand.

I suggested that White Li's plans must have to do with his *future* career, not something he was going to do right away.

Black Li just shook his head. Things dragged along like that for another month or so.

"See," I said to him one day, grabbing fast to the one bit of logic that was on my side. "Number Four hasn't pressed me. Obviously he must have been talking about long range-plans, not something he was going to do right away."

He shook his head.

As time went by, he began doing more and more odd things. One Sunday morning I even saw him go into a church. Thinking he'd probably gone in to look for a friend, I waited outside, but he didn't come out right away. I couldn't wait around forever, so I left. I mulled it all over as I walked along. His peculiar behavior must be the result of the various shocks he'd suffered—a lost love, a falling out with his younger brother, and maybe something else, something even I didn't know about. If you just stick to the two things I *did* know about, either one would be enough to send him round the bend.

If you looked at the way he carried himself, you might have thought that he saw his own life as one of the antiques he collected, for you would sense that same note of careful consideration with which he approached everything, no matter how trivial. If the fish on the tea bowls didn't face in exactly the same direction, he'd be upset. It was like that with anything that came into his life. He always had to take it and arrange it in his mind with that same kind of care, get it just right so that it wouldn't bother his conscience.

Going to church was, no doubt, intended to strengthen that conscience, one that had long since been prepared for him by the sages of antiquity. And yet, he didn't want to dismiss everything new at one fell swoop just for the sake of that conscience, either. The upshot of all this was that the kind of guy he'd *like* to be was no match for the kid of guy he already *was,* and he just couldn't figure out *what* he ought to do. He probably really did love her but, for the sake of his younger brother, had no choice but to give her up, and *that* was something he couldn't tell anyone—even me.

He'd often say, "One of these days you and I are going to take an airplane ride, too!" Then he'd smile. But *he* wasn't really the one doing the smiling. *From the parental pair come body, skin, and hair*—and all that stuff from the classics about how a good elder brother is supposed to act was somewhere inside Black Li doing the smiling for him.[2]

I went and looked him up after lunch. For more than a month now, as soon as we met, he'd start in about his brother. But this time he changed his tune. There was a slight twinkle in his eyes and just the trace of a satisfied smile on his face, the kind you'd often see just after he'd succeeded in buying a rare book.

"Saw you at the church," I was the first to speak.

He nodded and gave me a great big smile. "That was *really* interesting!"

Whenever Black Li first came across anything new—new to him, that is, might be old hat to everyone else—he'd always say the same thing, "*Really* interesting!" Tell him an outlandish story about someplace being haunted by ghosts and you'd get "*Really* interesting!" He wouldn't argue with you about whether there are such things as ghosts. He'd simply swallow whatever you told him hook, line, and sinker. "In this old world of ours there are probably a lot stranger things than that," he'd observe comfortably. The way he saw it, anything was possible. And so he accepted things quite readily, but had no reasoned opinions of his own. It wasn't that he didn't *want* to have a better understanding of things, it was simply that whenever Black Li should have used his intellect, he used his emotions instead.

"Morality's the same the world over," he said. "It always tells people to sacrifice themselves for others."

"Haven't you already sacrificed a lover?" I wanted to keep the talk down to earth.

"Doesn't count. That was just a negative sort of sacrifice. I didn't give anything of myself away. These past ten days I've read through all the Four Gospels, and I've worked out what I should do. I ought to take an active part in Number Four's affairs, not just negatively refuse to let him leave me. Think about it. If he really was going through this whole business just to get his share of the family property, why didn't he come to me and say it up front?"

"Afraid you wouldn't go for it."

"No, that's not it. I've thought the whole thing over very carefully these past few days. The only possible explanation for the way he's acting is that he must be planning something dangerous. Don't you see? He wants to make a clean break so *I* won't be involved. We see him as young and impetuous, right? He knows that, and he's taking advantage of it to mislead us. But the fact of the matter is that he has *my* welfare in mind and wants to make sure I don't get hurt. If he gets me off into a safe corner, then he'll be free to act on his own, so that he'll be the only one held responsible if anything goes wrong. I'm sure that's it! But can an elder brother just sit back and watch his younger brother go down in flames? No! It's my place to sacrifice for *him*. When Mom was on her death bed. . . " He didn't go on, for he knew I'd heard all that stuff so often I could recite it myself.

Black Li had brought up a possibility I hadn't thought of, but I wasn't ready to go along completely. Maybe he'd let his emotions run away with him because of all that religious stuff. How could I tell? In sum, I wasn't convinced that his explanation was the right one. I'd have to have something more solid to go on. On the off chance that he *was* right, I decided to go look up White Li.

No matter how I tried, I couldn't locate his younger brother: school, dormitory, tennis court, library, little restaurants around campus—not a trace of him anywhere. Everyone I asked said he hadn't been around for quite a few days. That's what made White Li, White Li. If Black Li left home for a few days, he'd notify every last one of his friends before he left. White Li, on the other hand, would simply disappear into thin air. I came up with an emergency plan—go to *her* place.

Because I hung around with Black Li, she knew who I was. It turned out she hadn't seen White Li for quite some time, either. She seemed quite put out with the Li brothers—especially Black Li. While I was trying to find out about White Li, she kept turning the conversation to Black Li. I realized that Black Li was really the one she had her eyes on, maybe even loved. Or perhaps, for the time being, she just wanted him as a trophy, and if somebody better came along, she'd give him his walking papers; if nobody came along, then she might stick with him. Because of that thought—even though it was a fleeting one— I didn't avail myself of the golden opportunity I had to draw her and Black Li even closer together. Logically, that's what I ought to have done, I suppose, but I was just too fond of Black Li to do it. As far as I was concerned, only an angel from heaven would have been good enough for him.

After leaving her place, I was beside myself. Where had White Li gone? I couldn't tell Black Li he was *missing*. Just couldn't! If he found out, he'd have notices published in every last paper in town and be up every night trying out some new sort of divination technique to figure out where his younger brother was. On the other hand, if I went to see him and *didn't* tell him, I'd be itching to let him know the whole time I was there. Well then, maybe I just shouldn't go to see him in the first place. No, that wouldn't do, either.

When I arrived outside Black Li's study, I heard him humming to himself. Now that was something he'd never do unless he was in a good mood. As a rule he'd hum something like a line of poetry or maybe even sing that one line of opera which, for him, stood for every last piece of music ever written: "Deep within the chamber's shade / Flawless lies a piece of jade." But this time it wasn't anything like that. When I listened closely, I made out that it was a Christian hymn! Since he had no ear for music, every melody went into his ears as a shapeless lump and then, when he sang it, came back out the same way. Well, at any rate, he was in a good mood. But what was he so chipper about?

When I walked in, he immediately put down the hymnal and turned to me. He looked happy as a clam. "You couldn't have come at a better time. I was just about to go look you up. Number Four just left. Took a thousand dollars from me, but didn't say *anything* about breaking up! Not a word!"

Obviously he hadn't asked his younger brother what the money was to be used for, otherwise he wouldn't have been so cheerful. He must have decided that as long as White Li agreed to go on living with him, he'd adopt a hands-off policy regarding everything else. As long as his younger brother was willing to live at home, Black Li apparently thought that there was nothing to be afraid of, even if White Li *did* have some dangerous plan afoot. I saw that quite clearly now.

"Prayer really does work," he said, serious as could be. "I've been praying every day lately and, sure enough, Number Four hasn't mentioned breaking up. Even if he squanders every last penny we have, I'll still have a kid brother left at the end of it all."

I suggested that we drink our usual bottle of White Lotus. He smiled and shook his head. "You go ahead. I'll eat a little something just to keep you company. I've given up drinking."

I didn't drink anything, either, nor did I tell him how I had looked high and low for his brother. As long as White Li was home now, what was the point? But I did bring "her" up again. He smiled but didn't pick up on my obvious cue.

He didn't seem at all interested in talking about "her" *or* his younger brother. Just wanted to tell me Bible stories. I listened, but my mind was somewhere else. Although I couldn't have told you exactly what it was, something seemed awfully wrong in Black Li's attitude toward his younger brother and the girl he loved. This bothered me all the way home.

Another four or five days passed by, but I still couldn't get it off my mind. And then one night Wang Wu dropped by. He had pulled a rickshaw for the Li family for four years now. A little past thirty, he was an honest and reliable sort. According to what I'd heard tell, that scar on his head was the result of a mule bite he'd gotten as a kid. Except for drinking a bit now and then, Wang Wu had no real faults. Must have had a few too many tonight, because even his mule-bite scar was pretty red.

"What brings you here, Wang Wu?" I was on fairly close terms with him. Whenever I left the Li home late at night, he'd always insist on pulling me back to my place in his rig. And I, of course, would always give him a good-sized tip.

"Came to see you." He sat down.

I knew he had something to tell me. "Just made some tea. How about a bowl?"

"That'd be great. Here, I'll pour it myself. Really worked up a thirst. "

I gave him a cigarette and a place to begin. "Anything up?"

"Yup. I had a few too many and just couldn't keep my mouth shut—even though it was something I should've kept to myself." He took a deep drag on his cigarette.

"Well, if it's got to do with the Li family, you can't go wrong sharing it with me."

"That's what I thought, too." He paused a bit and then the wine he'd drunk urged him on. "I've been at the Li's place four years and thirty-five days now, and I'm in a real pickle. It's like this. Second Master treats me pretty well and Fourth

Master—well, he's just like a friend. That's what makes it so hard. Fourth Master won't let me tell Second Master anything about what he's up to. And Second Master is such a good-natured guy that I don't feel quite right about *not* telling him, but if I *do* say anything, I won't be doin' right by Fourth Master—and he's more like a friend.

"You can see what a terrible fix I'm in! By rights, I oughta favor Fourth Master because Second Master—no matter how kind he is—acts like a boss. And a boss is a boss, no matter how nice. A boss can never be like a brother to you or even like one of the guys. Don't get me wrong, Second Master can be very nice. For instance, in hot weather like we're havin' now, when I pull Second Master, he'll always find some lame excuse to let me stop and rest halfway. He'll buy a pack of matches, stop and browse at a bookstall—whatever. Why? 'Cause he wants to give me a rest and let me catch my breath. Why would I say he's a good boss if he wasn't like that? He *is* nice. I respect him, too. And one good turn deserves another, as they say. A guy who's been kickin' round the streets as long as I have certainly knows about that and understands how a guy's supposed to act." I let him have another bowl of tea to show that *I* was a guy who understood "how a guy's supposed to act," too. After he had finished it, he pointed at his chest with a cigarette and went on.

"But here, right here, I love Fourth Master. How come? 'Cause Fourth Master is young and doesn't treat me like a rickshaw puller. Those two brothers—and I'm talkin' about deep down in their hearts—are really different. Take Second Master. Soon as it turns hot, he worries about givin' me a rest. Fourth Master hasn't got time for stuff like that. Doesn't matter *how* hot it gets—when I pull him, I've gotta fly. But when we start talkin', he'll say stuff like, 'Why should *you* have to pull people around in a rickshaw?' He thinks it's a raw deal, not just for me but for every last rickshaw man on the face of the earth. Second Master treats *me* well, but he's never even thought about all us rickshaw guys. So you see, Second Master comes out good in little things, but Fourth Master really shows himself in the big stuff where it counts. Fourth Master couldn't care less about my legs, but he cares about the way I feel. Second Master worries about every piddlin' little thing inside the family and he's got real sympathy for my legs, but he doesn't really care about me here." He pointed to his chest again.

I knew he had more to say and was afraid that the strong tea I'd given him would undo the loosening effect of the wine he'd drunk. So now I came in with a little drumbeat to keep him from losing his rhythm. "Come on, Wang Wu, get it *all* off your chest. After all, I'm not the kind to go round running off at the mouth like some old lady and get you in trouble."

He rubbed the scar on his scalp, put his head down, and thought about that for a bit. Then he pulled his chair closer and lowered his voice. "Did ya know they're just about through puttin' in the trolley tracks? Well, when they start runnin' them cars, it's gonna be the end of us rickshaw pullers. I'm not just thinkin' of myself. either. I'm thinkin' of all us guys who pull rigs." He fixed me with a stare. I nodded.

"Fourth Master knows the score. That's part of why we're buddies. Anyway Fourth Master says to me, 'Wang Wu,' he says, 'we gotta come up with some way outta this.' And I says to him, 'There's only one way out—wreck the trolley cars!' And he says, 'You've got it! We'll smash the cars!' We kept on talkin' till we had it all worked out. Can't give ya the details. But what I do wanna tell ya is this." He dropped his voice even lower. "I spotted a detective tailin' Fourth Master! Could be it had nothin' to do with the trolley business. But anyway you cut it, havin' a detective on your heels isn't a good thing. Where's that leave me? Between a rock and a hard place! If I tell Second Master, it'll be like rattin' on Fourth. But if I *don't* tell him and somethin' goes wrong, the police'll haul Second Master in right along with his younger brother. I got no way out!"

After I got rid of Wang Wu, I mulled it all over in my own mind until I had it worked out. The way I saw it, Black Li had hit the nail on the head. White Li really was up to something dangerous. And I didn't think it was just limited to this trolley business, either. It was bound to be something a lot bigger than that. White Li wanted to break up the family so he wouldn't get Black Li involved. White Li wouldn't balk at sacrificing himself, of course—or even others, for that matter— but he couldn't bring himself to just up and sacrifice his own elder brother without a word of warning. Besides, it wouldn't do any good anyway. And let's say he *didn't* break up with Black Li right away but put things off until he was in the middle of the trolley business—well, at that late date he wouldn't have time to worry about protecting *anyone,* even his own elder brother.

What was *I* to do? If I told Black Li, he'd go ape trying to protect his younger brother. And if I tried to give White Li any advice, it would be useless, and I'd have to blow Wang Wu's cover to boot.

Things got tenser every day. The trolley company had already announced the date it would begin service. I couldn't put it off any longer. I just *had* to go tell Black Li, no matter what.

He wasn't home, but Wang Wu was. "Second Master?"

"Gone out."

"Didn't take your rig?"

"Hasn't let me pull him for a long time now. Wang Wu's scar flushed a deep purple as he spoke. "I had one too many again and let the cat out of the bag."

"How'd he take it?"

"Cried."

"Must've said something."

"Asked me what *I* was gonna do. I told him I'd be side by side with Fourth Master. He said, 'Good.' Not another peep out of him. Afterward he took to goin' out every day, but never wanted to go in my rig."

I must have waited there a good three hours before Black Li finally came home. It was already pitch-dark. "How are things going?" I hoped to find out everything with that single question.

He smiled. "They're not."

I never dreamed that Black Li would give *me* such a flippant—even insulting—reply. There was no point in asking anything else, for he'd obviously already decided on his plans. I felt like a drink, but since it'd be no fun to drink alone, the only thing I could do was leave. Before I went, I tried another tack. "Why don't we go off somewhere for a few days' vacation. What do you say?"

"Try me again in a couple of days" was all I got by way of reply. A person can be coldest when his feelings are the most passionate. Black Li had never treated me like that before.

I went to see him again the night before the trolleys were scheduled to start running. He wasn't home. I waited till midnight, but he still didn't show up. He must have been avoiding me on purpose.

Wang Wu came back. He smiled and said, "Tomorrow."

"Second Master?"

"Don't know. After you left that day, he used something or other to burn off his mole. Afterward he just sat there starin' at himself in the mirror."

Now that was the end of everything! Without that black mole, there simply *wasn't* any Black Li to wait for. I was already out the main gate when Wang Wu stopped me with a shout, "Tomorrow, if—" He felt the scab on his scalp. "Hope you'll help my mom out."

It must have been after five or so the next afternoon that Wang Wu came over to my place and burst into my room. He'd been running so hard his pants were soaked in sweat. "Wrecked 'em—we wrecked those suckers!" He was breathing too hard to get anything else out. At long last, having finally caught his breath, he snatched up my teapot, took a long drink from the spout, and added, "We demolished every last one of 'em! Didn't leave until they charged us with horses. They took young Sixth Ma away with them—saw it with my own eyes. We got the short end of the stick 'cause we had no weapons. What could we do with just bricks? Young Sixth Ma has probably had it."

"Fourth Master?"

"Didn't see 'im." Biting his lip, he thought for a bit before going on. "Damn, that turned into one hell of a riot! If they caught anybody, it'd have to be Fourth Master—he was the leader. But don't count him out too soon. Fourth Master may be young, but that kid's got some kinda smarts! It's probably all over for young Sixth Ma, but maybe not for Fourth Master. He mighta made it."

"You didn't see Second Master?"

"He didn't come home at all yesterday." He lowered his head in thought for a bit, and said, "I'll have to hole up here with you for a couple days."

"OK."

The next morning the newspapers carried the headlines: "Trolley Cars Demolished," "Riot Leader Li Seized on Spot," "Student and Five Rickshaw Men also Apprehended."

Looking at the paper and recognizing only the word *Li*, Wang Wu said, "Fourth Master's had it!" He lowered his head and pretended to scratch at his scab while his tears fell on the paper.

The news blanketed the city: Li and Young Sixth Ma were to be executed before a firing squad after being paraded through the city as examples to others.

The scorching sun had heated the cobblestones until they would burn a bare foot. Nonetheless, the streets were packed with spectators. Hands bound behind his back, a man sat on the floor of an open wagon. Police in khaki and soldiers in gray formed a guard before and behind the wagon. Sabers shimmered cold in the sunlight as the wagon drew ever closer. Two white streamers were attached to the vehicle and swayed lightly as it bumped along. The prisoner's eyes were closed. A drop of perspiration showed on his forehead. There was a slight movement of his lips, as though he was praying. Swaying back and forth in that sitting position, the prisoner passed directly in front of me.

Tears so overwhelmed my heart that it wasn't until well after the wagon had gone by that I came to myself again and began to follow it. All the way to the execution ground the condemned did not once raise his head.

The brows were slightly drawn, the lips partly open, and the chest soaked in blood. He seemed to have been praying at the moment of death. I claimed the body.

Several months later I ran into White Li in Shanghai. If I hadn't called, he would have hurried right on past.

"Number Four!"

"Huh?" He seemed startled. "Oh, you. I thought for a moment Number Two had come back to life."

Though I hadn't meant to, I had probably called to him in the same tone of voice Black Li might have used. Or perhaps it *was* Black Li—still very much alive in my heart—who had called him.

Looking a bit older now, White Li resembled his elder brother more than ever. He didn't seem to want to talk all that much and we exchanged but a few words. I still remember what he said. "Old Two is probably up in heaven—just the place for him—and I'm down here still trying to smash down the gates of hell."

Notes

1. The narrator refers to the rapid and erratic economic and political changes occurring in China during the 1920s and 1930s.

2. The quotation is from the opening lines of the *Classic of Filial Piety* (Xiaojing), a work dating from approximately the first century A.D. that both the narrator and Black Li were, no doubt, required to memorize as children. In describing his friend's smile, the narrator uses it as a tag referring to all the family responsibilities inculcated by the classic. For a translation of the classic, see Mary Leola Makra, trans., *The Hsiao Ching* (New York: St. John's University Press, 1961).

Also a Triangle

After beating a hasty retreat from the frontline, Ma Desheng and Sun Zhanyuan got rid of two guns, a few armlets, and a couple of watches, and thereby made a fortune of over five hundred dollars. They rented a room at Lord Guan's Temple in the city and lived high on the hog. Rigged out in outfits of foreign satin and sky blue jackets, faces scrubbed squeaky clean, and sporting crew cuts, they roamed the streets in and out of town. Before two months were out, they had spent nearly half their fortune. On no account were they going back to the sticks, but they knew nothing about setting up a business. Besides, they were a bit short on capital. In the end, going back to being soldiers after using up all their money seemed to be their only—and not an altogether unattractive—recourse. Both men were aware of this option. But on second thought, perhaps they could make a major change in the way they lived; that is, if they were able to effect it before their money completely ran out.

In the past, their bodies were part and parcel of their army uniforms and bayonets. When they weren't in battle, they tumbled about on the drill ground. When they were in battle, they ran toward the enemy's guns and bullets. Their lives were never their own but always at the army's beck and call. What would constitute a major change? To live peacefully and comfortably for a few days, something more comfortable than spending nights at Lord Guan's Temple and days traipsing about the streets. They ought to settle down and set up a home! Once they had a home, things might just get rolling in a new direction. Who knows, they might never have to be soldiers again, even though being in the ranks was not entirely a bad deal. Both men could not but consider this other option, for a man without a family was bound to find his life incomplete. They would have to settle down right away, because their money seemed to be slipping out of their hands faster than an army is deployed. And why *wouldn't* their money slip away— the two friends were bighearted men. When they met other friends or beggars who made more than the usual number of pleas, money would inadvertently disappear. If they were to get married, then they'd have to get on with it; they couldn't wait until they had nothing but copper coins left in their pockets.

Both men mulled over all this, but it was impossible to talk about it with each other. From the standpoint of friendship, they were sworn brothers. They had been in battle together, had been wounded and hospitalized together, had slept side by side, had stolen together, and now they were living together at Lord Guan's Temple. To be sure, they could share clothes and socks together, but did that mean? . . . It was impossible to talk about it. The more one shared one's clothes, food, and drink, the more one showed one's code of brotherhood and loyalty. No matter what, two men couldn't share a single wife. But that's all they had money for. There was no way they could afford two. If each took a wife, then by the time they'd shelled out their silver on a double ceremony, they'd end up staring at their brides empty-handed. A lot of fun that would be!

Another scenario might be for one to get married and for the other to go on playing the bachelor. But who? In terms of age, they were both past thirty—no small-fry. In terms of friendship, they would risk their lives for each other. How could one of them possibly settle down and leave his friend out in the cold? Split their money, and each go his own way? Like hell, they would. To dissolve, in a single day, a friendship of ten-odd years was something they dared not even imagine. There simply wasn't a solution. The more helpless they felt, the more often it occurred to them that they were past thirty, that their money was almost gone, and that it was high time they changed their line of work. Though being soldiers wasn't bad, sooner or later they were bound to run into a couple of bullets. If two sworn brothers couldn't even choose one "body" at a whorehouse, how could they share one wife? Even after the two of them had gulped down four catties of *baigan*[1] and had opened up completely to each other, they still couldn't bring *that* up.

Ma Desheng—styled "Guofan"[2] on his newly printed name card (a fortune-teller had given him the name)—was the elder brother. His head was shaped like a quince, and though the skin on his face wasn't too coarse, it was blotchy and just didn't look quite together. Sun Zhanyuan was the younger brother. A fat head with big ears—he was your typical pork-shop stud. When Big Brother Ma wanted to be generous, he would first raise his eyebrows. Sometimes when he thought of his dead mother, he would cry and curse on the streets. Kid Brother Sun was forever friendly. Even when walking on the streets in civilian clothes, he would give people a hand salute.

Now, because of *that*, Big Brother Ma's eyebrows had already stood up for three days. The friendlier Kid Brother Sun got, the more reluctant both were to broach the subject.

Ma Desheng lay on the bed, scratching his quince head, unable to figure out what the hell the name "Guofan" meant. In fact, he wasn't brooding over that. Sun Zhanyuan was reading *The Eight Great Codes of Brotherhood* by the kerosene lamp.

Whenever he came across a character with the woman radical, a bridal sedan floated before his eyes, and each time the sedan went by, he lost his place in the book. Piqued, he decided not to read anymore. Picking up the small round mirror with the photo of the Beijing opera actress Jin Yulan on the back, he scrutinized his teeth. They were even and white—so what? He turned the mirror around to look at Jin Yulan. She was no big deal, either—just another fat broad. Out of the blue, he said, "Big Brother, did ya hear Xiao Yangfeng sing 'Spring in Jade Hall'? Now *that* was fuckin' dull."

"*All* those female entertainers are fuckin' ass dull." Big Brother's eyebrows shot up, expressing empathy for his sworn brother.

His sworn brother flipped the mirror over again to look at his teeth. This time it was to look exclusively at his two front teeth, big and glaringly white, a definite eyesore.

The two of them fell silent again, both thinking how "fuckin' dull" female entertainers were, both thinking of another kind of woman—the kind who poured tea, washed clothes, made dinner, was always by your side, raised your kids, and was buried with you when you were both dead. From here their thoughts turned with embarrassment to *that*. What good were street broads? Better to have an honest-to-goodness wife. Big Brother Ma's "quince" felt a bit itchy; Kid Brother Sun seemed barely able to sit still. On further thought, why shouldn't they share one? No, that wouldn't be right, shouldn't think that way. However, both of them *were* thinking that way, and moreover, were thinking of some even *more* embarrassing situations. Though embarrassing, they were nevertheless intriguing. Though intriguing, they were, to be sure, embarrassing. Big Brother Ma forced out a big yawn. Kid Brother Sun followed suit with an even bigger one.

The pig-head vendor who lived in the temple came back. Sun Zhanyuan went out to buy a pig tongue leftover in the basket. The two brothers each snacked on half a pig tongue and a rice bowlful of hot water, but they still felt life was dull and pointless.

The two of them were the temple's resident moneybags, not that the temple was filled with poor people. Take the proprietor of the pork shop, for example. Buried in his *kang*³ were seven to eight hundred hefty, greasy silver dollars. But his money never left his *kang*. Or take Mr. Zhang, who lived in the rear hall. He had once been a county magistrate and had been in possession of a hundred thousand dollars or so. But Magistrate Zhang had spent all his money on opium, while his concubine had run off with another man. However, when it came to spending, no one could match the two sworn brothers—they spent money like water and didn't smoke opium, either. The pork-shop proprietor could count on their business and never had to haggle over prices. Name the price, and they paid it, without ever demanding a discount on account of their being fellow tenants at Lord Guan's Temple. Everybody at the temple loved them.

The one who loved them most dearly was Mr. Li Yonghe. Mr. Li was probably *born* looking like a traitor. Otherwise, how was it that as soon as anyone saw him, the word *traitor* would immediately spring to mind. Lean and tall, with a pointy head and a scallion-like neck, he always wore a thin, long gown that seemed to stretch from the ground to the sky. Wearing satin shoes, he made no sound at all when he walked. He never failed to wear his clothes thin and long. He could pinch pennies at times, just like the rest of the people in the temple. But no matter how hard up he was, he always wore a long gown. As a last resort, he could pawn or sell the clothes hugging his body, but he never gave up his outer gown. His long gown was thin, probably so that when it was time to wear an unlined jacket, it wouldn't look too obviously empty inside, and in fact, it did provide some insulation. Such an approach had a lot to do with his profession. A long gown and satin shoes were requisite. When acting as a matchmaker or go-between, setting up home mortgages, selling real estate, or handling buyouts, he would not be able to earn his client's confidence if he didn't wear his long gown. He swore by a "buyer 3 percent, seller 4 percent" commission. His long gown was both his trademark and benchmark.

As soon as the two moneybags moved into the temple, Li Yonghe had them figured out. Whatever he looked at—people, houses, land, merchandise—was all the same to him. He couldn't care less whether a person had a nose or not. He first determined what you were worth, then figured out his share in brokerage fees. His friendship with people terminated the day he collected his fees. He was wholly aware that these people weren't about to come back for more business. He didn't bother with the residents in the temple, because practically all of them had been his clients before and dared not ask for his advice anymore. Except for Magistrate Zhang, who had given him more business than the rest. People who smoke opium would rather get the short end of the stick than get out of bed. But lately even Magistrate Zhang wasn't inclined to greet him, because Li had become much too brazen. Once on commission, Li had taken Magistrate Zhang's magenta lamb-fur gown out, only to come back with a measly number of the pills that supposedly helped people kick the opium habit. "You'd better stop smoking," he chastised Magistrate Zhang.

"Sure would save me from making a fool of myself running all over town trying to get rid of a lamb-fur jacket. No one's wearing lamb now, or even fox leg!" Naturally, Magistrate Zhang wasn't about to rush out into the streets to check the veracity of this statement. Consequently, he lay on the bed and nearly died from withdrawal symptoms.

Li Yonghe had been treated to quite a few meals by the two brothers. After the first meal, he had already sounded out their hearts. On the pretext of a business proposal, he had elicited and noted their cash standing. He got himself treated to more meals, and after a few rounds of drinking, he read them like a book. He saw that they were firefly-asses that weren't glowing too brightly, as inept at being soldiers as Zhang had been as a magistrate. Push the panic button, and they would open fire. Therefore he didn't reel them *all* the way in. Might as well enjoy a few free meals first. He'd wait until the two of them came swimming up to his door before he gave his reel a couple of turns. Though they were a pair of fireflies, a glow was a glow, after all. Whether it be for more or for less, even if he had to settle for only a new pair of satin shoes, he wasn't about to offend the God of Wealth—after all, when he paid his annual New Year's visit to the temple of the God of Wealth, he had to borrow a first-rate paper gold ingot.

The two brothers were too embarrassed to discuss this woman business with each other, and so each had discussed it on the sly with Mr. Li. As soon as Mr. Li had opened his mouth, he made them feel that the world was filled with things about which they knew nothing.

"Firing guns at the battlefield—now that's where you're the veterans. Sure is no piece of cake being in the ranks of the army!" said Mr. Li, after which he lowered his voice. "But if you're talking about getting a wife and settling down, I'd bet my ass that you two probably still haven't quite experienced all the possibilities."

On hearing this, Ma and Sun were even more convinced that they had no choice but to experience all the possibilities. This had to be one hell of a juicy affair, a really big deal, and something "fuckin' ass good." It had to be completely different from standing at attention and marching forward. If a man hadn't had a taste of this, then even if he had been in a hundred battles, he'd still be a loser!

How much would all this cost, then?

Once this came up, Mr. Li, in wizardlike fashion, stumped them with a counter question, "What kind of woman are you looking for?"

They were tongue-tied. With perfect timing, Mr. Li then began rattling off his sales pitch. Women, it turned out, were classified into several grades, so of course, prices would vary. Take, for example, the one Mr. Li introduced to Regiment Commander Chen. Just the candy sent out with the engagement announcements amounted to a thousand two hundred bags, at 35 silver cents per bag. Thirty-five cents; ten bags, $3.50; a hundred bags, $35.00; a thousand bags, $350.00; altogether 420 silver dollars—and just for the candy! Besides this, there were four diamond rings that even minor stage stars like Little Perfume and Diamond had on their fingers! And besides that . . .

The two brothers felt let down. Fortunately Mr. Li took just the right turn. "Of course, you brothers want someone who can wash clothes and cook, isn't picky about food or drink, doesn't gossip or nitpick, isn't sly, won't make you into cuckolds, a young woman with high aspirations."

"What do women like that cost a piece?"

"Three to four hundred a shot, and the father-in-law a rickshaw puller at that."

Whether the father-in-law was a rickshaw puller or a donkey driver didn't matter, but three to four hundred was a bit hard to swallow. Though the two brothers almost choked on the idea, the possibility of *sharing* a wife came back to mind.

If Mr. Li—in his long gown and satin shoes—didn't laugh at this arrangement, then perhaps it wasn't a bad idea after all. Mr. Li not only didn't shake his head, he even produced a great deal of evidence to prove that this wasn't at all a new discovery of theirs. Even wealthy people handled things the same way; their protocal was slightly different, that was all. For instance, Director Ding's wife often stayed over at General Jiang's, even though that was by no means her maternal home.

Mr. Li's logic became even more convincing. "We brothers have to think ahead, though we shouldn't think too far ahead. A man's got to do what he's got to do. Who knows whether we'll wake up to wear the shoes we took off the night before! To have children and raise them—who doesn't want to have children and raise them? But that'll come later. For now, it'd sure make sense to have some fun first."

The two men were reminded of scenes of bullets whizzing through the air. Who cares that they didn't die before; who can guarantee that they won't die in the future? And if they did die, who'd care? And supposing they *did* share a wife, who'd care about that, either? Of course, there'd be some problems, such as whose child would it be after it was born? But one "shouldn't think too far ahead." Mr. Li was a genius, qualified to be the chief adviser to an army division!

Was there any woman willing to do it?

Was it better than being a prostitute? Mr. Li stumped them again. Coming to the same conclusion separately, they both vested Mr. Li with full authority. What the hell, act now, think later. With Mr. Li shuttling back and forth between them, they didn't need to talk face-to-face.

Things began to take shape. The two brothers couldn't go on sounding each other out by exchanging glances. To get a wife, even if it meant using a method of a limited partnership, would require some preparation. They had managed, with no small amount of sweat, to break through this awkward predicament, which once overcome turned out not to be such a hot potato after all. They felt, on the contrary, that their brotherly friendship had become even deeper—something they hadn't expected! The two of them decided to limit betrothal gifts to 120 dollars, not a penny more. Next, they would keep the room in the temple and rent another one outside, so that when they took turns in the bridal chamber, the one off duty would have a base to return to. As for who would first be in the frontline, Kid Brother Sun unconditionally yielded to Big Brother Ma. Big Brother Ma vehemently proposed drawing lots, but this was an order Kid Brother Sun would not obey no matter what.

The auspicious date was set for the second day of the tenth month. The brothers had sky blue cotton gowns and green satin mandarin jackets made to order.

Besides a remuneration of 10 dollars, Mr. Li also pocketed 70 of the 120 dollars for betrothal gifts.

Old Lin Four was not the type of man to sell his daughter. But his two sons were both unfilial. One was living in a small shop, and the whereabouts of the other was unknown. How could the old man afford not to pull a rickshaw himself? His daughter was already twenty. Old Lin Four wasn't uninterested in finding someone for her, but what would he have to live for if he were to let his daughter go? This wasn't purely self-interest on his part, either. After all, how many rickshaw pullers' daughters married rich? But if she stayed with him, through thick and thin, she would still be with her father after all. To marry a young fellow who pulled rickshaws might not necessarily be better than staying at home. Though this sort of thinking wasn't the most enlightened, in not taking care of the matter, time passed by quickly. In a flash, the young girl was already twenty.

Old Lin Four absolutely detested Mr. Li. Each time he got sick and couldn't go out to pull his rickshaw, Mr. Li would be sure to show up and give him the glad eye. He knew Mr. Li's eyes were really on the girl. Old Lin Four's worth, in Mr. Li's eyes, lay in his daughter. Old Lin Four once punched Mr. Li out the door. This didn't make Mr. Li a whit worried or angry; on the contrary, he became friendlier and more determined to take care of the Lin girl's marriage, no matter what.

Old Lin got sick. Mr. Li visited him quite a few times. Without being asked, Mr. Li offered to lend some money to Old Lin Four, but Old Lin threw the money to the ground.

By the seventh day that Old Lin lay ill, his daughter had already gone without food for two days. There was nothing left to pawn, nothing left to sell, and no place to borrow money from. Old Lin Four wished only for a quick death, but knew that he couldn't go in peace—leaving a daughter who hadn't eaten for two days. Even if he didn't die and did recover, he still wouldn't be able to go pull his rickshaw right away, so what were they to eat?

Mr. Li came again, placed fifty silver dollars in front of Old Lin Four: "You have your coffin, your girl has a place to eat—a formal wedding. I want a snappy answer. An OK, and the money is yours." He pushed the money forward. "A no, and you've lost your chance!"

Old Lin Four couldn't say anything. He looked at his daughter; his mouth quivered. He seemed to be asking, Why did you have to be born in my home?

"We'll die, Father, we'll die together!" She looked at the silver dollars as she spoke; how she wished she could smash those silver dollars with her eyes. See who had more power in the end—man or money.

Old Lin Four shut his eyes.

Mr. Li smiled and slowly picked up the silver dollars piece by piece, making faint clanging sounds.

On the tenth piece of silver, Old Lin Four suddenly opened his eyes. He didn't know where he got the strength to say, "Hand them over!" His two hands pressed down on the money. "Hand them over!" He wanted the ten dollars in Mr. Li's hand.

Old Lin Four crawled over. He seemed to pass out. After a

long time, he raised his head a bit. "My girl, you have to find a way to live; just forget you ever had this father."

"You've sold your daughter?" she asked. She didn't have even half a teardrop.

Old Lin Four didn't make a sound.

"All right, then, whatever you say, Father."

"I'm *not* your father," Old Lin Four was still pressing down on the money.

Mr. Li was delighted and felt like commending the father and daughter, but he merely said, "The wedding's set for the second of the tenth month."

The young girl didn't feel at all that there was anything to be ashamed of. Sooner or later, it had to be this way. So long as she wasn't sold to one who sold people, it was a good thing. She couldn't see any light ahead of her. She only felt that her life had been nailed down even more securely. For good or evil, her life had been nailed to a place unknown. It was sure to be a dark cavernlike place, just like her home. But since she had been nailed to that place by fifty white and shiny silver dollars, there was nothing she could do about it. Those silver dollars were her father's coffin and the dark cavern of her own future.

Big Brother Ma rented a small north room in a compound close to the temple and stuck a happiness character on the door, then sent for a red sedan chair to carry the Lin girl over.

The young girl had nothing to weep for, neither did she have anything to be excited about. She sat on the *kang* and saw a man with a big quince head. She knew that she had become Mrs. Quince, and her life was stuck to a quince. She didn't like this quince, but she couldn't say she was annoyed with him, either. Her life wasn't hers to begin with. She and her father's coffin were altogether worth only fifty dollars.

Quince's mouth reeked of wine. She bore it. She knew that all men drank. She remembered her father once hitting her mother when he was drunk. Quince's eyebrows stood up, but she wasn't afraid. Quince wasn't completely harsh, but she didn't like him. She only knew that this quince that fell from heaven had some connection to her—perhaps good, perhaps bad. She acknowledged this little relationship, and wasn't too willing to think of the good or bad aspects. She only felt the equivocalness of life in this fixed relationship.

Big Brother Ma, however, felt just great. After ten years of carrying guns, only now had he grasped something that was more alive, soft, and lovable than the barrel of a gun. The scenes of bullets whizzing through the air and the warmth of this small room had absolutely nothing in common. Next to Quince was a living being, which could breathe and serve him. He no longer wanted to share this happiness with his sworn brother. This had to be something personal; otherwise he would lose everything! He felt as though his life had just been planted in fertile soil—he couldn't uproot it. Even when planting beans, one wouldn't do such a thing!

The next morning, he didn't want to get up, nor did he want to see Kid Brother Sun again. He planned things he never thought of before. He wanted to mark out a line for this lifelong relationship—a line that would run next to hers. Because they ran side by side, these two lines would crisscross each other and change as they advanced, like forming a battle array during an autumn drill. He would be the first line of defense, she the second, and in the future there'd be a third. The camp would grow more stable with every passing day. He couldn't see his sworn brother anymore.

However, he had to go to the temple, even though it was very difficult. To go from the small north room to the temple was to do an about-face from an autumn drill to mere play, from singing military songs to cracking jokes. As soon as he arrived at the temple, the line that had already been drawn was completely smeared. Nevertheless, he had to go. One couldn't go back on one's word with a friend. One shouldn't have said such things in the first place, and it seemed too late to regret it. Or just *maybe* it wasn't too late, if his sworn brother could bring himself to yield.

His sworn brother showed no signs of yielding! Kid Brother Sun's attitude was still to treat the whole thing as a joke. Since they had agreed to it in a joking mood, how could they now turn their faces and not acknowledge it as such? After all, who was more important—friend or woman? Big Brother Ma couldn't make up his mind. He could see nothing else now; what remained was only that at night he'd have to sleep in the temple and tell his sworn brother to go to that small north room. This wasn't relieving a garrison, nor retreating; it was opening the gates and letting the enemy into one's camp! Big Brother Ma slept remorsefully in the temple for half a day.

At night, Sun Zhanyuan set off for the small room with the happiness character.

When he was about to reach the door, his lighthearted feelings were gone for some reason. He came to a halt, feeling uncomfortable. This wasn't the same as whoring. There wasn't anything like this under the sky. He thought of Big Brother Ma. Big Brother Ma had gotten married last night. She ought to be *Sis-in-law* Ma. He couldn't!

He had to go in. How could he know that things would be this tough? He went in.

The Lin girl—or more appropriately Sis-in-law Ma—was sitting on the *kang* lost in a trance before the small kerosene lamp.

What was he to say?

Could he rape her? No, he couldn't. This wasn't like being on the frontline. Now he was quite clearheaded. He stood there, rooted to the spot.

Tell her everything? His head began to perspire.

But it never occurred to him to rub his head and leave. She was, after all, also his. Half of that 120 dollars was his.

She sat down.

She thought he was Quince's friend, and said, "He hasn't come back yet."

As soon as she made a sound, he immediately felt that she should be his. She wasn't very pretty, but she was, after all, a woman. He hated Big Brother Ma a little. Friends like Big Brother Ma were a dime a dozen in the army barracks. A woman, a wife, this was something he never had before. He couldn't retreat. He knew that he was better looking than Big Brother Ma, better at talking than Big Brother Ma. To set up a family and establish a career was *his* type of thing, not Big Brother Ma's. He thought of asking her whom she loved after all, but being too embarrassed to open his mouth, he just sat there, unable to say a word.

After he had been sitting for a long while, she began to grow suspicious.

The more he looked at her, the more he was loathe to leave. Sometimes he even wanted to go over and forcefully hug her. Perhaps if he overcame his embarrassment, things would be easier. But he sat there without moving.

No, he *didn't* want her; she was already used goods. Better that he leave. No, he couldn't leave. He couldn't let Ma Desheng have all the advantages. Ma Desheng already had gotten the long end of the stick!

She looked at him sitting there all along without moving and staring at her. She couldn't help getting red in the face. He was indeed better looking than that Quince and quite well behaved. At the same time, she was a bit afraid of him, perhaps because he was good-looking.

She blushed. He charged forward. He couldn't think anymore. He couldn't control himself anymore. Fire burned in his eyes. She was a woman, a woman, a woman. He had no time to think of anything else. He put everything aside. What remained was just man and woman, man and woman; he didn't care about husband and wife, didn't care about friend and friend. There was no future, only the present. Now he wanted to give free play to his power as a man. She blushed in such a lovable way!

She moved farther into the *kang* and turned pale. With the Quince, she had completely followed the natural course of things, because marriage, to begin with, was meant to solve her three meals and her father's coffin. Whether it was a quince or a golden pear, she had no freedom. But she wasn't prepared for this. This man was indeed more comfortable to look at than the Quince, but she had already become the Quince's wife!

When he saw her move away, he was pleased. If she had sat there without moving, he wouldn't have been able to strike. When she moved, he felt as if he had caught something, as if she had committed a wrong that had to be chased and attacked. When a victorious army is on the pursuit, one no longer looks at the defeated soldiers ahead of him as human beings. Sun Zhanyuan was savoring this again. She was no longer a person; neither was she related to any person. She was a thing that tickled your heart—pursue her! He opened his mouth, ready to shout one, two, three—four, just as soldiers always did when they ran, ready to mouth off the volley of curses that were a part of chasing down the enemy. Once on the attack, his mouth opened on its own. "You don't have to hide, I'm also—" All of a sudden, he stood still, as if struck by an acute illness. His eyes stared at the bed.

He was overcome with regret. Why didn't they plan things ahead of time!? They could have planned it so that on the day Big Brother Ma had her, he would blow out the lamp around nine o'clock at night, pretend to go out for a leak, and they'd take the opportunity to switch places. They could have spared themselves this mess.

While he was lost in thought, she took the chance to move to the *kang*'s edge. She thought of running out while he was off his guard. But there was no way she could escape without bumping into him. She was afraid to bump into him but afraid, too, to remain sitting still. She was just thinking of an idea when he seemed to suddenly wake up.

"You don't have to be afraid. I'm leaving." He laughed. "The two of us got you for the both of us. I got a bad deal. I'm leaving."

Not even in her wildest dreams had she expected anything like this. He really did leave. What was she to do? He probably wouldn't give up just like that, and the Quince naturally wouldn't let go. What if both of them came at the same time? Go to her father for advice? How could he help when he was so sick and frail? Leave this small room? Where would she go? But if she stayed, what was she to do if the two of them came back together? She circled the room a few times and sat on the edge of the *kang* in a daze.

Sometime after ten o'clock, the persimmon vendor who lived in the compound returned.

She began to feel even more afraid. If they didn't come, well that would be that, but if they did, it had to be together!

She figured that no one would yield and no one would do in the other. They would surely come to an agreement. In a friendly manner, they would come together, manage to overcome their shame, and then . . .

When she got to this point, she had to grasp something, stand up, walk out, go look for her father. She had just opened the door, when she saw standing outside it a pair, one whose head was shaped like a quince, the other with a fat head and big ears. Both were leering at her with their white teeth, and reeking heavily of wine.

Notes

1. A catty (*jin*) is equivalent to 500 grams or 1.1 pounds; *baigan* (also called *baijiu*), or "white liquor," is usually distilled from sorghum or corn.

2. A "style" *(zi)* is a name taken at the age of twenty. The fortune-teller has given Ma Desheng the name of the famous scholar-official Zeng Guofan (1811–1872), whose Hunan army helped end the Taiping Revolution in 1864.

3. Brick bed that can be heated from within.

An Old Man's Romance

They may come sugarcoated on the outside, but words said by way of consoling oneself are bitter on the inside. Old Liu no longer spoke such words. Some defeats are the result of a man's own uselessness, while others are brought on by forces beyond his control. Old Liu was convinced that he himself was not a useless man, and therefore he had no need of such sugarcoated words—words that advertise a man's weakness. From now on he was determined to do his damndest, to be hard-nosed with everything and everybody. There was no longer any reason to be polite. His past defeats had come about because outside forces had taken advantage of him. Now it was time to avenge himself. Already sixty, he simply had to live on, to continue his life for at least several decades so that he might show society that Old Liu was, after all, a man to be reckoned with. Since society had not done right by him, there was no need for him to do right by society, either. His only real responsibility was to do right by *himself,* to do right by this life of his. The discovery of such a truth at sixty could not be regarded as too late. From here on out there would be no more self-consoling words. Old Liu declared war on everything and everybody.

Of all the enterprises he had been involved in, name one

Translated by William A. Lyell

that he had not planned out and carried through by himself! Yes, he had talent. He had vision. The trouble was, once he had something going, everybody and his brother would jump in and milk it for all it was worth. Yes, they had all victimized him. Before turning sixty, Old Liu always saw these various enterprises as so many new roads he was opening up for himself, and so he always forgave his friends for horning in. "Take any new enterprise and you'll find that *I'm* the one who leads the way. And if other people also manage to get something out of it—well, fine and good!" After turning sixty, however, he could no longer afford to think so generously. The idea of lying stretched out in his coffin, loaded down with resentment over past generosities, was not a sweet one. He'd have to skim some cream off the top while there was still time.

Name one thing in which he hadn't done right by people or in which he hadn't given it his all. Name one thing where he had just been a tagalong or where his strategy had been anything less than brilliant. You couldn't! And how about politics? Name a single influential political party he hadn't been the first to join. Or take social welfare. Name one profitable work of charity that he hadn't launched. And how about his relationships with people in general? Was there anyone worth cultivating that he hadn't gotten in good with? In all honesty, he could say he had never fallen behind in any area of his life— and yet he had never really gotten ahead, either. Fate! No, it wasn't fate. It was all because he was *too* honest, too easygoing, too readily bamboozled. Now that he was sixty he finally saw the light: unless a man is thoroughly ruthless and unmitigatedly vicious, he doesn't stand a chance.

Old Liu had also done everything for his family that a man possibly could. When he lost his wife in his forties, he hadn't thought of taking another. He had done right by the departed spirit of the dead, and he had also done right by the living: he had refused to do wrong by his children just for the sake of his own comfort. Children! His son had been born a moron and his daughter—a daughter for whom he had already arranged an excellent match—had seen fit to run off with some pauper of an artist! He couldn't be bothered about her anymore. She'd made her bed; let her lie in it. He had done right by her; it was *she* who was shameless. No matter how moronic his son was, Old Liu would have to support the lad, and when the time came, he'd also have to get a wife for him. Anything that should be done in this life, Old Liu had to do. Who told him to have such a moron for a son?

The weather was unusually cold. A night of northerly wind had covered the water jar inside Old Liu's room with a layer of ice. He had to get up bright and early this morning. As he emerged from the warm nest of his quilt, a gust of cold air grabbed his old bones and wrung them into a chilled lump. He was racked by a fit of coughing. He *had* to get up. Even the wind was trying to bully him, but Old Liu was not going be cowed. He coughed, swore, and put on his clothes.

Old Liu stepped down to the floor. The stove hadn't been lit. Amah Zhang was probably not up and about yet. He really *was* too easygoing—even indulging an old female servant until she had become utterly worthless. He'd have to give her a good scolding. Peace at any cost just didn't make sense.

He went outside and paced back and forth in the court-yard. Though it had subsided somewhat, the wind was still bitter cold and cut to the bone. Although the sun wasn't up yet, a bit of cheerless red had begun to show on the eastern horizon. Yellow sand, which had blown in during the night, dimmed the blue of the sky directly overhead. Old Liu felt depressed. He called Amah Zhang.[1] She had already gotten up and was now in the kitchen making rice gruel. He didn't scold her, but when he asked for his morning basin of water to wash up in, his tone was gruff. Old Liu's only son was still asleep in his room on the southern side of the family compound.

Listening to the sounds of his son's slumber from outside the window, he felt even more at loose ends.

He didn't believe in divine justice. Just plain didn't, that's all. For if Old Heaven above possessed any intelligence at all, how could it have inflicted such a son on him? You could find any number of people in this world with less upstairs than Old Liu, and yet, contrary to all rhyme and reason, *his* son had turned out to be mentally retarded. It just didn't make any sense. But sense or no sense, he had no choice but to walk the road life had set out for him. And so, even though his son was a moron, he would still have to find him a wife. Old Heaven had seen fit to give Old Liu a hard time and that meant that he, in turn, had no choice but to give some poor girl out there a hard time of it as well. Since Old Heaven had dealt him a moronic son, some girl would have to end up with a moronic husband. There was no way around it. What's more, it wasn't at all unjust.

After washing his face, Old Liu gazed musingly at himself in the mirror. Although he was getting along in years, one had to admit that he was still rather handsome. He began recalling his youth. In his twenties, thirties, and forties he had always been quite presentable, and now that he was sixty, he still wasn't hard to look at—thin face, dark beard, high-bridged nose, and eyes full of spirit. And to think that Old Liu, favored with a countenance like that, hadn't even considered taking a second wife when his first died, much less taking a mistress or the like. . . . To be sure, he'd gone to his share of brothels, but that was only because he had tagged along to keep his friends company. With regard to proper women, he had always kept a respectful distance. He couldn't neglect his own interests just for the sake of a female. But where did those interests lie? He had arranged marriages and the purchase of concubines, but it had always been for *other* people. He had never gotten anything out of it himself; for that matter, he hadn't even received the appreciation that was properly due him.

Amah Zhang brought breakfast. Old Liu dived in with a vengeance. Ordinarily he ate only one bowl of rice gruel and a *shaobing*.[2] Today he ate a double portion and had Amah Zhang boil him a couple of eggs to boot. Old Liu felt that today he had to eat, had to fortify himself. Only when a man ate something, swallowed it down, and had it there in the pit of his stomach could he really feel that he hadn't been taken advantage of. After breakfast, Old Liu took a damp towel and smoothed his beard in preparation for the impending expedition. The wind was blowing hard again, but Old Liu wasn't about to let himself be intimidated by that. After taking a lifetime of knocks, was he *now* to be browbeaten by the wind? In his mind he went over all the errands on his agenda for that day—no, better to say all the *battles* he had to win. No more would he allow others to make off with the fruits of his own labor. He vowed to stake those old bones of his on a fight to the bitter end.

He would have to go to the Relief Association first. He was its founder. Why was it then that the money, rice, and clothing was all in the hands of Fei Zichun?[3] What's more, why was the society's car also at Fei's exclusive disposal? Yes, he'd start out today by having it out with Zichun. He just couldn't afford to go on being so stupid. Old Liu had helped out in the relief of who knows how many disasters. And what did he have to show for it? Well, this time he wasn't going to give an inch!

He donned an otter-collared coat that reached to his feet, put on a three-flapped fur cap, and took up his walking stick, comfortably conscious that he presented a rather well-to-do appearance. Old Liu had been in this world sixty years and could not remember having been helplessly down-and-out once during all that time. He wasn't old. A great deal of the future was still before him. If only he could manage to be thoroughly ruthless and unmitigatedly vicious, the day was bound to come when Old Liu would finally do right by himself.

The sun was already out, but its feeble rays seemed to shiver in the wind as Old Liu pushed open his door. He wasn't conscious of the cold, for his belly had food in it, the clothes on his body were thick, and his heart was burning with ardor. Since the fullness of his belly and the warmth of his body had both been won through the sweat of his own brow, Old Liu had no need to be grateful to Old Heaven above. And now, if he could only manage to topple Fei Zichun, he'd feel even more secure and comfortable. He was happy now. Yes, first he'd have it out with the north wind, and then he'd take on Fei Zichun. As he moved through the courtyard of his family compound toward the main gate that opened out onto the street, Old Liu caught sight of his son standing in the doorway of the southern room, his bed quilt draped about him. Not bad looking. Had Old Liu's stature, same long face, high nose—in fact, everything but Old Liu's brains. He loved this doltish lad of his with all his heart. Although his daughter was intelligent, she had run off on the sly with that pauper of an artist. As far as Old Liu was concerned, a son who was short on brains was preferable. What's more, as long as the father had ability, it didn't really matter if the son *was* a bit off, though it would have been better, of course, had the boy had a little more upstairs.

"Get inside; you'll freeze!" he ordered in a harsh voice, though his heart was brimming with affection.

"Pa!" the lad called out in hurt tones that bespoke the sufferance of some injustice. His ruddy face was flushed with passion, his eyes burned brightly, and his gaze was straight and sure. "When are you gonna bring a daughter-in-law into the house for me? Going back on your promise? Better watch it or I'll give you a good working over!"

"What kind of talk is that! Get back in there!" Old Liu barked every word and, gesticulating with his cane, drove the doltish youth back into his room. And then the father's heart softened. This was his only son. OK, so he *wasn't* the smartest thing that ever came down the pike. Yet who was to say that in the long run such a lad might not turn out to be a much better bet than some youngster who was brainy and slick? As though in a trance, Old Liu gazed at the back of his retarded offspring. As he stood there contemplating the red-and-blue striped quilt draped across the lad's back, he came very close to forgetting what he had to do that day. The son went back into his room, neglecting to close the door. Old Liu hurried over and gently drew it closed.

After going out the main gate and onto the street, Old Liu began thinking about Fei Zichun again. Looking up Fei, however, wasn't the only thing he had to do today. He had to go to the city council as well. He'd boosted them all up to the positions they held today. And now they thought they were going to cut Old Liu out, did they? Well, he'd show *them* a trick or two! And how about Sun Laoxi[4] of the Merchant Association? Old Liu was not about to let *him* off, either. From here on out, he'd never be the easygoing fellow he used to be. Somehow or other, he also had to sandwich in time to arrange for a daughter-in-law to pair off with his son. Well, he could always go to see Feng Er[5] about that after he had given Sun Laoxi his comeuppance.

While in the midst of working these things out in his mind, Old Liu emerged from the lane where he lived out onto a main thoroughfare, where the cold north wind immediately cut short his train of thought. Willows on either side of the street bowed low in its gusts. The wind piped a mournful tune, and the trembling electric lines strung from pole to pole began to hum along as well. Old Liu had to walk upwind. He lowered his head, held tight to his cane, and used it as an oar to drag himself northward. Thrust into the wind, his high-bridged nose soon began dripping clear drops of liquid onto his beard. By now the wind was blowing so hard he couldn't take a breath. It grabbed his overcoat and wound it about his legs. Unwilling to show any weakness before this adversary, he refused to take the time to stop and turn his head downwind so that he might suck in a breath of air. A steady stream of choking sounds issued from his throat. He forged straight ahead, turning his face first to the right for a bit and then to the left, as though he were swimming.

Old Liu forged on. His back was beginning to sweat. Not many rickshaws on the street, but he wasn't interested in taking one anyway. When a puller did ask him if he wanted a ride, he refused, for he knew that rickshaw pullers would take advantage of weather like this to soak a man for all he was worth. Old Liu was not about to be soaked. Rickshaws, indeed! If he only had the ability to bring it off, he'd take over Fei Zichun's automobile—now that would really show he had talent. In the meantime, he was determined not to let rickshaw men fleece him.

Old Liu forged on. Though his hands had begun to tremble, he continued to fight his way into the wind. He had once had his own personal rickshaw, one that he had engaged by the month. The puller, however, had begun taking advantage of him. Old Liu was not a man to shell out good money to hire someone to give him a hard time, and that was the end of that. There wasn't a single person in the lower-classes who knew right from wrong, not a solitary one. Old Liu forged on. He wasn't going to take anything from anyone. The wind, however, continued to treat him barbarously. Already gasping for breath, he longed to find a shelter where he could take a moment's refuge. There was a small tea shop by the side of the road, to be sure, but he wasn't about to squeeze in there among all those lower class types. Old Liu forged on. The lane he was looking for should appear pretty soon. After he made a ninety-degree turn and went into that lane, the wind was sure to die down. After all, it couldn't *always* blow opposite to the direction Old Liu wanted to take. The metallic ringing of his cane tapping against the frozen ground grew louder as he summoned all his remaining strength to keep up the good fight.

But now the wind seemed to call up *its* reserves as well as it wrapped Old Liu's overcoat so tightly around his legs that he could barely move them. His steps became erratic. It was apparent that whether he liked it or not, the wind was about to take him and spin him like a top. Old Liu's heart pounded feverishly, and yellow spots appeared before his eyes. Not daring to make another move, he clutched his cane and held his ground. He struggled to remain calm. At his wit's end, he summoned up the last bit of fight left in him and told himself, like a mother comforting a frightened child, "There's nothing to be afraid of." He knew that he had more than enough mental stamina to brave it out. If he just stood there and continued to hold his ground, things were bound to improve before too long. Listening to the howling of the wind with his eyes closed tight, he was momentarily disoriented, but nonetheless remained fully aware of his surroundings. Let it blow its damndest! Come hell or high water, Old Liu would hold on to that cane.

Like a candle on the verge of being blown out that flames up again, Old Liu's mind blanked out and then, while sweat poured from every pore of his body, became alert again. Once more he resolved to put up the fight of his life and forge on ahead. Yet he didn't open his eyes immediately after that resolve. And now, as the wind blew across his sweat-covered face, he began to tremble. Despite his best efforts, he began to lose strength. Halfheartedly, he cracked his eyes and peeked through the lids. Everything was rocking in the mighty wind. Instinctively, Old Liu turned around and braced himself against the wall of a family compound. He heaved a long sigh.

Should he press on to Fei Zichun's? He didn't have the energy to think about it anymore. But he had to make up his mind. He couldn't go on standing there at the base of the wall all day. How comfortable it would have been to squat, but he just had to battle on to Fei's place. Couldn't give up just because of a little north wind. Now he regretted not having taken a rickshaw, but at the same time he also knew that regret is useless. He was still convinced that he had more than enough stamina to complete the trip he had set out on. After all, from the age of forty until now he had lived alone and—when you come right down to it—celibate living is the mainstay of the regimen to which those vigorous monks in the monasteries subject themselves.

Be that as it may, there was simply no strength left in Old Liu's legs. Should he go or shouldn't he? Was Fei Zichun to get off so easily? A gust of wind—so violent it seemed that it would take the very street he was standing on and roll it up like a rug—came along, picked him up by the scruff of the neck, and blew him along from behind. Buoyantly light, he found his feet doing something very akin to walking, though the intention of walking had not so much as crossed his mind. Barely conscious of what was going on, he was blown down the street along with the sand as though he were light as a chicken feather. The wind, for one, was no respecter of Old Liu's status. Off he went! Without exerting himself in the least, driven by the wind, he and his beard set forth in full sail— toward the south. The way to Fei Zichun's was to the north, but Old Liu could do nothing to stop his southward progress.

All right then, if he was going south—south he'd go! After all, it wasn't that Old Liu was a weakling, it was just that Fei Zichun happened to be particularly lucky today. At this point there was simply no way for Old Liu not to believe in luck. So many things were like that—a gust of wind here, a rain shower there, and one man would ascend to the heights, while another would descend to the depths. Old Liu heaved a long sigh. Everyone was taking advantage of him, even the wind.

Before he knew it, he was back at the entrance to the lane where he lived and without thinking, he turned in. The wind here was nothing more than a small tributary of a great river, no big waves to speak of. Old Liu walked close to the enclosing walls of the various family compounds along his lane. He couldn't feel any wind at all. Moreover, it was much warmer in here. His beard no longer blew before him as though leading the way, and his overcoat hung looser about his body. Now he was able to move his shoulders and breathe freely. He was alive again! The wind had not been able to subdue Old Liu after all! He relaxed his pace a bit and considered going home for a cup of tea. No! He'd have to continue his expedition. Even if the wind *had* helped Fei Zichun, Old Liu was not about to spare the likes of Feng Er. Old Liu was once more at the gate of his own family compound, but he did not go in.

He couldn't help wondering what his moronic son was up to. No! He wouldn't go in. He'd go hunt up Feng Er. When the wind subsided a bit in the afternoon—if that were possible—he'd go look up Fei Zichun again. But first, he'd take care of Feng Er. Old Liu continued on past his own gate. He really was a bit drained and allowed his straight back to incline forward ever so slightly. Putting a little more of his weight on his cane, he slowed down a bit. There wasn't any hurry. Subduing someone like Feng Er was no big deal.

He had no sooner started thinking of Feng Er than he immediately put him out of mind and started thinking about Feng Er's daughter. Feng Er was nothing but a shop sign; the *real* goods were deep inside the shop—that daughter of his. And yet things weren't as simple as that, either. Old Liu's back bent even lower. Whenever he thought of the Feng girl, his heart would go all soft, and he'd start thinking back to his own youth. He couldn't help it. He didn't *want* to think of her that way because it complicated things, and yet he just couldn't help himself. Here he was arranging a match for his son, and thinking about himself—he ought to be ashamed! Come to think of it, that Feng girl wasn't worth a diddledy-damn, either—stirring up such thoughts in poor Old Liu's head! *Everybody* was taking advantage of him, Feng girl thrown in. The nerve of her—putting him into a frame of mind like that!

A turn to the south and he'd be at Feng's place. He let the wind take him. A puff or two and there he was. Feng Er was home! Old Liu couldn't help but feel annoyed. To think that on a day like this a good-for-nothing like Feng Er should get to hole up at home, snug as a bug in a rug, while Old Liu had almost been blown to bits by the wind! Feng Er's little room was so cozy that when Old Liu stepped into it out of the cold, his face prickled at the warmth. From somewhere deep down inside, Old Liu's anger welled up like lava in a volcano. There sat Feng Er, safe and sound as you please, arms draped around the stove, comfortably warming himself. Despicable!

"Elder Brother Liu,[6] what brings you out on such a windy day?" Feng Er asked with a smile.

"Must have been fated to a bitter lot at birth. Guess I'm supposed to suffer!" Old Liu had never shown any mercy with the likes of Feng Er.

"Come off it now, elder brother! Call *your* lot bitter? Just take a look at *me*. I don't even have a whole piece of clothing to my name." Feng Er tugged at the lapels of his jacket. The cotton padding showed through in several places.

Old Liu didn't have any time to waste on looking at that jacket, and still less to waste on sympathizing with Feng Er. He despised Feng Er more than anyone else he knew. Feng Er owed him money but never tried to make anything of himself so that he might repay the debt. There he was—sitting in a room warming his hands on a windy day without the slightest inclination to go out and find work! Old Liu removed his overcoat and selected a dilapidated old chair that was farthest from the fire: Old Liu wasn't cold. The longer Feng Er lived, the punier he got! Past fifty, Feng Er was thin, good-natured, and poor. His long, pale hands were so illumined by the bright fire that they seemed translucent. The more Old Liu looked at Feng Er, the madder he got. In order to lessen the fury he felt seething inside, he asked, "The girl?"

"Gone out to pawn some things. We don't have any rice left." Feng Er's gaze was fixed on his own hands.

"In weather this cold couldn't you have gone yourself instead of having *her* do all the work?" There was simply no way that Old Liu could avoid bickering with the likes of Feng Er, even though he considered such exchanges beneath him.

"The girl still had a long robe left. It was *her* idea to go. She was afraid I couldn't take the weather out there. Always filial like that, she is." Feng Er spoke slowly, every word carrying overtones of love for his daughter—overtones that made it impossible for Old Liu to find a suitable reply. There were lots and lots of things that he might have said, but the warmth of feeling behind Feng Er's words blunted the hard edges of Old Liu's heart. It was as though he had smelled the perfume of flowers—a perfume that opened a fresh path for the feelings welling up within his own heart. How Old Liu longed to put aside that anger and pursue that fragrance.

But just as quickly as it had softened, his heart began to harden again. It occurred to him that he himself had often entertained feelings for his moronic son that carried overtones identical to those that he detected in Feng's words. Yes! But had any of his relatives or friends—or even his own moronic son, for that matter—ever entertained this kind of feeling for *him?* Never! Every last one of them exploited him. Feng Er, on the other hand, had a daughter who went out and worked to support him, a daughter who was filial. What right did Feng Er have to such good fortune? Was there a single solitary thing about him that entitled him to it? It also occurred to Old Liu that Feng Er had absolutely no ability of any kind, either. How was it then that such a good-for-nothing should have such a filial daughter?

Yes, that must be it! It must be that Feng Er wasn't at all the simple, honest fellow he appeared to be. Feng Er had *his* bag of tricks, too. At the least, Old Liu was sure that Feng Er had discovered the trick of controlling his daughter. So, even a useless fellow like Feng Er had considerable talent, too—the talent to govern his daughter. When Old Liu's thoughts reached this point, he was hardly able to sit still any longer. He had never been able to control anyone in his entire life. His own daughter had run off with some pauper of an artist and his son was a moron. Fei Zichun, Sun Laoxi . . . all of them were taking advantage of him, but he had never been able to get the better of anybody.

And contrary to all rhyme and reason, there sat Feng Er warming his hands by the fire while his daughter went out to pawn things. Old Liu wasn't even up to Feng Er's level! How could he go on living? There was no choice. He simply *had* to find some way of cleaning Feng Er's clock. That would prove that Old Liu knew how to bring people under *his* control, too.

By the fire, Feng Er didn't even dare make so bold as to take a loud breath. He had never insulted anyone in his whole life, had never said anything out of place. His good-naturedness had made him weak, had deprived him of the power to resist. There he was, wearing a short cotton jacket with the padding flying out, and still worried about saying something that might offend Old Liu. He loved his daughter. He also stood in fear of her. If he hadn't feared her, he would certainly never have allowed her to go out on a day as cold as this. Fear imposed limits on Feng Er's ability to love; otherwise he would have long since become a saint or immortal. He felt sorry for Old Liu but wouldn't dare say such a thing, despite the fact that they were old friends. Just as the two of them were sitting there like that, not saying a word, the door opened and a gust of cold wind blew in, sending a shudder through both old men. The Feng girl had arrived.

"Hurry up and warm yourself over here by the fire," said Feng Er, looking at his daughter's ruddy, cold face.

Paying no attention to her father, the daughter went over to greet their guest. "Elder Uncle Liu,[7] do you mean to say that you've come out in weather as cold as this? You really must have a sound constitution!"

Old Liu didn't say anything in reply. He didn't know why, but as soon as he set eyes on the Feng girl, his thoughts were thrown into total disarray. He looked at her. Her face was flushed through and through with the cold; there was some dirt on her nostrils; and there was also some yellow sand in the creases of her blue cotton gown. She wasn't tall. Her face was round, her eyes large, and her hair so abundant that it covered her ears. Her body was rounded, strong, and full of life. Her frost-nipped fingers were quite red. A small bundle wrapped in blue cloth was clasped under her arm. You couldn't say she was very good-looking, or even very *clean* for that matter, but there was a certain vitality about her that knocked his thoughts into absolute chaos. She was unaffected, quick in her movements, and her voice was pleasant to the ear. She put the blue cloth bundle down next to her father and then stood before the stove, rubbing her hands together. When they were thoroughly warm, she pressed them against her ears. "It's really cold out there! I'm not going to let you go out today, all right?" She directed the question smilingly at her father—but rather than a question that one would ask a father, it sounded more like one that one would direct to a child.

Feng Er nodded.

"Have you made the tea?" she asked, looking at their guest.

"Don't have any, do we?"

"That's right. Forgot to buy it. Elder Uncle Liu, how about a bowl of hot water?" Her face was right in front of his as she asked.

Old Liu adored her big eyes, but they were a bit intimidating, too. He shook his head. Now his heart and mind were more confused than ever. The way the father and daughter talked, the cozy atmosphere of the room, the mixture of open honesty and warm affection in her words—all conspired to benumb Old Liu to such an extent that he might as well have been made of wood. He envied Feng Er; he was jealous of Feng Er; he *hated* Feng Er. With Feng Er in possession of a daughter like that, there was simply no way that Old Liu could subdue him—unless, that is, he were able to capture the daughter first. But how? Should he bring her into his house as a daughter-in-law, or as his own? . . . But his moronic son had been kicking up a fuss about getting a wife for quite a while now, and the Feng girl was the only suitable candidate around. She was in good health and her father was firmly in the palm of Old Liu's hand. If his son married her, they'd certainly give him a grandson, and the grandson wouldn't necessarily be a moron just because his father was. The Liu clan would have some rootstock again—something to build on.

And yet, somehow or other, he didn't know quite how, as soon as Old Liu set eyes on the Feng girl, he was conscious of an increase in the life force within him and he began to have thoughts that were young. He wanted to do right by his son, and yet he believed that he himself could father a son—maybe more than one—a son who wasn't a moron. Old Liu wasn't old. There was no doubt in his mind whatsoever that he could sire another son. And if Old Liu took her for his own wife, then *his* room could be like this one, with the same crackling fire, the same warmth, the same intimate and affectionate conversation. He began to hate Amah Zhang: there was never any warmth in the fires that *she* made. Whether he decided to take the Feng girl as a daughter-in-law or as his own wife, there should be no difficulty either way. The only trouble was that since he really did love his moronic son, how could he? . . . Old Liu's feelings were thoroughly confused.

All his life he'd always gotten the short end of the stick. Was it possible that now even his own son was going to treat him the same way? Since Feng Er was able to control his daughter, how could it possibly be that a man of Old Liu's caliber couldn't govern a moronic son? A myriad of images crowded into his mind as he thought, and not one of them made him feel good.

Although he had managed things so that he had never been short of food or clothing in his entire life, he'd never made any real showing for himself, either. Besides, food and clothing are by no means equivalent to happiness. Already sixty, he'd have to hurry up and find some way of skimming a little cream off the top of life. He needed something in his life that would offer him understanding, that would obey him, that would press against him, flesh to flesh—a woman perhaps, a woman like the Feng girl. After all, you *couldn't* say Old Liu was old.

To be sure, out there in society, he had a need to accomplish something, to overcome Fei Zichun and his ilk. But beyond that, he needed to invigorate his home life as well—even in bed. He *wasn't* old. He could feel the blood coursing swiftly through his veins. It was almost as though he could even hear its sound—a sound something like that of grain bursting into growth after a good rain. Well, his moronic son would just have to wait! A moronic son was certainly not more important than the father! It was about time that the father gave priority to his own interests for a change. Throughout an entire lifetime, no matter how he'd schemed, Old Liu had never managed to get out in front of anyone. Could it possibly be that now even his moron of a son was to get the better of him?

He looked at the Feng girl: rosy face, big eyes, shiny black hair—a tasty morsel if ever he'd seen one. Why shouldn't he take a bite for himself? Even from *her* point of view, it would be a good deal: he had some money—not much, but enough so she'd never want for food or clothing after they were married. And if he died first—if—why, she'd be secure for the rest of her life. Yes, in working things out, he couldn't just think of himself. No, Old Liu was a fair man. She'd be pretty well-off—plump, prosperous, and happy—all thanks to Old Liu.

The girl went into the other room. It was time for Old Liu to speak up. Yes, he decided, he would take her as his own wife. Blood rushed to his face and he felt his cheeks flush a bit, making him feel twenty or thirty years younger. No matter how he turned it over in his own mind, it always came out looking like the right thing to do, and it made him feel young. The blood was young, but the scheme was that of an old man. He was aware of his own power: the thing would be no sooner said than done. What could Feng Er do to stop it? If Old Liu couldn't swing a little thing like this, how could he call himself a man?

And yet, in the end, he didn't speak up. He just sat there like a bump on a log. And as long as Old Liu didn't start a conversation, Feng was the kind of man who could sit there for a lifetime without letting out a peep. Old Liu didn't speak up because he just couldn't shake that moronic son loose from his thoughts. He *hated* that chuckleheaded brat. What could he do with a millstone like *that* around his neck? The moron wanted to take a wife, had already been known to expose himself before girls on the street. Could Old Liu get away with getting married while the boy stood by and looked on? It probably wouldn't work, and reasoning with the booby was obviously out of the question. Damn! Old Liu bit down on a couple of strands of his beard. Heaven, if there was such a thing, really knew how to kick a guy when he was down. Old Liu didn't mind that heaven had strewn his life with clever opponents, for they were no match for him. But why, toward the end of his life, did it have to throw in a moronic son that he had no possible way of dealing with? Hah! Intelligent adversaries could do you in, but a moron could take advantage of you, too! Old Liu had run up against both kinds. He wasn't afraid of anyone, and yet he had been intimidated by everyone, his own moron of a son included.

"Elder Uncle Liu," the girl called from the next room, feeling that her dad was being too stiff and inhospitable to their guest. "How about a bite to eat? I can cook. What do you say?"

"I still have to go hunt up Fei Zichun. I'm not finished with him yet!" Old Liu got up to leave.

"In a storm like this?"

"Who cares about a little bad weather?" He grabbed his overcoat.

Feng Er continued to warm his hands by the fire as he stood up. He was in a quandary: if he saw his guest out, he might catch cold, but if he didn't, he'd seem impolite.

"Stay where you are, Dad. I'll see Elder Uncle out." She had wiped the dust off her face, and now her cheeks seemed even softer and brighter than before.

"No need for that!" shouted Old Liu, casting her a quick glance. The girl rushed forward as Old Liu all but bolted out the front door. Young and fleet of foot, she easily overtook him.

"Be careful, Elder Uncle Liu, the wind's blowing hard. When you get home, give my best to Dum-dum Elder Brother."[8]

A cold gust of wind snatched Old Liu up like a chicken feather and sped him on his way.

Notes

1. Pronounced "Jang" so as to rhyme with the Chinese surname "Wang."

2. A flat griddle cake covered with sesame seeds.

3. "Fei" rhymes with the English word *hay*. The *Zi* in "Zichun" is unavoidably difficult; it is said something like the *"ds"* sound in the English word *buds;* the *"chun"* is pronounced like the initial *"ch"* in *church* with a *"wun"* tacked on to it (say the English word *won*, and replace the *o* with a *u*).

4. For "Sun," say the *"wun"* in the previous note and then put an *"s"* in front of it. *"Lao"* rhymes with the English word *how*, and *"xi"* sounds like the English word *see*, with a bit of *"h"* in front of it.

5. "Feng" rhymes with the English word *sung*. "Er" sounds very much like the letter *r*, as pronounced when one recites the alphabet.

6. A respectful form of address.

7. Polite form of address to someone about father's age or older.

8. Affectionate usage with no derision intended.

Hot Dumplings

Love, since ancient times, has always been prone to go offtrack. But in the old days there were no newspapers or magazines, so such affairs didn't splash into headlines the way they do now. One need not go too far back in time, for even when I was a child, love affairs rarely created a citywide scandal. I remember our old neighbor, Young Qiu.[1] By now the "Young" Qiu of those days is naturally "Old" Qiu. But even if I were to meet him now, even if he were already a hoary old man, I would still call him "Young" Qiu. For me, he could never grow old. When we imagine flowers, what springs to mind are blooming red flowers and lush green leaves, not faded blooms that have lost their fragrance and are dropping their petals like rain. It was the same with Young Qiu. In people's minds, he was forever in the springtime of life, though he looked nothing like a flower.

Where had Young Qiu moved here from and in which year? I can't seem to recall. I merely remember that when he moved in he had a young wife with him. They lived in the small north room in the outer courtyard of our compound. Ever since these young newlyweds moved in, I often heard people say they quarreled in the middle of the night. Now, young couples' spats are ancient as time and certainly nothing remarkable. What I really anticipated was a cut on Young Qiu's head or a few scars on Sis-in-law Qiu's[2] hand. In those days I was a great deal more naive than now and welcomed the spectacle of a good fight. I expected to see a few battle scars at least. But the young Qius were forever—during the day—cheerful and friendly. Not a mark on either of their bodies. And when I say bodies, I mean bodies—I even saw Sis-in-law Qiu's bare back once. In those days I often thought to myself, "Those two probably have their fists wrapped with cotton when they fight."

Sis-in-law Qiu's small room was really cozy. Always clean and warm and always with a certain atmosphere to it—a special atmosphere difficult to describe but clearly distinctive. A young-couple's atmosphere—yes, only now have I found the right words for it. No wonder that the neighbors then, the middle-aged men in particular, were rather disposed to go over to Sis-in-law Qiu's to chat. The young couple was always as pleased and thrilled to welcome their guests as on New Year's Day. But once the guests were gone, people said, they always quarreled. Some people swore to heaven that they even heard them laying into each other.

In the eyes of the neighbors, Young Qiu was a jittery youngster. When he walked, his feet seemed to float above the ground. Except when he was at home, practically no one ever saw him stand still, even for a moment. Even when he was sitting, his hands and legs never got a moment of rest. If his hands were not rubbing the edge of his clothes, they were sliding around the edge of the stool, or they were busy scratching his face. His feet were here, there, and everywhere, as though looking for something to do, as though pretending to be walking even when he sat down to chat. It wasn't on account of this that the neighbors looked down on him, although one had to admit that that was the main reason he could never be promoted from Young Qiu to Old Qiu. No, people were disrespectful to him on account of something else: his neck was always pulled in like a turtle's. Before one knew it, "cuckold neck"[3] became another way of referring to Young Qiu. Ever since this name stuck, people said their fights in the middle of the night became even peppier. During the day, however, they appeared more cheerful and friendlier than ever.

I wasn't the only one who had seen Sis-in-law Qiu's bare back. Some of the middle-aged men also claimed to have seen it. In the old days it was improper for women to reveal their shoulders. Yet Sis-in-law Qiu had actually allowed others to see her bare back. Even I—still a child then—felt that she was a bit too free and easy. Again, these are words that came to me just now—free and easy. No doubt about it, she was free and easy: from the emperor on down to commoners, everyone seemed to get along with her. I knew that the street vendors selling sesame oil and vegetables always gave her bigger portions. She was, in my childhood eyes, supremely beautiful. She had the most charming teeth. Even to this very day, I can still remember her smile. Whenever she smiled, a tiny bit of white would emerge. Just a tiny bit, and yet this glimpse of white, once inside a person's mind, could burgeon into endless fantasies that converged on her smile and glowed with the whiteness of her teeth. The most beautiful events of my childhood were to bring peanuts, roasted broad beans, or big sour dates over to her small room. To unshell a peanut and put it into Sis-in-law Qiu's mouth was to be rewarded with the everlasting pleasure of looking at her teeth. To have given her an entire bag of peanuts would have been heaven, though I never got to do such a thing in reality.

Sis-in-law Qiu never had children. Sometimes I heard her say half jokingly and half seriously to Young Qiu, "What do you expect with that soft thing of yours?!" Young Qiu would pull his neck back in even farther, as though cut to the heart. He could spend half a day without uttering a word, blankly stroking his face with his hands until she would say, "All right, go buy some matches!" Only then would he smile again and run out, his feet scarcely touching the ground.

I remember it was a winter's day when I had just gotten out from school and ran into Young Qiu at the entrance to our alley. He was so ghastly pale I thought he was sick. His eyes peered off into the distance, but his hands kneaded the red knot on my felt hat as he asked, "Have you seen Sis-in-law Qiu?"

"No, I haven't," I replied.

"You haven't?" He asked in a frightened tone, as though he were a woman drawing lots on the fate of her sick son—eager to know it yet refusing to see it, wanting to believe it yet ready to deny it.

After he asked that one question, he dashed into the street.

That night as usual I went to Sis-in-law Qiu's room, but the door was locked. Though I had already reached school age, I couldn't help crying. Not one of the peanuts that I faithfully delivered to Sis-in-law Qiu each night got unshelled that night.

First thing next morning I went over to find her again. She still wasn't there. Young Qiu was sitting on the edge of the *kang*, head propped in his hands. I called him a few times, but he didn't respond.

For nearly half a year, whenever I was on the streets going to school, I looked for her, hoping to run into her, but not once did that happen.

Though Young Qiu still returned every night, I did not visit her small room anymore. It was clean and warm as ever, but that "special" atmosphere it once possessed had disappeared along with Sis-in-law Qiu. On a wall or in the air, I often saw her white teeth. Just a tiny touch of white. Nothing else remained. That touch of white would no longer chew softly on my peanuts.

Young Qiu became even more jittery, but less talkative. Sometimes he would return early, and without making dinner, he would just sit there and stare vacantly into the air. Whenever this happened, we always called him over to have dinner with us. When he ate with us, he still talked and laughed, his hands and legs as jittery as ever. From time to time his eyes would glance outside the door or window. None of us mentioned her. But sometimes I forgot, and asked, "Where did Sis-in-law Qiu go?" He would hastily mumble a few words, go back to the small room, and sit on the edge of the *kang*. It went on like this for half a year.

It happened one night, if not before the Fifth Month Festival[4] then after it. I had gone out with my classmates after school and had come home late. Just as I was entering our alley, I saw Young Qiu. He was carrying a plate in his hands.

"Where're you off to?" I stopped him.

He seemed to have momentarily forgotten how to speak, but from his eyes I could tell that he was beside himself with joy, so happy that he was speechless. Recovering his senses, he whispered into my ears, "Sis-in-law Qiu's come back. I'm going to buy some hot dumplings for her!" He said the word *hot* most distinctly.

I fairly flew back home. She really had returned. She was pretty as ever and her teeth were just as white. She was a bit thinner, that's all.

To this very day, I still don't know where she went for that half year. At the time, both Young Qiu and I just wished for her return—no questions asked. When I recall this now, I feel that love in the old days, even when it went offtrack, was something sacred. Because there were no newspapers or magazines that could publicize Sis-in-law Qiu's photograph, Young Qiu's joy, once recovered, could not be lost again.

Notes

1. The surname "Qiu" is pronounced like the English word *chew*. It is customary among Chinese friends to use the familiar form of addressing one another as "Young" so-and-so or "Old" so-and-so (the so-and-so being a surname) according to their respective ages.

2. It is customary among Chinese to refer to a friend's wife as "Sister-in-law" so-and-so, since a friend is regarded as a brother.

3. The term for *cuckold* here, *wang ba,* is a derogatory term referring to the turtle or tortoise. The Chinese believe that the turtle or tortoise does not beget its own offspring.

4. Also known as the Dragon Boat Festival, the Fifth Month Festival falls on the fifth day of the fifth lunar month. In many river ports, boat races are held on this day. A dragon's head is mounted on the bow of these boats, and the dragon's tail is decorated on the stern. There is no dragon-boat racing in Beijing, but the festival is observed as one of the three major festivals of the year—the other two being New Year's and the Midautumn Festival.

Life Choices

"Mei!" whispered Wen. What he had prepared to say suddenly became all jumbled up. He looked away from Mei's face and smiled feebly at Chun. Eight-month old Chun, cuddly as a cub, smiled back at his father, dimpling both his cheeks. Wen winced and dropped his eyes. Right now the innocent smile of a child cut more sharply than a knife. Having lost his father's attention, Chun nudged his mother's breasts and looked up at her. She was staring blankly out the window, looking off into the distance to hold back her tears. Chun began babbling, exposing his pink gums. Wen thought of how he used to stick a strip of cotton under Chun's soft, round chin and, against the light of a lamp, create a silhouette on the wall. Mei would whisper tenderly, "Little Graybeard, Little Graybeard," and Chun would coo with delight. But tonight the mother merely held him loosely, staring out the window. The green curtain wasn't lowered yet.

Chun babbled away, trying to utter phrases to draw out the love from his parents. Unable to bear it any longer, the mother lowered her head and kissed Chun's hair, pouring her anguish and tears onto his tiny head.

"It isn't a stomach problem!" She had wanted to say more, but the pain from this brief outburst sealed her heart again, like the wake behind a ship, opening up then closing in again. Without wiping her own tears, she patted Chun's hair dry with the palm of her hand.

Wen felt like a beast. Had he not given her all the happiness in the world? It had all turned out to be a sham. A sham! How he suffered, yet how much greater must be her pain. He thought of the days before they were married. . . . At the time, she was . . . but in two years . . . He couldn't think about it anymore. If he thought any further, he would no longer recognize the reality of the past nor derive any solace from it. He couldn't give up all hope. Only hope could mitigate the damage he had done, even though believing in it hadn't been of much help in the past.

"Before we had Chun, your appetite wasn't always good, was it?" His smile was tired, devoid of energy. He remembered Mei before she was pregnant with Chun. The paleness then was just occasional: like the azalea, after a while, it would turn red. And now . . .

"You shouldn't be so scared; it can't be that." He took Chun into his arms, eyes scanning Mei. In two years, Mei seemed to have changed into a different person. Gone were the baby cheeks that looked like Chun's. She had aged, taken on the appearance of—of a mother. When she looked at herself in the mirror, how gloomy were her thoughts?

"Good boy, stay with Daddy. Daddy'll sing you a song." But Daddy didn't sing. He couldn't find his voice. Only Chun's cool, soft face gave some comfort to his lips, and he felt somewhat better.

Mei collapsed onto her bed and buried her face in the pillow. Wen rocked Chun and circled the room, letting Chun pull at his ears and grab at his face at will. His eyes were glued to Mei. Was that Mei? They had been in college together for four years. He remembered their first meeting—outside the registrar's office—very clearly. Mei had been as beautiful as a kingfisher on the wing. And now, this human form on the bed, could it still be Mei? What was she thinking? Was life such an impenetrable gloom? Feeling his legs weaken, he sat at the edge of the bed. He pressed his face against Chun's plump cheeks, looking ashamed, feigning courage. "Mommy won't cry, Chun won't cry." Chun wasn't crying at all, merely trying to avoid the bristles of his father's five-o'clock shadow. Taking his finger out of his mouth, Chun began to draw on his father's face.

Mei turned her head slightly. "Let's try and mix some powdered milk with water—come, Chun!" She slowly sat up and inadvertently glanced at her breast. She felt like vomiting, but couldn't.

"If your stomach's weak, then naturally your milk won't be good." As he read the directions on the can, Wen made a miserable effort to think positively.

"Just hurry up and mix it. It's time for his feeding, and he'll go to sleep after he's fed!" Mei was impatient.

This wasn't the kind of impatience that grows out of a young couple's spat. Wen could tell that this was utter frustration and anxiety that could detonate at a touch. Wen forgave her. It wasn't her fault, but in this act of forgiveness he also felt a little fear. Quickly he mixed the powder.

Chun swallowed the first spoonful. Mei calmed down a bit. Deftly and earnestly, she reached for the second spoonful. Wen looked at her hand. It was still white and soft, but slightly swollen, so that there was an unnatural quality to that very whiteness and softness. Chun could now make out the taste. He kept the second mouthful of the white liquid in his mouth, hesitated over what to do, then sputtered it out. The white liquid dribbled down the corner of his mouth. Tiny specks landed on his nose as well. Wen felt a lump in his throat. He hadn't even had time to say, "Be a good boy now."

"Darling Chunchun!" Mei steadied herself, trying to shift her attention away from all her problems to Chun. She had completely turned into a mother again. "There now, eat, eat . . . " she murmured, gently giving him another spoonful. He began kicking his plump legs. Though he didn't cry—he never cried much—he continued to splutter, refusing to take the unfamiliar milk.

"Won't work; don't even try." Like all men, Wen was impatient.

"Come on, Chun, come on . . . " To no avail. Mei heaved a sigh, not entirely admitting defeat, yet unwilling to coerce her baby. Unbuttoning her blouse, she said, "All right, go ahead, but my milk's no good!"

Chun fell on the nipple like a bee returning to its hive. While busily sucking, he stole a look at his father. The father wanted to squirm into a hole. Chun sucked to his heart's content, while his finger played with the other nipple. Mei's eyes were riveted on the baby's cheeks. Her mind seemed drained of all thought. She was willing to give all of herself to Chun, wholeheartedly and without hesitation. But as she had said, her milk was no good. She gazed blankly at the two cheeks, a feeling of vast emptiness inside her. Wen looked at his wife's breasts. Those breasts, which had once bewitched him, had lost their charm because of Chun and had now become Chun's poison—her milk was no good. He listened to the quiet sucking of the nipple gently pronouncing the sins of adults. He felt his dignity gradually fading away. Chun's eyes slowly began to droop. To feel completely safe and at ease with these adults, he had to sleep with the nipple in his mouth. Having finished sucking one side, he changed his position and opened his eyes again, his moist lips curled up in a sleepy smile. Wen turned his head away. Mechanically, Mei patted the tiny legs, and Chun fell off to sleep.

An unbearable silence. If he didn't say something, Wen felt his heart would explode. Bending over toward Mei's ears, he said softly, "Let's go see old Doctor Meng tomorrow and try some medication." He still hoped that it was a stomach ailment. Right now, a stomach ailment was a necessity; it would be a lifesaver!

Mei nodded. "But herbal medicine will make my milk even worse." She had to be cautious for the sake of Chun. She herself didn't matter.

"Tell old Meng that you're breastfeeding." Wen's hope was boundless, as if faith in Chinese medicine could save everything.

Husband and wife didn't sleep well the entire night. Chun woke up from time to time—he was hungry. He thrust his two tiny hands upward as if startled and babbled for awhile with his eyes shut. Listening to his mother hum, he made an effort to sleep but a little later woke up again. Mei summoned up enough energy to hum, gently patting him, sometimes heaving a soft sigh, a kind of sigh wrung out of exhaustion, forbearance, remorse, and love. Wen stared into the darkness, holding his breath. He dared not think of anything, but he thought of everything. The more he thought, the more con-fused he became. How could an act of love trap one into this tangle of life and death, pain and suffering. Who would have thought it two years ago?

The spring dawn brought no cheer. Black circles under Mei's eyes, her face ashen—Wen dared not look at her closely. Like some sort of fool, he yawned and yawned again, the tears still on his face. He went to ask for a day off, and then rushed back to babysit so Mei could go see the doctor.

Chun was a terror, playing with his father, tearing up paper, grabbing his father's nose . . . but, as he played, he began to babble anxiously. The father devised new ways of coaxing him to laugh, but he himself felt depressed. From time to time, he looked at the can of powdered milk. Making money was not easy, but he had to provide his son with powdered milk. And yet Chun wouldn't drink it. Chun was getting thinner, crying and babbling day and night until . . . He dared not think further. He quickly checked to see if Chun was any thinner. Chun's eyes seemed to have sunk in a bit, the lines of his double eyelids more pronounced, paradoxically making him even more handsome!

He didn't want to think about money, but did he dare not to? Its value was marked on each and every thing! He made sixty dollars a month. He didn't object to the amount, but rent, clothing, food, socializing, and raising a child all depended on these sixty dollars. Money was so tight he couldn't breathe, whether he objected to the amount or not. For Chun's sake, they hadn't made any clothes or seen a single movie or play for nearly a year. For Chun's sake, Mei had quit her job. For Chun's sake, Mei needed to drink five dollars' worth of milk each month. But Chun was everything. If there wasn't enough money, they'd have to spend less on themselves—that was all there was to it. They would buy anything for Chun.

Who would have expected that they'd ever become parents in the first place? When they were first married, they could spend their money as they pleased. How could two college graduates be afraid of not making enough money? After marriage, they had both worked, and although their salaries were not as high as they had hoped for, hadn't they felt free to spend more when there was money to spend and less when there wasn't? Go out in the morning and come back at night; their home of three small rooms had been nothing more than a long-term inn. Doing as they wished whetted their appetite for romance. If they felt like going out to eat, then they would, and if they wanted to cook at home, then they would do that, too. They lived as carefree as the swallows, their hearts leaping and bounding over everything, as though they were running hurdles or a footrace. Each meeting at night had been a new experience in love . . . the only thing that remained the same was the combined smell of their bodies. It lingered on the curtains, along the rims of their cups, and on their towels.

"We'll always be like this!"

"We'll always be like this!"

Always like this—who was afraid there wouldn't be enough money? With enough to eat and drink, everything had been fine. Who wanted to save money? Why would two college graduates worry about having no work to do. "We'll always be as carefree as today, and we'll always love each other in the same way!" Life had been like a flower accepting the brightness and warmth of the spring sun, free of all cares.

Slowly, however, in time this simple room also became home to a very small creature, and a frightening one at that. A living being was extending its influence, and it would turn their small nest into a prison! They were scared. And yet why should they be afraid? After all, they now had Chun. A mother's dignity and pride had endured the strain on her body. Mei's bursts of joy and her crying had caused Wen to be both hopeful and uneasy. To relieve some of her strain, he had told her to stop working and had hired a maid. They had been both hopeful and fearful. They had not been ready to be parents. What had been most clear to them was the pressure of money. Of the two college graduates, one was already unable to work. Wen had not been afraid. Mei had said as soon as the child was weaned, she would go back to work. But they couldn't help being afraid. The arrival of a new experience had diminished their self-confidence and made them aware of the many unexpected burdens children could bring. Before they knew it, they had been assailed with doubts about their future, which hardly looked rosy. Yet neither of them had seemed to know how to deal with the problems. . . .

Wen and Chun sometimes looked simultaneously out the window. Chun already knew how to look for his mother. Wen was waiting to see Mei's facial expression. He could recall all those different expressions of hers. If she looked this way . . . or that way . . . Wen's heart leapt up and down, hope and alarm battling for dominance. Chun was already a bit impatient, clutching at the table and pounding it in anger. "How about Daddy taking you to the garden?" On the way to the garden with a white cap on his head, Chun began to laugh again.

"Mommy's back!" Wen heard the footsteps on the brick road. The lightness of the footsteps was a good sign, and as expected, a smiling face emerged from behind the screen wall. Her purse tucked under her arm, her head raised a bit, a hint of her former carefree charm was back.

Wen's heart swelled with joy.

Not bothering to take off her long Chinese overcoat, Mei took Chun into her arms, snuggling her face against his. There was a big spot of oil on the collar of her coat, but she didn't seem to notice it. A year ago, she would have refused to wear it on the streets even at gunpoint.

"I saw old Dr. Meng. I'm not pregnant. The old man said so with a chuckle, but I didn't let him embarrass me!" Mei's eyes flashed, adding gusto to what she said.

"Give me the prescription. How many doses?" On his own, Wen reclaimed his qualifications as a human being. "I said it wasn't possible. How cautious do we have to be? How could just a kiss . . . can't possibly be!" He took the prescription out of Mei's purse and read it as he walked, "Distended pulse, air blocked in the diaphragm . . . " Reading and walking at the same time, he didn't bother to put his hat on.

After two doses, Mei wasn't any better. The skin under Chun's temples drooped noticeably. Mei continued to feel nauseous from time to time.

Wen was losing hope. The signs were bad. Mei was in a stupor again, full of tears all day. Chun still refused to take the powdered milk. During the day, they managed to appease him with thin gruel and tender pieces of chicken. At night, no milk, no sleep.

At night, brows in a tight knot, Wen went over all that had happened. The signs were bad! How could it happen so easily? It was always his fault. How could he correct or cross out this mistake? He could not suppress the groan rising in his throat. Mei was still awake. She heard his groan and began to sob.

Wen wanted to comfort her, but his mouth would not open. The night seemed to have sealed the seven orifices of his head, preparing to trample him to death in the dark. He felt confused. Ever since they had Chun, the deadly hands of money had been choking them. The things they had to buy were innumerable, while unexpected expenses seemed to creep up on them constantly. It had never occurred to them before to save any money! But Chun was everything. He was not only the object of their love, he was their catalyst to love—a precious, living love with a form, sweet and warm, that they could grasp. Their intimacy as husband and wife was now shared, deepened, harmonized, moderated, and made complete by a third party. Love flowed out of Chun into his or her heart. Chun did not hinder their love for each other but conveyed it. Because of him, husband and wife forgave each other's petty complaints. They came to understand even more about life, that life was responsibility, hope, and continuity. Financial worries disappeared at the sight of Chun. Their baby's smile brightened the years ahead. What was there to worry about? Besides, Mei was doing her best. After Chun was a month old, she had let the maid go and had begun to do everything herself: washing, cooking, shopping. Wen felt he had let her down, but she was happy to do so. She had to accept hardships for Chun's sake. Wait until he could walk, then she could go out to earn some money again. . . .

But what if just as things were getting easier with this one, another should come along? The older one would be held back, and the younger one wouldn't be properly fed—then what? Mei would have to look after both of them; this one would fall off to sleep, the other would wake up. How could he face Mei with sixty dollars—sixty dollars? Would she live like this as a mother forever? How could a child not go to school once he grew up? The lack of money cast an ominous gloom as large as the sky.

Mei vomited.

The next day Mei decided to go to the hospital for a checkup. When she discussed it with Wen, neither dared to look at the other. Mei had guts. Except for being afraid of black insects, she was braver than Wen—in dealing with any matter, whether it be bargaining, looking for a doctor, or whatever, she had more mettle than her husband. She decided to consult a Western doctor. Wen smiled but averted his eyes.

"Poor Chun!" the two whispered simultaneously. Chun was fast asleep in his bed. For the sake of poor Chun, the other life would not be permitted to see the light of day.

Wen had to take half a day off.

When Mei left, Chun was still asleep. Wen stood in a daze in front of the bed looking at Chun's long eyelashes, spread out one by one under his eyelids. He felt lost. To see Mei going off to the hospital was certainly not the same as seeing her go off to the market. It clearly attested to the fact that she was slave by day and victim by night. He felt he wasn't even half-human.

Chun awoke, rubbed his eyes, and grinned stupidly. Wen carried him in his arms, assailed by a stinging pain. He murmured some nonsense, while Chun cooed in monotones. Wen's thoughts were on Mei. In the past, Mei belonged to him alone. Now Mei was a mother. What if Mei were gone, and only he and Chun remained? He dared not think any further. Life and death, pain and suffering, love, murder, wife, mother . . . in no particular order, words drifted about in his mind, like bubbles on water.

Mei didn't return until almost noon. There were shadows under her eyes. No need for him to ask. She didn't offer to explain, either, sitting in a daze on the edge of the bed. The only sounds came from Chun's baby talk. The room seemed to be in the clutches of death. After a long time, Mei suddenly laughed, like a convict sentenced to death, feigning indifference because there was no alternative. "Death sentence!" Having said this, she covered her face with her hands and wept silently. Chun drove his head toward his mother for milk.

There was much cause for heartache. At the moment, Mei wept because she feared anything could happen. There was no way to stop this sort of agony. It obliterated all their past happiness and signaled the uncertainty of the future—the road ahead was a battle in the fog. She feared anything was possible. She couldn't accept it as the truth, but would doctors lie? Two months pregnant! Who would have believed it?

After she let out the pain, she thought it through carefully. She had to get rid of this troublesome fetus. She loved Chun too much; she couldn't let Chun go hungry for the sake of a future sibling. Chun was their first and had to be the best. But should she or should she not deal with the problem this way? A mother's instinct made her hesitate. She had to discuss it with Wen.

Wen had no opinion. If Mei wanted to, then she should go ahead and do it. But he was afraid of the risks! He was willing to spend some money to pay a fine for his crime, but where was the money? He couldn't bring up money problems with Mei. She wasn't going off to enjoy herself, after all. If, for the sake of saving money, Mei were to delay her decision until the point when the new life was born, what were they to do then? What child never cost money? He didn't have an opinion. Money had locked up the life of the unborn. Pain and suffering had bound Mei up—being a woman. Pain and suffering always belonged to women.

They checked all the hospitals. The French hospital was Catholic—definitely no abortions there. The American hospital was Protestant—not permitted to deal in such things. The small private hospitals were willing to do this kind of business, but they didn't look safe. Only the Japanese Yalu Hospital specialized in it; fees for the procedure were high, hospital charges steep, but they had the experience and the facilities and, moreover, were willing to kill Chinese fetuses.

To go or not to go?

To go or not to go?

To choose life or abortion in this confusing and meaningless culture. . . .

Mei made her decision. Go.

Wen gathered his courage, pawned his watch and ring. . . go.

Mei stayed in room number seven in the second-class wing. She didn't bring any bedding, nor did the hospital provide it. Wen had to go home to fetch their own.

On returning with the bedding, he found room number seven filled with elderly women with bound feet, waiting to be hired by Mei. The nurses of the hospital only accompanied the doctors and took temperatures. One had to hire elderly women with bound feet to take care of the rest, because the Chinese people preferred doing things this way. Mei had no choice but to hire one Auntie Wang.

Having been chosen, Auntie Wang immediately delivered a comprehensive report: Number eight was an abortion—fifteen-year-old girl, seven months pregnant; for two days they had her propped and stretched; she screamed for two nights. Yesterday it was aborted, and today she was already singing and playing. Her man was a thirty-something shop clerk.

Number nine was an abortion—a schoolteacher. Her man stayed with her in the hospital. Already had the abortion, and they were talking about getting married. Why couldn't they have saved all the trouble? Who knew. Number ten was an abortion, but it wasn't a Miss (Auntie Wang didn't seem to respect married women who had abortions), and the child wasn't even her husband's. Number eleven wasn't an abortion; husband and wife had been in the hospital for over two months—some gastric problems, took Chinese medicine every day. They were here solely because they could happily smoke opium.

She was just about to report on number twelve when a group of people came in. Those who delivered milk took orders; those who sold newspapers hawked their papers; the Three Immortals potsticker store announced that they would cater meals; melon-seed sellers gave away melon seeds, cigarettes. . . . Auntie Wang explained on their behalf, "Missus, it's more convenient here than at the market. Otherwise, why is there never a vacant room, always a full house? More expensive but really convenient. No one complains when someone smokes opium. Even the police are afraid of the Japanese, aren't they?"

The young girl in number eight began to sing again, followed by number nine turning on the phonograph, playing the opera "Spring in Jade Hall." Wen wanted to pick Chun up in his arms and rush home at once. But Mei didn't move. The pure and the brave were his child and his wife. Because of him, they were put in this place—a place that promoted the abuse of women, a place where money could cover up a disgraceful affair, a place where they let foreigners murder fetuses!

He wanted to tell Mei to go home with him, but he was the chief culprit; he had no right to tell her what to do. He and those "men" were of the same kind.

Auntie Wang asked, "Is Mister also staying over here?" If so, she would go look for a bed board. This place could accommodate an entire family, and one could cook as one wished.

Wen couldn't reply.

"The young master is really a handsome little thing!" Auntie Wang praised Chun. "How many months is he now?" When she saw they they had no intention of replying, she continued, "How many young masters do you have?"

Mei, listless and annoyed, forced a smile. "He's our first."

"What! You have just this one? Why, ah, why not keep the younger one? There'll only be two, then, won't there?"

Wen couldn't help grabbing for his hat. But Chun wouldn't let his father leave, stretching his tiny hands toward him and babbling. Wen fastened his hat onto his head, picked up Chun, and sat on the edge of the bed.

Number nine played another opera on the phonograph.

Neighbors

Mrs. Ming was constantly on her guard. To be sure, she had already borne sons and reared daughters for Mr. Ming; and though she was fast approaching forty, she still waved her hair to keep attractive. And yet, in spite of all this, she was in a state of constant apprehension from morning till night, for she well knew that she had one major flaw: she was illiterate. She felt that she had to do everything possible to compensate for that flaw; therefore she was scrupulously diligent in looking after her husband and taking care of the children. With regard to discipline, however, she had to let the children do pretty much as they pleased, not daring to punish or scold them. She couldn't very well be strict with them, for she knew that in the eyes of her spouse, her own position was not as high as theirs, due to the fact that *she* didn't know how to read. And after all, it was only thanks to *him* that she was the mother of such fine children in the first place. Given these circumstances, she could not but be constantly on guard. Since her husband was everything to her, she simply could not afford to strike or scold that husband's children. She was well aware that if her spouse really became put out with her, he was quite capable of making her life intolerable. He could, for instance, take another wife anytime he felt like it, and there would be absolutely nothing she could do to prevent it.

She was of a highly suspicious nature, and hence, always felt uneasy in the presence of anything with writing on it. For behind the written word lurked secret meanings that she could never guess. She detested all those housewives and young ladies who knew how to read. Looking on the bright side, however, she consoled herself with the thought that her own husband and children were not one whit inferior to all those literate ladies. Furthermore, she had to grant herself that she was naturally bright, enjoyed good fortune, and had a respectable social position.

She never allowed people to say that her children were either naughty or mischievous, for anything said against the children would constitute an indirect slur on the mother, and she wouldn't stand for that. In everything, she obeyed the wishes of her husband or those of her children. But apart from this domestic subservience, she felt superior to everyone and availed herself of every opportunity to display her importance to the servants and neighbors. When her children got into fights with the neighbors' children, she was very likely to join the fray with complete disregard for life and limb in order to let people know how formidable she was. She had her *position* to think of. She was, after all, Madame Ming, and her own belligerence reflected the prestige of her husband much as the light of the moon causes people to think of the glory of the sun.

She despised the servants because she felt that they didn't show her the respect that was properly due her. You see, they didn't refer to her as *Madame* Ming every time they addressed her. Moreover, they occasionally betrayed just the hint of a superior air, making her feel that they were saying to themselves, "Take off that fancy mandarin dress of yours, and underneath we're equals, or maybe you're even more of a humbug than we are." It seemed that the more carefully she planned something out, the more likely they were to reveal that trace of snootiness. How she longed to sink her teeth into them! And so it was that she often fired servants, for this was the only way that she could spew out some of that suppressed wrath that was forever welling up inside.

Vis-à-vis his wife, Mr. Ming was a despot. However, in such matters as spoiling the children, quarreling with neighbors, or firing servants, he did allow her a modicum of freedom. He thought it fitting that in these areas his wife should display the prestige of the Ming household. A hardworking and proud man, in his heart of hearts he did not respect this wife of his, but he wouldn't allow outsiders to treat her lightly: no matter what she was, she was, after all, *his* wife. He couldn't take a concubine because he worked for a wealthy and piously religious foreigner. A divorce or the taking of a secondary wife would be enough to shatter Mr. Ming's rice bowl. Since he was forced to make do with a wife like Mrs. Ming, he wasn't about to allow outsiders to slight her. Mr. Ming felt perfectly comfortable giving her a good beating, but a stranger wouldn't be permitted to give her so much as a dirty look. Since he was incapable of really loving this wife of his, he doted to distraction on the children. Everything he owned had to be better than anyone else's, and that applied *doubly* to his offspring.

Mr. Ming held his head high. He provided adequately for his wife, dearly loved his children, and had a moneymaking occupation. Nor did he have any bad habits. He viewed himself with all the awed respect that one usually reserves for the sages of high antiquity. He had no need to ask favors from people and hence no need to be polite to them, either. He spent his days at work and his evenings playing with his children. Since books had nothing to offer him, he never read. After all, he knew everything worth knowing. Whenever he saw a neighbor about to nod to him in greeting, he turned away. He had so little respect for his own nation and society that he never gave either a second thought. However, he did have an ideal: to amass enough money to make himself as secure and independent as a small mountain.

Yet in spite of everything, he still felt somehow dissatisfied. He told himself that he *should* be happy, but in life there are, it would seem, some things that one just isn't destined to have—things that nothing else can replace. He was clearly aware of just such a lack in his own life. It was like a spot—a tiny foreign object—within an otherwise perfect piece of crystal. Except for that spot, Mr. Ming was self-confident, even proud; except for that spot, Mr. Ming was flawless. Yet there was no way to rid himself of that little black spot, for it grew within his heart.

He knew that his wife was aware of the spot, and that it was precisely because of it that she was so given to suspicion. She had done everything possible to eradicate it, but realized that it was growing bigger and bigger all the time; by observing her husband's smile or the expression in his eyes, at a single glance she was able to gauge variations in the spot's size. But she never dared to reach out and actually *touch* it, for it was like one of those black spots on the sun whose intensity is past all imagining. She was afraid, however, that sooner or later someone *else* was bound to recognize its passionate intensity. She had to be on guard.

Now it so happened that Mr. Ming's children were in the habit of stealing his next-door neighbors' flowers and grapes. The dividing wall between the two homes was low, and the children clambered over it on a regular basis to raid their neighbors' garden. The neighbors were a young couple named Yang, and although they were very fond of their plants, they never complained about the thefts. Mr. Ming and his wife never actively encouraged the children to go on such forays, but once they had returned home with the loot, neither did the parents ever tell them that they had done anything wrong. Moreover, the Mings felt that grapes and flowers were not at all like other things, and there was nothing so terrible about picking a few here and there.

As the Mings saw it, if the children took some flowers and the neighbors came over to make a fuss, then it would be inexcusable to just ignore the whole thing. But the Yang couple had never once come over to complain. Mrs. Ming, in her thinking on the subject, went one step farther than her husband and concluded that the Yangs didn't *dare* come because they were intimidated by the prestige of the Mings. Mr. Ming had long been aware that the Yangs were somewhat intimidated by him. It wasn't because the young couple had openly expressed any fear, but simply because he felt that everyone *ought* to be overawed by a man like himself—a man who always walked with his head held high. What's more, the Yangs were both teachers, a line of work for which Mr. Ming had never had any respect. He had always thought of teachers as a bunch of piddling paupers with no prospects for the future.

But the thing that particularly disgusted him about Mr. Yang was the fact that Mrs. Yang was so very pretty. He had no use for teachers, but *women* teachers, especially pretty ones— well, that was another story. And to think that that pauper Yang should have such a wife—ten times better than his own—he couldn't help but be nauseated by the man. When he thought about it from Mrs. Yang's point of view, he concluded that it was probably a certain lack of foresight that had caused such a good-looking young woman to marry a teacher. Thus he had no logical reason for objecting to *her;* yet in the end he came to feel put out with Mrs. Yang as well. Now, Mrs. Ming was aware of all this, for her husband's eyes often roved over in the direction of the low dividing wall that separated the homes. She concluded that it was only right that the children should steal the Yang family's flowers and grapes as a way of punishing that Yang tramp. She had already made up her mind that if Mrs. Yang ever dared to so much as open her mouth, she would promptly dismantle the bitch limb by limb.

A Chinese of the most up-to-date type, Mr. Yang manifested the utmost courtesy in everything he did in order to let people know that he was an educated man. Throughout the affair, he didn't want to say anything about the Ming children's thefts from his garden. It was as though he thought that Mr. and Mrs. Ming—assuming that they were educated people as well—would come over and apologize of their own accord. But to pressure them into an apology would smack too much of purposely embarrassing them. The Mings, however, never once came over to apologize. Mr. Yang couldn't allow himself to become angry over any of this, either, for while the Mings might disregard the rules of etiquette, he had his own dignity to preserve.

When the Ming children began to make off with his *grapes,* however—well, that was pushing it. It wasn't so much the physical loss of the grapes that annoyed him, but he did begrudge the time that he had invested in them. He had planted them three years ago and this was the very first time they had borne fruit. The three or four little bunches that appeared were promptly picked and carried away by the Ming children. Mrs. Yang finally decided that she would report the whole thing to Mrs. Ming, but Mr. Yang—though on one level he *wanted* his wife to go over—held her back. His anger was outweighed by his concern for propriety and their status as teachers.

Mrs. Yang didn't see it that way at all. She simply *had* to go over. What's more she would carry herself with an air of plenary courtesy and with no intention of getting into an argument or fight. In the end, Mr. Yang, fearing his wife would consider him a spineless jellyfish, had no choice but to let her go. And so it was that Mrs. Yang and Mrs. Ming finally met.

Mrs. Yang was very polite. "Mrs. Ming, I presume? My own surname is Yang."

Mrs. Ming knew perfectly well what it was that Mrs. Yang had come for, and she detested this pretty young woman from the bottom of her heart. "Yeah, I've heard about the likes of you for a long time now."

The education that Mrs. Yang had received caused her to blush at such a brusque reply. She couldn't think of anything to say but had to come up with something. "It's nothing really. The children . . . It really doesn't matter, but they *have* taken some of our grapes."

"You don't say?" Mrs. Ming's tone was sweetly musical. "Children love grapes. They're fun to play with. Of course, I would never let them eat them. They just take them for fun."

Gradually the red began to recede from Mrs. Yang's face. "Our grapes are not easy to grow. It took three whole years before they bore fruit."

"But it's *your* grapes I'm talking about. They're so sour I won't let my kids eat them, but I do let them take them to play with. What a wimpy vine you have—so few grapes!"

"Now as for children," Mrs. Yang began, remembering some of the educational theory she had learned in normal school, "all children are mischievous, but Mr. Yang and I are very fond of our plants."

"Mr. Ming and I are very fond of ours, too."

"What if your plants were stolen by the neighbors' children?"

"Who'd dare?"

"And if your own children steal other people's?"

"They've stolen yours. Is that what you're trying to say? In that case the best thing for you to do is just move away and not live around here anymore. You see, our kids are very fond of playing with grapes." There was nothing else that Mrs. Yang could say, and lips trembling with anger, she went home. Upon encountering her husband, she almost burst into tears.

Mr. Yang reasoned with his wife at great length. Although he felt that Mrs. Ming *was* in the wrong, he didn't contemplate any further action. The way he saw it, Mrs. Ming was barbaric, and wrangling with a barbarian would demean one's social status. But his wife wasn't willing to let it go at that and insisted that he wreak some sort of vengeance on her behalf. After mulling it over at great length, it occurred to Mr. Yang that *Mr.* Ming couldn't possibly be as barbaric as his wife. He'd talk with the husband, but it wouldn't do to carry on such negotiations face-to-face. He'd write a letter. He'd write an exceedingly polite letter, not mentioning the last round between his own wife and Mrs. Ming. Nor would he say that he thought the children had been misbehaving. He would simply implore Mr. Ming to order his children not to come and lay waste to his plants anymore. In this way he felt he'd be acting the part of an educated man. He worked in such high-sounding phrases as "the amity that exists between close neighbors," "infinitely thankful," and "will be extremely appreciated." In his mind's eye, he saw Mr. Ming receiving the letter, being moved by its contents, and coming over to apologize in person. With a feeling of utter satisfaction, he drew to a close a letter of no inconsiderable length and asked the maid to take it over to the Ming household.

After Mrs. Ming had sent her neighbor scurrying back to the security of her own little nest, she was enormously pleased with herself. For a long time she had been itching to lay into a woman like that Yang tramp, and the latter had finally afforded her the opportunity. She began imagining to herself the way that Mrs. Yang would probably explain it all to her husband and how the two of them would see the folly of their ways. Even if it *is* wrong for children to steal grapes, still, a person ought to consider *whose* children they are. When the Ming children steal grapes, a person really ought not resent it. Upon grasping this basic principle, the Yang family was sure to stand totally in awe of the Mings. How could Mrs. Ming help but feel pleased with herself?

When the Yang's maid brought Mr. Yang's letter over, Mrs. Ming was filled with suspicion. She decided the letter must have been written to her husband by that Yang woman in order to put the skids to her. Now, Mrs. Ming hated the written word, and she hated even more that Yang hussy who was able to write such words. She decided not to accept the letter.

Even after the Yangs' maid had taken the letter back, Mrs. Ming still felt uneasy. What if the young couple brought it back over after her husband came home! Although she was quite assured of her husband's love for the children, still she had to bear in mind that the letter was written by that Yang tramp. Perhaps because of the prestige the trollop enjoyed in her own husband's eyes, he might blow his top, even go so far as to give her a beating. If her husband really did give her a thrashing and that Yang slut got wind of it, that would be more than she could take. To be worked over for some-thing else would be all right, but to be beaten for that Yang baggage . . . She'd have to take precautions. As soon as her husband came home, she'd lay the foundation—she'd say the Yang family had come over and started a big row over a few sour old grapes. She'd tell him that they had threatened to write him a letter demanding an apology. Hearing all this, her husband would certainly refuse to accept the letter and then the victory would be totally hers. While waiting for her husband to come home, Mrs. Ming did a rough mental draft of what she'd tell him.

As she explained things to him upon his return, Mrs. Ming managed to sandwich in all his pet phrases. And her words did indeed arouse his enthusiastic devotion to his children. He might have been able to excuse Mrs. Yang had she not said that his children were bad. But having done that, she now elicited his categorical contempt. And to think that she had given her hand in marriage to a pauper of a teacher like Mr. Yang! Couldn't be a good piece of goods to start with.

By the time that Mrs. Ming's narration reached the point where she reported that the Yangs intended to send a letter demanding an apology, Mr. Ming was boiling. He was thoroughly disgusted with pauperish pedants like Yang who would immediately resort to the writing brush over absolutely nothing. Working for a foreigner, Mr. Ming was convinced that only a signature on a typewritten contract carried any weight at all. He couldn't possibly imagine of what use a handwritten letter from a poor teacher might be. Yes! If the Yangs sent a letter, he'd refuse to accept it.

And yet that black spot in his heart made him curious about what Mrs. Yang's writing might look like. Writing was worthless in itself, but then one had to take into consideration *whose* writing it was. Early in the game, Mrs. Ming had foreseen just such an eventuality: she had said that the letter was written by Mr. Yang. Mr. Ming, of course, had no time to waste on a stinking letter written by the husband. He was firmly convinced that a letter from even the very highest of Chinese officials did not carry the weight of a foreigner's signature.

Mrs. Ming sent the children to lie in wait at the door with firm instructions that they were not to accept any letter from the Yangs. Not letting up in her own vigilance, either, she kept glancing in the direction of the Yang home. She was quite pleased with her own success, and though one might have thought that she'd let it go at that, she continued to think of still other steps to take and even went so far as to suggest that her husband buy the house that the Yangs were living in. Mr. Ming knew that he couldn't spare the money to do it, but agreed anyway. Just listening to his wife even *speak* of such a plan was music to his ears. It was simply too good to pass up. No matter whether the Yangs owned the house or were renting, he'd think of *some* way to get hold of it. No problem! It did his heart good to hear his children say, "One of these days, we're going to buy that house over there," for outright purchase was the greatest of all possible victories. Houses, cars, gold jewelry—whenever he thought of being able to buy such things, he felt an increased sense of his own eminence well up from within.

Even though he considered the Mings' refusal to accept his letter as a personal insult, Mr. Yang did not favor sending the letter back over again. For a while he thought of having it out with Mr. Ming, once and for all, right out in the street, but that was just a passing fancy. His social position, you see, would not allow him to resort to such barbaric behavior. Hence he was reduced to impotently explaining to his wife what "rotten eggs" the Mings were and how there would be no point in starting a fight with such people. In this way he was able to comfort himself to some extent.

Like her husband, Mrs. Yang kept her anger well tucked in; nor was she able to come up with any strategy of revenge. Suddenly it occurred to her that "being cultured" meant always getting the short end of the stick. She expressed a number of similar pessimistic views and insights on the subject to her husband. Saying such things straight out helped her to get rid of some of her own spleen.

The two of them were doing their best to babble away their anger like that when the maid brought in a letter. Mr. Yang glanced at the envelope: the street number was right, but it was addressed to Mr. Ming. For a moment he thought of keeping the letter, but he immediately realized that that was something a "cultured" man really couldn't do. He told the maid to take it over to the Mings.

Mrs. Ming had been lying in ambush for a long time, and on seeing the Yang maid approach with the letter, began to fear that the children stationed at the door might not know how to handle the situation. And so it was that she personally joined the fray.

"Take it back. We don't want to even look at it."

"It's for Mr. Ming," the maid said.

"I know, but the head of this household doesn't have any time to waste reading a letter from the Yangs." Mrs. Ming was extremely decisive.

The maid handed her the letter. "It was mailed to the wrong address. It's not from the Yangs."

"Oh, sent to the wrong address, was it?" Mrs. Ming rolled her eyes around in confusion for a moment. She had it! "Think I can't see through that? You take it back over to your place. Don't try to put anything over on me!" *Slam!* The door closed in the maid's face.

To the consternation of Mr. Yang, the maid brought the letter back. He didn't want to go back over with the letter himself, nor was he willing to open it up and see what was inside. At the same time, he decided that Mr. Ming was a rotten S.O.B. just like his wife. He knew that the husband had already come home and so it was apparent that he must have formed a united front with his barbaric spouse. But still, what was he to do about the letter? To confiscate another man's mail would certainly be less than honorable. After thinking of a number of alternatives, he finally decided that he would put it in another envelope, address it correctly, and toss it into the nearest mailbox the very next morning. After he had stuck a penny stamp on the envelope, he was even able to smile.

The next morning the Yangs were pressed for time in getting to school, and Mr. Yang forgot the letter. He didn't remember it until he got to work, and by then it was too late to go back and get it. Since the letter had come by regular delivery, he decided, it couldn't have been anything very important and it certainly wouldn't make any difference if he forwarded it a day late.

When he came home from school that day, he didn't feel like going out again, and stuck the letter in one of his schoolbooks, promising himself that he'd be certain to mail it the very next morning. Having thus disposed of the matter, he was just about to sit down to supper when he heard a great commotion over at the Mings'.

Mr. Ming was fastidious about some things and would never demean himself by screaming or shouting while beating his wife, but Mrs. Ming, the recipient of the beating, was not equally as fussy about preserving such niceties. She wailed and howled for all she was worth, and her children helped out as well. Mr. Yang listened very carefully, but still couldn't make out what it was all about. Suddenly he thought of the letter. Maybe it *was* important after all. Perhaps because Mr. Ming hadn't received the letter on time, some affair or other had miscarried, and now he was taking it out on his poor wife. It was a thought that made young Mr. Yang very uncomfortable. Perhaps he ought to open the letter and see what it was about. He didn't have the nerve. Yet by *not* looking at the letter, he managed to so frustrate himself that he couldn't eat a decent meal.

After supper the Yang family's maid ran into the Mings' maid. A falling out of employers doesn't do any harm to the amity between servants. The Mings' maid let the cat out of the bag. It seemed that Mr. Ming had beaten his wife over a letter— a very important one at that. After the Yang maid had returned and reported this intelligence, Mr. Yang wasn't able to sleep. He was positive that the letter in question must be the one *he* had. But if it was that important, why hadn't it been sent by registered mail? Moreover, why had whoever sent it been so careless as to write down the wrong street number?

He thought about this for some time and could only conclude that businessmen must be terribly careless with regard to the written word. This in itself was probably sufficient to explain the mistaken address. Add to that the fact that Mr. Ming didn't ordinarily write or receive letters, and one could very well see how the postman might have simply looked at the street number without noticing the name. Perhaps he didn't even remember that there *was* a Ming family on the street.

Thoughts such as these made Mr. Yang aware of his own superiority. Mr. Ming was, after all, nothing more than a rotten S.O.B. whose only talent was raking in money. Since he *was* such a rotten S.O.B., then why not just open the letter and take a peek? To be sure, reading another man's mail was a legal offense, but a man like Mr. Ming wouldn't be aware of that anyway.

But what if Mr. Ming should come over and demand the letter back? No, it wasn't a good idea. He picked up the letter a good many times, but in the end he lacked the nerve to open it. At the same time he no longer felt like sending it to Mr. Ming. If it really was an important letter, then it might be useful to hang on to it. Of course this was not open and aboveboard, but then, who told Mr. Ming to be such a bastard in the first place. Who told him to deliberately give the Yangs a hard time? He thought of his grapes. Bastards *deserved* to be punished.

Then he began to reconsider the whole affair from square one. He thought, he pondered, and in the end he changed his mind again. He would send the misaddressed letter to Mr. Ming in the morning. What's more, he would also send that original letter of his own exhorting the Mings to look to the conduct of their children. He'd show the bastard how courteous and amiable a really educated man could be. He had no hopes of reforming Mr. Ming, but at least he could make him realize that teachers are gentlemen. That would be enough.

Mr. Ming ordered his wife to go over and get that misaddressed letter back from the Yangs. He was aware of its content, for he had run into the man who had written it. What's more, he had already taken the precautions the letter had advised, but, even so, he didn't want it to remain in the hands of that vile teacher. The heart of the matter was this: Mr. Ming and a friend had used the name of his foreign employer to smuggle some goods into the country, and somehow or other his rich and piously religious employer had gotten wind of it. The misaddressed letter was, in effect, a warning from his friend advising him to find some way of pulling the wool over the eyes of the foreigner.

Mr. Ming was not in the least concerned that the Yangs might publicize the contents of the letter, for in his heart of hearts he had no respect for the Chinese government and had never stood in awe of Chinese law. Even if his compatriots *did* find out that he had been engaged in smuggling, as far as he was concerned, it still wouldn't matter all that much. What he was really afraid of was that the Yangs might mail the letter to the foreigner, *proving* that Mr. Ming had, in fact, been guilty of smuggling. He thought that Mr. Yang was just devious enough to peek into the letter and then screw things up by mailing it to the foreigner. He, himself, couldn't very well go over to the Yangs and get the letter back, for if he met that Yang bastard face-to-face, there'd certainly be a fight. From the bottom of his heart, he found people like Yang repulsive. Mr. Ming sent his wife to get the letter back, because it was *her* refusal to accept it that had created this mess in the first place. It was a fitting way to punish her.

Mrs. Ming dreaded going over to the Yangs. It would be simply too humiliating. She'd rather take another beating than go over there and lose whatever face she had left. She procrastinated until her husband had gone to work and then spied on the Yangs until she had satisfied herself that they had gone to work, too. At that point she sent her maid to talk things over with their maid.

Mr. Ming was called on the carpet that very day and subjected to hard interrogation by the foreigner. Fortunately, since he had already seen the friend who had written the misaddressed letter, he was well prepared for what was coming. He was able to cover things up quite well during the questioning, but was still uneasy about that letter. The hardest thing to take was the fact that it had to fall into the hands of nobody else but a pauperish pedant like Mr. Yang! He'd just have to think of some way of paying the bastard back.

After arriving home, the first thing he did was ask his wife if she had gotten the letter back. Ever on her guard, she told him that the Yangs had refused to return it, thus shifting the responsibility from her own shoulders. Mr. Ming was furious. To think that a penurious pedant like Yang would have the gall to cross him! *Hmph!!* He ordered his children to climb over the dividing wall and stomp down every single plant in the Yangs' yard. Then they were to report back to him while he considered what further steps might be taken. Beside themselves with joy, the children spared not a single plant.

After the children had returned from their heroic mission, the postman made the delivery that usually comes somewhat after four in the afternoon. Mr. Ming read the two letters, and it was hard to tell whether what he felt was sorrow or happiness. The misaddressed one made him happy, for he realized that Mr. Yang had not, after all, opened it. But the letter that Mr. Yang himself had written put Mr. Ming into a very somber mood, indeed, and made him even more disgusted with that pauperish pedant. Only a penniless pedagogue like Yang would be even capable of such politeness! To think that a human being could even be that polite—enough to make a man throw up! He was glad that he had had his children destroy their garden!

142   Lao She

On the way home that day, Mr. Yang was in high spirits. On the one hand, he had returned a letter to its rightful owner, and on the other, he had—with the utmost politeness—exhorted a neighbor to do the right thing. How could Mr. Ming fail to be moved? Upon arriving home, however, Mr. Yang was utterly stunned. The plants in his backyard looked as though they had been dumped there by a garbage truck. His garden was in a state of absolute chaos. He had no doubt about who had done this, but what could he do? He tried to collect himself so that he might objectively consider his options. After all it wouldn't do for an educated man to react emotionally.

Try as he would, however, he was no longer capable of objectivity. That tiny drop of barbarian blood that was left in him after so much education boiled up and made dispassionate thought impossible. He tore off his coat and gathered up an armful of bricks. Taking careful aim across the wall at the windows in the Ming house, he let fly. The sound of breaking glass was music to his ears. He wasn't conscious of anything anymore, except sheer joy, a sense of fulfillment, and even a feeling of glory! It was as though a man had suddenly become a barbarian. He was deliciously conscious of his own strength, of his own courage. He felt the way that he did when he stood naked just after a bath, completely free and unrestrained—a new man. He felt young, passionate, free, and brave!

When he had smashed almost all the windows within the range of his arm, he went back to his room to rest. He waited for Mr. Ming to come over and fight him, and he wasn't afraid. Puffing wildly on a cigarette, Mr. Yang looked for all the world like a victorious warrior. He waited for a long, long time, but there was nary a stir from the direction of the Mings'.

As a matter of fact, Mr. Ming hadn't the slightest intention of going over to the Yangs' house, for now he felt that Mr. Yang wasn't really *all* that disgusting, after all. As he surveyed all that broken glass, though he wasn't pleased, he wasn't altogether pained. He even began to consider the possibility of enjoining the children from making off with the Yangs' flowers and grapes. In the past, nothing had been able to move him to think in that direction. But now the broken shards of glass changed his mind. As he thought things over, Mrs. Yang's image flashed before his eyes; thinking of her, he couldn't help but hate Mr. Yang. But now he realized that there was a difference between *hate* and *disgust. Hate* carried with it a slight hint of respect.

The next day was Sunday. Mr. Yang was in the yard cleaning up his garden. Mr. Ming was inside his house repairing the windows. It seemed that the whole world was at peace, and mutual understanding had finally come to mankind.

Crooktails

When we were both kids——Bai Renlu and me, that is——as soon as we got out of school, we'd go down to a little tea shop to listen to the storytellers. We didn't spend all of our daily allowances on food and used whatever we had left over to go listen to the storytellers. Actually, the manager of the tea shop, Old Gentleman Sun the Second, didn't necessarily want our money, but on the other hand, Renlu and I were too proud to listen without paying.

I suppose when you come right down to it, we two weren't really up to snuff as members of a storyteller's audience anyway. My hair, for instance, was still done up at the back of my head in a child's ponytail and tied with a piece of red cord. Renlu's hair was done up in the kid's fashion of having two little tufts that stuck out like horns from the sides of the head——we used to call them "crooktails." When Sun the Second passed the basket for money, he'd lower his voice when he got to us, and say, "Well, if it isn't Crooktails!" Then as he took our money, he'd give us a big smile and a handful of beans or peanuts to boot. "Eat up, little Crooktails." I couldn't help being a bit put out with him that he didn't call *me* "Little Ponytail." But to tell the truth, Renlu looked a lot more presentable than I did. He had that big, smooth kind of baby face that you see painted on New Year's cards, only maybe not that fat.

Eyelids that came straight down without a fold, round little nose, and clean-cut features—Renlu was a good-looking little guy. When he cranked up his legs and ran, those two crooktails would swing right and left, drumming against his cheeks like the two little balls tied to opposite sides of a handheld butterfly drum. And after a haircut that scalp of his would look so sleek and clean that no one could resist giving him the traditional three raps on the head. *Barber shop, barber shop— chop, chop, chop!* He wasn't the kind to complain even if you gave him three pretty good ones.

In school Renlu was well behaved, but even so there'd be times, of course, when he couldn't remember all the stuff he was supposed to memorize. But nobody'd give a cute little guy like "Crooktails" Bai Renlu a whacking just because he couldn't remember the text. Besides, Renlu was a favorite with the lady who was principal of our school—her "little crooktail treasure"—and she wouldn't let the teachers punish him. Whenever she needed someone to go out and buy her a little thread or maybe a couple cents' worth of vinegar, she'd give the chore to Renlu.

The trouble was that Renlu would *ask* for a beating. Whenever he couldn't remember the text, *he'd* get madder than the teacher. He'd get all red in the face, scrunch his a nose up a bit, and announce, "I will *not* recite! Just won't, that's all!" Then before the teacher even had time to react, he'd add, "I *won't* recite, and I'd like to see what *you* can do to make me!" Now what kind of room did that leave the teacher? The teacher had no choice but to reach for the little ruler reserved for such occasions. Renlu wouldn't scratch the palm of his hand the way the rest of us usually did to make it hurt less, but you could see his eyes blink especially fast as, crooktails swinging, he'd stride over to the teacher without the slightest hesitation to receive his punishment. After it was over, tears would roll around in his eyes like froth that spins about on top of water but refuses to go down. From beginning to end, however, he wouldn't let a single one of those tears fall. After a while, when his anger had subsided, he'd sit at his desk, rub his palms against his knees, and bury his head in his book. He still wouldn't let a peep out of him, but that little mouth of his would twitch as fast as a fish gasping for air on a hot day. Strange that such a mellow-looking kid should have such a tough, stubborn disposition.

By the time he was old enough to go to high school he was handsomer than ever. Hadn't put on much weight, but his eyes and eyebrows had spread out to those places on his face where, ideally, they should be. And while the rest of us turned into pimply-faced teenagers, Renlu's skin stayed smooth and fair as ever. As a matter of fact, on our first day in high school an upperclassman even bumped into him, and said, "Excuse me, Miss!" Renlu didn't say a thing, just took this school-mate's face and beat it to a pulp. It wasn't as though he was simply fighting, but more like his very life was on the line. Even students trying to break it up got hurt. Renlu didn't come to class the next day. He took the exams to transfer to another school. We didn't see each other for ten-odd years after that. Later I heard people say that he'd graduated from college and gone off someplace else to work.

At the fair held just before New Year's last year it was particularly cold. The Mountain of the Thousand Buddhas[1] was covered with dark, chilly clouds. Like a devil on the loose, a sharp wind cut and tore at people's ears and noses. But since I had nothing to do and lived pretty close to Shanshuigou where they held the fairs, I decided to go and check it out anyway. Sometimes you can find rare books at fairs like that.

I thought that since it was so cold, there wouldn't be many

people, but that was by no means the case. No matter how cold it is, people always have to lay in the wherewithal to celebrate New Year's. I made the rounds but there was nothing that took my fancy. Edible kelp, paper images of the God of Wealth, and slices of pork frozen hard as nails—nothing I was interested in. I was just thinking of calling it quits when I spotted a display of books spread out on the ground at the southernmost end of the fair.

The books were a good twenty or thirty feet from the other displays and in a spot where people were not likely to pass by. I wouldn't have gone over to it myself, except that I had already walked to the southern edge of the fair and was interested in buying books. I went over and thumbed through the few volumes that were spread out on the ground—all used English language texts. "Who in the world would want to buy old English language texts at New Year's?" I asked myself. As I looked at the books I noticed the salesman's feet. He was wearing a really old—albeit satin—pair of cloth shoes. His socks were the single-stitched kind that you wear in the summer. While everyone else was stomping their feet up and down to keep them warm, his seemed frozen fast to the ground. I closed the last book and walked away.

Everybody has probably experienced a time like that when some totally unrelated thing—for instance, you might see a swarm of ants that's captured a caterpillar or a mangy old dog being beaten—when some totally unrelated thing makes you feel bad for a good long time afterward and sticks to your heart like some strange and mysterious disease. Well that ragged old pair of satin shoes stuck fast to my heart in the same way. After walking a few steps, without thinking, I turned and looked back. The man selling the books had stooped to rearrange them. But why? I certainly hadn't gotten them out of order. With so few books, there was nothing to *get* out of order in the first place. I could tell the man wasn't accustomed to doing this kind of business. People who are used to going from fair to fair selling odds and ends would never be so fussy.

He was wearing an old, gray cotton robe of very thin material, and that hat he had on was so out of date you couldn't have given it away. My eyes shifted from him to the embankment behind him and then on past that to Thousand Buddha Mountain, where dark clouds had gathered into a bleak, cold mass. The man seemed to have cast a spell over me, and even though it would be a bit embarrassing, I decided to walk back to him. I realized, however, that when I got right in front of him, I might not have the nerve to scrutinize him more closely. There was a certain air of lofty pride about the man, a bit like a rundown old temple that inspires a feeling of reverence in one, despite its dilapidation. I can't tell you exactly how I traversed the short stretch of ground that lay between us, but at any rate, there I was standing directly in front of him again.

I recognized the eyes—the lids came straight down without a fold. For the time being, I couldn't be positive about the other features on that face, for even the clearest of memories is not immune from the passage of time, and I hadn't seen Renlu for well over ten years. The man looked at me for just a second and then immediately averted his eyes and looked off toward Thousand Buddha Mountain. That expression. It had to be him!

"Is it Elder Brother Renlu?" I asked boldly.

He gave me another once-over and looked back toward the mountains. But then, almost immediately, he looked back at me again. On that haggard face there now appeared no expression at all, though there was an ever so slight twitch in the cheeks. He wanted to talk, but pride held him back. And yet three words—Elder Brother Renlu—had obviously moved him. He didn't say a word but took me by the hand and, with a quiet smile, looked toward the mountains again.

"Let's go. I don't live far from here," I said. I tugged him along with one hand, while grabbing up the few books he had spread out there with the other.

He spoke my name, paused ever so briefly, and said, "I'm not going!"

I raised my head and saw that tears were hanging in his eyes. Releasing his hand for a moment, I tucked his books under one arm. I feigned a smile, and said, "It's like this: if you want to go with me, I'll take you; and if you *don't* want to go, I'll take you anyway!"

"Look you up later." He still hadn't moved.

"Wouldn't want to put you to all that much trouble!" I intentionally kept up my bantering tone. "And what's with this 'later'? There's no way I'm going to find you later, and you know it."

He looked as though he'd like to get mad at me but was too embarrassed to. No matter how proud a person may be, it's not easy to get mad at a schoolmate you used to hang out with when you were still in crooktails. The upshot of it all was that he came with me. It wasn't until we started walking that I noticed how stooped his shoulders had become.

Before five minutes were out, we were back at my house. On the way I was constantly afraid that he'd take off on me. Only when I was safely ensconced inside my house did I stop worrying. It was as though at long last I had a precious object firmly in my grasp. But I couldn't think of any way to begin our conversation. What would I ask and how would I ask it? It was obvious from his looks that he was very uneasy and I certainly didn't want to scare him off.

I remembered that I still had a bottle of white wine stashed away somewhere. When I found it, I also discovered some dates I'd forgotten about. Good! I had the wherewithal to entertain him. It'd be a lot better than just sitting around like two bumps on a log. As he took the wine cup, I noticed that his hands trembled a bit. After he'd drunk half of it, his eyes moistened, and he looked like a kid who comes home on a cold winter's day and has some hot rice gruel.

"When did you get here?" I asked, testing the waters.

"Me? Couple days back, I guess." He was looking at a tiny bit of cork that had stuck to the edge of my glass as though he was talking to it instead of me.

"Didn't you know I was here?"

"Nope." He glanced at me in a way that announced there was much he could say but found it difficult to, and that he hoped I wouldn't continue with this line of questioning. Damn! I'd hit his sore spot right off. Well, what the hell, people who have been childhood friends can't help doing things like that.

"Where are you staying?"

He grinned. "Staying? The way I look, you think I'm *staying* anywhere?" He kept on grinning, an inane sort of grin at that.

"Great, then *this* will be your home. Just move in with me. We can go hear the drum singers together. In the area around Bao Tu Springs there must be three or four places where you can still hear good drum singing.[2] How about *The Travels of Lao Can*? How's that grab you?" I thought I'd tease him into a good mood. "Remember when we were kids how we used to go listen to *Crimes Solved by Magistrate Shi*?"[3]

My words didn't have the expected result. He said nothing. But I didn't give up. Since wine is a great loosener of tongues, I urged him to drink some more. That went fairly well. He wasn't all that adamant in his refusal, and before long his face gradually turned red. Another idea dawned on me.

"OK now, what'll it be for eats? Noodles? Dumplings? Griddle cakes? You name it, so I can get started."

"Can't. Still have to go sell these books."

"You can't? Well, in that case, *I* can't let you out of this room!"

After a good long time, he nodded his head, and said, "You're full of the devil as ever, aren't you?"

"Me? I'm not the same guy I was back in the days when we wore our hair kid style, either. Where has the time gone? Just look at us—thirty-something already!"

"When you get into your thirties, it's time to call it quits. Dogs go in their teens."

"I'm not that pessimistic."

"Piddling little game—that's all life is." He sighed.

If the conversation stayed on this tack, we'd get farther and farther from what I was interested in. What I was curious about was what had happened to him during all that time. I changed my strategy and began telling him what had happened to *me* during all those years. And no matter how forced it was, I managed to drag in references to the themes *he* seemed interested in—pessimism, the meaning of life, and so on. Finally after many a twist and turn, I threw in the line I'd been holding in reserve all that time. "Well, I'm all done; now it's *your* turn."

Actually, very early in my monologue, he'd seen through my little ploy and had simply stopped listening. Had he been listening carefully, I would have had to take even more zigs and zags before throwing in my bottom line. You could tell from the expression in his eyes that he had edited out a great deal of what I had to say. When I was finished, however, there was nothing left for him to do but ask, "Exactly what is it that you want me to tell you?"

I pulled a long face. Now I was on the spot. To him, I guess I must have sounded like a district attorney grilling a known felon. Since we two were old friends, why not just come straight out with it? He might prefer it that way anyway. "Renlu—how is that you've fallen so low?"

For the longest time he said nothing. I didn't get the impression that he was finding it difficult to respond to such a troublesome question. It rather seemed that he needed time to arrange his reply. When you come to think of it, there is no rhyme or reason to life unless you impose some sort of order on it. That's why when old friends meet again after a long time, you'll see them just sit silently and look at each other. Don't we often see that sort of thing?

"Where shall I begin?" It was almost as though he was asking the question of all those little lanes and byways on the road of life that he had taken to get where he was now. "Do you remember how I was always getting punished when we were kids?"

"Yes, it was all due to your somewhat unusual disposition."

"It wasn't all *just* a matter of disposition." He shook his head slightly. "We were little kids back then, and I never really told you about this but, to tell the truth—and back then I hadn't realized this myself—the fault *really* lies with my eyes."

"What do you mean? You've got a perfectly good pair of eyes, right?"

"Ordinarily they're just fine, but sometimes they get sick on me.

"How can eyes get sick?" I began to suspect that all his troubles must be mental.

"It's not that they suffer from any sort of *physical* ailment. It's another kind of sickness, one that can't be treated. Sometimes it comes on me quite suddenly and then I see—I can't put a name to it. . . . "

"Illusions?"

"No, they're not illusions. I've never seen green-faced monsters or anything like that. It's more like images, and yet they're not really *images,* either. It's more like a certain facial expression or a general air. You'll understand it better if I give you an example.

"Remember that teacher we had when we were little? Really nice guy, right? But when the sickness was on me, he was totally repulsive, and I'd start acting up. After while, my sickness would pass. He'd be the same nice guy he'd always been, and I'd have gotten a licking for nothing, for nothing more than a certain expression, a certain air he'd have about him—a repulsive air."

Without waiting for him to finish, I asked: "You must have seen that certain air about me sometimes too, right?"

He smiled ever so slightly. "Probably. Don't remember too clearly now. But you and I did have our share of quarrels when we were kids, and I'll bet there must have been at least one of them that started because I saw that disgusting air about you, too. What a good thing it was that we didn't stay together once we got to high school, because if we had . . . My sickness, you know, grew worse. In the beginning I'd see someone with that repulsive air, raise a little hell, and that would be that. But later on I was totally unable to control myself. If I saw that air about someone—even if we *didn't* get into a fight—I'd never be able to have anything to do with him again. And that's why the only *good* memories I have are those from early childhood. Back then, you see, my sickness wasn't as serious as it got to be later. After I passed the age of twenty, every last repulsive image I saw lodged itself permanently in my mind, so that now my memory is nothing more than a pile of repulsive photographs."

"Was *every* person repulsive?"

"When the sickness was on me there were no exceptions. Parents, brothers—everyone. I considered ignoring those images and muddling through as best I could, but if I did that, then that same irresponsible attitude would spill over into everything I did, and life would become unbearable. On the other hand, if I *didn't* ignore those images, then I'd be forced to assault everyone I met, and that wasn't a viable option, either. So gradually I became what you see before you now, a man with no home, no children, and no friends. What's the point in making friends when you know that someday you're going to see a repulsive side to every one of them?"

I interrupted, "What you call 'repulsive' should perhaps be modified to 'weak.' Everybody has weaknesses, but that doesn't necessarily make them repulsive."

"No, I'm not talking about weaknesses. A weakness can disgust you but it can also call forth your compassion and sympathy—give you the sort of feeling you have toward a friend who's an alcoholic. Actually, you can observe the sort of thing I'm talking about even without these sick eyes of mine. Just try this and you'll be able to see something of what I do, though perhaps not so starkly. When you look at a person, don't look at the whole face, but just the eyes, nose, and mouth—especially the eyes. For example look into the eyes of someone who's lecturing you on such grand themes as benevolence and righteousness, and if you look closely enough, you'll see vivid pornographic images flickering there. And even while that person's mouth is spouting all that righteous crap, you'll see a grin on the lips. A grin! You'll find that the higher up the social ladder you climb, the more revolting people are. Uneducated people are a little better. To be sure, they're repulsive, too, but at least they're a bit more open about it. The educated ones are more skilled at hiding it. Come to think of it, if I didn't have this pair of eyes, life would be one gigantic fraud.

"I'll give you an example. One night I went to the opera, and a man in his thirties took the seat next to mine. He was well dressed and quite presentable, but when I looked out of the corner of my eyes, I saw him in all his ghastliness. I was furious! It was none of my business, of course, but what claim did a loathsome creature like that have to such a respectable-looking face? A repulsive beast with a handsome face—an appalling blunder in the way nature fashions human beings!

"At just that moment the usher came by to collect our tickets.

The beast seated next to me didn't have one. Nonetheless, his eyes bulged out ferociously as he turned to the usher, and said, 'My name is Wang and *I* didn't buy a ticket in the first place! Even if you were a Japanese usher, none of us Wangs would bother to buy a ticket.'[4] I couldn't restrain myself. It wasn't that I wanted to punish him so much as it was that I wanted to beat away that mask of respectability and make his true form visible to everyone.

"I gave him a good clout right across the mouth. Guess what he did? Nothing. Just muttered to himself and walked away. Exactly what you'd expect of such a repulsive person. What was wrong with him could by no means be termed a *weakness.* It was pure repulsiveness in search of a good beating. Trouble was, people didn't beat him often enough to let everyone see his true image—a mangy old bitch snapping at the heels of a beggar. Fortunately the sickness was on me at the time I encountered him, otherwise even *I* might have taken him for a respectable man myself."

"That means you're actually *fond* of your sickness and wouldn't give it up even if you could, right?" I goaded him.

He didn't seem to have heard me, and I repeated my question. He smiled. "I really can't say whether I consider my illness a blessing or not, but when it *isn't* on me, things are even worse—*knowing* that people really are degenerate yet not being able to see it, knowing that I'm in a dream yet not being able to wake from it. When my sickness *is* on me, no matter what else, at least I am not bored. Just think—taking a swing at someone whenever you feel like it—that's fun in its own way. One fascinating thing about it is that whenever I'm done beating someone up, even the bystanders—and *they're* repulsive, too—don't have the backbone to say anything to my face. I've yet to meet a repulsive man with guts enough to be straight-forward. Every last one of the bystanders is a hypocritical wimp, too! But behind my back they'll call me crazy. I once stuck my finger right in the face of a soldier and told him how contemptible he was. He got so mad he pulled a gun on me. Now I *liked* that! I asked, 'OK, *now* what are you gonna do?' Hah! He put his gun back in its holster and was a good half block away before he worked up the nerve to turn back and give me a dirty look. Now there's a lowlife S.O.B. for you!"

Renlu was silent for a bit, and then went on, "In the beginning I dreaded the onset of my malady because as soon as it was on me I'd pick a fight, and you can't hold a job very long that way; but then after I'd lost a job, as time passed by I came to dread the *absence* of my disease. For when it wasn't on me, I'd find it difficult to just sit around and remain idle, and *that* meant I had to go out and look for work. Trouble was, I couldn't just find something in the abstract called 'work'— people always came attached to it and repulsiveness always came attached to the people. I was at a crossroads. Which way should I go? Should I just remain constantly at odds with society or should I muddle along as best I could? I couldn't decide. When the sickness was on me I'd stir up trouble without even half trying.

"And yet sometimes there were periods of one or two months in a row when I'd go along free of my malady. What was I to do, just stay unemployed while I waited for it to come back? Couldn't do that. And yet no sooner would I start a job than my sickness would come on me again. Life seemed to be playing a cruel game, pulling me first one way and then straight back the other way, like a saw. There was one time when I was free of my sickness for the better part of a year. 'OK,' I thought to myself, 'it's time to get firmly planted in the rut of normalcy.' Since I no longer wanted to take the fire I felt inside and use it to commit arson, perhaps I could use it to warm house and hearth. And so it was that I returned home determined to play the filial son and loving grandson. I even shaved on a regular basis to let people know how serious I was about muddling through.

"Since I could no longer see the faces in the humans around me, I began pretending to see human faces among the beasts. I became very friendly to small animals like cats and dogs. When I had free time I'd even comb and groom cats and take dogs for walks. Once again I made my peace with mankind. The people around me had a world through which *they* muddled with great gusto and relish. Who was I, then, to insist on knocking my head against it at every turn. It was then that I began writing lots of scripts for my future. First off, I wanted to set up a family. Thought that maybe an oil-salt-firewood-and-rice sort of responsibility would cure me of my disease. What's more, I had a pretty good impression of women, for the vast majority of people I had seen through when the sickness was on me were men. Perhaps it was simply because I had more opportunity to meet men, but whatever the reason, the result was that I had come to the conclusion that women were somewhat preferable. I took stock of my life and, one after the other, began drafting scripts for it. Don't most people like to compose such scripts? At any rate, I thought all I had to do was find an ideal woman, and then I'd probably be able to muddle along in some half-assed fashion for several decades.

"My scripting didn't stop there. I went even farther and decided that my judgment regarding the wretchedness of the world was, at most, only an *inference*—after all, I hadn't met everyone in it. On the other hand, it was still just possible, of course, that my judgment was right on the money. Since my sickness wasn't always on me, however, how could I ever be absolutely certain of the world's universal repulsiveness even if I *did* meet everyone in it? And just suppose that my inference wasn't true; suppose that there were good people out there, people so wholesome that even if you put them in front of me while my sickness was on me, I still wouldn't be able to see anything in the least repulsive about them.

"I never knew when the sickness was going to come on. It was only when I saw a person's appearance changing before my very eyes that I knew it was back. But since that was true, another question arose: how could I ever be positive that there weren't times when the sickness was already on me and the person before me didn't change precisely because there was nothing repulsive about that person to begin with? On the basis of such questions, my hopes for a new life became even more extravagant. I decided I would no longer be the perverse person I had been. I would get married, establish a household, and have myself a few nice chubby children. All around me other people seemed to be moving through their days quite contentedly. With so many of the world's sweet grapes set out before me, why did I insist on picking only the sour ones. The script I worked out for myself now wasn't half bad."

He rested a bit. I didn't dare press him, but I did fill his glass with more wine.

Suddenly he asked, "Remember my cousin? The one we used to play with when we were kids?"

"Back then she was called Zhaodi, right?"[5] In my mind's eye, I saw a little girl with green jade earrings.

"That's the one. Two years younger than I. Well, I found out that she still wasn't married—waiting for me, it would seem. Now I really had good material for a new script. I looked her up, told her everything about myself. She still wanted me and we got engaged." There was another long pause in the conversation while he swallowed three or four mouthfuls of wine. "And then one day as I was going to see her, my sickness suddenly came over me again. It was like this. A little girl of six or seven carrying a big rice bowl was walking down the middle of the street. She heard the horn behind her and ran straight ahead. But after only a stride or two, she changed her mind and started running back *toward* the car instead. When it was almost upon her, she squatted in terror. Fortunately the driver hit the brakes. At just that moment, however, I happened to look at his face. Hideously repulsive! Now, as a matter of fact, he *had* stopped in time, but in his heart of hearts, he would have loved to run her down and then back up and run over her little body again and again until it was nothing but a pulp.

"I no longer had the heart to go see my cousin, for my world was now a hideous one, one that I couldn't drag her into. I took off. I sent her a short note. 'There's no point in waiting around for me anymore.' But those brief hopes I entertained of marrying and setting up a household were enough to rob me of my former ferocity, for they made me think about myself in a different light. How could I be sure that *I* wasn't repulsive, maybe even *more* repulsive than other people? That doubt was enough to strip me of all my former viciousness. Previously I used to beat up any repulsive person I encountered, or at the very least, nail him with a look that would set him trembling for a long time afterward. Although I wasn't particularly proud of that, it did give me an unusual degree of self-confidence, for I knew I was tougher than anyone I'd run into.

"But then when I considered marriage and the possibility of muddling through right along with the rest of the world— that ruined everything! I realized that I wasn't really meaner than anyone else; I just had a pair of sick eyes that they didn't. After that, I no longer had the balls to beat people up. I passively avoided any repulsive person I happened to spot. I really longed to have someone come up to me, stick a finger in my face, and tell me how repulsive *I* was. But nobody did." He fell silent again.

"Life has the real script worked out far more carefully than anything we can devise. Think of it: I just got out of jail. It was like this. I fell in with a gang of crooks. Since I was so repulsive myself, I figured it didn't matter what kind of people I hung around with. All things considered, our leader had scaled the heights of loathsomeness to the very pinnacle: he got the ransom money and then tore up the ticket anyway.[6] Took the guy and bricked him up inside the flue of a *kang*. I didn't give our leader the beating he deserved, but I did turn him in to the police. He was shot before a firing squad just a few days back. As I testified in court, I exposed every last one of his crimes. And him? Didn't say a single word that would implicate *me* in anything! Just the opposite, he did his best to clear me of any wrongdoing. That's why I only spent a few days in jail and wasn't charged. Just think, the most repulsive person imaginable had some goodness left in his heart. A rotten sonofabitch like that who had torn up his ticket actually refused to rat on the very friend who'd turned him in! I had never imagined such a thing possible. Jesus used to pray for criminals as well as his own enemies. Jesus was something else. I wonder if *his* eyes were the same as this pair of mine? Unlike me, however, Jesus was able to hang in there and stay tough from beginning to end—precisely because he was also soft from beginning to end. Most people only know how to be soft, but have no idea how to be tough—that's why the world is as spineless as it is. I only knew how to be tough, but had no idea how to be soft. And now—now, there's no place where I can settle down anymore. Life doesn't amount to much of anything." He drank down the rest of his wine and stood up.

"Rice is almost done."

"Don't want any." His tone was determined.

"You're not gonna leave here, Renlu. This is your home." I was worried he might take off.

"I'll come see you again some other time. I really will." He went over and picked up his books.

"Do you have to go? Without eating anything?"

"Yes, I do. In my world, friendship isn't possible. I'm the kind of guy who doesn't understand himself, but likes to tell others how to live. I'll never be able to enjoy the ordered kind of life that you have here. It seems that bumping and bungling my way from pillar to post is the only thing I'm fit for."

I knew there was no point in trying to detain him. Now it was my turn to be quiet for a bit. Finally I pulled a little money out.

"Don't want it!" He smiled, and added, "I'm not going to starve to death. Might not be a bad way to go anyway."

"Well, let me give you something to wear. That'd be all right, wouldn't it?"

He paused a bit before answering, "OK, then. How can a guy refuse a childhood schoolmate? I'm sure you must think me very strange. I'm no longer as tough as I used to be—not tough on others, that is, but there's no way I can be anything but hard on myself. Just think—even that repulsive gangster I told you about had a little backbone in him. OK then, give me something, but make it something *you* wear on a regular basis. That way it'll have some trace of your body warmth about it and won't seem completely like a gift. God, see how I like to script things out!"

I took off my overcoat. He put it on, unbuttoned, over his long cotton gown. As I saw him out, the air was thick with snowflakes, and dark clouds covered the sky. Neither of us said a word. In the bleak world outside it seemed as though nothing existed save the sound of our footsteps. Leaning slightly forward into the whirling white, Renlu continued on out through the front gate without turning his head.

Notes

1. Mountain of the Thousand Buddhas (Qianfo shan) is on the outskirts of Jinan, capital of Shandong Province, where Lao She taught at Qilu University (Qilu daxue) between 1930 and 1934.

2. The Bao Tu Springs are located in Jinan. Such singers told stories (often based on popular novels) while accompanying themselves on the drum.

3. These two novels—which the drum singers could present orally, of course—are nineteenth century works. The first, *The Travels of Lao Can* (Lao Can youji), is available in English, translated by Harold Shadick under that title (Ithaca: Cornell University Press, 1952), except the last word in the title is romanized "Ts'an" instead of "Can"). *Crimes Solved by Magistrate Shi* (Shi Gong'an) has not yet been translated into English. Lao She himself wrote a novel about drum singers in the late 1940s, translated into English as *The Drum Singers* by Helena Kuo (New York: Harcourt Brace, 1952); the Chinese manuscript was lost before publication; the English version of the novel was subsequently translated into Chinese by Ma Xiaomi and published in 1980.

4. This story was written at a time when the Japanese were in virtual control of large areas of North China either economically, militarily, or both.

5. "Zhaodi er" was a name often given to little girls in hopes that the mother's next pregnancy would result in a boy. The name means something like "beckoning a younger brother to follow."

6. *Sipiao* is gangster slang for "killed the hostage."

Ding

The ocean air's stifling. Ding sits on the sand, his toes kissed by sprays, a weary Apollo. Yes, there is an ambience of Greece—men, women, old, and young baring their backs. Too bad the chests—this one and everyone else's—are a bit on the narrow side. Not fully naked, either. Something's off-kilter about this Greece in China. A narrow-chested Apollo gasping for breath!

In any case, China has shown *some* progress. Ding—China's Apollo—slowly rests his head on the damp and soft sand, feeling sluggish, but the mind's still clear, equipped for beauty and ideas. Eyes shut, he can picture those goddesses he just saw. Yes, there's been progress! That coed who looks as if she's still in high school. Her mother probably still has bound feet. A wholesome beauty, legs, progress! Those small feet dipping into the sea, a national disgrace!

Back feels wet. The new swimsuit feels clammy. Too lazy to get up, but have to get up, the ocean air will blow it dry. Sun's quite fierce, though not totally hot. Got to get sunglasses, at the pharmacy on Zhongshan Road. Round ones and oval ones, placed on top of the boxes of aspirin. Eye rims feel awfully dry. There's salt in seawater. Drink enough seawater, won't need to eat salted vegetables anymore. Won't work. Drinking seawater can make one go mad, supposedly. Drink a stomachful, oh, wasn't it in the newspaper—there's a *People's News* everywhere; are they all from the same publisher?—about some twenty-two-year-old youth who drowned. Drink a stomachful, can be dangerous, going to a sea-green-colored death!

The fort, a stretch of green, can't see the cannon, a green of such poetic beauty. Yes, red when it's time to kill and green when it's idle, like phlegm. Struck the chest once. Lungs too narrow. Could it be tuberculosis? Couldn't be. The sailboats look terrific. Find a woman. Both of us in swimsuits. Get on a small sailboat, and drift, drift, drift to over there by the island. That island. Looks like a fly on blue paper. Gross! On the small boat, mess around . . . a bit of romance! No, better to go up on Mount Lao. There's a Western-style restaurant. Western style, everything is Western style. China's made progress!

A pair of American sailors, hugging two prostitutes, bounding about on the beach. From behind, a woman walking by. What nationality? Her legs are as thick as the pillars of a palace. A bunch of boys burying a little girl with sand. Only the head remains, shrieking, "Stop! Stop!" The sound of breakers, music. Oh, a tea dance. Hm, the American sailors have drifted far away. Someone is just about to jump off the diving board, far, far away, first extending the arms, like Jesus on the cross . . . splashes with a spray of water. Must be deep over there. A lifeboat. Ah, that fatso's got the right idea, a life preserver slipped around the neck, like a huge, green python. Qingdao probably doesn't have poisonous snakes. India. Someone, barefooted but not wearing a swimsuit, walking by the edge of the water and throwing a cigarette butt onto the sand. Ding takes a look at the steel basket—fruit peels, odds and ends, thrown into the basket. China hasn't made too much progress!

"*Ha-low,*[1] Ding," a human fish climbs out of the ocean.

A prostitute pulls a sailor into the water. Infectious. Ought to be prohibited.

"Hey, Sun!" Ding exposes his white teeth, takes a look at his arms. They're black. A black face and white teeth, couldn't look too good, but romantic?

The fat woman dips into the ocean. Turns out she can also float. Mechanics, mechanics, now what was the theory behind it? Oh, the minute you leave school, forget everything in the books! A group of students coming over, each and every one black as a demon, the bones propping up the swimsuits— nothing but edges and corners. Sea bathing, sunbathing. But not enough food, insufficient nutrition. A mouthful of seawater. Without a doubt, death. Problems! Sooner or later, two meals of steamed cornbread. Practice running ten thousand meters!

"How's it going, Ding?" Water streams down Sun's hair.

"C'mon, take a rest. Don't work too hard. The air's stifling, and the seawater's hard!" Ding still thinking of health problems. The Chinese ought to practice tai chi, really.

A cluster of people walking by. Most likely a family. Four to five children, all holding small iron pails. A fortyish woman, bound feet let out. Footprints in the sand are particularly deep. Two young girls. Sun's eyes follow them. A fiftyish man, an embroidered dragon bathrobe draped over him. A retired army officer.

A stretch of black clouds rising over the island. The fort looks even greener.

Bobbing up and down in the ocean, people's heads, life preservers, foams of water, shoulders, sharp shouts. Blond-haired ones are westerners. Still can make out the men and the women. All moving, hearts beating somewhat faster. Who knows how many lovers have found each other. Mount Lao, small boats, restaurants. They've eyed each other, from top to bottom. Police inspecting the hotels. No problem.

Sun has a lover. Ding's for the single life. But who knows,

if the right woman turns up, he'll get married. No, the single life's better. Kids are a terror. A hundred fifty, enough for me. Rent a place, buy furniture, hire a maid, have kids, no way there'll be enough money. What about sex? Don't have to get married to take care of that problem. But society, feudal thinking . . . Isn't easy! Even a small proposition to any female would cost a diamond ring!

"Sun, where'd you go last night?" Thinking about sex.

"To take the torch and go wandering at night, 'tis a fine thing indeed."[2] Sun sits by Ding. The retired army officer and his wife and children are gone.

Ding laughs. Sun, that devil of a rake, also makes $150.00. *And* has a lover.

No, Sun isn't a total rake. Scrounges all the time. Stays for free at the guest house, wheedles for dance tickets, rides the public bus for free, gets free train tickets, pays nothing for sea bathing. The air belongs to everyone. A bowl of rice porridge, twenty fried dumplings, plus tips—fifteen cents. Fifteen cents, on $150.00. He's got enough to spend. He's no rake, just a sly fox.

"Ding, what happened to your camera?"

"Didn't bring it along."

"We'll use it tomorrow, climb Mount Lao, ride the warship." Sun buries his feet in the sand.

The sailors come out of the water. The tattoos on the arms are even bluer. On the prositutes' legs are some gray marks, like lichens.

The fat woman's face is red as the sun. Her legs have creases of fat, like a tied-up ham.

More clusters of people walking by. The sun is setting. An ocean steamer passing by, whistling its golden red chimney with the white lines.

"Sun, when're you going back? There're still three days of vacation. The chief's a backbreaker!"

"Me, once the yellow crane leaves, it doesn't return. Arrive at Qingdao, live in Qingdao, die in Qingdao—the Tri-Daoism. I'm not planning on going back!"

That son of a gun over there looks like Liu, doesn't he? Disappointments. Running into an old friend in a strange land. Liu, childhood classmate, the happy days, running together like wild rabbits. Middle school, begin considering technical school, fail math, graduate. A hundred fifty. For the single life, antirevolutionary, patriotic, China's made progress. Flood victims. Sun gets free tickets to the fund-raiser dance. Went with a date, no doubt!

"Who cares about Chief Li?" says Sun, reminded. "Even if he wiped my butt, I still wouldn't go back! I tell you, get a rich girl, you'll have everything! You, me, technical school graduates, how much capital did we spend? Who are the parents going to give their young girls to, if not to us? Do we want girls for nothing? Get this. There's hope for China, as long as the likes of us can comfortably multiply and propagate for our country. Even beggars, if they could, would have seven to eight kids. When Zhang Gongdao was thirty-five, he was well supported by six sons. What happened? More bandits and rickshaw pullers, that's what happened! People like us, we shouldn't fail our responsibility to society. We've got to produce more sons and daughters. Counting both husband and wife, that's comfortably worth five hundred thousand, equivalent to a special prize in the air force lottery! Get what I mean?"

"Got to go now." Ding stands up.

"Bai-bai! Goo-bai!"[3] Sun sits waving his hand. The sun lights up his nails.

"See you here tomorrow! *Goo-luc-ke!*"[4]

Ding gazes out. Not many people in the ocean yet. Remaining scatter of heads moving up and down in sync with the red flag on the lifeboat. The fat woman, the sailors, the prostitutes, can't see them anymore. Music. In the far distance, someone is blowing on a harmonica. He goes to change his clothes. Sounds of endless cars honking and flashing by on the street.

Coming out, glimpse bright red lips, moving up and down, chewing gum, then they're gone. Legs, back, all tanned, high and low shoes, round and shiny heels like newly laid eggs. Several girl students giggling, walk away. Holding the damp swimsuit, he walks along the seaside park. The big leaves of the western parasol tree wave in the golden sun rays. The pines suck the golden setting sun into the tree trunk. Brown rocks, wet and hard, gazing at the white ocean sprays.

A hundred fifty. The blurry past, swimming by . . . Sea, mountain, island, brown-wet-hard-white wave-dashed rocks. Beauty, beauty is a stretch of emptiness. Work, buildings, Chinese archways, Western houses. A mutt runs by. China's made progress. Feel a bit hungry. Yellow croaker, prawns, China's fishing industry's a failure. Sun's a genius, even at a time of national defeat, he can eat free yellow croakers. Where to have dinner? Feeling lonely. Seamen dragging around their prostitutes. The retired army officer has a wife, Sun has a lover. Ding only has a body with a clammy swimsuit. A tanned skin should count as an achievement. Got to go back to the public affairs office, got to. Qingdao won't give me $150.00. Business office, cigarettes, paper, pen, idle talk, disagreements. Gross $150.00. Take off $2.50 income tax. A check of $147.50. Post office savings $25.01. Placing the damp swimsuit on the brown rock, he looks at the sea. The mystery of great nature. Vast sea, empty sky. Taking out the lacquer box from the bag, there's only one small tobacco pouch left, and no match! The ocean air's stifling. Chest's a bit on the narrow side. Put the lacquer box and the lone cigarette back into the pouch. Hands on the waist, gazing at the sea, the mountain, the distant sails. China's Apollo!

Notes

1. Transliteration for the English "Hello."

2. Sun's variation on a line from one of the famous series of anonymous poems known as "The Nineteen Old Poems of the Han": "If the day is short and you hate the long night, / why not take the torch and go wandering?" Burton Watson, trans., *The Columbia Book of Chinese Poetry; From Early Times to the Thirteenth Century* (New York: Columbia University Press, 1984), p. 101.

3. Transliteration for the English "Bye-bye! Good-bye!"

4. Transliteration for "Good luck!"

A Man Who Doesn't Lie

A man like Zhou Wenxiang,[1] who considered himself very honest, was understandably insulted by such a letter. Long before it arrived, he had heard of the existence of a preposterous organization that flagrantly named itself the Liars' Society. Among his friends, there were—allegedly—quite a few who were members. He dared not investigate further into this alleged membership. What if it turned out to be true? That would be quite embarrassing. Break off relations? That would seem a bit too drastic. Go along with them? That would be doing violence to his conscience. Zhou Wenxiang knew that he had no remarkable talents, but he *was* trustworthy and steadfast. His work and reputation depended entirely on these qualities. He believed in honesty. He likened himself to a clumsy, heavy rock, which, while no exquisite gem to the eyes, was strong and solid. And now, to his surprise, he had received this letter:

> *Without lies there is no culture. Telling lies is life's ultimate art. We question the credibility of everything. The only thing known for certain is that everyone lies, and lies about everything. History is a record of lies. Newspapers are the transmitters of lies. Those who are adept at telling*

lies are the happiest people in the world, because being good at it denotes wisdom itself. Just think of all the fights you would get into in the course of a day if you didn't tell a few lies. Between husband and wife, how would there ever be twelve hours of peace if it weren't for telling lies? Our conscience never bothers us for all the hogwash in our love talk and love letters. Nonetheless, love remains sacred! The victor is a noble prince and the defeated a traitor. Yes, and it all boils down to whether or not one has a knack for telling lies. Culture is the product of lies. Those gentle literary types and gentlemen are the biggest pretenders of all! Most comical of all, people spend day and night futilely covering up this gem, acting like a pregnant woman wearing an oversized coat. People are so afraid of others detecting their lies that they pile lie upon lie until they've created a real monster.

We are not like this. We know that lies are valuable, that telling lies is no easy feat. Therefore, we tell lies honestly and use them artistically. The purpose of forming this society is to research the techniques of telling lies and to publicize its good points. We know everyone lies. But we urge everyone in the future not to lie in such a shoddy manner. . . .

Forever in admiration of your habit of lying and in hopes of mutual assistance in refining our art and glorifying East-West culture, we remain most humbly yours . . .

Before he finished the letter, Zhou Wenxiang had put it down. This society, as he saw it, was absurd, and so was this letter. Just because others were shooting off their mouths didn't mean he could brush them aside with a laugh. He couldn't excuse these people who bulldozed their way into his head. This was an insult to his character. "Forever in admiration of your habit of lying?" He didn't recall ever telling a lie. Even if he had, it must have been unintentional. He was against telling lies. He could not even admit that newspapers created rumors, because so many of his opinions and ideas had come from them.

Most likely, he thought, those "alleged" members of the Liars' Society had written this letter to poke fun at him. And yet, printed on the left-hand corner of the envelope was "President: Tang Hanqing; Standing Committee Members: Lin Dewen, Deng Daoqun, Fei Muchu; Treasurer: Ho Chaolong." These were all people Zhou Wenxiang recognized and wanted to get to know. They were quite well known in society, and moreover, had some money. Their fame and money, in Zhou Wenxiang's eyes, could not possibly have originated in reckless talk. On the contrary, carelessly shooting off one's mouth could only serve to destroy a person. In that case, a group organized by such rich and famous people couldn't be some fly-by-night operation. That wouldn't be reasonable. Perhaps then, this letter *did* make sense and wasn't necessarily a joke his friends were playing on him.

Once again, he picked up the letter, intending to read it anew. But he couldn't get past the first few sentences. Regardless of how famous or wealthy the president and members were, this letter was, of course, totally and utterly absurd. This *had* to be some kind of bad dream! Never in his life had he encountered such contradictions. It was all so bewildering!

Zhou Wenxiang was already past the age of caring about his appearance. Although he wasn't deliberately sloppy, he sometimes could let several days go by without shaving and still feel thoroughly comfortable. He not only felt good about it, he felt even more sure of his own solid simplicity. He didn't look into the mirror often. He knew that his round face and square body weren't much to look at. His self-esteem rested entirely on that unadulterated and straightforward heart of his. He didn't want his outer appearance to announce his inner intelligence but rather preferred that it proclaim the honesty in his heart. It was as though he was always saying, "Look at me! Honest inside and out! Zhou Wenxiang is nothing if not dependable!"

Nevertheless, as he put down the letter, he decided to look at himself in the mirror. His time-tested self-confidence forced him to scrutinize himself anew, like an established Government Cabinet unafraid of—nay, even welcoming—a motion of no confidence. Just as he was about to go toward the mirror, he heard footsteps outside the window. He recognized them as those of his wife. He suddenly felt cheered, not because he welcomed his wife, but because he had recognized her foot- steps. Everything in his house had a routine—familiar and intimate. One always ate noodles with thick gravy on the summer equinox, and his wife always walked in that manner. He wished everything in the world were like this, all familiar and intimate. If one day his wife should walk in a manner unac- customed to his ear, how rattled and at wit's end he would be! He couldn't say whether he loved his wife or not, but these familiar-sounding footsteps seemed to give him a kind of strength, seemed to grant him the firm belief that life was not a bungled nightmare. He recognized the way she walked, just as he recognized the two bright red peonies on his tea cup.

He quickly put that disturbing letter inside his pocket. This movement was done quickly and naturally, almost instinctively. Without having to give it any further thought, he immediately decided he couldn't let her see such a preposterous letter.

"It's getting late," his wife opened the door, one leg on the threshold. "Shouldn't you be going?"

"Don't I look like I'm all ready?" He glanced at his over- coat—strange that just now when he was absorbed in that letter he had forgotten whether or not he had put on his overcoat. Now that he saw it on his body, he couldn't recall when he had put it on. Since he had put it on, no doubt he was getting ready to leave. Leave early and come back early, make a living for his family, young and old—this was his hope and glory. In fact, because of that letter, he had actually forgotten about going to the office. But when prodded by his wife, he couldn't let his ever constant hope and glory diminish a speck. "Don't I look like I'm ready to go?" He put on his hat. "Has Xiaochun[2] left yet?"

"He says he's not going to school today." His wife looked at him with that all-too-common troubled look of a mother, unwilling to anger her husband yet unwilling to make the son out to be a good-for-nothing, either. But if the husband wouldn't get angry, it wouldn't matter if the son had a slight tendency toward being a good-for-nothing. "He's complaining of a stomachache again."

Without saying a word, Zhou Wenxiang walked out. Suppose he had gone to question Xiaochun and found him guilty— suppose he merely disliked school and didn't have a stomachache at all. This would have proven that Zhou Wenxiang's son was capable of lying. Suppose he hadn't educated his son properly, and his son really had learned to lie; then that would be even worse. The only thing to do was remain silent and look resolute. Looking resolute could make a man appear to have a solution when he didn't, especially in front of women. Zhou Wenxiang was head of the house and, of course, had to show his authority. He couldn't let his wife and child see any of his weaknesses.

Walking out the gate, he felt even more aware of his own competence and ability. All that silent treatment toward his wife just now was executed with such finesse, flowing naturally from his heart. Not a bit of faking, not a bit of manipulation, it came entirely from an unadulterated sincerity that was purely the product of his own self-cultivation. He had no need to deliberate, for he could handle problems easily and naturally without it. The thought of that letter—how preposterous!

The big clock at the office said 8:32. He was two minutes

late. This was a new experience. In the past ten years, the latest he had ever arrived was 8:28. Even in his dreams, the long hand on the clock was always on *this* side of the half-hour mark. The world seemed to have stretched two minutes. Everything had changed! He suddenly didn't recognize himself. He had always been a man on *this* side of 8:30. Life was an accumulation of habit. A new bed can make one lose sleep. Having lost two minutes, Zhou Wenxiang lost his bearings as well. It was as though he suddenly found himself walking along a stretch of desolate beach.

Presently, however, he began to feel calm again and found himself back on track. He felt like reproaching himself for having let such a piddling matter shake him up so. At the same time, he felt that he ought to commend himself. To have become so worried over such a trifling matter was certainly a clear indication of his habitual trustworthiness.

Sitting at his desk, however, he was assailed by irksome thoughts. Office regulations did not permit tardiness. He had seen his colleagues get reprimanded by the manager because of it; some even got a pay cut because of being late. Hm, this was no laughing matter! Of course, ten years of loyal service couldn't be casually written off because of a single instance of tardiness. But what if the manager were to leak this out? Even if the manager *didn't* come out and say anything but merely used his index finger to point at him—Zhou Wenxiang softly called out his own name—that would be more than he could take, not to speak of being reprimanded or having his pay cut. In and of itself the finger pointing wouldn't be all that bad, but its *significance* would: it would strike out ten years of honor like a splash of hot water poured onto snow!

Yes, he ought to take the initiative to seek out the manager and not wait to be summoned to court. It was only right that he should be reprimanded and penalized. He stood up, intending to go see the manager.

For a while he didn't budge. He had to prepare his speech. "Mr. Manager, I was two minutes late. In all these years this is the first time, but there's no denying I have made a mistake!" This was appropriate, he thought, as he assessed and rehearsed his repentance. But, what if the manager asked for the reason? Not only should he prepare a reason for his tardiness, he should volunteer it first and not wait for the manager to ask. He had it. "Xiaochun, my son, had a stomachache, and so . . . " This would be quite acceptable, and moreover, it was true. It occurred to him, furthermore, that while he was at it, he might as well ask for half a day off, because Xiaochun had a stomachache and should perhaps go see a doctor. But he didn't dare. True, it would appear even more thoroughgoing, but it was perhaps a bit too drastic. Normally he loved Xiaochun, but now for some reason he didn't really care about Xiaochun's stomachache. Although, according to his standard of honesty, he ought to believe in his son's stomachache, and, moreover, ought to get a doctor for him right away.

He went to see the manager, said all the things he had prepared, said it very aptly at that, neither too rushed nor too hesitant so as to arouse suspicion. He dared not ask straight out for half a day off, but he did intimate that he had to find a doctor. Having finished talking, before the manager had opened his mouth, he already felt thoroughly at ease. He hadn't anticipated that he could speak so suavely and convincingly. Since he had always viewed himself as being trustworthy, he had never thought of himself as a skilled speaker. Now that he had spoken in front of the manager with an articulateness that surprised himself, he began to feel that he was not only trustworthy but was also possessed of a hitherto undiscovered talent.

Just as he had anticipated, the manager did not reprimand him but merely smiled. "An honest man after all!" thought Zhou Wenxiang to himself.

A silent smile is sometimes just like a silent angry look,

causing one to feel boxed in. Zhou Wenxiang had finished talking, the manager had already smiled, the matter seemed to be closed, but there was no follow-through to wrap up the matter. Zhou Wenxiang couldn't just walk out without saying something, yet just standing there was awkward, too. He felt that he ought to add a little something, but what? He couldn't just hang around shooting the breeze with the manager, either. In his moment of anxiety, he thought of his son again. "So, if it's all right with the manager, I will take a half day off, go home, and take a look!" This was again appropriate and earnest, though he still didn't know whether his son really had a stomachache or not.

The manager consented.

Zhou Wenxiang walked out of the office feeling a little unsure of himself. Even though this was all a function of his love for his son, his behavior was somewhat unsubstantiated. But being an honest man, there was no need for him to contemplate and recontemplate his actions. All he had to do was go home and take a look.

When he arrived at the doorway, Xiaochun was sitting on the barrel-shaped stone chair in front of the gate, singing, "Go to school when the sun is up." Both his complexion and his voice were evidence enough that he couldn't have had a stomachache.

"Xiaochun," Zhou Wenxiang called out, "how's your stomachache?"

"Comes and goes. Can't sing as loud as I usually do!" Xiaochun rubbed his hand across his belly button.

Zhou Wenxiang grunted, "Hm."

Catching sight of his wife, he asked, "Does Xiaochun really have a stomachache?"

When Mrs. Zhou saw her husband return, she already felt uneasy, so when interrogated, she became even more aware of her precarious position. Motherly love, after all, still made her want to protect her son. Real love has no time for sorting out the means. She had to tell a lie. "When you left, he really did have a stomachache. It was so bad, he was turning pale. He's just getting better now!"

"Then why not see a doctor?" Zhou Wenxiang took this approach to prove that the mother and son were lying. Although he felt this was somewhat lacking in sincerity, it didn't detract from his honesty, because he really did intend to get a doctor—if his wife agreed to it.

"There's no need to have the doctor pay a house call." His wife thought for awhile. "Why don't you just take him over to the doctor's."

He hadn't expected that his wife would so readily agree to have Xiaochun see a doctor. All right, since he had proposed it, they would go. A doctor wouldn't write a prescription for a child who wasn't sick. And even a wasted visit would indicate he genuinely loved his child, and at the same time, it would catch the mother and the child in their deception. Although it would be painful to know that a Zhou family member could be so dishonest.

He took Xiaochun to see Niu Boyi, for he felt that a sixty-year-old doctor of Chinese medicine would, of course, be reliable. Old Dr. Niu with his eyes shut, placed his finger with the long nail on Xiaochun's wrist and took his pulse for about ten minutes.

"Not a light case!" said Niu Boyi, shaking his head. "Let's try a prescription. Come back after trying two doses!" Having said this, he wrote out a detailed prescription, very slowly and at great length.

With nothing to do in the meantime, Xiaochun amused himself by playing catch with the armrest pillow, playing with it as if it were a sandbag.

Having paid the doctor's fee, Zhou Wenxiang took the prescription and thanked him. When he took Xiaochun out, he couldn't decide whether to go get the prescription right away or simply ignore it altogether. Xiaochun was, in his opinion, not sick at all. On the other hand, giving some medicine might be just the right punishment. See if he would still pretend to have a stomachache then! But if Xiaochun wasn't sick, and the doctor wrote a prescription anyway, then the *doctor* must be lying. If he went to fill this phony prescription, it would mean he believed in the lie, and he would be a victim of the doctor's ruse. Xiaochun lied, his wife lied, and the doctor lied. Only he was honest. He thought of the Liars' Society. He had to admit it—that letter did make some sense. But he himself was, after all, an exception, so he still didn't believe altogether in that letter. Only if someone were able to prove that *he*— Zhou Wenxiang—had lied, would he fully respect the arguments of the Liars' Society. That, however, was impossible, for there *was* no proof. He carefully sifted through everything in the past. There was nothing that he could pick out. From both near and far, he examined all the things he had done this morning, all the things he had said. There were no chinks in his armor, because all that he had done and said was the result of his daily habit of honesty. There wasn't a single deliberate detour in his behavior or speech. Only he understood himself.

He took the letter and the prescription, ripped them both up, and tossed them to the ground.

Notes

1. The surname "Zhou" is pronounced like the English name "Joe." The *"xiang"* in "Wenxiang" is pronounced as *"yang"* with an English *see* in front of it.

2. The *"Xiao"* in Xiaochun is pronounced as the English word *see* elided with a *yow* (rhymes with the English word *how*).

Rabbit

1

There were those who said that Young Chen was a "rabbit."[1]

I knew him, knew him even before he became a ticket-friend.[2] He was frail, intelligent, ambitious—and very young. Though his features weren't what you'd call "delicate," his face was fair and without blemish. We worked in the same business office for more than half a year, and during that time none of us was disrespectful to him in either attitude or behavior. Quite the contrary, we all treated him as a younger brother, and since we knew how prone he was to blushing, we always did our best not to embarrass him. No. Young Chen couldn't possibly be a "rabbit."

He was quite clever. I remember once when our company was planning a party to commemorate something or other, they decided to have a program of live entertainment in which all management and personnel were to participate. The idea wasn't so much to put on a quality show as it was to get everyone into the act. Blushing, Young Chen volunteered that he could sing a bit of Beijing opera. Said he had never studied it formally but had *seen* quite a bit, and if we wanted him to, he'd be willing to give it a try. You could perform opera just by virtue of having seen it? Nobody bought that, but since it was all in fun anyway, why not let him have a shot? No big thing, no matter how he did.

Well, he sang an aria from *Red Phoenix Union*. His voice was thin as a hair. Even those in the very first row couldn't make out a word of what he sang. Ah, but his makeup and costume! His walk, his gestures, the figure he cut on stage! Apart from his singing, every last bit of stage business he performed was simply exquisite down to the finest detail. You might have taken him for a veteran singer whose voice was going and now relied exclusively on his stage presence to win an audience.

Though Young Chen may never have formally studied the opera, everything he did was polished to perfection. In sum, his *Red Phoenix Union* was far and away the "reddest"[3] performance on the program that evening. All the applause and bravos were Young Chen's alone. After taking off his makeup and costume, he lowered his head and shyly offered, "I can also sing in the flower-drum style, though I've never studied that formally, either."

Not long after that, I left the company. I continued, however, to see Young Chen from time to time. The success of that scene from *Red Phoenix Union* piqued his interest in studying Chinese opera on a more formal basis. He began taking lessons from Mr. Yu, who was himself a ticket-friend and also happened to be a close friend of mine. Though he was past fifty, Mr. Yu's singing voice still retained the delicate tone of a young woman's. When the mood took him, he was still capable of shaving off his beard and doing an amateur performance of *Trial by Three Judges*. An upright and principled man, Mr. Yu had none of the bad habits so often associated with ticket-friends.

I once dropped in on one of their practice sessions and watched as Mr. Yu parted his bearded lips and sang in the gentle tones of a young woman while Young Chen followed along in that frail little voice of his. It was such fun that I began to sing right along with them. I had a better natural singing voice than young Chen, but somehow or other couldn't quite get the hang of what Beijing opera was really supposed to sound like. Nonetheless, I tried singing along with them until even I couldn't keep a straight face any longer. Mr. Yu laughed even louder than I did.

Mr. Yu began to treat Young Chen like he was a real disciple, too. And me? Well, I continued to treat him as a young friend. Besides studying the opera together, the three of us would often go to little holes-in-the-wall specializing in this or that snack, or else go for strolls in the park. Since we were older than Young Chen, Mr. Yu and I always made it a point to present proper role models in everything we did. And Young Chen? He was always on his best behavior as well. Never so much as a misspoken word out of him. Even so, Mr. Yu would often remind him, "Remember, for people like us the opera is only a hobby. Don't get so wrapped up in it that you lose sight of your proper vocation."

2

Because he was so bright, Young Chen wanted to learn as much as he could as fast as he could. Had it been humanly possible, he would have learned an entire opera in a week. Mr. Yu, on the other hand, preferred to proceed at a more leisurely pace. He knew that Young Chen was bright but didn't want him to swallow more than he could chew. The accuracy with which Mr. Yu read the libretto and the clarity with which he pronounced it were such as is seldom seen among ticket-friends. He would much rather see Young Chen learn a bit less so long as the enunciation of what he *did* know was smooth and clear.

Like most young people, however, Young Chen had a

penchant for the flashy. Sometimes he would learn a new aria from a phonograph record and then show it off to Mr. Yu at the first available opportunity. Although Mr. Yu never said anything, you could tell he was less than pleased. After Young Chen had pulled that on him a couple of times, Mr. Yu confided to me, "The way I see it, I probably won't be able to keep this student of mine over the long haul. Of course I'm not charging him any sort of tuition to begin with, so it makes no difference to me whether I go on with him or not. But the thing I *am* afraid of is that he's going to learn it all wrong. Now to be sure, learning the opera wrong is no big thing in itself, but if your character goes in the process, if your *character* goes . . . I'm worried about him. I really like that youngster a lot. He's incredibly bright. The trouble with that is that bright people all too often get the short end of the stick."

I didn't offer anything in reply because I knew that Mr. Yu said what he did partly because of his genuine affection for Young Chen and partly because of his antipathy to the new arias that were being sung. I didn't see things the same way Mr. Yu did. The way I saw it was that since opera is only a pastime anyway, why get so all-fired serious about it? Why should anyone take sides on whether the new arias or the old ones are better? And why should you always be fretting about what's moral and what isn't? But I knew I'd better hold my tongue for fear of getting the old man riled up.

It wasn't long after that, however, that I became vaguely aware that the worries he had expressed were not entirely without foundation. I saw Young Chen on the street in the company of other ticket-friends, but these amateurs were nothing like old Mr. Yu, who was an honest and upright man.

Other than his being able to do some Beijing opera, nothing about Young Chen was any different than what you'd expect in any young man of his age. But that was far from the case with the amateurs in whose company I saw him now. With them, "opera buff" was probably the *only* identity they had. Although they were not professional performers, they cut their hair in the moongate style[4] and dressed, talked, and moved like professional actors. Though it is likely that none of them knew a single opera by heart, they had managed to pick up all the bad habits of the profession. When I told Mr. Yu of this, he just sat there and said nothing.

A few days later when I went to visit old Mr. Yu again, I found Young Chen there. From the expressions they wore, I could tell that teacher and student had had a falling out. No sooner had I sat down than Mr. Yu pointed at Young Chen's shoes and said, "Just look at them! Are those proper shoes for a *man* to wear? Rose colored! Soft soles and softer uppers! Now if he were headed out to a dress rehearsal, I'd have nothing to say. But to walk the *streets* in such shoes! What does that look like, I ask you?"

Hard put to find any reply, I thought for a bit, smiled, and said, "Don't we often see colorful men's shoes these days? Nothing like the heavy, clumsy things we wear around here that never come in anything but black." I hoped my words would calm old Mr. Yu down a bit and then if Young Chen didn't wear those shoes again, the whole thing could be easily smoothed over.

But old Mr. Yu just wouldn't let go of it. "It's not as simple as all that. That pair of shoes was *given* to him. I've devoted myself to the Beijing opera for more than twenty years, and I know the shenanigans of some of those ticket-friends. They can't put anything over on me. Today it'll be a pair of shoes, tomorrow, a handkerchief. But if you put out your hands and accept those gifts, then you'll see what happens. Behind your back, they'll gleefully drag your name through the mud until your reputation is utterly ruined. Since Young Chen here only sings for his own amusement anyway, why can't he be satisfied studying with me? Why does he have to go and get himself hooked up with trash like that? Why make it easy for them to spread their rotten rumors?

All the blood drained out of Young Chen's face. I could tell he was fuming, but I never imagined he would explode the way he did. "All your stuff is *old*," he said. "I want to learn something up-to-date." No sooner were the words out of his mouth than he blushed red as a beet. As if to escape before his usual, shy self had a chance to reassert itself, he lowered his head, grabbed his hat, and strode out the door without so much as a parting bow in the direction of his teacher. Lips trembling, Mr. Yu gave an angry grunt as he watched Young Chen's retreating form.

"Youngsters have short fuses. There's no need to—" I began, doing my best to console him.

"Hmph! People like that will be the death of him yet. First they'll tell him my stuff is too old, and then they'll introduce him to a new teacher. Next, they'll keep encouraging him until they get him to *go to sea*.[5] And once he's done that, they'll sink their teeth into him and never let go. Why, they'll eat him alive! They'll . . . It's a pity, a real pity!" Mr. Yu was so upset that he wasn't himself for several days.

3

There was no need for Young Chen to go to Mr. Yu's place again. He had other friends now. He began to sing, without any musical accompaniment, at the Fragrance of Spring tea shop. They held amateur performances there every afternoon, but Young Chen, of course, could only make it on Sundays. Because of my friendship with Mr. Yu, I knew several of the ticket-friends over there myself. And so it was that whenever I had a free Sunday, I'd go to the Fragrance, have a pot of tea, and listen to an aria or two. Since I had friends there, I even tried out my own vocal chords now and then, but—truth be known—this was only in order to better observe Young Chen.

It was just about this time that some people began saying Young Chen was "a rabbit." I didn't buy it. OK, so he did have an unusually fair complexion and sang with a slight voice. So what? He was also highly intelligent, had a good job, and carried himself with reserve and propriety. No matter how he might have changed, he couldn't have changed into "one of those," just couldn't, that's all. I was confident of that and continued to frequent the Fragrance to watch him and to keep an eye on those who said he was "one of those."

Young Chen's clothing was becoming more and more vulgar, and it looked as though he had begun to powder his face a bit as well. But his general demeanor still gave one the impression of uprightness and reserve.

When I looked at the fellows who had started the rumor— the very same people who flattered him to his face—I saw what was behind it all. The powdered face and vulgar clothing were on a par with that pair of rose-colored shoes—none of it was his own idea but rather had come about because he had fallen into *their* clutches. Mr. Yu was right. They were going to be the death of him.

Among them, the one who most attracted my attention was a big dark fellow. He had a moongate haircut and eyelids that were as dusky as the pupils of his eyes. He always wore that same long, thin cut, silk gown with a collar that must have been a good six inches high.

Although I never heard him sing a single line, people said that he could do painted-face roles.[6] Nor was he the kind to go around humming this or that aria the way your average ticket-friend does. However, you could tell that he was always counting the beats of the music to himself, for if you looked at his hands or feet during a performance, you'd detect faint traces of motion in time with the music. Needless to say, he had gone far beyond the accomplishments of those humming ticket-friends and had arrived at the point where he could, from memory, accompany the drums and cymbals in setting out the rhythms for entire operas. He was probably also capable of leading an orchestra.

That big, dark fellow was ever at Young Chen's side and rather reminded one of a madam following one of her girls around. Backstage, I discovered that it was always *he* who decided in what order Young Chen appeared on the program as well as what he would sing. If he knew that Young Chen was out of voice today, he'd arrange to have him do something in which he could slack off a bit. And if he discovered that Young Chen had just learned *An Ideal Couple* to the point that he was fluent in it, then he would make sure that he had a chance to perform it. If there weren't enough singers to do all the roles, that fellow was always able to dig up someone at the last minute. Just before it was his turn to go on, he'd take Young Chen by the hand and instruct him on where to fish for bravos and where to take it easy. And if it looked as if his voice wasn't going to hold out, he would signal him the adjustments to be made in the tempo. Whenever the need arose, he would also hand him a lozenge to soothe his throat. I dare say in terms of advice and guidance, that dark fellow was far more thoroughgoing and enthusiastic than an athletic coach just before his team takes the field.

When Young Chen came offstage, the dark fellow would praise him to the skies, never offering a single word of negative criticism. And while he was at it, he would be sure to attack the most famous contemporary singers of *dan* roles:[7] *this* one had a voice that sounded like that of a *heilian*,[8] yet insisted on singing *qingyi* parts;[9] *that* one, with a lantern jaw and a back as broad as an ox, wasn't satisfied with playing anything but *huadan* roles.[10] Such attacks, of course, displayed the dark fellow's knowledge and taste, but they served even more as a means of letting Young Chen know that he was fully worthy of comparison to the leading professionals of the day and in many respects far exceeded them. Occasionally it seemed that all this attention embarrassed Young Chen and that he would have preferred it if the dark fellow *didn't* take him by the hand and lead him onstage. On the other hand, Young Chen didn't dare insult him, either, for it was in the dark fellow that he saw a glimmer of hope—the hope that someday he, too, might become a professional singer of female roles. The realization of that hope depended entirely on the dark fellow. Thus if he told Young Chen that he shouldn't associate with someone, he wouldn't; and if he told him he ought to wear a bit of face powder, he would.

I saw that as long as the dark fellow was at his side, there was no way he could avoid being called a "rabbit." Young Chen probably knew this as well as anyone else, but he was also aware of what a marvelous thing it would be to become a full-fledged professional. And what, after all, was there to stop him? He was quick-witted enough to learn parts overnight. His voice was good enough to get by, and his stage presence, gestures, and facial expressions were far above average. In short, he had what it took. Purses worth thousands of dollars were there for the taking. All he had to do was stretch out his hand and take them. What could be easier? What could be more promising?

And since that's the road he wanted to take, who could possibly be any more helpful to him than the dark fellow. Always engaging in sophisticated talk of the opera, the dark fellow knew such things as how to arrange *tang-hui,*[11] how to go about hiring actors, how to decide how much of the house everyone was entitled to, and where to rent costumes.

Professionals, ticket-friends, and "under-the-table ticket-friends"[12] were all at his beck and call. He could cause one singer's star to rise and another's to fall, for not only did the dark fellow understand opera, but more important, he was fluent in the ways of the world as well. How could Young Chen afford *not* to obey him? How could he afford *not* to be friendly? If Young Chen wanted to succeed, he could not refuse to let the dark fellow lead him by the hand, for if he did, he might just as well forget about the Beijing opera. If he ever *offended* the dark fellow, he wouldn't even be able to continue to perform with amateur opera clubs, singing purely for the fun of it, not to mention dashing his hopes of becoming a star. One word from the dark fellow and he wouldn't be able to fulfill his yen for the opera in any way whatsoever.

4

As long as the dark fellow was behind him, no one in the amateur opera club dared to say anything against Young Chen. They deferred to him but kept their distance. Young Chen's drummers wouldn't dare throw in an unexpected beat; nor would his *huqin*[13] accompanist dare play tricks on him by dragging the bow very slowly across a string to prolong a note until Young Chen ran out of breath before the accompanist reached the end of his bow. Nor would any fellow performer make so bold as to trip him up with a new cue; nor would anyone be foolhardy enough to shout bravos that were loud enough to completely drown out Young Chen's frail voice. With one eye to the dark fellow, everyone was especially considerate of Young Chen and clustered about him like stars around the moon. It was not, by the greatest stretch of the imagination, that they respected him—opera amateurs don't respect anyone—but there can be no doubt that they did stand in fear of the dark fellow. While no one onstage dared to let out a peep, people in the audience gave voice to their sentiments *for* them. Even the dark fellow could not interfere with the audience's free expression of opinion.

Now, on the whole, there are two kinds of people who will go to a tea shop like the Fragrance to listen to the opera. The first consists of those people who will come on a Saturday or Sunday for a cup of tea, looking for nothing more than a means of whiling away the weekend's boredom. For a slight expenditure, they can stay and listen to their heart's content. They're nothing to worry about: if they like the entertainment, they'll shout a bravo or two, and if they don't, they'll either sit there quietly or just get up and leave.

But then there's that *other* group—let's call them the "regulars." Winter or summer, you'll find them rooted there at the Fragrance. The regulars are quite knowledgeable about the Beijing opera. Many of them were once ticket-friends themselves, but, for one reason or another, are no longer able to take the stage. They come on a daily basis to listen to others sing, with no other purpose in mind but to offer a resounding "Boo!" or two in order to demonstrate that they are real connoisseurs.

The regulars can be further divided into three subgroups. In the first you'll find those who have just learned to sing a little bit, but aren't yet good enough to go onstage. Dressed and groomed just like the singers who are performing, they come by day after day to soak up the ambience of the place. As they see it, the only difference between them and the ticket-friends up there performing is that—for the time being, at least— they haven't yet had a chance to show their stuff. They are convinced, nonetheless, that when they do, they will be overnight sensations. The second subgroup of the regulars consists of relatives and friends of those ticket-friends who are onstage performing. Day after day they come to the Fragrance with no other purpose than to applaud their friends and relatives. They don't know much about the opera, but are past masters in the art of clapping and shouting "Bravo!"

The third subgroup of the regulars consists of people who originally just happened in for the tea and a place to sit. As the days wore on, however, the knowledge and interest of the other patrons gradually rubbed off on them until they began to consider themselves cognoscente as well! It was *this* group who began to whisper "rabbit!" every time Young Chen came on. As soon as he showed his face, they would begin to whisper among themselves. Though they couldn't very well go from table to table proclaiming their opinion that Young Chen was a "rabbit," they did manage to whisper loudly enough to be heard in every nook and cranny of the tea shop. Patrons made newly aware of Young Chen's alleged status would, of course, be curious to know more, and before long, to one degree or another, every last ear in the tea shop would be strained to see what could be picked up from the whispers.

And then—just like that!—the whisperers would all fall silent. Not a peep. They would just look at each other and smile, and the curious, having nothing more to listen to, would be forced to retrieve their ears. At that point the whisperers were really proud of themselves. While it is true that the dark fellow controlled what went on *on*stage, it was these whisperers who controlled what went on *off*stage in the audience. Just as the dark fellow was the controlling tide of influence onstage, so did they become the offstage tide. Moving in totally opposite directions, these two tides crashed down mightily on the frail person of Young Chen.

Among the whisperers you would find the very young as well as those in their fifties and sixties. But young and old alike, they would plaster their faces with a makeup base and a layer of powder—the older they were, the thicker the powder. Among them you would find both rich and poor, but rich or poor, they were meticulous about their clothing. The poor had the poor's way of expressing fussiness. Though they might be able to afford nothing but a cotton gown, they would make sure that at least part of the lining was silk. And if they couldn't afford that, then they would be particular about colors. The linings might be entirely of cotton, but they would be lilac or perhaps a deep lavender. And they would always have the sleeves of their gowns turned up a bit to show off the immaculate whiteness of the jacket underneath. These whisperers probably said that Young Chen was a rabbit out of pure envy. If you asked me, though, many of them looked a lot more like "one of those" than he did.

As soon as Young Chen came on, they would shift their faces into neutral, so that they might expand them into a smile or contract them into a frown as occasion demanded. When they chose the path of expansion, they would wear expressions that announced that they had just graced him with an act of benevolence such as is seldom seen on the face of this earth; when they opted for contraction, you would have thought that Young Chen had incurred the wrath of a king or an emperor. In hopes of winning their plaudits, he had to favor them with entreating glances. Even then, they did not readily grant their bravos.

When someone appeared onstage whose star they wanted to see rise, they would assume the most serious demeanor imaginable, stretch out their necks, and listen in rapt concentration. But when the rest of the audience roared out a bravo, *they* would remain silent. At those places the rest of the audience passed over without notice, however, they—in a transport of total admiration—would moan their approval as though they had been so moved they had forgotten they were in a public place, and thus didn't bother to restrain themselves from such very unseemly sounds of approval.

Astonished at their reacting at such unlikely places, the rest of the audience could not help but be bowled over by such fine-tuned sophistication. It was said that if a singer treated them to a banquet, they were even more likely to exhibit this strange behavior. One thing was clear: if Young Chen wanted to lessen their murmurs of disapproval, he, too, would have to wine and dine them. In my heart of hearts, I could not help but ask, "Why? What's the point?" Young Chen, however, had his own agenda.

5

One day I picked up a paper and saw news of a dress rehearsal open to the public in which Young Chen would appear. I decided to go and have a look. It goes without saying that the dark fellow would have planted a claque for him in the audience. In light of that, I realized I wouldn't be able to judge his performance solely on the basis of how many bravos he got. I'd have to trust my own judgment.

His forte was still stage movement and there is no denying that he was very accomplished in that area. As for his singing—well, to tell the truth, it wasn't worth a single bravo. I'll grant you that in a small room his voice could be rather pleasant, but once he mounted a stage it was simply too slight. The first two rows might have been able to hear him if they put their minds to it, but people farther on back had to content themselves with watching his mouth open and close without hearing a thing.

Making a living singing the Beijing opera is no easy thing. I was well aware of that, but what could I say? I was in no position to talk him out of it. Since the dark fellow always arranged a claque out in the audience, all Young Chen ever heard was wall-to-wall acclaim. How could he *not* think that his singing was marvelous? Anything I said to the contrary would be a waste of breath.

After the dress rehearsal, the critics were unanimous in their praise. They all said that he was comparable to Tian Guifeng of years gone by.[14] I knew right off where *that* had come from: how could the dark fellow possibly have overlooked that little trick!

From then on, any time there was a benefit performance, or a *tanghui* in a private residence, Young Chen's name would be sure to appear on the program. Though I didn't have time to attend all his performances, I did continue to worry about him. I knew that in order to be a ticket-friend, you had to lay out a great deal of money to court people's favor. It wasn't unusual for people to actually go bankrupt in the process.

And who *was* Young Chen after all? Just a poor little nobody. But to appear onstage required so many things: his own set of costumes and props; his own supporting players; as well as his own attendants to help him with makeup and costumes. And above all he had to look the part of a wealthy man. All that on the salary of an office clerk? Not likely.

To be sure, the dark fellow was helping him out. But what would happen later on if they had a falling out and the dark fellow demanded repayment for all he had done? I began to realize that Mr. Yu had really known what he was talking about, and that his worries about his student had not been in the least unwarranted. I decided to look up Young Chen and see if there was anything I could do. And yet it was almost as though I didn't so much want to help Young Chen as I wanted to thwart the dark fellow by rescuing an intelligent young man from his clutches.

6

There were three or four people in Young Chen's room watching him sew. In order to save money, anything he could do for himself, he did. At the moment he was working on a sleeveless jacket, the kind one would wear when playing a maid. His visitors smoked and chatted, but Young Chen didn't say a word. He was busily sticking tiny glass beads of various colors to an area on the jacket that he had previously painted with a coat of glue in the shape of a plum blossom. Once he had it completed, he'd have a striking bit of costume at a real savings. When I entered, he simply raised his head and then went right back to his work. It was as though he had lumped me together with the three or four men who were already there. Since I neither knew them nor had any desire to talk to them, I just sat there like a bump on a log.

The people with him were all past forty, and two of them had already grown beards. Judging from the expressions they wore and the content of their conversation, I decided that they were ticket-friends, too. From the way they were dressed, I judged that they were probably minor officials in this or that government office, the very kind who would defend the old traditional moral standards at home and abroad, and who would readily agree that it is immoral for an unrelated man and woman to so much as touch. Yet here they all were, watching Young Chen work on a costume! Now, I'll grant you that there was no impropriety in their speech. As a matter of fact, it was rather elegant. But it is also true that they were constantly glancing at Young Chen, and when they did so one could detect the faint traces of lascivious smiles—smiles that even they were uncomfortable with but could not entirely conceal.

Young Chen didn't join in their conversation to any extent except when the talk would turn to this or that performer or when they would criticize a certain singer's style. At those points he would put down whatever he had in hand, prick up his ears, and listen intently. Then, looking for all in the world like the dark fellow, Young Chen would express his own opinion. He wouldn't say much, but what he did have to say had the ring of authority about it as he pointed out this or that singer's shortcomings. He wouldn't boast of his own abilities, but the very firmness and self-confidence with which he made his criticisms constituted ample demonstration of his own superiority. By now Young Chen had convinced himself that he was the foremost contemporary performer of *dan* roles and that, apart from himself, no one really understood the Beijing opera.

After I had managed to drive his admirers away—and that wasn't easy—I came straight to the point. "How do you manage to make ends meet?" He suddenly blushed, recalling no doubt the shame he had felt when our company fired him. When he didn't respond, I decided that I might just as well go all the way. "Got a lot of debts?"

His smile was forced but his general demeanor expressed a quiet determination. "It's impossible to avoid going into debt, but it's nothing to worry about. I can always make it back. If I had three thousand right now for a good set of costumes, I'd head straight for Shanghai, sing there a couple of weeks, and then . . . "—his eyes brightened at the prospect—"Hankou, Qingdao, Jinan, Tianjin. I'd do the whole circuit, and by the time I came back here, I'd be . . . " He gave a thumbs up.

"Do you really think it's going to be as easy as all that?" I asked, throwing courtesy to the winds. He looked at me with a cold smile that announced my question was unworthy of a reply. "Is it that you have real confidence in your own abilities or is it rather that you have so many debts you've got no *choice* but to try a tour? For instance, could it be that you owe a few thousand dollars to a certain man—a debt you couldn't possibly repay on the salary you'd get from any ordinary job—and that you're thinking in terms of turning pro and doing a tour to make a lot of money fast? And could it also be that the man you owe the money to is *encouraging* you in that direction? Isn't that just about the size of it?"

He thought for awhile and then hesitated a bit as he suppressed his obvious anger—but in the end had nothing to say in reply. I knew that I'd hit the nail on the head. "If that's the way things stand, then it's about time to do some serious thinking. You're already into him for quite a bit now, and if you turn pro, you'll have to borrow even more. And him? He'll have you in his clutches for life. No matter how much you make, you'll never be able to completely clear the debt. You will, in effect, have handed your life over to him lock, stock, and barrel. And all those people who have been promoting you will all want a piece of the action as well. If you'll allow that I'm not just trying to frighten you, and agree to start repaying what you already owe right now, then I'll do whatever *I* can for you out of my own pocket. And if you want to find a new job, I'll help you out on that score, too, and then you can pull yourself free from all this opera stuff you've gotten bogged down in. Think it over."

"But art is worth sacrificing yourself for!" He said this without looking at me.

Now it was my turn to look at him with a cold smile. "That's the kind of garbage a high school education has taught you. Has nothing to do with reality. Just words. Means nothing!"

He blushed again. He didn't want to continue the conversation, for the more he talked the less sure of himself he was, and he was at just that age where young people cannot admit their own mistakes. "Er-mei, put on a pot of water!" he yelled at the top of his voice.

7

WORLD FAMOUS

FOREMOST PERFORMER OF *HUADAN* LEADING ROLES

APPEARING IN A UNIQUE HISTORICAL MASTERPIECE

CHEN ———

Printed in huge characters, advertisements appeared in the local papers and in announcements pasted up on the streets. Young Chen was "going to sea."

Two days before "firing his opening salvo," as opera jargon has it, young Chen gave a banquet at the Eastern Sea for the newspaper world and some of his friends. Don't know why, but he gave me an invitation as well. I was torn. I didn't really want to go, but I did want to see him again. I don't know how many times I picked up and put down that invitation before deciding that, *yes,* I would go.

There must have been seventy or eighty guests at that banquet—stars of the opera world, reporters, people who could be hired to shout bravos, and a few local gangsters thrown in. None of them particularly aroused my interest. It would seem that I had come only to see Young Chen.

His appearance was transformed. His clothes were so exquisite that just *looking* at them was nauseating. Young Chen was dressed as unnaturally as a girl in full bridal array and just as extravagantly as well. The real attention-getter, however, was that diamond on the ring finger of his right hand. If genuine, it must have been worth three thousand dollars at the very least. Who could have given him a ring like that? And why?

He was obviously wearing makeup as well, for while his cheeks were thin as ever, they now had an unaccustomed rosy glow. The artificiality of that perpetual flush of the cheeks lent a theatrical air to his every word and gesture. Whenever he turned his head, he did so with meticulous care, as though afraid of damaging that high mandarin collar on his dress. Whenever he initiated a conversation with anyone, he would first tilt his head at a coquettish angle and, before uttering the first word, delicately knit his brows and draw the corners of his mouth upward just enough to make his cheeks dimple. It made my flesh crawl just to watch.

In the end, however, I forgave him all, for I saw that the dark fellow was forever hovering over him. He was the commander in chief who oversaw every last detail: he slapped some guests on the back, chatted with others, winked at Young Chen, exhorted everyone to drink more wine, joined in the general laughter, and ran busily hither and yon while wiping his dusky brow with a great silk handkerchief that reeked of perfume. I have heard that brown bears in the circus will run over to anyone they see, shake hands, and then laugh wildly. I've never seen that myself, but I can well imagine that those bears must look very much like the dark fellow did that night.

While I watched the dark fellow, my attention was also drawn to a short, fat man of fifty or so. Little fatty was seated in the place of honor, and it was to him that the dark fellow addressed most of his remarks, even though he seldom received anything by way of response. It suddenly dawned on me. Yes! I had discovered the source of that diamond ring.

As I studied that fat little face more closely, I seemed to recognize it. Aha! I remembered! I had seen that same face in newspapers and magazines. It belonged to a man named Chu, a cabinet minister no less. Minister Chu was reputed to be a "devoted patron of the arts." Yes, it must have been Minister Chu, for he left the table after nothing more than a glass of wine and a bit of soup. The dark fellow and Young Chen saw him off with exaggerated courtesy. When the dark fellow returned to the table, he began telling jokes to all who would listen, as if to indicate that now that the bigwig had left, everyone could relax a bit. After finishing just one course of the banquet, I, too, slipped away.

8

Minister Chu put up the money and the dark fellow served as manager. Young Chen lived at Minister Chu's villa, had his own trunk of costumes, a diamond ring, and even a car at his own disposal. The only thing was, he couldn't get his hands on any of the cash, for the dark fellow controlled that. Whenever Young Chen appeared in an opera, Minister Chu was sure to be there in his private box. Sometimes he brought Young Chen's younger sister along, and when the opera was over she would go back to the villa with the minister and spend the night. Needless to say, Young Chen's sister was a beauty. And so it was that Cabinet Minister Chu obtained a beautiful young woman, the dark fellow made a lot of money, and Young Chen got to sing his opera—*and* came to be called a "rabbit" in the bargain. That's the way it all sorted itself out. Young Chen had fallen into a fiery pit from which no one, absolutely no one, could extricate him. Mr. Yu was right. Young Chen would perish at their hands.

9

Because I was busy, I didn't have a chance to go to the opera for a year or more. I often saw Young Chen's name in the paper but had no way of telling how he was getting on. One evening when I was in Tianjin on business, I fled the boredom of my hotel room and went out to pick up a paper to see what advertisements for opera there might be. I saw that a new arrival in the city, named "Fragrance" something or other, was going to sing that very night. I couldn't tell from the ad whether it was a woman or a female impersonator, but since I was only seeking an escape from boredom to begin with, I decided to go and have a look. I made it a point never to expect too much from a "new" star, so that I wouldn't be disappointed afterward and end up with a bad feeling about the whole thing.

As it turned out, Fragrance Something-or-other wasn't all that good. The production was elaborate but neither the singing nor the acting was up to snuff. By the second half of the performance it looked as though this new star didn't have the energy to see it through to the end. What a demanding art Beijing opera really is! As this thought occurred to me, I couldn't help but wonder how Young Chen was doing.

At just that point I spotted the dark fellow. With brisk and practiced steps, he slipped through the door that led onstage, leaned over, said something to the drummer, and then, just as briskly, slipped back out again. "Hah, *that* bastard!" I said to myself. "He's probably already milked Young Chen for all he's worth, and now he's working on this Fragrance Something-or-other. Sonofabitch!"

Not long after I returned from Tianjin, I ran into Mr. Yu. In the course of a long conversation we finally touched on Young Chen. Mr. Yu had kept up with him more that I had, for as soon as I mentioned his name, he sighed and said, "He's all washed up. And minister what's-his-name has dumped his younger sister, too. Now she's a girl who's not a girl, and a wife who's not a wife—just holes up at home with nothing to do. As for Young Chen himself, well, when the dark fellow milked him for everything he could get, he dropped him like a hot potato. Made off with most of his costumes, too.

"Now, who *doesn't* know there's money to be had in the Beijing opera," he continued. "But the number of people who make it to that point is very, very small. If you do it as a ticket-friend, it'll cost you every last cent you have. Even if you do it as an 'under-the-table ticket-friend,' you still won't make enough to make ends meet. Let's say you go beyond that and do turn pro, then you'll have to take guff from everyone and his brother, and can count yourself lucky if you make enough to eat. I know the opera trade, know it inside out. Tried my best to warn him early on, but . . . " There seemed to be so much more that he wanted to say, but he just sat there and shook his head.

10

After another half year went by, I happened to be in Jinan just when Young Chen was singing there. He was first on the program. The second and third pieces would feature a *xusheng* and a *wusheng*,[15] neither of whom was any great shakes, but worth seeing if you had nothing better to do. Out there in the sticks even singers from the Dapeng back in Tianqiao[16] can command substantial purses. I was sure that Young Chen— even if one took all his shortcomings as a performer into account—would still be a notch above anyone from Tianqiao. I decided to go and take in his performance. Well, not just to take it in, perhaps, but also to root for him with my applause. Who told me to be his friend?

That evening, according to the advertising poster, he was scheduled to sing an aria "of his own" that no other contemporary singer had in his repertoire. He was scheduled to go on at nine and present a scene, which would combine elements of both civil and military styles and even have some fighting thrown in. Before he went on, the notice said, he would pass out copies of the new libretto so the audience could follow along.

It so happened that I had something to do and couldn't set out for the theater until a quarter past nine. On the way I constantly worried that I had set out too late and wouldn't be able to buy a ticket. I didn't get there until half past nine. The theater that night turned out to be an empty pot on a cold stove. I heard the sound of drums and cymbals in the distance long before I got to the theater itself, but I didn't see a single soul around the box office. I could tell from the uncommonly friendly attitude of the ticket seller that the house was far from full. Without a second thought, he immediately handed me a ticket for the eleventh seat in the fourth row—the best seat in the house.

When I got inside, I saw that the seats beyond the fourth row were all empty. There were a few people in the side sections but no one in the boxes. Klieg lights glared down on the bleak stage. Four men holding flags stood listlessly to either side of a young male actor in a red robe seated before a small table center stage. All five looked like so many figures cut from paper. Except for that sprinkling of people close to the stage, the house was nothing but empty seats. The people who *were* there looked sorry that they had bought tickets in the first place. The saddest sight in the world, bar none, is a sparsely filled theater. It no longer even *looks* like a theater; doesn't look like much of anything, except perhaps a fragment from some forgotten dream.

I hadn't been there long when the tempo of the drums and cymbals changed to signal the arrival of a new performer. The cushion on the chair center stage and the skirt around the table before it were both changed as well. Both cushion and table skirt were embroidered in the southern style and bore Young Chen's name. A shimmer of small cymbals was heard as he minced his way onstage. There was, of course, no welcoming bravo to greet him. With so few people in the house, no one felt up to it. I was on the verge of tears. He had grown thin, so much so that he seemed a lot taller and looked for all the world like a swordfish that someone had stood on its tail and then sheathed in an opera costume.

He didn't slack off just because the house was small. Far from it, he gave the performance everything he had. His thin face was a mixture of determination and pride. Whether it was singing, recitative, or stage movement—he threw himself wholeheartedly into all of it. The more the audience *didn't* shout bravo, the harder he tried. He seemed to have all that enthusiasm combined with disdain for hardship that one associates with a zealous missionary preacher. I couldn't help noticing that every time he finished an aria and turned to take a drink of water, his frail body was racked by a fit of coughing. After he had gotten over it, he would rub his chest and turn toward the audience again. His voice was still as small and narrow ranged as ever, but his stage movement was perfection itself! Every lift of the hand, every extension of the foot was masterfully planned and executed with consummate skill. When he had finished a set of moves, he would look down at his audience, as if to ask, "Come now, doesn't even *that* rate a bravo?" From beginning to end, however, no one cheered him.

And then suddenly, as though I had gone stark raving mad, I burst out with a couple of wall-shaking bravos. He saw me and nodded in my direction. Even though I wasn't able to make out clearly what the plot of this piece was supposed to be, I stuck it out until I heard the final *wuu duu-duu* of the trumpet that signaled the end of the performance. I went backstage. Still in costume, he shook my hand. Bones. Nothing but bones. I had to wait a long time for him to change, because he really *was* like a girl in the slow and meticulous way he removed each flower and tiny string of pearls from his hair. And then, too, after removing each item, he would fix his attendant with a watchful eye until the latter had carefully stored it away.

By the time we got to the Sanyi inn where he was staying, it was already half past one in the morning. Once we were inside, it seemed that Young Chen had no time to waste in entertaining me, for he immediately lay on his bed and, with trembling hands, lit an opium pipe. After a few puffs, he was somewhat recovered, and said, "Can't live without it."

Unable to think of anything by way of response, I simply nodded. Besides, I really didn't want to say anything, unless I could find something to say that might help him. But what could an ordinary fellow like myself do to save him? And so I had no choice but to sit there like an idiot and see what *he* had to say.

After another big puff on his opium pipe, he gently peeled an orange, separated the sections, and put one into his mouth. "When did you get here?"

I briefly filled him in on my own affairs, and then asked, "How's it going?"

He smiled. "They don't understand Beijing opera in these parts."

"Losing money?"

"You got it." He didn't blush the way he would have once, but rather said this quite naturally and without the slightest hint of regret. "I'll give it another couple of days and see how it goes. If it's still the same, I might as well dump my opera trunk right here and call it a day."

"But that would be disastrous."

"Who says it *wouldn't?*" He coughed some more and rubbed his chest. "But if nobody comes, it doesn't matter how good I am, so what am I supposed to do?"

I wanted to say, "Your voice is too slight and you've always underestimated the difficulty of things." But I didn't. What good would it have done? He couldn't very well change his voice, and the pattern of his life was set. Besides he was hooked on opium and had a bad case of tuberculosis to boot. Since there was no way I could possibly help him, what was the point of adding to his torment? "Things are probably a little better back in Beijing." I tried to console him.

"Not all that great there, either. Money's tight and there are lots of companies competing with each other. No, it wouldn't be all that great back there. Matter of fact it's probably not going to be all that great anywhere." I could tell by the way he was rolling the orange peel between his fingers that he was becoming quite impatient with me but forcing himself to remain calm. "At any rate," he continued, "I've done justice to Lao Lang Shen[17] and I've always given my audiences the real thing. As to the rest . . . "

He was right. He *had* given his audiences the real thing, for it goes without saying that he still considered himself the foremost *huadan* in the opera world. All the failures, suffering, and oppression from which he had been unable to extricate himself had combined to forge in him a scrap of self-confidence. It was that small bit of belief in himself that gave him the courage to keep on living now. As long as he was able to continue deceiving himself with that belief, he was also able to fear nothing, to dismiss everything with a smile. His younger sister had been ruined, he had been done out of his money, and all he had left to show for it was a bag of bones and a heavy habit. He was useless to others and rapidly bringing destruction down on himself. And yet, despite it all, that tiny shred of belief in himself enabled him to say that he was giving his audiences the real thing.

"All right then, see you back in Beijing." I started out the door.

"Aren't you going to stay for my *Phoenix Pavilion*? I'm going to do the whole thing the day after tomorrow."

I didn't respond.

It wasn't long after I got back to Beijing that I saw news of his passing in one of the tabloids. To the best of my knowledge, Young Chen couldn't have been more than twenty-four or five when he died.

Notes

1. *Tuzi,* or "rabbit," a slang term for "homosexual."

2. A hard-core opera aficionado. For further details, see the Translator's Postscript (pp. 302–303).

3. *Hong,* or "red," in Chinese also has the meaning, "popular."

4. Moongates are perfectly round openings in a Chinese wall, like the full moon. Professional opera singers shaved the tops of their

heads bald to facilitate the wearing of wigs and other headpieces. Viewed from the top, their heads looked like moongates.

5. *Xiahai,* i.e., to become a professional.

6. For the most part, painted-face roles were military heroes.

7. The *dan* were female roles; there were many subdivisions. Young Chen, of course, sang *dan* roles.

8. *Heilian,* literally "black face." These roles were also known as major painted-face roles, as distinguished from minor ones, and required the booming voice of a military hero.

9. The *qingyi* roles were proper young ladies, ingenues.

10. The *huadan* were not-quite-so-proper young ladies, coquettes.

11. *Tanghui* were private performances put on at the homes of those wealthy enough to afford them.

12. "Under-the-table ticket-friends" (those who dealt in improper funds or *shi heichu*) referred to ticket-friends who, against all rules of the trade, were paid for their performances. This was done "under the table" because, as amateurs, they were not entitled to compensation for their work.

13. The *huqin* is the two-stringed Chinese violin; the bow is more or less permanently attached since the hairs go between the strings.

14. Tian Guifeng (1866–1931) was known for his brilliance in performing coquette *(huadan)* roles; he often performed together with Tan Xinpei (1847–1917), who was famous for playing *wusheng* (military roles).

15. Both are male roles. The *xusheng* would play a scholar; the *wusheng,* a military man.

16. The Dapeng was a well-known theater in Tianqiao, the lower-class entertainment section of Beijing. Executions—as "warnings to the people" with an element of entertainment mixed in—were also performed in the Tianqiao area.

17. Lao Lang Shen, patron god of the theater.

Attachment

On the thoroughfares of Chengdu's Xiwanglong Street, Beiping's Liulichang District, and Jinan's Buzhengsi Street, we generally notice two kinds of people.[1] Those of the first kind are honest and prudent, just like plain folks. If they are in any way distinctive, it is that they delight in collecting calligraphy, paintings, bronze wares, seals, and the like. Their fondness for collecting, like loving flowers, dogs, or crickets, is nothing extraordinary or remarkable. In terms of profession, these people are perhaps government employees, or perhaps middle school teachers. Sometimes we also find lawyers or doctors, in their leisure time, rummaging about for small treasures. Most of these people have some learning that enables them to make an honest living. Some have good incomes, some not, but whenever they have spare money, they will spend it on things that delight their hearts and enhance their sense of refinement. At times they won't hesitate to borrow a few dollars or to pawn a couple pieces of clothing in order to press their seal of ownership on a cherished collectible, if indeed it is an item that can be inscribed.

The second kind of people, however, are not like this. They collect, but they also peddle. They appear to be refined, but at the core they are no different from merchants. Their collecting is equivalent to hoarding.

Mr. Zhuang Yiya, whom we will introduce now, belongs to the first kind.

Mr. Zhuang is a member of the Jinan gentry. It is not on account of his wealth or eminent ancestors that he has acquired gentry status. He is just an ordinary college graduate. Sometimes he works as an administrator, sometimes as a middle school teacher. Nevertheless, he has a warm concern for people and his work. Whether part of an organization or a school, he is someone who can always be counted on to do a favor and do it ungrudgingly. He may not always deliver splendid results, but he is willing to help his friends. Having tried his hand at many things, he has become quite experienced. People in society tend to be lazy, so it's often the case that because *they* loaf on the job, they regard someone else's bit of experience as something considerable. Consequently, Mr. Zhuang has become an important figure among relatives and friends, a familiar customer at shops and restaurants, and a member of the local gentry to boot.

On the whole, he is a good man; on the whole, he is also a good-looking man. Medium build, round face, and two jet-black, sparkling eyes typically fixed on his chest or the ground, as if to discourage any impression of acting like a hotshot. Though his legs are short, he is a fast walker, who scurries about all day. Sometimes he wears a Sun Yat-sen tunic, sometimes he wears a Chinese-style gown. None of the material is of good quality, but his clothes are all neat and clean. On the front of his garment, he always wears a badge.

He is married but has no children. His wife lives in a village more than forty miles away from the city. Because he is busy he doesn't often go down to the village. When he does go home once in a while, his city friends all miss him. By the time he returns, he finds that he has become even more indispensable to them, because there are so many things waiting for his short legs to tend to.

Although he walks fast, his eyes, which appear preoccupied with his chest or the ground, are in fact always on the lookout. From far away a piece of paper yellowed with age or a fan displayed on a roadside stand can stop him dead in his tracks. Slowly making his way toward the stand, he will stop abruptly before it as if totally by chance. Calligraphy and paintings are what he loves. He will casually browse through this and that, then, with a smile, ask about prices. At long last, he will offhandedly pick up that scrap of old paper or fan, take a look, shake his head, and put it back down. He will walk off a couple of steps, stop, then turn back to ask the price. Or he may come straight out with it, "Fifty cents for this torn fan; how about it?"

He will take home a couple of such eighty-cent treasures, full of insect holes, smudgy, smeared, and crinkled up like an old woman's face. Only at night, after locking the door to his room, will he savor the pleasures of his modest purchases, handling them over and over again. After numbering them, he will carefully press his seal on them, then put them in a large cedar chest. This bit of exertion will send him to bed, happily weary and satisfied. Even his world of dreams will be quaintly ancient.

From time to time, he will stop by the big and small antique shops on Buzhengsi Street. With respect to those undamaged and famous works whose values are set in the hundreds and thousands, he can only feast his eyes regretfully. When finished looking, he will smile sheepishly, reverently roll the works up, and hand them back. He can only afford to buy those three- to five-dollar fragments of ancient texts or the works of minor artists without market value. Whenever he enters a shop with a superb collection of dazzling objects, he feels like a destitute scholar. Though never an ambitious man, as soon as he enters an antique shop, he dreams of a day when he will strike it rich and buy the rarest, most precious calligraphy and painting, then press his seal on them. What joy and glory that will be!

According to the shrewd business sense of northern merchants, a *customer* is anyone who is "just looking." Although Mr. Zhuang just looks at the expensive items and buys the cheap ones, the merchants do not treat him the less for it. They welcome his looking as free advertising. At the same time, when they obtain a cheap but genuine item, they will set it aside especially for him. They know that "love" is something that grows slowly, and so long as he continues to buy small items, there will come a day when he will buy a big one.

In the course of contacts, Mr. Zhuang becomes a friend to quite a few antique shops. Needless to say, cigarettes and hot tea greet him at every visit. Sometimes he is even treated to a drink. He no longer feels ashamed. And sure enough, just as they expected, he brings new business to the shop owners. The rich, who don't know what to do with their money, will eventually think of buying calligraphy, paintings, or antique objects as emblems of their wealth. They will leave no stone unturned in their search for a specialist willing to volunteer as their agent, lest they not get their money's worth. Naturally, they seek out Mr. Zhuang—he is a member of the gentry, willing to help, and moreover, has a good eye.

When volunteering his services as a buyer's agent, Mr. Zhuang feels wonderfully gratified. He will view and handle a famous painting countless times, unrolling it, rolling it back up, and unrolling it again. Each occasion brings him joy and enriches his knowledge and power of judgment. At the conclusion of a transaction, both buyer and seller will invite him for a drink. Drinking is a trifling matter, but good conversation is important: he acquires a lot of knowledge through people's talk. Furthermore, after concluding several transactions, his position is considerably elevated. He can now boldly refuse those small items that merchants put aside especially for him. "I don't have any spare money these days" or "We'll see in a few days!" become his way of expressing "I don't take just anything you shove on me. I, too, have a discerning eye." In response, the merchants ingeniously call him "connoiseur of Shandong's minor artists." From the standpoint of Mr. Zhuang's financial situation, he had no hopes of ever being considered a connoiseur. Yet now, to his surprise, he is being referred to as one. Thus, taking no heed of the sarcasm contained in that title, he accepts it with cool equanimity.

After acquiring this title, Mr. Zhuang matches name with reality and really *does* become a connoiseur. He begins paying attention to Shandong's minor artists and constructs another trunk especially to store their works. Now, he is willing to spend ten to twenty dollars, even thirty dollars to buy a work of calligraphy or a painting, so long as it is the handprint of a respected village scholar not yet in his possession. He does not hesitate to borrow money from his friends or to send his coat to the pawnshop. One has to be audacious to be a connoiseur. Not all of these works have artistic value. In the past, he might not have even looked at some of them, but now he will spend ten to twenty dollars to buy them. Collecting is collecting. A collection could—even should—be detached from artistic value and become a singularly unique obsession and passion.

It used to be that there might be just one small flower or a couple of characters intact and untainted on the tattered paintings he bought for thirty or twenty cents. To him, there was no question about the beauty of the flower or the charm of the characters. He loved them dearly, viewing them over and over again. But he looked at them locked up in his room, for one reason, so as not to be disturbed, and for another, because he was afraid others would laugh at him. Ever since he acquired the title of connoiseur, however, he no longer locks himself in his room, but makes it a point to let others know of his new acquisitions. Whenever he obtains a new prized item, his room is packed with people. His sparkling black eyes are no longer fixed on the ground but move about with excitement, and his two cheeks are flushed. He is still a bit reserved, but after a couple of light coughs, he musters up his courage and explains the history of the minor artists, their style, and the seals and annotations on their works. He will not appraise a work but will wait for others to nod their approval. If people remain quiet after a viewing, he will continue explaining, suggesting that whatever is old must be good, and that, in the hands of an artist—even a minor one—there can be no inferior work. He has much to say, and his heart quickens with excitement. Not until people recognize it as a masterpiece will he roll up the work with a smile, put it down lightly, and let his eyes resume their normal function of staring at the ground.

There has been no discernible change in his income for many years. He doesn't seem too interested in money. If it weren't for his need to buy calligraphy and paintings, he could very well ignore the issue of money. He has the ability to teach or work. He is also honest and doesn't have any unwholesome habits. In his mind, worrying about one's livelihood is a superfluous activity.

Ever since being recognized as a connoiseur, he feels an increased zest and regard for life; on the other hand, he is somewhat irked with his inability to earn the money to buy better pieces of calligraphy and paintings. Even so, selling his calligraphy and painting to make some money is something he will not do. For better or for worse, this is *his* collection, and it will follow him to his grave. He will never sell it. He is not a merchant. Occasionally he will stoically part with a work of calligraphy as a gift to a friend, but he has never sold anything. The best thing he can think of is to simply do some moonlighting to increase his income. But when he gets busy, he has no time to wander among the landscapes in the galleries or go to Buzhengsi Street to feast his eyes. Time is what he needs, because each item consumes several hours of viewing.

Because he is unable to broaden his sources of income, he can only reduce expenditures. This, however, causes hardships on his wife. Not fond of going home to begin with, he now further curtails his visits home. So now, at every holiday he can go to the antique stores or to the homes of fellow aficionados to sit and chat the whole day. Or, he will open his chest and scrutinize everything in his collection, even to the extent of forgetting to eat. By reducing his visits home, he also saves on the roundtrip fare and travel expenses. When he grimly cuts his wife's household expenses, he feels a bit ashamed at first but decides in the end that it seems far better to take advantage of his own wife than commit some other reprehensible deed.

In the spring of 1937—the year war breaks out with the Japanese attack on July seventh[2]—friends celebrate Zhuang Yiya's fortieth birthday. It is as though he has never thought of his age, for only when friends arrive at his home does he realize that he is in fact a man of forty. He is not a man with far-reaching ambitions or one with just hollow concerns. But when the people who came to celebrate his birthday have all left, he cannot help but have some thoughts and feelings. He is forty now, he thinks silently to himself, but what did he have to boast of? After mulling over it for awhile, he can only think of one thing. Over the years, he has collected over a hundred pieces of calligraphy and paintings by Shandong's minor artists. This surely is an accomplishment. A few days ago, Yang Kechang, a Jinan collector—our so-called second type of collector—unexpectedly brought two Japanese to come and view his collection. Zhuang Yiya didn't feel any sense of satisfaction. On the contrary, he was somewhat embarrassed to bring out those tattered paintings. But reflecting on this incident today on his fortieth birthday, he sees that this surely was of great significance. It has not been for nothing that he has scurried about spending money. Even if those things are in such intolerable shreds and patches, just think, in the entire nation, is there anyone who has collected more than a hundred Shangdong minor artists? There is no other collection like it! Even the Japanese have come for a viewing. Hm, so this little collection of his has already brought him international recognition! He shuts his eyes, carefully turning the matter over in his mind from beginning to end and begins to feel that he ought to dismiss it as something not even worth a good laugh. Yet there is no denying the fact that the Japanese have recognized his collection as a genuine one. Even if he is overly modest, facts are facts. Amid mixed feelings of embarrassment, lament, and ineptitude, this thought brings him a sense of satisfaction. He has made no contribution to the world, but becoming a collector by a fluke isn't too bad an achievement. He hasn't lived in vain. After all, as the saying goes, When people die they leave behind their name; when wild geese fly away, they leave behind their cries! He is weary from entertaining his friends, but when this thought occurs to him, he feels reinvigorated and begins inspecting his collection anew. Regardless of which work he picks up, he can't bring himself to put it down, as if it has become several times more beautiful than when he first bought it. Even those insect holes display a charm all their own, and the dust smells distinctly fragrant. When he comes to the thirty-second item, he falls asleep with it in his arms.

The day after his birthday, he makes a new vow to himself, "I, Zhuang Yiya, am going to get something that's truly valuable!"

At the beginning of summer, a small antique store obtains a large landscape painting by Shi Qi. First Yang Kechang, then Zhuang Yiya, hears the news. Mr. Yang wants to make a sum of money. Mr. Zhuang wants to spend a sum of money to secure the painting as a connoiseur's pride and joy. The painting is exquisite and elegantly mounted, but unfortunately the lower left corner, where the seals normally are inscribed, is missing. One cannot see the seal, and some unknown busybody has patched up the missing corner with a few hideous brush strokes. Mr. Yang is superstitious about seals. Since there is no seal and since the repair brushwork is so obviously shoddy, he therefore concludes that the painting is a fake, though he is aware, too, that it is an exquisite piece. Aside from making an aesthetic assessment, he naturally has another purpose. He wants to secure the painting at the price of a fake painting, then turn around and sell it to the Japanese as genuine. There is no question that the painting is a fine piece. Moreover, even if it should be a fake, the Japanese will pay a hefty price for it, because in Japan Shi Qi pieces are highly marketable.

Since Mr. Yang is an authority on antiques in Jinan, and most antique buffs have no eye for genuine art, the Shi Qi painting becomes everyone's wisecrack. "Going for a look at the fake Shi Qi!" With this attitude, people go to banter with the owner of the small antique shop in their spare time. Many come to see the painting but none will make a bid for it—who wants to spend money on a fake?

Finally Mr. Yang, seeing that the time is ripe, offers a price—two hundred fifty dollars, take it or leave it. He is pleased as punch, because at the very least he can sell it at eight hundred dollars, a clear profit of five to six hundred dollars!

Mr. Zhuang also has set his sights on the painting. After countless trips and viewings, he concludes that it is a genuine piece. His self-confidence increases each time he sees it, while his decision to secure it becomes more resolute. But each time he sees it, he also feels increasingly dejected: he doesn't have the money. For many days he cannot sit or sleep in peace, grumbling to himself over and over, "In collecting, it's quality, not quantity! Shi Qi! Shi Qi! Isn't a single work by Shi Qi superior to these two trunks of junk? By a long shot! These two trunks are nothing! I won't be satisfied until I get a Shi Qi. Even if it means that from now on I will absolutely, never ever buy another item! I've got to have that Shi Qi. . . . " He wants to borrow money but feels embarrassed. Pawn his clothes? He has nothing that is worth any money. What should he do? What should he do?

When he hears that Mr. Yang has offered a price of 250 dollars, he can no longer afford to just sit there wavering. In one breath he runs to the small antique shop. His palms are sweating, his heart beating wildly. The more he wants to keep calm, the more flustered he feels. He even stammers as he speaks, "I, I, I want to look at that, that fake Shi Qi again!"

As he rolls open the painting, he can no longer see clearly. Hot steam seems to have clouded his eyes. In fact, he doesn't need to take a look; he can remember every detail of the painting even with his eyes shut. Lost in a trance for a moment, he says in a whisper, "I'll give five hundred! I'll pay tomorrow! How about it?"

With bated breath he waits for the answer, like a criminal waiting for his death sentence. In a snap, he wins the owner's "All right. It's a deal." For a second, he swoons, then, wild as the wind, he runs home, hastily snatches up all his wife's jewelry, and flies back to the store.

He secures the painting. But he has also made an enemy of Mr. Yang.

Because he has failed to obtain a profitable item, Mr. Yang spreads the word everywhere that Zhuang Yiya is a quack, foolish enough to spend five hundred dollars for a fake. At tea shops and wineshops, this becomes the talk among all of Jinan's collectors, and Zhuang Yiya becomes the butt of their jokes. He no longer dares to browse the antique stores in broad daylight. But neither does he yield to the idle talk and snub the painting or sell it on the sly to recover his reputation. He is convinced that he has obtained a masterpiece at the lowest price.

In June a connoisseur named Lu arrives from Beiping. Mr. Lu is an internationally known figure. As long as his seal is on a piece of calligraphy or painting, even a European or American collector dare not shake his head lightly. Zhuang Yiya takes the Shi Qi to show to Mr. Lu, who, without a word, presses his seal on the painting. Only when Zhuang Yiya is about to leave with the painting nestled in his arms does Mr. Lu offer casually, "I'll give you twelve hundred for the painting." Zhuang Yiya doesn't dare respond but merely holds the painting more tightly. "I'll not press the matter then," says Mr. Lu, demonstrating he has no desire at all to deprive another of his prized possession. Zhuang Yiya takes his leave, looking apologetic but beside himself with joy.

Yang Kechang meekly comes to pay a call on Zhuang Yiya. He knows that his own power of judgment and reputation are far inferior to Mr. Lu's. Since Mr. Lu has pronounced the Shi Qi piece as genuine, he would simply be destroying his own rice bowl if he were to continue claiming it a fake. He intends to explain to Zhuang Yiya that what he said in the past was merely a little joke among friends, so Zhuang Yiya should not take it too seriously. Zhuang Yiya refuses to see him!

July seventh—war breaks out with Japan. Emotions at Jinan, as at all other places, are at fever pitch. Zhuang Yiya, like everyone else, is in a state of shock, as he waits day and night for news of victory.

The news, however, becomes increasingly bleak. The jam-packed crowds and the panic at the train station make everyone nervous. No one knows where to go but everyone wants to get out. The train station becomes a scene of chaos and vacillation. Mr. Zhuang sees his friends flee in haste to Shanghai, Qingdao, and Nanshan, only to flee back again. He feels terribly uneasy but dares not flee so casually. He is Jinan-born and bred and cannot bear to leave his hometown. In any case, even if he wants to flee, where is he to go? And once he has fled, how is he to support himself? He decides to wait and see. Fortunately he doesn't have children yet, so he and his wife can afford to wait until the last moment when they have no choice but to flee, before having to decide on a plan of escape.

Cangzhou falls into enemy hands. The garrison withdraws from Dezhou. Enemy planes are in the skies above Shandong, their bombs claiming lives at Lokou. On Mountain of the Thousand Buddhas,[3] antiaircraft cannons begin exploding. Information is chaotic, rumors even more so. Zhuang Yiya decides to go down to the country and hide out for a while. More than anything, he is afraid that those two chests of paintings and the Shi Qi will be destroyed by the bombing. Tucking the Shi Qi under his arm, shouldering a bagful of minor artists, he makes it out of the city. There are no vehicles for hire, so he walks for ten miles. When he hears there are bandits ahead, however, he beats a hasty retreat. When he gets back to his own room in Jinan, he paces frantically back and forth. He isn't concerned about himself, nor does he worry over his wife. Country folks have land, and gunfire cannot destroy land. There is no need for concern. He only worries that his Shi Qi and minor artists have no safe haven. The siren shrieks again. Holding the works of calligraphy and painting in his arms, he hides underneath a table. In the far distance he can hear the sound of bombing. He thinks to himself, "Bombs! Go ahead and do your damndest! If I have to die, these works will be buried with me!"

The enemy has already passed through Dezhou, but rumors of enemy assurances of "protecting territory and people" give Zhuang Yiya a little hope. It isn't that he lacks patriotic feelings. He doesn't want to listen to these shameful rumors. However, for the sake of his beloved objects, it seems to him that surrender is not necessarily impermissible.

Yang Kechang comes once to urge him to sell the Shi Qi, to pay for travel expenses and flee as early as possible. "You aren't like me," he persuades Mr. Zhuang. "The Japanese know I'm a collector, pure and simple. You, you've been a government employee and a teacher, you're an intellectual. When the Japanese arrive, they'll have to kill you!"

"Kill me?" Zhuang Yiya is dumbfounded for a second. "Go ahead and kill me then, but I am not going to give up my Shi Qi!"

After Yang Kechang leaves, Mr. Zhuang decides to leave his wife behind and flee, taking only his Shi Qi and minor artists of Shandong with him. But he is unable even to carry that out, because enemy planes are bombing the trains. *He* doesn't matter, but the Shi Qi is more important than anything. Once again he must bide his time.

The enemy arrives. He isn't exactly sorry about not having fled. Every day he waits for the Japanese, holding the Shi Qi in his arms and saying to himself, "Come on then! The Shi Qi and I will die together!"

The waiting brings Mr. Yang to his home again.

Zhuang Yiya has always been an even-tempered person, but now he is in a fury. The fear and hardship he has suffered the past few days are dumped, bag and baggage, onto Yang Kechang. "What the hell are you here for again? With our country on the verge of extinction, are you still thinking of turning a profit?"

"No need to get angry," Yang Kechang says with a smile. "Listen to me carefully. You know how thorough the Japanese are. Whatever we collect, they always catch on. They know that you have a Shi Qi. When their army arrives, the civilians will also arrive. They'll be collecting antiques door-to-door. If you want to hold on to your skull, you'll have to give up the painting; if you want to hold on to the painting, then you'll have to give up your skull!"

"Good! My skull and my paintings are my business! You needn't worry on my behalf!"

"You really are a man of iron!"

"Iron or not, I don't need praise from the likes of you!"

"Cool down, will you?" Yang Kechang smiles again. "Let me tell you that I didn't come to ask for the painting but to congratulate you!"

"Congratulate me? Why are you playing games with me?"

Yang Kechang's face is dead serious. "Mr. Zhuang! The Japanese have sent me over here to invite you to come out of retirement and serve as head of the Education Bureau!"

"Huh?" Zhuang Yiya sounds as though roused from a dream. He pauses for a moment. "I can't work for the Japanese!"

"I'm a very busy man. Let's make this quick." Mr. Yang's eyes are riveted on Mr. Zhuang's face, as if ready to begin hypnosis. "If you agree to become the bureau head, you can save your one-of-a-kind collection. Not only that, but the Japanese will shower you with gifts! If you *don't* agree, they'll confiscate your things and punish you as well—perhaps kill you! How about it?"

For the longest time, Mr. Zhuang is unable to utter a single word.

"Well, how about it?" prompts Mr. Yang.

Mr. Zhuang lowers his head, and says in a whisper, "Let me think it over!"

"It better be fast!"

"I'll give you an answer tomorrow!"

"I need it now!" Mr. Yang looks at his watch, "In five minutes. give me a 'yes' or a 'no'!"

When Mr. Yang finishes his cigarette, he looks at his watch again. "Well, how about it?"

With tears in his eyes, Zhuang Yiya looks at the two chests of his collection and nods his head.

To be attached to something is to die with it.

Notes

1. Chengdu is in Sichuan province, Jinan in Shandong province. Beiping refers to modern day Beijing. See note 2 in the story "No Distance Too Far, No Sacrifice Too Great" for more about name changes for Beiping/Peking/Beijing.

2. The Eight Year War of Resistance against Japan (Kangzhan banian) which broke out in 1937, and Lao She's role in the All China Resistance League of Writers and Artists are discussed in the translator's postscript. "Attachment" was published in 1943 in the midst of this war against Japan.

3. This mountain (Qianfo shan) is on the outskirts of Jinan. See note 1 of the story "Crooktails."

Appendix
Autobiography of a Minor Character

1

If it's in fact true that man evolved from the ape, as some erudite people so solemnly claim, I suppose that when I introduce myself, there's no need to bring out a family tree.

Might as well get right to the point, then: my surname's Wang, my first name One Success. I can't say that I like my surname, nor can I say that I absolutely detest it. Since people have to have a surname, whatever I got smacked with is it. In any case, since Zhang, Wang, Li, and Zhao are probably the four standard surnames, when the government regulates the surnames in the future—and I believe there will be such a day—I probably won't have to bother with changing mine. However you look at it, there's got to be some advantage to that.

As for my first name, though, I often think of jacking it up a bit. Even if I can't claim to be a *Complete* Success, why not at least Six or Seven Successes? On second thought, however, they say it was Father who named me, and since our relationship as father and son seems to be no more than that—he died when I was eleven months old—then, supposing I brazenly altered my first name, wouldn't I be destroying the little evidence that remains of our relationship, as though I never had a father? Well then, if covering up one's finagling with highfalutin words isn't exactly the most honorable thing to do, I might as well admit my pettiness and try to get by with One Success the rest of my life.

Perhaps when Father named me, he had something special in mind. For example, maybe he hoped that I would do a commentary on one of the classics or be versed in one of the histories or that I would be skilled in one of the arts. But I have no way of investigating this because he died so early. I've asked Mother time and again, but even she had no idea as to what Father's intentions were, so this sort of turned into a tiny riddle in my universe. Though I hated the discounted quality of my name, I wasn't willing to lightly change it, either, for fear of destroying that bit of mystery attached to it.

Yes, I really am a minor and insignificant character. Take the circumstances surrounding my birth. I had no say whatsoever about it. If it weren't for Eldest Sister, who rushed back home from her in-laws', no one would have noticed that the Wangs *had* a new son, much less thought about saying how he would "add glory to his ancestors" and all that kind of talk.

At that time, Eldest Sister was already married and had a little daughter. It wasn't because I was able to be an uncle as soon as I was born that I was grateful to Eldest Sister, although being an uncle is something worthy of pride. I was grateful to her, because she was the first to find me and to hold me in her arms. If it weren't for her, the odds were nine to one I wouldn't have made it, no matter how life loving and death fearing I was.

The situation was this: Father was away on business and Elder Brother had already left to be an apprentice, so only Mother and Youngest Elder Sister were at home. Our neighbor in the east room, Auntie Guan, was a jolly woman and a bit on the plump side, but she was as deaf as a rock. My aunt, who had long been widowed, lived with us, but she often wasn't at home during the day, preferring to go here and there to play shuttle cards.[1] Sometimes she didn't even come home for dinner.

Mother must have wished for a son in her old age, but probably because she was somewhat embarrassed to have a baby when her eldest daughter had already gotten married, she was reluctanct to disturb anyone and merely told Youngest Elder Sister to call for an old midwife. That was the middle of the twelfth lunar month. It was so cold, even the air seemed to have frozen. Anyone who says I lack warm feelings ought to know that the first time I faced this world, the world was cold and heartless.

Just when the sun was setting, the sound of my frail cry filled the room, declaring a simple and mournful preface to life. How chillingly spare life's beginning is. I cried, then my mother passed out. Youngest Elder Sister's wailing drowned out mine. She didn't know what to do except to cover her face with both hands and burst out crying. No doubt she loved her little brother, but in that twilight time between life and death, neither was there any doubt that she loved her mother even more. So she simply didn't attend to me. Whether I lived or not after being born didn't seem to be the issue. She merely wanted to bring Mother back to life with her tears. To this day, I have never teased her for only loving Mother and not loving her younger brother, because when I reached the age when I understood about loving Mother, I, too, loved Mother as though she were mine alone.

Just at that moment, Auntie Guan came into the outer room and, lifting the curtain, took a look inside the inner room. I don't know what sort of sixth sense prompted her to jump to the conclusion that Mother had been poisoned by coal gas. What others said was a moot point because she couldn't hear them. Thus she wasted no time arguing and simply went ahead with her good-hearted attitude of "What's got to be done has got to be done." She bustled about looking for some pickled cabbage soup and then for an antidote. When neither could be found, she simply opened up a drawer, scrounged up several dried jujubes, and placed them on top of the stove—supposedly, to absorb the coal gas.

This thoroughly sincere but utterly useless concern prompted Youngest Elder Sister to break into another round of wailing.

"Whatever are you bawling your eyes out for, you silly brat?" boomed a loud voice outside the window. It was my aunt, back from several rounds of shuttle cards and having probably lost a few strings of cash. She entered the house in a foul mood.

Although Youngest Elder Sister was always afraid of my aunt, she went out courageously to greet her and drove her head into my aunt's midriff. "Mama's stopped breathing!"

"What? How could she stop breathing just like that? I tell you, today's an unlucky day. Everywhere, unexpected troubles! To think that I couldn't even draw a forty-thousand card, and then to lose to a hand of Nine Lotus Lamps!"

My aunt was our family hegemon. Except for Father, who dared to argue with her when driven to wit's end, no one had the nerve to so much as raise an eyelid in her direction.

"Mama's had a baby!" Youngest Elder Sister suddenly summoned up her courage to take my aunt's hand and led her into the room.

"Ah! As if there weren't enough kids already! When's this ever going to come to an end?" My aunt had had two children who were, according to her own assessment, the world's most beautiful babies. Nowhere could one find their like, especially the one called Shuanzi, who was able, at one and a half years old, to say anything and understand everything. His hair was combed in, *aiya!* a pigtail this long and this thick. If my aunt was playing shuttle cards with some old ladies, Shuanzi could play all day on the *kang* without even a sigh. What a well-behaved child he was! But unfortunately, one day Shuanzi died without a sound. How strange that Shuanzi, "the Fastened One," should break loose from his mooring to life! Shuanzi's sister—her eyes were like two brimming drops of rain water!—seemed to have felt embarrassed about living much longer. Therefore my aunt always felt it strange that other people's children should live, and so it was that whenever she heard news of newborn babies, if she could just gloss over it, she would. Otherwise, it would set her to thinking about that precious one with the lovely pigtail. It wasn't that my aunt never showed a little warmth—she could, out of the blue, drop unexpected tears of sympathy. That's why whenever people were grateful to her, they refrained from saying anything that might touch her soft spot. As soon as Youngest Elder Sister took her hand, my aunt's heart softened a bit, and she asked, "Where's your father?"

"He didn't come home!"

"*Heng!*" Pulling open the door with one hand and dragging Youngest Elder Sister along with the other, my aunt thought for a moment and said, "Go and call your sister to come! Quick!"

Youngest Elder Sister wiped her tears and dashed out like a lunatic.

According to Auntie Guan, who later recounted the entire incident to me in all its details, storyteller fashion, as soon as my aunt stepped inside the room, she smacked the midwife clear across the courtyard, swept the jujubes on the stove into the fire, and then took out some coins and laid them out on the table to total up her losses. She didn't so much as glance at Mother and me on the *kang,* not even once! Otherwise Auntie Guan couldn't have insisted that Mother had been poisoned by coal gas.

If I had had any say at that moment, it would undoubtedly have been to wish for Eldest Sister's speedy arrival. Arrive she did, and cried out, "Ma!" She swept me up into her arms, her tears falling on my fist-sized face. I nearly caused Mother's death, and yet, Eldest Sister baptized me into this world with her tears.

Not until three hours later did Mother open her eyes.

Later on, whenever Eldest Sister and Youngest Elder Sister would tease each other, Eldest Sister would always say that Youngest Elder Sister cared about Mother and not about Younger Brother, and Youngest Elder Sister would say that Eldest Sister cared about Younger Brother but not about Mother. Without a word, Mother would look at the two of them and at me and smile, the tears welling up in her eyes. Then my aunt would take me by the hand, and say, "If I hadn't thought of calling Eldest Sister, would you be alive today?" Having said this, she would glare at everyone until she understood that everyone expressed total agreement. Only then would she close her remark with an "Ah!" following which she would quickly put her right hand into her sleeves, large as a sack of white flour, and take out a coin and place it on my palm, saying, "You stinking little brat, *heng!*"

2

I couldn't make up my mind: was it better to live or to die? I was more helpless than a fluffy yellow chick. As soon as a chick breaks out of its shell, it can flap its wings in the sunlight and look for seeds on the ground or by the edge of a wall. I wasn't capable of doing anything. Whether I lived or died was totally in the hands of others. When hungry, I only knew how to cry—the most concrete thing to do! I only pleaded to be fully fed once, but Mother didn't have any milk for me. Her breasts clung softly to her chest, and her nipples were like two shriveled up grapes. They had not a drop of milk in them. What to do? I was hungry! Mother and Youngest Elder Sister cooked up some rice-powder paste in a small clay pot and fed me through my little red lips. Even in those "modern" days, powdered milk or fresh milk were not so common. And if they had been easy to find, there wasn't much money at home to spend on me. The rice paste provided just enough sustenance for me to make a passive stand against death, but it wasn't enough to fatten up my soft pink skin from my bones.

If I could take matters into my own hands, I definitely wasn't going to put up much longer with all this. I would have been sorry to disappoint Mother, but how could these miserable snatches at life be called living?

Of course, Mother wasn't without a conscience. She did everything she could to keep me full and warm. When it was clear I was still hungry and cold, she was more concerned and worried than anyone, including myself. But she couldn't come up with a good plan. She could only say with tears in her eyes as she fed my skinny face, "Why couldn't you have found yourself a *good* home to be born in?" She would then smother me with her kisses until I could hardly breathe. A rare flush of color would surface on her haggard cheeks.

The saying goes "Sit by seven months and crawl by eight." I wasn't able to sit at seven months nor was I able to crawl at eight. I was very well behaved, as if within these seven to eight months I had already fully tasted life and had already understood what forbearance and making-do meant. Except when Youngest Elder Sister propped me up to walk unsteadily, I hardly ever showed a smile. No wonder my aunt always said I was "a little thing that grandmas didn't love and uncles didn't like."

I can well imagine that I wasn't much to look at. Although Mother always talked about how handsome and fair I was when I was young, I never believed it. If to a mother's eyes there can be an ugly child, though the human species may not become extinct, its population will in all likelihood dwindle markedly.

When I was seven or eight years old, each time my Eldest

Brother-in-Law visited us, he would always want to take a look at my "little silkworm." After he had seen it, he would look somewhat relieved and say with a lisp—he was a good-looking man but unfortunately had a lisp—"*Heng!* his weenie's OK now. It used to be as tiny as a pea!" I hated to hear this. Even if it was a bit small, it didn't have to be in the ranks of a pea! However, this probably was more true to fact than Mother's praises. No one could deny that I was a skinny, measly little thing.

Each time I saw a mangy dog, with his bones nearly sticking out of his skin and with a few strands of hair as sparse as the grass in an impressionist landscape painting clinging grudgingly onto his skin, I had to ask, "Why the heck are you living? How the devil do you manage to go *on* living?" This bit of concern did not rise from contempt but from the commiseration of "One who pities another remembers himself." In this pathetic creature I saw my own shadow. Why the heck was I living? How had *I* managed to go on living? Like this dog, I had no answer but felt lost, afraid, and indescribably sad. Yes, my past—what I remembered, what I heard, and what I seemed to remember and seemed to forget—was a stretch of darkness. I did not know how I had groped my way out. In coming out, there had been no joy. Yet thinking back on it, there was a bit of love in the midst of all that misery. If I were to erase this bit of love, then even my present life would seem superfluous and meaningless.

To put it simply, I rallied through with the skin clinging loosely to the bones. I was very much like starved bedbugs in an empty room, deprived by hunger and cold of even the ability to die. Perhaps this was precisely the power of life.

I was almost a year old when I suddenly became active. Father had died while away from home. Elder Brother was too young and so unable to go get his body. My aunt and Mother, a couple of widows, one old and one new, were also unable to leave. The great distance, the inconvenience of traveling, and the difficulty of raising any money, also cut off any hope of relying on friends and relatives to take care of the matter. Mother and Youngest Elder Sister cried until they could hardly open their eyes again. It was just at this time that I began to stir. Wearing a mourning gown two feet long, I wailed all day and all night, but there were no tears—just a dry, unrelieved howling.

After several days, Mother and Aunt and Youngest Elder Sister could cry no longer over Father. They took care of me, carried me, forcing themselves to smile and play with me, as though they had to make me laugh before they could grieve over Father in peace. My wailing made them nervous, threw them into a strange state of fear and anxiety. It was as if an even greater disaster would befall on this already gloomy family if I didn't stop crying. My aunt, who normally had such a temper, was ever so calm and, surprisingly, got up in the middle of the night to carry me and rock me as she walked around the room. The oil lamp on the table cast an eerie glow. Youngest Elder Sister sat on the *kang* with her covers pulled over her and gazed vacantly at the black shadow on the wall. After a while she rubbed her swollen eyes. "Go back to sleep, girl!" coaxed my aunt gently. Youngest Elder Sister nodded her head, and her swollen eyes welled up once more. As my aunt held me in her arms, my mother stood in the corner of the room, raising her sleeve from time to time to wipe her tears. I continued to cry and howl. My skinny little face turned purple, my narrow chest seemed about to explode. Life was only a burst of angry energy that would explode in a moment and scatter my frail bones against my aunt's bosom. My aunt now patiently played with me, now scolded me in aggravation, now spoke rationally with me, now included even Father in her cursing. It was all in vain. Finally she tossed me back to Mother, stormed back into her room, and muttered a string of curses. Then, wiping her eyes once again, she charged back. "Here, let me have him again!"

All the simple solutions were used up. Yet the difficulties remained before our eyes. There was no way but to look elsewhere for a better solution. Second Elder Brother from my maternal uncle's home and Eldest Sister were both asked to come up with a suitable plan. Second Elder Brother was the most bighearted person as well as the only male in the group. Naturally what he said carried the most weight, no matter how unenlightening his opinions were. He proposed going to fetch Father's body, because my immoderate howling was undoubtedly due to seeing a ghost. Children's eyes were clear, and a lonely spirit that had no place to rest would be sure to find its way back home. If Second Elder Brother could muster up some money, he was more than willing to make the trip. Even if he had to carry the body on his shoulders he was willing to bring it back home and bury it in peace among the ancestral graves.

His arguments and his ardor made everyone nod in tears. If one could raise the money, nothing he said could be turned down. But from where was one to muster up the money? My aunt had some savings, and she was willing to hand out the money for this purpose. Mother, however, would not accept. If she spent my aunt's savings, how would she make up for it? Even if it were not necessary to pay back the loan, did we have the ability to support my aunt? We couldn't do it this way, no matter how sincere and selflessly loyal my aunt was.

Eldest Sister's family was doing all right. She was willing to approach her in-laws. But Mother shook her head. This amount of money, no matter from whom we borrowed, could only be spent but could not be paid back. How could she let her daughter be at the mercy of her in-laws' idle gossip for the rest of her life?

There were no other alternatives. Even Second Elder Brother

was living a hand-to-mouth existence. What wife would be so cruel as to leave her husband's corpse abandoned in a strange place, if it were within her means to retrieve it? Mother, however, steeled her heart. Her tears never did soften her toughness. She only resented being a woman, unable to carry her husband on her own shoulders back home. Whatever anyone said, Mother would not consent to burden others on this account. At a time when her heart was breaking, she was able to grit her teeth.

Second Elder Brother then proposed the second best alternative. If it was not possible for the time being to fetch the body, then the family should at least invite several monks in to chant sutras to release the soul from suffering. In the whole wide world there could be nothing better than this plan, because it could be carried out without much trouble. Everyone felt a bit heartened.

According to Mother's idea, it was necessary only to invite five monks—because that was the minimum required—and sufficient to conduct the Third Day Reception. This was to say, the monks would arrive at dusk, beat the Buddhist drums, chant a few lines, then follow the paper men and paper houses to an empty ground. When the paper things were burned and the beating of drums ceased, the monks need not return. It saved both time and money. The beating of the Buddhist drums—as Mother saw it—could not comfort the lonely spirit but could at least keep it from coming back to frighten the almost year-old little baby. People under hardship need to be a bit cruel to maintain their dignity. Mother wanted to take care of everything without seeking help from anyone.

My aunt and Eldest Sister naturally could not agree. Eldest Sister felt that the burning of the paper images was her responsibility. From the standpoint of a married daughter, this bit of filial piety was not only her duty but her privilege. No one could rob her of this.

My aunt, following the natural order of things, increased the number of monks to seven. Moreover, they were to chant the sutras through the night. It was her brother who died. No matter what, one could not merely use Buddhist drums to frighten his soul away.

Consequently, Eldest Sister had some attractive houses and chariots made, Second Elder Brother gathered bits and pieces to offer a sacrificial table, my aunt accompanied seven monks to chant a round of sutras, and Mother prepared some vegetables and willow leaf soup for the monks. When it was time for the bonfire procession, Second Elder Brother took along Elder Brother, while Youngest Elder Sister held me in her arms. All the neighbors from our alley who came out smiling to watch the fanfare walked back into their homes wiping their tears away.

When we returned, I was asleep in Youngest Elder Sister's arms, and I never let out another wail.

By three o'clock in the morning, the monks were ready to summon the spirit of the dead to the "assemblage of all souls": the monks on the dais put on flower hats in the style of Monk Mulian,[2] shook the spirit bell with one hand while assuming a symbolic position with the other, then grabbed some little balls of dough with the hand that assumed the symbolic position and cast them onto the floor in front of them, so as to chase away all the vengeful, unrequited spirits and to allow Father to meet the king of Hades in peace. Youngest Elder Sister shuddered. Covering her eyes with one hand, she groped about with the other and picked up some "evil-chasing, courage-fortifying" dough for me to eat.[3]

The little balls of dough must have been quite effective, for never again did I wail out as if I had seen ghosts. Until I was past twenty, this bizarre incident was recounted by superstitious friends and relatives. They believed that my eyes were different from those of ordinary people because I could see ghosts, and that when I saw ghosts I was not afraid, because when I was an infant I had tasted those sacred little balls of dough.

Once, someone who had studied chemistry in Japan and was good at catching ghosts invited me to view the group of ghosts he had assembled. For some unknown reason, I didn't even see a hair of a single one of them. I don't know whether it was because his technique was flawed or because I was nearsighted. To this day, it remains a question worthy of further research.

3

When Mother and my aunt were discussing whether to fetch Father's body or not, they were concealing a matter that neither was willing to bring up. The fact was we had real estate—that very house we were living in. No matter how old and run-down our house was, the deed was, after all, solid and sound, certified with the red chop of the yamen.[4] There was no question that we could borrow some money against this deed. They were both fully aware of this.

Nevertheless, Mother was waiting for my aunt to broach the subject, because when the house was purchased, Father and my aunt had both come up with the money, though the deed was under Father's name. As for my aunt, she was reluctant to bring up such a dead-end proposal. She knew that once they borrowed money that they couldn't pay back, one day the house would become the property of some other family. True, the house was half hers, but ever since she had been widowed, she had relied on her brother's and sister-in-law's support. She was willing to leave the house to her nephews and nieces so that when she died, she could die with a clear conscience. That was why she didn't say a word.

Since my aunt didn't bring the matter up, Mother could hardly speak out of turn. It was crystal clear to her: from now on, she would have to rely on herself for her living. How was she to do this? She had not thought it through. Yet there was no avoiding the responsibilities at hand. Under the circumstances, to have several shabby rooms to live in, even if they housed a hungry family of old and young, was at least better than living on the street in shame. If we shut the tattered doors, no one outside the walls could see our tearful faces. So that her sons and daughters could live under a roof, she had to leave her husband's dead body in a strange place. This ruthless solution sprung from a mother's love. There is no romance in the home of the poor.

I grew up in a rickety old house.[5] It was light and airy but without any style to it. The courtyard was long east to west but narrow north to south. The foundation dipped. Each time it rained heavily, the courtyard would fill with water, like a canal. The three north rooms had two doors. One door led to the two rooms we lived in, the other to the one my aunt occupied. The two east rooms were rented out to Auntie Guan and her son, who was training to be a housepainter. Hard of hearing, she had enormous eyes. Perhaps because she could never hear anything, in her impatience, her eyes often popped outward.

Behind the east rooms was a small outhouse. The air there wasn't too bad, because the outhouse was roofless. At night when one did one's business, one could count the stars in the sky and not feel so lonely.

Because the courtyard was narrow between the north and south bungalows, the two south rooms ended up at the western end. The western short walls of the north rooms faced the eastern short walls of the south rooms, such that the two walls created a sort of a pass. When it rained, the water was deepest in this area, and one had to set up a stool to get from one side to the other.

Viewed as a whole, this house was not at all suited for rain. Not only did the courtyard turn into a canal with a stool for a bridge, but the rooms were never completely dry, either, because every single roof leaked. The rooms that got the most water were naturally the two south rooms, which, ever since I could remember, never had a roof over them. They were two peculiar rooms.

The courtyard had three trees. Outside the south rooms and in front of the north rooms were two jujube trees. By the south wall was an apricot tree. The two jujube trees were truly deserving of praise. When they blossomed at the beginning of summer, the entire courtyard was permeated with such sweet fragrance. When the leaves became lush, they would beckon flying insects known as "flowered kerchiefs." With their bright red wings with black polka dots, they were quite stylish. When autumn arrived, we would have jujubes to eat. Until their leaves were all gone and a few deep-red jujubes remained on the tips of their branches, these two trees continued to entice the crows and Youngest Elder Sister. The apricot tree, on the other hand, wasn't even worth mentioning. I don't remember it ever bearing fruit. It was forever filled with little black red pouches that harbored insects. Its leaves were always curled up, and the hairy green worms that crawled about in them gave everyone the creeps.

Mother loved flowers, but after Father died, the number of our flowerpots only dwindled and never increased. Flowers cost money. Since we had to watch out that our water bill didn't get too high, we were left with only a pot of a pink-and-red twin-petaled oleander and four pots of sweet pomegranate. These five plants were all older than Youngest Elder Sister. They must have seen Mother's youthful days. Because they were old, they were like a part of the family. Whenever Youngest Elder Sister taught me to count how many people were in our family, we would always include the oleander and the pomegranates. So none of us was willing to cut off their water supply. Anyway, these woody perennials were easy to grow. With a little care, good or bad, they were sure to bloom when the time came.

When winter arrived, we would move them inside the house and cover the oleander with a large paper wind hat and tuck all the leaves under it so that dust wouldn't collect on them. The pomegranates had no leaves in winter, so it wasn't necessary to cover them. Instead, we made them do simple chores for us, like hold our chopstick basket or bamboo scoop. We didn't have to water them all winter. When we rinsed our teapot, we would pour the remaining tea with the tea leaves into the flowerpot. Supposedly, tea leaves made good fertilizer for the plants.

About the time of the "grain rains," when the spinach was about three feet tall, we would move our plants into the garden. Between April and May, they would always dazzle the eyes with their splendid red blossoms. Matched against the wildflowers by the wall and the grass on the roof tiles, our ramshackle garden seemed to come alive with vitality. When the Midautumn Festival[6] arrived, though we couldn't afford to go to the market to buy fresh fruit, we had some home-grown jujubes and sweet pomegranates to grace the holiday.

Beyond the south wall of the courtyard was the backyard of an incense-and-candle store. Used for drying incense, the backyard was very large. We couldn't see the people on the other side of the wall but could hear their voices. From our side of the wall, we could see the many colors of the Szechwan chrysanthemums and a large mulberry tree. In the summertime, the tree was filled with mulberries. Our old white cat always went over there at night to entertain his friends. Their calls were unusually sharp and rude. Perhaps cats' manner of socializing and conversing with each other follows a separate set of rules. Whenever we called out to our cat, eight out of ten times he would jump down from the mulberry tree onto the wall and from there jump to the ground by way of the apricot tree as though it were a ladder for his exclusive use. In my childhood imagination, I somehow felt that our old cat came from some mysterious land, and I often fantasized that some day I would follow him and venture to "that other side."

Past this incense factory was a public bathhouse that was even more mysterious. At that time, I was unable to see the awning of the bathhouse even if I stood on tiptoe. But I could hear the sound of the pulley drawing water from the well throughout the night. The sound was especially clear at night. *Guada, guada* . . . then no sound, then suddenly *hua . . . hua . . . hualahuala* . . . like something being chased. Then it would start all over again. *Guada, guada.* After going on like that for the longest time, suddenly a person with a sharp voice would say something. I would then know that the pulley would stop, and I would feel very lonesome. Many a night's sweet dreams followed in the wake of that *guadaguada,* and many an early morning's sunlight drifted into my consciousness with that same *guadaguada.* As we neared New Year's, the sound of the pulley would intensify along with the hope of eating good food. Every New Year's Eve, the sound of fire-crackers and the pulley would continue all night nonstop. We had no money to buy firecrackers. Any New Year's money we received was the little we got from my aunt.[7] A cold kitchen with empty pots—our home wasn't a bit festive. Old and young alike felt no joy. Hardly the season for crying, we quietly listened to the unspeakably mournful sound of the pulley.

Our alley[8] was pointed at the two ends and wide in the middle, much like a lake with two mouths that you see on a map. In the round belly of the alley were six households and two large locust trees. In the summertime, the locust leaves shaded the entire ground and even gave a greenish hue to people's front doors. When a breeze rustled through the leaves, green insects could be seen swinging back and forth in the air.

Under these two locust trees, Youngest Elder Sister helped me pick up the locust-tree insects, make locust-leaf flowers, and play and fight with the neighborhood children. I don't know how many hours we whiled away under these trees or how many times we cried and laughed there. When I gazed up to look at the gently swaying leaves, I always thought that they were waving to me as though to tell me something awfully kind and friendly.

It isn't that I am intentionally jotting down these images of no great import. Nor have I put any mental effort into describing them in this way, because they live so naturally in my heart and remain forever fresh and vivid. An old painting can seem blurred, but the colors of this painting of mine seem to have seeped into my blood where they never fade. Consequently, I often have this rather comical fear that if I had not had such a home in my childhood or that if I had moved here one day and moved there the next, I wouldn't have accumulated these treasured paintings. People with brains may consider abolishing private ownership. Some intellectuals may advocate the destruction of the family system. But in my mind, if all private ownership were like our rickety old house and our two jujube trees, I would be happy to declare myself a conservative. Because even though what we possessed didn't relieve us from our poverty, it did provide us that stability that made each blade of grass and each tree come alive in our hearts. At the very least, it made me a small blade of grass always securely rooted to its own turf. All that I am began here. My character was molded and cast here. If I had grown up in the most progressive nursery or child-care center, I may have developed a hundred times better than if I had stayed home, but I doubt very much that I would have had the kind of childhood that Mother and Youngest Elder Sister and those pots of pomegranate plants gave me.

When traveling, I often see towering mountains and great rivers, exotic flowers and unusual plants, but this is just scenery that, however grandly beautiful or exquisitely subtle, once past has no bearing on me. Its grandeur or subtlety cannot enter my heart and become one with me. On the other hand, if I see a green locust-tree insect, I immediately see before me those two old locust trees and hear Youngest Elder Sister's laughter. I can't push these off to one side and still find a complete me. That was home. I was born there and grew up there. Each blade of grass and each brick there is a signpost in my life. Yes, I prefer to have this kind of private ownership, this kind of family, if you understand what I mean. I'm afraid I haven't made it completely clear. But perhaps I haven't gone as far as to be misunderstood. If, unfortunately, I am misunderstood and am labeled an upholder of private ownership and the family system, I don't want to analyze this question in detail. Because as soon as I think of my childhood days, my emotions get the better of my reason. The more I talk, the further I get from common sense. So the less said the better.

4

Spread across the arch over our front gate[9] were tiles in the shape of old coins. By the time I could remember things, however, these old coins were all crooked and bent out of shape. Grass, which was not quite green, popped through the coin holes. Each time after it snowed, those pitiful sparrows who lived among the "silver coins" with their empty bellies would hang on as best they could, pecking at those skinny blades of grass. As for the old and worn-out panels of the door, it is no easy matter to describe them just right. To put it very generally, they were porous and delicate, full of holes and cracks everywhere, like the rocks in some paintings. Naturally, this fact didn't hinder us from shutting them tight every night—chains, bolt, lock, and all—with a great rock propped against them to boot. Our concept of a door was, in any case, complete. For years no couplet graced our door frame. Only the year when Youngest Elder Sister left home to get married did I personally write one. I believe it was well written, but unfortunately it was pasted on in reverse order by Mother. The green dust that piled up on the left and right buttresses never completely faded nor fell away. I remember, in fact, that there were several mounds like slabstones, covered with crow's-feet markings made by our water carrier to tally up our end-of-the-month bills. Sometimes when my aunt was feeling cheery she would, with a brush of her hands, erase one or two groups of markings. And the water carrier never said anything to us.

The doorway was merely two feet wide. Each time it drizzled or the wind blew heavily, Younger Elder Sister and I would sit here and play. I had exclusive use of the rock lying against the door. I don't remember how many times I sang "Little, little one, sitting on the door mound."[10]

The screen wall[11] wasn't worth mentioning. In its twilight years, it was always slowly falling halfway over. Its bricks were picked up for other uses, and consequently, it contented itself in being short. In the autumn, it would even grow a few strands of pumpkin vines as if doing its best to be sprightly.

After I became a grown man, I once visited the Forbidden City. Red walls followed red walls, the great halls faced each other. Everywhere one ran into walls, and everywhere it was neat and orderly. It was stately and dignified, all right, but I really doubt that the crown prince had ever seen a pumpkin vine growing on a screen wall. If he had any intention of switching places with me, I would still abhor those deadly boring compounds. Faced with such red walls, I felt, even someone smarter than Li Bo[12] would find it difficult to write any poetry. In any case, our shabby house had an abandoned, free and easy feel to it. Here, one could savor and appreciate all those scenes of "crumbling walls and dilapidated houses" or of people "alone by lamplight midst falling leaves" that lean and sprightly poets so love to depict. On a summer's night in our courtyard, there were indeed three to five fireflies and not a few crickets.

As for those rooms of ours, no matter how one began to describe them, they wouldn't be as interesting as the things in the courtyard. What I was most familiar with, of course, were the two rooms I lived in. In the inner room was a large *kang* running the length of the eaves. Facing the *kang* was a big, long table with three drawers. On this table was a pair of cylindrical ceramic hat stands on which was painted "Wealth until Old Age." They were hollow inside, but their surfaces were held together by a lot of braces.[13] Placed in front of the table was a large feather-duster vase patterned with indigo plants on a bean-green background. Its shape was clumsy and awkward, and it only contained one chicken-feather duster, which was unwieldy and impractical. Between the *kang* and the table, against the western wall, was a large wooden trunk that also subbed as a stool. At times when the room was fully occupied and all the seats in the room were taken, someone would have to get on this trunk. But no matter how one sat on it, one could not look natural. The two small red-lacquer stools could be placed anywhere, but every morning they had to be in front of the table to serve temporarily as stands for the washbasins. I dare not say I disliked these things nor the way they were arranged, but neither was I completely enamored of them. Their biggest failing probably was not that they were ugly in themselves but that because the room was so cramped, each item had an air of being a bit overbearing. As a result, I also felt a bit oppressed by them.

The outer room was much better. At the foot of the north wall was an eight-immortals table.[14] The table's wooden surface was so uneven that anything placed on it could never stand properly. So the top of this table was forever unused. On both sides of the table were two chairs made of lacquered elm wood. In the wintertime, because the stove stayed in the inner room, no one sat on these chairs. In the summertime, whenever it got humid and mildewy the lacquer would stealthily shrink away and emit a greasy, sweatlike smell. No one dared to sacrifice their trousers on them. An empty table and empty chairs, which forever maintained a dignity that kept people at a respectful distance. Consequently I developed love at a distance for them. Only in spring and in autumn when it was neither cold nor humid did I dare climb on top of the chairs and sit for awhile, feeling snug and comfortable.

At the foot of the eastern wall was a Buddha table, on which lay offerings to the Kitchen God and the God of Wealth. These two gods together enjoyed a small tin candle stand, but there were only two incense burners, one large and one small. The old Buddha inscription at the top of the altar, blurred and faded by incense smoke, always appeared to the observer a bit mysterious. During New Year's a small tile bowl would make its appearance on the table. The bowl was filled to the brim with "New Year's Rice,"[15] on top of which were placed several jujubes, and a piece of persimmon cake. Those jujubes, always of much concern to me, were quietly gobbled up by me before the fifth or sixth day of New Year's. I was under the impression that my stomach was the perfectly reliable storage place for the jujubes. Underneath the Buddha table lay, in horizontal fashion, a wooden board thick with dust. Dust on implements is somewhat frightening, so even though I wanted for a long time to move the things on the board, on many an occasion when I extended my hand toward them, my hand would shrink back. I finally mustered up my courage to investigate them and discovered three copies of *The Three Knights-errant and the Five Altruists*[16] and several copies of *The Five Tiger Generals Pacify the West.*[17] The former's paper was soft, the characters were small and elegant looking, and moreover, one copy was entirely filled with drawings of little people. The latter was not much to look at—the paper was yellow, the book itself small, the characters large but faded. The copy with the little people became my treasure. Although my aunt didn't know how to read, she was familiar with many plays and stories, because supposedly my uncle had been an actor. When she had time, she enjoyed listening to drum songs,[18] the Judge Bao crime-case stories, and the like. What's more, she could judge good from bad performances, because my uncle, don't forget, had been a *real* professional actor. She glanced through that copy with the little people and told me which one was Judge Bao, which one was Old Chen Lin.[19] Thus I began to understand that besides the people I knew, there were also some people who grew inside books.

Opposite the Buddha table was a large earthenware vat. A long stone slab, on which was placed a small tiled pot, lay horizontally over it. I couldn't see the water in the vat, but I could stretch open my mouth under one side of the stone slab and wait for the dripping water to fall in. In the summer, when it was scalding hot everywhere else, only this vat remained icy cool. Oozing under the belly of the vat was a layer of cool sweat, which, when rubbed, felt as if one had touched a fish— both cool and wet.

In short, the outer room was refreshingly and respectfully silent. Each morning when I first walked out from the inner room I always felt a lighthearted cheerfulness. Although the inner and outer rooms were divided only by a curtain, they clearly imparted two different atmospheres. After dinner, before one lit the lamps, six quiet sparks in front of the Buddha altar emitted fragrant incense smoke. Each day the Kitchen God and the God of Wealth enjoyed three joss sticks. However, sometimes I only saw one joss stick standing alone in the burner. I would know then that Mother had no money in her pocket again. I would be unusually well behaved so as not to arouse her anger. Naturally, there were times when there wasn't even one stick of incense. Gods and humans alike would all keep silent and go to sleep early.

I rarely went to my aunt's room. For one thing, she often wasn't at home during the day. For another, she was fond of temper tantrums, so unless she yelled at me to come in, I wasn't about to run in on my own to look for trouble. Moreover, I didn't like that room. My aunt's room had as many things as our room—no, maybe even more. For example, her large mirror and tea cannister were things we didn't have. When Mother and Younger Elder Sister combed their hair, they merely used a tiny mirror that made their noses look crooked each time they used it. All the items in my aunt's room no doubt were squashed and crushed against each other as if none of them could breathe. Here, I always felt stifled. Also, if my aunt were rushing to go out to listen to drum songs or to play shuttle cards, she wouldn't bother to clean up her room. Her things would be left in a topsy-turvy mess. Mother was not fond of this way of doing things, so Younger Elder Sister and I, too, disapproved. What bothered us even more was how my aunt always put the spout of the teapot in her mouth when she drank tea, holding her breath while pouring the tea down. Only when guests came to visit would she bother to use a cup. We felt very fortunate that we were not her guests and never had to drink her tea. We secretly cried out for the guests, but there was no way to give them even a little warning.

Might as well quickly admit that my impression of this room was not on the mark. Of course, if someone forces me to report on all the things that were there, I wouldn't fail in doing so. However, I really don't want to think in detail about them, because things are like people—if they cause a headache as soon as you think of them, it's always best to keep them locked up in your mind. People who are overly frank, in my opinion, are not able to write poetry.

Auntie Guan's two rooms on the east side had no partitions. When one opened the door, one got the entire view. That large *kang* was enormous—an ocean without boundaries or shores. It made me imagine that one of these days it would grow bigger and swallow up everything. This wouldn't have been difficult because the simple room contained nothing big enough to obstruct the huge *kang*'s wild ambitions.

Although there weren't many things in it, the room was always very hot in the summer. The sun's rays and the heat from the long and narrow courtyard all seemed to pour into this place. Auntie Guan always bared her top, exposing her two immense and rolling breasts. Her body was greatly different from Mother's. One simply couldn't find any muscle or bone; everywhere was flesh. I was most fond of feeling her back with my hands, so soft and so smooth. I consequently often urged my mother to learn from Auntie Guan and induce more flesh to grow outward. Mother would say nothing and merely respond with an unsmile-like smile.

Auntie Guan's lovable nature vanquished the hatefulness of those two rooms. I would spend hours each day playing there. I could whoop and holler, but she couldn't hear a thing. She always praised me for being well behaved and quiet. Sometimes I would shout at the top of my lungs to deliberately test if she'd be annoyed at me or not, but I always failed. Instead she would straightaway count my teeth, then compliment me on how cute each and every one of them was. When she later moved away, many times I woke up crying from my dreams, pleading again and again for Auntie Guan. During the day I would sneak into that empty room and repeat with fond recollection, "Auntie Guan, here's some spinach for you to make dumplings with!" I imagined her sitting on the *kang*, nodding to me and smiling at me, but I couldn't find her plump hands. Terribly disappointed, I would go into the courtyard to pick up one or two fallen flowers to bring over to her, because she loved wearing flowers. It didn't matter if it was the most unconventional flower, she would always find an opportunity to put it in her hair. When I brought the fallen flowers into her room by the *kang*, no hands extended out with a smile. Auntie Guan! I cried out for her all around the wall, but no one stirred!

I had a mother but no father, an aunt but no uncle, an Auntie Guan but no Uncle Guan: all the women in our courtyard were widows. At the time, I thought this was the way things were supposed to be. When I saw children with fathers it actually felt strange. Needless to say, as time passed I came close to becoming like a woman. I managed and took care of all matters in great detail like women. As a result, I always looked down on a woman who couldn't or didn't like to take care of household matters, no matter how interesting and how learned she was. Naturally, I certainly won't go help anyone shout, "Ladies, back to your kitchens!" But neither will I help anyone yell, "Ladies, off to the theater!"

Now I should mention those two dilapidated south rooms. The room with the *kang* had absolutely no roof on it. I hear that back then my grandmother's coffin[20] was placed there. Of course, back then the remains of a roof were still there. When Eldest Sister was sixteen, someone came to look her over, and moreover, left a pair of rings. She hid crouched behind the coffin for an entire day. No matter who called her, she refused to respond, much less come out. When night came, only when the tears were dried from her eyes and her stomach felt strangely empty did she show due respect to

Mother's feelings and return to the north room to eat two bowls of rice in tea. The room, with such a history later on, had only half a *kang* left in it. Robust green grass grew on the *kang*. As for the room without the *kang,* a shadow of a roof remained. Inside the room was a long table piled with dust. On the table were piled a disarray of useless things. As soon as my legs could walk, I wanted to come here to see if there was anything to play with. This room was so pitifully run-down and so frightening that my pity and curiosity congealed into a force of courage, which from time to time urged me on to go take a peek inside.

In which year and month was this? Unfortunately I don't remember all that well. I finally did venture into that awful room. I have absolutely no excuse for forgetting the year and month, because it was a landmark year worth recording. I had discovered some toys in that room. How poor was I? It's not so easy to describe. I can merely tell you that I had no toys whatsoever! When Mother took apart the quilt to wash, I shredded a small piece of cotton. When our family ate bleached flour once in a blue moon, I begged for a little kneaded dough—this was my toy. I could roll that little bit of cotton or piece of dough back and forth and mold them into what I felt were accurately formed little chickens, little fish, and all sorts of things. Not until after I had entered that dilapidated room did I have real toys. I acquired ten or so clay molds[21] and several already dyed sheep anklebones.[22] Perhaps my brother had hidden them there when he went off to work as an apprentice? I didn't care; anyway, I had some things to play with. My life suddenly became grandiose! I begged Younger Elder Sister to mend a small cloth bag and put those sheep anklebones in it. As for those clay molds, I hid them under the Buddha's table and entrusted them under the protection of the Kitchen God and Goddess. Even so, I had to go take a peek at them tens of times each day. When spring came, I mixed a bit of mud and created quite a few mud pies and forced Younger Elder Sister to buy them. Her money consisted of some broken ceramic pieces. I waited until I had completely sold my wares to return those ceramic pieces to Younger Elder Sister and told her to buy them all over again once or several times more.

Notes

"Autobiography of a Minor Character" (Xiao renwu zishu) is an unfinished autobiographical novel that was unknown to the public until 1985, nearly twenty years after Lao She's death. Only four chapters were published as serialized fiction in the January 1937 issue of *The Ark*. Due to the outbreak of war with Japan that year, this issue turned out to be the journal's last. Lao She assumed that this work had been lost and never bothered to mention its title or place of publication. It was discovered by Zhang Wei and Chen Fukang in 1985 and republished in the 1986, no. 1, issue of *October* (Shiyue) together with an article by Zhang and Chen on the work.

In the 1960s Lao She attempted his second autobiographical novel *Zhenghong qixia,* which again remained unfinished and unknown to the public until after his death. It has been translated by Don J. Cohn as *Beneath the Red Banner* (Beijing: Panda Books, 1982).

1. *Suorhu;* also called *zhipai, liuerpai, doushihu, dashiyu.* A set usually consists of 164 cards, four each of 41 different cards. There is also a set consisting of 40 cards. Each card measures about 2 cm. × 10 cm. (8/10 in. × 4 in.) For further information and to view a photo of the 40-card set of these "shuttle cards," see Tokiko Nakayama, ed., *Ro Sha Jiten* (The Lao She encyclopedia) (Tokyo: Taishukan Shoten, 1988) pp. 403–405.

2. According to an ancient Buddhist legend, Monk Mulian went to hell to release his mother. When the food he gave her turned into flames at her lips on account of her past sins, he chanted some

paragraphs from the holy books, at which the flames disappeared, and she was able to eat the food. He was able to save his mother's soul from further sufferings, for his great filial devotion to his mother was considered enough reason for the gods to grant her release.

The sutra-chanting service conducted throughout the night of the Third Day Reception, known as "Flaming Mouth" *(yankou)*, has its origins in the legend of Monk Mulian.

3. Among the many superstitions about the ghost-appeasing rite, called the summoning *(zhaoqing)*, described here is that children who gather up the pieces of the "evil-chasing, courage-fortifying" dough are said to become courageous and unafraid of ghosts. It is also said that a very young boy (but not a girl) with "pure" eyes can get a glimpse of the spirits, provided he is bold enough to get behind the seat of the chief abbot and peep into a mirror held in his hand. For more about the Third Day Reception see H. Y. Lowe, *The Adventures of Wu: The Life Cycle of a Peking Man* (Princeton: Princeton University Press, 1983). Lowe's book, first published in 1940, contains a great deal of information about the beliefs and practices of traditionally minded, lower middle-class Beijing families during the first half of the twentieth century.

4. A yamen is a local government office.

5. Like many traditional residences in the Beijing area, Lao She's childhood home was built in the quadrangle style known as the *siheyuan,* in which rows of rooms were built around the four sides of a central courtyard. High brick walls usually surrounded or connected the rooms on each of the four sides, hiding the courtyard from outside view. A screen wall was usually built right behind the front door, again hiding the courtyard and the inside of the compound from the outside view.

Nowhere else in his essays or fictional works does Lao She describe his childhood home with such loving detail as he does in "Autobiography of a Minor Character." Lao She's childhood home still exists in present-day Beijing on No. 8 Xiao Yang Jia Alley. To this day one jujube tree still grows in the courtyard.

For more about Lao She's childhood home, see Liyun Li, *Lao She zai Beijing de zuji* (Traces of Lao She in Beijing) (Beijing: Beijing

Yanshan chubanshe, 1986) and Tokiko Nakayama, ed., *Ro Sha Jiten,* pp. 518–522. Professor Nakayama's *Ro Sha Jiten* is an invaluable reference source for various aspects of Beijing life and society that form the background of so many of Lao She's works: the city and its customs, food, clothing, arts and entertainment, education, occupations, religions, and so forth. The book also provides a great deal of information about Lao She himself.

6. Midautumn Festival falls on the 15th day of the eighth lunar month, the time of year when the moon is fullest and brightest. This festival is also called Festival of Reunions, for it is hoped that on this day the family circle will be kept round, just as the full moon. Moon cakes—round pastry with black-bean or date paste inside—and fresh fruits in season are exchanged as gifts and eaten on this day.

7. Part of the many traditional preparations for the lunar New Year's holidays include settling one's debts, cleaning one's house, and taking a bath in order to start out the new year afresh. One of the most important features of the New Year's festivities is shooting off firecrackers and fireworks of various kinds in order to scare away ghosts. On New Year's Day children are given red packets of New Year's money, known as "money for weighing down the age" *(yasuiqian).*

8. The alley in Beijing is called the *hutong,* a term derived from the Mongolian word for "well." Beijing, made the capital of the Mongolian Yuan dynasty (1280–1368), relied mainly on well water for daily needs until 1910 when the Germans established a water service bureau. At the time, over half of Beijing's *hutong*s had wells. For more about the *hutong,* see Nakayama, *Ro Sha Jiten,* p. 21.

9. A four-sided bungalow home with courtyard was typically surrounded or connected by high, thick walls often topped with tiled roofs. The front gate with tiled arch mentioned here is contiguous with the walls. The entryway behind the doors of the front gate is therefore a covered space and is called a *mendong* or "door hole." To view photos of a typical front gate and to read more about the construction and design of Beijing residences, see Nakayama, *Ro Sha Jiten,* pp. 303–317.

10. This is probably the first line from a nursery rhyme called

"Small Boy Craving a Wife," translated by H. Y. Lowe in *Adventures of Wu*, vol. 1, p. 96, as:

> *A little, little boy,*
> *Sits on the doorstep.*
> *He weeps, weeps bitterly,*
> *For he wants a wife.*
> *"Wants a wife—but what for?"*
> *"To make me rice, to make me vegetables,*
> *To make me trousers, to make me socks,*
> *To light the lamp, to talk with me,*
> *To blow out the lamp, and keep me from loneliness,*
> *Next morning, she will also comb and make my little queue!"*

11. The screen wall, *yingbi* or *zhaobi*, is a solitary standing wall built inside the courtyard usually facing the front gate to block the view of the rest of the courtyard. To view photos of a typical screen wall and the more elaborate "Nine Dragon Screen Wall," *jiulongbi*, seen in palaces, parks, and temples, see Nakayama, *Ro Sha Jiten*, p. 305.

12. Li Bo or Li Bai (701–762), a famous Tang dynasty poet.

13. When cracks developed in these ceramic hat stands, braces were used to hold them together. That the narrator's family braced the cracks rather than buy a new hat stand is a sign of their poverty. I am indebted to Parker Po-fei Huang for this information.

14. A *baxianzuo* is a large, square table that can seat two people on each of its four sides, thus its name "eight-immortals table" (Nakayama, *Ro Sha Jiten*, p. 327).

15. H. Y. Lowe in *Adventures of Wu*, Vol. 2, p. 156, describes the "New Year's rice" in the following manner: "A big bowl of freshly prepared rice was placed on a table in a prominent position in the central room. This was their *nien fan*, or 'New Year's rice,' in which a green branch of cypress was inserted. On this was laid a small string of loosely tied old cash and a paper decoration was attached to the cypress branch. An assortment of dried nuts was strewn over the rice. This would be displayed until the sixth day of the first moon of

the new year. It is a sign of abundance and an embodiment of prayers tantamount to saying: 'Give us this day our daily rice.'" Clearly, the narrator's family could only afford a simplified version of this "New Year's rice."

16. *Sanxia wuyi,* a late nineteenth-century novel attributed to story-teller Shi Yukun (fl. 1870). A quasi-historical novel of adventure, crime detection, and political intrigues, its plot revolves around the courtroom cases of the famous incorruptible official Bao Zheng (999–1062), also known as Bao Gong or "Judge Bao," and the adventures of the heroes and gallants.

17. *Wuhu ping xi,* a military romance about the eleventh-century general Di Qing (1008–1057). Incorruptible official Bao Zheng (999–1062), or Judge Bao, is also assigned a major role in this story.

18. *Dagu* are stories from the historical romances or from folklore recited in a singing style by a woman and accompanied on a stringed instrument played by a male musician. The female singer also beats time on a drum about ten inches in diameter.

19. Chen Lin is an upright eunuch who appears in the Judge Bao crime case stories and in *The Three Knights-errant and the Five Altruists.*

20. It was the custom among the elderly to prepare their coffin while still alive and store it in their homes. One referred to the coffin as *shoucai,* "material for longevity," and avoided using the common word for coffin, *guancai.*

21. Little reddish molds made of baked clay were favorites with Beijing children to make little figures of houses, temples, pagodas, people, and so forth. According to H. Y. Lowe, if a man does not remember having these clay molds, "tell him for me that he had not been a typical Peking boy" (*Adventures of Wu,* Vol. 1, pp. 135–137).

22. According to Lao She's son Shu Yi, sheep anklebones were commonly used as toys.

How I Wrote My Short Stories

I wrote my earliest short story while teaching at the Nankai Middle School. I tossed it off with nothing more in mind than to please the editor of the school magazine. That must have been twelve or thirteen years ago by now. The story, needless to say, had absolutely nothing to recommend it, nor is it at all important in my career, because it did nothing to pique my interest in writing; what precious little there is of my writing career began with a novel, *The Philosophy of Lao Zhang* (Lao Zhang de zhexue).

And that was the trouble. In short, before I wrote my first novel, I had absolutely no experience in writing short stories, and it cost me dearly. If you want to write good short stories, you have to give it everything you've got. With novels, you can slack off a bit: if you have some good paragraphs, and in each of those, you have some brilliant sentences, your novel will stand muster. Of course I'm not saying that it *ought* to be like this, but as a matter of fact, it often is. Even the reader of a novel—just because it *is* long—will be unusually forgiving. The world will allow the existence of a very imperfect novel but won't be that polite with a short story. And so it was that with no experience at all in writing short stories, I insisted on doing five or six novels; my slow rate of improvement in writing skill was a foregone conclusion. In the history of literature, the short story is a latecomer and most demanding of skill. One could almost say that it became an independent genre because it relied on skill. But as soon as *I* started out, I used the novel form for practice. It's a lot like somebody who's studying Chinese fighting techniques trying a stand-up lift of the heaviest weights before he's gotten his legs fully in shape. He can thank his lucky stars if he doesn't get crushed by the load. And even if he was able to lift a thousand *jin,* it would only be thanks to a kind of clumsy strength that would be of no use to him in fighting. It wasn't until after I had written a fair number of short stories that I caught on to this.

In the last sentence of the above paragraph, I write "a fair number" advisedly as you shall see. The twenty-five stories collected in *Deadliners* (Ganji) [first edition 1934] and *Cherries and the Sea* (Yinghaiji) [first edition 1935] along with my most recent stories—"The Death Dealing Spear" (Duanhunqiang), "An Old Tragedy in a New Age" (Xin shidai de jiu beiju), and so on—can be divided into three groups.

Group One consists of the first four stories in *Deadliners,*[1] along with "The Man in Riding Breeches" (Maku xiansheng), and "The Grandchild" (Baosun) from the same collection.

Group Two consists of those stories beginning with "By the Temple of Great Compassion" (Dabeisi wai) and up to "The Crescent Moon" (Yueyar).[2]

Group Three consists of stories like "The Crescent Moon," "The Death Dealing Spear," and "An Old Tragedy in a New Age." [When he discusses this group later on, Lao She includes "Sunlight" (Yangguang). *Trans.*]

I wrote the half dozen or so stories in Group One just for the hell of it. The earliest in the group was "May Ninth" and was done as a space filler for the *Qilu University Monthly.*[3] "Hot Dumplings" was written for the "Forest of Talk" (Yulin) column of the *Social Welfare Daily* (Yishibao).[4] It's as short as it is because that's the way they wanted it. When I wrote these two pieces, I had no sense that I was "writing short stories"— their sole function was to serve as space fillers. It wasn't until after the January 28th Incident and the multiplication of publications that came in its wake that I felt I'd simply have to write "short stories":[5] everybody wanted manuscripts and the short story was the most convenient way to go. That's right, it was simply a bit more *convenient* to write short stories. And that was my only reason for doing it, for I still disdained the short-story form and thought they really weren't worth writing. That's why I ended up doing such silly things as the anecdotes represented in "The Grandson" and stories like it. Just write up some trivial yarn and you've got yourself a short story—that's how I thought at the time. I planned on continuing to do these little lightweight pieces until I had a block of time available and *then* I'd do some real writing—a novel. But finding that block of time proved far from easy. And then, too, more and more people began pumping me for short stories. At that point I decided it was time to get rid of my "just for the hell of it" attitude—couldn't go on writing silly little anecdotes forever! And so it was that the stories in Group Two took form, beginning with "By the Temple of Great Compassion" and "Vision."

Stories like "Vision" and "Black Li and White Li" from Group Two underwent several revisions, for since I was no longer writing short stories just for the hell of it, it behooved me to apply myself and really work them up. But even so, there are still quite a few in Group Two that were written at one fell swoop and ended up as utter messes because I really didn't have the time to revise them. The trouble was I didn't get much money for them to begin with, and the more I wrote, the more I made. Besides, sometimes I had to crank them out as fast as I could in order to please friends. These two circumstances contrived to nudge me in the direction of doing a wholesale business—in other words it was better to do a lot of bad ones than a few good ones. I'll bet there are other writers out there like me, too. It wasn't a policy that I adopted consciously, it was just that there was nothing else I could do. I felt that I was really letting literature down, but, on the other hand, it wouldn't do to let down my friends—or the money, either.

I remember one time when an editor by the name of Wang wanted me to crank something out.[6] Writing in fits and starts, I ended up with over thirty thousand words but still wasn't able to shape it into a story. I was afraid he wouldn't believe me if I simply told him that, so I gathered up all the bits and pieces I had written and mailed them off to him. This isn't to say that I am dead serious about writing, but just to point out that it did happen to me like this that one time; what's more, it *only* happened that one time. If things went on like that every time I wrote, I'd either die from exhaustion or succumb to starvation. Dying because you've worn yourself out is a straightforward and honorable way to go, but dying of starvation is painful—not all that respectable, either. Look at it this way: suppose I got twenty dollars, or even less, for every five thousand words I ground out; now let's say, in the interest of art, I edited out three thousand of the five—how could I possibly steer clear of starvation? But I've run on about this too much already.

There were probably four sources for the ten-odd pieces in Group Two: (1) personal experiences, (2) hearsay, (3) imitation, and (4) abstract concepts on the basis of which I fashioned characters and events. Why don't I make a chart.

CATEGORY 1: **Stories from My Own Experiences**
By the Temple of Great Compassion
Vision
The Liu Family Courtyard
The Eyeglasses

Sacrifice
Caterpillar
Neighbors

CATEGORY II: Stories I Heard People Tell
Also a Triangle
Assuming Office
The One from Liu Village
An Old Man's Romance

CATEGORY III: Story Imitating Other People's Work
Crooktails

CATEGORY IV: Stories Written from Abstract Concepts
Black Li and White Li
Iron Ox and Sick Duck
The Philanthropist

Since there is only one story in Category III—story imitating other people's works—let's start there. I wrote "Crooktails" in imitation of F. D. Beresford's "The Hermit."[7] I happened to be lecturing on that particular short story at the time and had translated it into Chinese so that I could share it with the class. For a long time after that I couldn't get it out of my mind and thought about writing something similar to it myself. But from beginning to end I was not able to come up with a parallel plot and ended up by simply imitating the original one. Although the material of the story was my own, the concept was completely plagiarized.

Most of the seven stories in the Category I consist of events that I personally witnessed and in one or two cases, events in which I participated. Actually this wouldn't be worth talking about if "Sacrifice" hadn't received such unfavorable criticism. Every last character and event in that story is true to real people and actual happenings. Yet contemporary critics of my short stories invariably picked that particular one to rip apart, and some of them went so far as to say that it was *unrealistic.* Whenever I saw that kind of critique, I would counter—as I think most people would—with, "But this really happened!" When I carefully read the story over again, however, I saw what they meant: it really wasn't any good.

"Sacrifice" is a bad story: it wobbles all over the place, and the ending does nothing to strengthen the idea that I started out with. It's so fragmented it looks as though I patched it together as I wrote along—something like quilting. You can't depend on things that actually happened to give you a story, because reality is *not* fiction. It all depends on how you write it up. If you put too much faith in your raw material, you're quite likely to neglect the artistry of your story. The stories in Category II, on the other hand, will all stand muster despite the fact that the material in them was all secondhand stuff I heard from my friends. Precisely because those stories were based on hearsay, I was very conscientious in handling the material—there's nothing wrong with being careful.

Similarly, there are fairly presentable stories in Category IV even though the people and events in them are purely products of my imagination, the progeny of abstract concepts. "Black Li and White Li" and "Iron Ox and Sick Duck" both consist of two characters representing two opposite ways of thinking. Since the ideas came first and the characters second, everything that the characters do fits within the confines laid out for them and stays there. The characters can't go crashing off track even if they want to, a lot better than having them plunge pell-mell all over the place, I think. Experience enriches imagination but imagination determines experience.

The language of these stories is somewhat tamer than that of my novels. In some of them, this is the result of frequent revision; in others, quite to the contrary, it is due to my having been in a hurry to get them done and handed in. In the former case I fanned the fire so much that I fanned it out—perhaps one might say I "edited" it out.[8] In the latter, there wasn't any fire to begin with. But on the whole, I have managed to hold fast to my desire to keep the language both popular and spoken. As for the rhetoric, I always put clarity first and let everything else follow from that. For if we can say that clarity is the result of having put some thought into what you write, then clarity is strength. I don't know if I can lay claim to writing that is strong and clear, but that's what I tried for.

I ought to take up Group Three now. The stories in this group—"Crescent Moon," "Sunlight," "The Death Dealing Spear," and "An Old Tragedy in a New Age"—have nothing in particular to recommend them. My situation at the time as well as something I caught on to made me treat them as a separate group. As I have said above, I wrote the stories in Group One for the hell of it, so their lack of quality is a foregone conclusion and anything good about them is purely a matter of luck. Though I took the writing of the stories in Group Two seriously, I still tended to disdain the short story as a form and thought that my own forte was the novel. By the time I got to Group Three, my attitude had changed. My situation at the time had pushed me into a position where I was forced to take material for novels and use it for short stories instead, for more and more people wanted short stories out of me and material was not all that easy to come by. I was forced to take what I had kept in the back of my mind for novels and trot that out to save the day.

Needless to say, the transformation of a wholesale business into a retail operation left me with a bad feeling. When it came to taking material intended to produce a hundred thousand words and reducing it to five thousand for a short story— "The Death Dealing Spear" is an example—I caught on to something, and that "bad feeling" transformed itself into an insight. (Experience really is precious!) What I caught on to was this: taking material for a novel and using it for a short story isn't at all a bad deal, for if you select just one section from material that was intended to serve for over a hundred thousand words, then naturally you're going to pick the best—a clear validation of the saying that holds that it is "better to take one bite of the Peaches of the Immortals than eat a whole basketful of rotten apricots."

Then, too, although a novel has a central theme, the descriptive passages and subplots that result from the form's proliferation of characters and events produce a welter of subsidiary themes as well. If from these various themes you pick just *one* and work it up as a short story, the result is bound to be tight and polished. Any of the subsidiary themes can make a good short story, but scattered throughout a novel they cannot easily display their excellence.

Whereas a novel is well proportioned, a short story is concentrated. Take "Crescent Moon," for example. It was originally only a part of a novel, "Daming Lake." After the manuscript for "Daming Lake" was burned, I forgot most of its plot without the slightest regret, but there was part of it I couldn't get out of my mind, and that part resulted in "Crescent Moon." Needless to say, it was also the most interesting segment of the novel. In the original, however, it was not so neatly structured as when it became an independent short story. In "Daming Lake" it was sandwiched in among a lot of other things and therefore unable to stand on its own. As I see it now, I would much rather have "Crescent Moon" than "Daming Lake." Not because the story is any great masterpiece, but because it is so much better than it was when it was "drowned" in "Daming Lake."

"The Death Dealing Spear" was like that, too. It was originally a small part of a novel I planned that would have been titled, "Second Master of the Fist" (Er quanshi). Had I been able to complete it, this would have been a *wuxia* tale.[9] I had thought of writing such a novel for a long time, but if I had actually written it, who is to say what it would have been like. You can't say anything on that score until you've actually - written it. In creative works you don't dare operate on the basis of "contractual" promises. In "The Death Dealing Spear" I portrayed three characters and one event. I selected the characters and the event out of a large stock of material I had for the novel. I had given long and careful thought to everything concerning the trio and that's why they are able to stand on their own as characters. The event was just one of many that I planned to write about in the novel, and therefore it is presented very smoothly. For my short story, I took that event and tied it together with those three characters. The result is that the whole thing moves along at a natural pace and is neither under- nor overtold, but just right. Thus, while the original material was severely cut, art was the beneficiary. The five thousand words I ended up with are probably much stronger than the hundred thousand I had originally envisaged. Art, after all, is not like a pig—the fatter the better. But when all is said and done, a hundred thousand words *would* have brought in something between three and five hundred dollars. The five thousand I ended up with only got me nineteen!

I'm afraid that right there you have the reason that I didn't always maintain too intimate a relationship with art. Sacrificing oneself for art's sake sounds great, but nobody ought to die of an empty stomach. Why should people ask writers to lead the way? I just don't get it.

If I hadn't written "Crescent Moon," maybe "Sunlight" would have come off looking better than it does. Some people say that the failure of "Sunlight" is due to the subject matter of the story. But the way I see it, the reason that "Sunlight" doesn't come up to the level of "Crescent Moon" is this: "Crescent Moon" was taken out of "Daming Lake" and revised; therefore it hangs together very nicely—no rough edges or places where things seem forced. And "Sunlight"? Well, actually that was originally material for a novel, too, but it was material that I hadn't thought about very long. The result was that rather than culling out the best of it, in writing "Sunlight" I just took anything that happened to come to mind and threw it *all* in. That's why that story is rough around the edges and rather forced, as well.

If you let a novel incubate over a long period of time until you've worked out all its complexities and are thoroughly familiar with the people and events involved, and then you go on to take part of it and turn it into a short story, your success is a foregone conclusion. As soon as you set pen to paper, you'll have the whole thing just right; you are bound to achieve the aesthetic appeal that comes from balance and proportion. That's something that I caught on to after writing "The Crescent Moon" and "Sunlight."

In passing I'd like to point out that writing takes time. That is to say, in order to write something really good, a writer must be fully prepared to spend time on it. And how do you achieve that degree of preparation? The answer lies in a single word, the most important word in our entire language—*food*. I often hear people complain that we don't have any great works. Every time I hear this, I think that in the mind of the person who says it, a writer is probably some sort of tiny creature able to subsist on dewdrops.

Now I realize I'm not any great talent and probably have no hopes of writing a great work in the first place, but I really do believe that if you gave me *food* (which in turn would give me time), I could come up with some pretty good stuff. Don't believe me? All right then, let's give it a try!

There are several things wrong with "An Old Tragedy in a New Age." The greatest defect is that several of the characters are introduced and then just left hanging. There is no "Come back next time and I'll tell you what happened."[10] The trouble lies in its being a "middle-length story."[11] I had originally intended it as a novel. When I changed it into a middle-length story, I had no choice but to concentrate on a single character. At the same time, because I had to write at least thirty thousand words, I also had no choice but to drag some secondary characters out on stage as well. Perhaps I could have avoided this by making it into a short story instead.

My plan for the original novel was to take old Mr. Chen, his two sons, and Song Lungyun and make all of them into important characters. Old Mr. Chen was to represent the past; his elder son, Lianbo, someone seven-tenths old-fashioned and three-tenths modern; his younger son, Lianzhong, someone who was half-and-half. Song Longyun would stand for the modern age. When I changed it into a middle-length story, I got rid of three-quarters of my characters and spent all my time describing old Mr. Chen. At that point the other three all became shadow figures who only served to help prop up the framework of the plot. It was a dangerous way of proceeding and, of course, produced no good results. On the other hand, old Mr. Chen *is* a good, strong character. If I had made it into a novel, I cannot guarantee that he would have possessed the same vigor.

And therefore I still don't regret taking this wholesale material for a novel and retailing it as a short story. On the contrary, I feel that it takes a lot more talent for a singer of civil roles in our Beijing opera to turn around and do military ones, and that his accomplishment is not at all comparable to one who is simply good at crass acrobatics.

It took me some thirty-odd short stories to catch on to all these little things. But "catching on" to them is one thing and whether or not you are able to make use of them to improve your writing is entirely another. Thoughts like these make me apprehensive about my future work. But who knows, maybe an old ox pulling a rickety cart gets stronger the farther he goes.

During the War of Resistance, a hectic and unsettled life coupled with illness made it extremely difficult for me to do novels. I didn't write all that many short stories for that matter, for apart from the above mentioned factors, I was also newly trying my hand at plays and poetry. In the three years from 1938 until 1941 I only wrote some ten short stories. They are to be found in the two collections *Train* and *Thin Blood. Thin Blood*—that title was most appropriate, for from the winter of 1940 until now (the spring of 1944), I have suffered from anemia. In the winter of each of those years, if I worked until I got a little tired, I'd get dizzy, and then if I didn't rest immediately, that dizziness would invariably progress to fainting spells. I'd raise my head and the whole world would go spinning. When it got a little warmer, my dizzy spells would decrease and I'd pick up my pen again and write. Logically, I ought to have simply taken off for an extended recuperation, perhaps six months or even a year. But I didn't want to slack off that long and I certainly didn't want to live from hand-to-mouth on what I could borrow. And so it was that whenever my illness improved a bit, I'd write something. When I was too sick to get up at all, then, of course, I had no choice but "to live unfettered from daily cares." And so as my health went down-hill, my works deteriorated right along with it. I am ashamed to say that in those two collections, *Train* and *Thin Blood,* you won't find a single presentable story!

Since they were as bad as all that, why bother to publish them in the first place? That's easy. When I was bedridden, I couldn't even write bad stuff! Besides, lousy as they were, they were still—after all—my heart's blood! When I was too sick to get out of bed, that meant I had to stop working altogether. If I didn't take the crummy stories I'd written when somewhat better and exchange them for cash, how was I supposed to live? Well, at any rate, *Train* and *Thin Blood* ought to be considered in that light.[12]

Notes

1. The first four stories in *Deadliners* are (1) "May Ninth" (Wujiu), (2) "Hot Dumplings" (Re baozi), (3) "Love's Little Devil" (Ai de xiaogui), and (4) "Mutual Pact" (Tongmeng).

2. In addition to "By the Temple of Great Compassion," this group would include the following twenty-eight stories (1) "Quitting" (Cigong), (2) "Buying a Lottery Ticket" (Caipiao), (3) "Crooktails" (Waimaor), (4) "Vision" (Weishen), (5) "The Grand Opening" (Kaishi daji), (6) "Talkies (You-sheng dianying), (7) "The Liu Family Courtyard" (Liujia dayuan), (8) "The Grandson" (Baosun), (9) "Also a Triangle" (Ye shi sanjiao), (10) "Black Li and White Li" (Heibai li), (11) "The Eyeglasses" (Yanjing), (12) "Iron Ox and Sick Duck" (Tieniu yu bingya), (13) "Sacrifice" (Xisheng), (14) "The Prescription" (Zhuayao), (15) "The One from Liu Village" (Liutun de), (16) "Life Choices" (Shengmie), (17) "Assuming Office" (Shangren), (18) "Withdrawing Cash" (Quqian), (19) "Portrait Painting" (Huaxiang), (20) "Second Brother Shen Gets a Raise" (Shen erge jiale xinshui), (21) "An Old Man's Romance" (Laonianren de langman), (22) "The Last Dollar" (Mo yikuai qian), (23) "At the Yuxing Bath House" (Yuxing chi li), (24) "Caterpillar" (Maomao chong), (25) "Creation Sickness" (Chuangzao bing), (26) "An Old and Established Name" (Lao zihao), (27) "Neighbors" (Linjumen), (28) "The Philanthropist" (Shan-ren).

3. A Christian University in Jinan, Shandong Province, where Lao She first taught upon his return to China in 1930 after a five-year teaching stint in London.

4. A Catholic paper published in China between 1915 and 1949.

5. The Japanese attacked Shanghai on 28 January 1932. The Commercial Press was destroyed during the fighting that ensued and Lao

She lost the manuscript for a novel titled, "Daming Lake" (Daminghu). What he salvaged of that novel from memory became the short story "Crescent Moon" (Yueyar).

6. Paul Bady identifies him as Wang Pingling. See Paul Bady, trans., *Lao niu po che: Essai autocritique sur le roman et l'humour* (Lao niu po che: Self-critical essay on fiction and humor) (Bulletin de la Maison Franco-Japonaise, Nouvelle Série, Tome IX, Nos. 3–4) (Paris: Presses Universitaires de France, 1974): 60.

7. This should be John Davys Beresford (1873–1947). The proper title of the story is "The Misanthrope." Included in *Nineteen Impressions* by John Davys Beresford, first published in 1918 and reprinted in 1969 by the Short Story Index Reprint Series (Freeport, New York: Books for Libraries Press).

8. In Chinese the pronunciation of the two characters *shan,* "to fan," and *shan,* "to edit," is identical.

9. It is difficult to find an exact equivalent for *wuxia.* Novels of the *wuxia* type usually describe groups outside the law, well versed in the military arts, which are passed down within the group from master to disciple. In their skills the heroes or heroines are often near-magical.

10. *"Xiahui fenjie,"* a stock storyteller's expression designed to bring his or her auditors back for the next session.

11. *Zhongpian xiaoshuo.* Chinese fiction customarily falls into three divisions: the short story *(duanpian xiaoshuo);* the middle-length story *(zhongpian xiaoshuo);* and the novel *(changpian xiaoshuo).*

12. The last two paragraphs were added by Lao She's widow, Hu Jieqing, on the basis of manuscripts she discovered after her husband's death.

Translator's Postscript
The Man and the Stories

1: The Man

As the years roll by since the death of Lao She[1] at the hands of the Red Guards in 1966 and especially since his political rehabilitation in 1978, more and more is known of Lao She's life. In discussing some modern Chinese authors one begins with a detailed biography designed to demonstrate why his or her stories are significant against the historical or social sweep of the period in which they are set. Not so with Lao She. First and foremost, he was a creative writer: one reads the stories because they are good as stories, not because they are historically significant. In this brief introduction to his life, people are emphasized (his mother, uncle, siblings, as well as his own children) because that is how one pictures Lao She—always among people, always interested in their lives, in their stories. Perhaps that explains in part why his writing is never about sharing this or that great "ism" with his readers. He was always immersed in and fascinated by the kaleidoscope of humankind. This is particularly true of his short stories.

Lao She, pen name of Shu Qingchun, was born to a Manchu family in Beijing in 1899.[2] From a purely Chinese point of view, the Manchus were an alien group that swept down from the northeast (that part of present-day China to the north of Korea), conquered China in 1644, and then established

273

the Qing Dynasty, which lasted until the Republican Revolution of 1911. By the time of Lao She's birth, the Manchus had been largely sinified, and some of them—Lao She's own family is an example—even lived in straitened circumstances. The Shu family was large; Shu Qingchun (Lao She) was one of eight children; only five of them survived into adulthood. After the death of his father, an imperial guard who was killed in the fighting that took place when the Eight-Nation Allied Powers occupied Beijing in the wake of the Boxer Rebellion of 1900, the Shus were downright poor. As Lao She remembers it:

> *Father died in the year 1900 during the Boxer Uprising. The army of the Allied Forces entered the city and went from door to door grabbing property, chickens and ducks. Our house was "searched" twice. Mother sat against the wall with my brother and third sister, leaving the door onto the street ajar, and waited for the foreign "devils" to come. The "devils" came in through the door, bayonetted our old yellow dog, and then ransacked the house. Only after they were gone did Mother find me under an old trunk, which would have crushed me had it not been empty. Our emperor had run away, Father had died, there were foreign invaders everywhere you looked, and the entire city was engulfed in blood and fire. Despite all of this, Mother remained fearless.*[3]

At that time, the elder children having already moved away, the household consisted of five people: Lao She, his mother, two brothers, and his father's widowed sister. His mother supported this group with any work she could find and by taking in sewing and laundry. Had it not been for a rich uncle, it is likely that Lao She would have remained illiterate, as was his strong and much-loved mother. His early education was arranged by that rich uncle, who entered his nephew in an old-style private school when the boy was nine.

When he was fourteen, Lao She passed the entrance examination for the Beijing Normal School and graduated in 1918 when he was nineteen. Immediately upon graduation, he was appointed principal of a primary school. During the next few years he worked in various capacities in China's new and evolving system of modern education. He did this at a time when many of his contemporaries were engaged in political movements or campaigning for various social causes. Lao She did not: he couldn't afford to. For this reason, perhaps, in his fiction he is virtually alone among the authors of this period in viewing students—the sacred leaders of the various movements associated with the New Culture Movement launched 4 May 1919—with an irreverent eye.

In 1922 when he was twenty-three, he became a Christian. He was baptized in the Gangwashi Church in west Beijing. In the same year he translated "The Ideal Society in Christianity" (Jidujiao de datong zhuyi), an essay by Bao Guanglin, a Chinese who had studied theology at London University. During this time Lao She and Bao were frequent companions, and it was Bao who, the following year, introduced Lao She to Professor Robert Kenneth Evans at Yanjing University. Evans allowed Lao She to audit classes in English in his spare time. This was a very important event in Lao She's life, for it was Professor Evans who recommended him for a position at London University's School of Oriental Studies, where he was to teach the Chinese classics as well as colloquial Mandarin. Lao She would remain in London from 1924 until 1930, and those years would change his life.

While in London, in order to improve his grasp of the language at first, he read widely in English literature; he particularly admired the works of Charles Dickens. "I could do that," he told himself. And he did. The result was his first novel, *The Philosophy of Lao Zhang,* which told the story of a humorously corrupt schoolteacher and some of his students.[4] The very activity of writing probably did much to combat his loneliness in London and to some extent, no doubt, served to satisfy his nostalgia for Beijing as he recreated its sights, sounds, and smells with his pen.

At best this novel was a mixed bag. When it was published serially back in China in *The Short Story Monthly* (beginning in 1926), however, it was an immediate success. Lu Xun (1881–1936), perhaps the best-known writer of modern Chinese literature at that time, opined that it was spotty in terms of technique but acknowledged that it was rich in Beijing color. Let us note in passing that Lao She wrote largely in a modified Beijing dialect and that his writing influenced a whole generation: the Ministry of Education, in compiling textbooks on how to write modern Chinese, often quoted Lao She's works as examples of good contemporary Chinese usage.

Behind most of Lao She's prose many readers sense a writer who is not too different from themselves—a basically decent human being whose heart is in the right place. For that reason, perhaps, most readers are prepared to forgive the writer his flaws rather than to seek them out. In the majority of his works, unlike many of his peers, Lao She offers the reader no new way of viewing the world but rather supposes that both writer and reader have a firm sense of how things should be. It is significant in this regard that he often assumes the guise of first-person narrator and addresses the reader as *zamen,* or "we"—a northern expression that is used when the speaker or writer assumes that we all belong to the same group and roughly have the same way of seeing the world.

He returned to China in 1930 to find himself already famous as a novelist. The following year, at the relatively late age of thirty-two, he married Hu Jieqing, at that time a student at Beijing Normal University. From 1930 until 1936 the couple spent most of their time in Shandong Province, where Lao She taught at Qilu University in the city of Jinan and then Shandong University in the port city of Qingdao. It was during this period that he wrote many of the short stories in the present collection. The Eight Year War of Resistance against Japan (Kangzhan banian) broke out in 1937. In order to better serve the wartime needs of the country, Lao She left Jinan and went to Wuhan, where he was elected head of the general office of the All-China Resistance League of Writers and Artists. The following year he went to the Guomindang capital-in-exile, Chongqing, in Sichuan Province. He remained there until the end of the war in 1945. When he went to Wuhan to join the war effort, he left two unfinished novels in Jinan: "Sick Man" (Bingfu) and "Autobiography of a Minor Character" (Xiao renwu zishu). Only the serialized first installment of the latter ever appeared in print and a carefully annotated translation appears in the Appendix.

During the War of Resistance, Mao Zedong, as the head of the Communist Party, and Chiang Kaishek, as head of the Nationalist Party, called off their civil war to present a united front against Japan. The Communist capital was in Yan'an, the Nationalist one, in Chongqing. Although Lao She visited Yan'an in 1939, it is probable that his prolonged stay in the Nationalist capital during the war adversely affected the way he was viewed after the establishment of the People's Republic in 1949.

When Lao She went to Wuhan in 1937, his immediate family consisted of his wife, two daughters (Shu Ji, born in 1933, and Shu Yu, born in 1937), and a son (Shu Yi, born in 1935).[5] His wife and children stayed in Jinan until 1938 and then went back to Beijing where they remained under Japanese occupation until 1943 when Hu Jieqing, her three children in tow, braved an arduous fifty-three day journey to wartime Chongqing, thus reuniting the family. Her recounting of that adventure, which I have heard firsthand, is quite dramatic. Lao She's youngest daughter, Shu Li, was born in Chongching in 1945.

Lao She's entire life was distinguished by dynamic energy and constant hard work. The result was the prolific production of literature across a gamut of genres. In 1937 his best-known novel was published, *Camel Luckylad* (Luotuo xiangzi). In the United States the title was translated as *Rickshaw Boy* by Evan King in 1945 and became an American best-seller soon after its publication. King took the unfortunate liberty of giving the work a happy ending. Since 1979 we have had a faithful translation under the title *Rickshaw* by Jean James (University of Hawai'i Press), and another from the hand of Shi Xiaoqing under the title, *Camel Xiangzi* (Foreign Languages Press, Beijing) in 1981.

During the War of Resistance (1937–1945), Lao She's literary life changed utterly. With more enthusiasm and energy than most writers of his generation, he threw himself wholeheartedly into the war effort, serving varied literary organizations in high administrative posts with unflagging energy. Putting aside other literary projects he was engaged in at the time, he unstintingly turned his many-sided talent to the writing of popular propaganda—drum songs, plays, scripts for comedians, and so on.

In 1946, after the war had drawn to a close, Lao She was invited to spend a year in the United States by the State Department under its cultural cooperation program. He remained on for an extended tour, returning to China only in 1949 after the founding of the People's Republic. In the 1950s he wrote plays, short stories, and articles on the art of writing. He also rose to become chairman of the Beijing branch of the All-China Federation of Writers and Artists. His pre-1949 works, however, were largely judged unacceptable by the new arbiters of literary taste. It was objected that in most of them his sense of justice as well as his compassion for the oppressed were weakened by his humor, and he himself once admitted as much. Despite this, however, he was given points for his poverty in youth, his love of the oppressed, his love of China, and his tireless efforts in remolding himself. He was even honored with the title of People's Artist.

In the 1960s there were increasing signs that he was in trouble. Then in September of 1966 the Red Guards accused him of being anti-Mao, anti-Party, and anti-People. On 23 August 1966, as part of a frenzied campaign to obliterate the "four olds" (old ideas, customs, culture, and habits), Red Guards torched a pile of Beijing opera costumes and props in the courtyard of the Confucian Temple. At the same time and at the same location, they called to account more than thirty famous writers and artists. Lao She was harangued and then beaten until he lost consciousness. His son, Shu Yi, has said:

> Put simply it was Father who was beaten the worst, the blood from his cut head turning his white shirt completely red. His head was roughly bandaged with the white sleeve from one of the Peking opera costumes, but blood had seeped through and his appearance was enough to shock anyone.[6]

In an effort to rescue him from his ordeal, members of the Municipal Literary League, his place of employment and the place from which the Red Guards had snatched him earlier that day, succeeded in getting him back to the league's offices. Unfortunately more Red Guards had massed there, and Lao She "felt the full brunt of their belts, fists, boots, curses, and spittle."[7] Finally, at two o'clock in the morning, Hu Jieqing was allowed to bring him home in a pedicab. The Red Guards had ordered him to appear for work at the league's offices that day. He did in fact manage to leave for work the morning of the twenty-fourth, but that's the last time his family saw him alive.

> *The morning of the second day, 25 August, was also spent*
> *waiting and it was not until that afternoon that the*
> *Municipal Literary League phoned up to say that I should*
> *go over to their offices. They brought out a certificate and*
> *handed it to me. On it was written, "Shu Sheyu [Lao She*
> *is his pen name]*[8] *of our League has divorced himself from*
> *the people by taking his own life. This is a specially issued*
> *certificate to this effect." They had spent practically the*
> *whole day drafting this document and determining the*
> *"correct" analysis of Lao She's death.*[9]

Shu Yi was told to go to Taiping Lake to pick up his father's body. He has come to believe that Lao She actually did drown himself there even though there was no parting note. In 1978, two years after the end of the ten-year Great Proletarian Cultural Revolution that had begun the year that Lao She died, an official funeral was held with the highest government authorities in attendance. His name was posthumously cleared of all charges brought against him by the Red Guards.

After the death of Chairman Mao and the subsequent fall of the "Gang of Four"[10] in 1976, Lao She's work began to regain some of its former recognition. Views of him, now positive, continued to be somewhat one-sided, however, in that the works that were brought out again were primarily the socially conscious novel, *Rickshaw,* and the politically correct play, *Teahouse* (Chaguan). When I taught a course at Beijing University in 1987 with some such title as "An American View of the Modern Chinese Short Story," I found that most of my students knew that Lao She was known as a humorist, but they didn't understand why. The reason, of course, was that his humorous novels and stories had not been republished.

That, thankfully, is no longer the case. Perhaps in the future a complete works of Lao She will be be published and provided with the same loving annotation as the *Complete Works of Lu Xun,* 16 vols., (Beijing: Renmin wenxue chubanshe, 1982).

2: The Stories

Why read Chinese short stories at all? To learn about China? Perhaps. To study modern Chinese stories as a literary form? Possibly. Because they are enjoyable? In the case of Lao She the answer is a resounding yes! For the analytically minded reader, another question may rear its inquisitive head: what *makes* them enjoyable? That's pretty easy—Lao She! Perhaps some of our more logically minded readers may object: "Aha! What have we here—an innocent, unsophisticated, even primitive, view of literature? Is not the presumption behind that somewhat effusive affirmation of Lao She that the personality of the author is reflected in and guarantees the quality of the work?" Possibly. But the proof is in the stories. When the reader has digested them, even in our imperfect translations, he or she may just agree with us.

In teaching classes on modern Chinese literature, one often has to explain to American students why this or that Chinese writer is considered "good" or "important." Not so with Lao She. Students read and like Lao She in such a way as to appropriate him as their own, so much so that they resent the intrusion of the busybody critic who earns his keep by telling them *why* Lao She is good. From an individual vantage point, each student knows—and knows possessively—exactly why Lao She is good and doesn't want anyone meddling with that personal conception.

Personal conceptions will unavoidably influence the way one translates Lao She as well. Wei-ming and I make no apologies for that. She has her Lao She; I have mine. To keep our translations from coming out totally at odds, however, we have read each other's work and made suggestions for revisions; nonetheless, our different Lao Shes speak with slightly different voices. Far from apologizing for this, we consider it desirable. We hope that the reader will come away from our *Blades of Grass* with a more accurate impression of Lao She's own voice than would be the case if either of us had done all the translations.

There is perhaps no better place to begin a discussion of the stories than "Autobiography of a Minor Character."[11] Much of this fictional autobiography closely corresponds with what we know of the early life of Lao She. A close reading of the stories themselves will also reveal that this fictionalized memoir does much to explain the writing style of the author. There is, for instance, a delightful section in which the narrator compares the severe and abstract lines of the buildings one finds in the Imperial Palace with the chaotic but down-to-earth lines of the impoverished family compound in which he grew up. After describing his home in some detail, the narrator comments:

> *I often have this rather comical fear that if I had not had such a home in my childhood or that if I had moved here one day and moved there the next, I wouldn't have accumulated these treasured paintings. People with brains may consider abolishing private ownership. Some intellectuals may advocate the destruction of the family system. But in my mind, if all private ownership were like our rickety old house and our two jujube trees, I would be happy to declare myself a conservative. Because even though what we possessed didn't relieve us from our poverty, it did provide us that stability that made each blade of grass and each tree come alive in our hearts.* (page 244)

Whoever would cite this to show that Lao She was a political conservative would miss the point entirely. The narrator—and Lao She, we believe—is simply stressing his preference for the concrete realities of everyday life, not making some grand statement about economic or political systems.

> *I once visited the Forbidden City. . . . Everywhere one ran into walls, and everywhere it was neat and orderly. It was stately and dignified all right, but I really doubt that the crown prince ever saw a pumpkin vine growing on a screen wall.* (page 246)

The veteran reader of Lao She's fiction will, we believe, see in the above paragraphs too much that rings true of his approach to life, as revealed in his novels and short stories, to dismiss it as a somewhat comfortable and stereotypic presentation of the advantages of a humble life over a privileged one. Throughout the corpus of Lao She's fiction, one will find a marked preference for the concrete over the abstract and an intense interest in the little things of life, even its apparent trivialities. Toward the end of "Autobiography of a Minor Character," the narrator—in a manner that today appears a tad sexist—ascribes his interest in the domestic details of life to the influence of women.

> *I had a mother but no father, an aunt but no uncle, an Auntie Guan but no Uncle Guan. . . . When I saw children with fathers it actually felt strange. Needless to say, as time passed I came close to becoming like a woman. I managed and took care of all matters in great detail like women. As a result, I always looked down on a woman who couldn't or didn't like to take care of household matters, no matter how interesting and how learned she was.* (page 252)

An interest in the concrete details of life accounts for much of Lao She's practiced skill as a writer. He is a man who is forever interested in the look and feel of those little things in which our lives are immersed. Whereas T. S. Eliot's Prufrock laments that "I have measured out my life in coffee spoons," Lao She's characters might well, on the contrary, rejoice in having measured out their lives in "cups of tea." Not for Lao She the abstractions of politics or philosophy—or the neat, straight, and imposing lines of the Imperial Palace. A plate of Chinese dumplings just out of boiling water, a pair of chopsticks, the interior of a silk store, rickshaws hurtling over or dragging along Beijing's streets and alleys, punishing winter winds against which the old are helpless—these details are the stuff of his fiction, the staples of his metaphors, and he loves these little things of life as much as the words with which he describes them.

Chinese readers have often said that no matter what Lao She *seems* to be writing about, he is in fact almost always talking about the same thing, and that is *wulun,* or the five cardinal relationships of traditional society: (1) ruler-subject, (2) father-son, (3) husband-wife, (4) brother-brother, and (5) friend-friend. One might object that you can say that about a whole host of authors contemporary with Lao She. Perhaps. Yet most readers of Lao She's fiction—even in translation—are likely to agree with the statement, for if nothing else, it underscores the emphasis of his works. "Black Li and White Li" is an excellent example.[12] Played out against a background of rapid, even revolutionary social change, the story is fundamentally about the relationship between two brothers and the deep friendship of one of them with the narrator, a man who displays a typical persona of the author—warmhearted, friendly, and intensely loyal.

By Lao She's own testimony, "Black Li and White Li" is one of three stories he wrote on the basis of an idea.[13] The plot was apparently conceived in answer to the question, What would happen if a conservative elder brother (nicknamed "Black Li" in honor of a mole on his face) and a radical younger brother (nicknamed "White Li" because of the absence of any such distinguishing mark) confronted the phenomenon of social revolution? The family rickshaw puller, Wang Wu, makes a telling comparison of the brothers when he describes them to the story's first-person narrator:

> [White Li] couldn't care less about my legs, but he cares about the way I feel. [Black Li] worries about every pid-dlin' little thing inside the family and he's got real sympa-thy for my legs, but he really doesn't care about me here." He pointed to his chest. . . . (page 62)

It is apparent that the narrator, like so many of Lao She's first-person narrators, is rather conservative—more like Black than White Li. The latter is a man of modern China, a man given to the abstract and ideological, while his brother, representing tradition, is given to the concrete and emotional. And yet the relationship between the brothers *as brothers* transcends all these differences.

Like Black Li and the narrator of the story, Lao She was a man more interested in life—of Beijing life in particular. Another indication of the rather conservative cast of Lao She's thought is to be found in the fact that in setting the back-ground of his stories, he often seems to take for granted social situations that, in the hands of another author, might provide the basis for an indignant tale of exposure. In the short story "Neighbors," for example, wife-beating is treated as a subject of mild humor.[14]

The Mings and the Yangs are neighbors; the Yangs are modern and educated, the Mings more traditional. Mr. Ming admires the pretty, young Mrs. Yang from afar. Conscious of this admiration, Mrs. Ming is jealous and hence refuses to accept a letter sent over from the Yangs, much to the displeasure of her husband—so much so that she receives a beating over the letter, which Lao She describes in the following words:

> *Mr. Ming was fastidious about some things and would never demean himself by screaming or shouting while beating his wife, but Mrs. Ming, the recipient of the beating, was not equally as fussy about preserving such niceties. She wailed and howled for all she was worth, and her children helped out as well.* (page 139)

The flippant tone in which he describes the beating does not by any means, of course, indicate that Lao She condones it. He doesn't. The emphasis of his fiction, however, is far more often on plot than on political agenda or any other theme. Wife-beating is simply part of the social background that people at that time took for granted as a social given.

There is a similar example of Lao She's taking the social background of society for granted in "Also a Triangle" when the rickshaw puller, Old Lin Four, sells his daughter to a venal and unscrupulous matchmaker. Lao She does not condemn him for this: given his poverty and the society of those times, Old Lin Four has little choice. Yet this is not the center of the story. It is the background against which the following basic plot develops: two soldiers, neither of whom can afford a wife, pool their money and buy one in common. Neither does Lao She condemn the two soldiers. They are not wicked men, but what happens to Old Lin Four and his daughter *is* evil and is presented as such. All these people live in a society dominated by a money economy that corrupts everyone in it.

While on the subject of money, we might point out that the contemporary American scholar Ranbir Vohra argues rather persuasively that Lao She came to see the emergence of a modern money economy as "the key problem of his age." That is certainly true of "Also a Triangle" and even more true of another story included in this book, "Life Choices," a story that describes a young couple who were classmates in college and have been married for two years since their graduation as the story opens. Even though they have only one child, in the China of the 1930s they find it very difficult to make ends meet. The last thing in the world they want is a second child. Thus Mei is somewhat relieved when a Chinese doctor assures her she is not pregnant. She continues, however, to experience the early signs of pregnancy and decides to consult a Western doctor who, to her dismay, tells her that she is in fact going to have a baby. Husband and wife consider an abortion:

> They checked all the hospitals. The French hospital was Catholic—definitely no abortions there. The American hospital was Protestant—not permitted to deal in such things . . . . Only the Japanese Yalu Hospital specialized in it; fees for the procedure were high, hospital charges steep, but they had the experience and the facilities and, moreover, were willing to kill Chinese fetuses.
>
> To go or not to go? (page 124)

During the time when Lao She did most of his creative writing, many Chinese of a conservative bent found meaning in the traditional systems of Chinese thought, particularly Confucianism, and under the banner "Preserve the National Heritage" (Baocun guocui), they proclaimed the sacred duty of every Chinese to defend virtually everything that was traditional. With typical acuity, Lao She's contemporary Lu Xun tersely pointed out that the real question was not whether the Chinese could preserve the national heritage, but the other way around. Contemporaries of more modernist inclinations looked for meaning in ideologies newly imported from abroad, such as Marxism and Democracy. If one judges from his fiction, Lao She was singular in that he found meaning in the moral standards of ordinary Chinese urban dwellers of the middle and lower classes; in his writings you will find a wide and varied array of characters from this group.

In "Ah Q—the Real Story," Lu Xun took what he saw as the weaknesses of the Chinese people and concentrated them in the person of one man, Ah Q. His standard of judgment was informed by readings in Chinese and foreign literatures as well as the theories of such thinkers as Charles Darwin. Of a far less philosophic leaning, Lao She took ordinary people, told stories about them, and judged them with an almost instinctive knowledge of what was right and what was wrong. Unlike Lu Xun, he wasn't trying to teach his readers anything they didn't already know at a gut level. He knew that, like the storytellers in the marketplace, he shared a common morality with those who came to hear, or, in his case, read his stories. Thus the use of the inclusive *zamen* by many of Lao She's narrators announces that we are all friends here and share the same ethics. In this regard Lao She stands closer to writers of popular fiction like Zhang Henshui (1895–1967) than he does to the writers of the high May Fourth Tradition.

We know what is right and what is wrong because we learned it from parents, relatives, and friends as we grew up. It is a knowledge that makes us decent human beings and gives us our integrity. The most reprehensible thing we can do in life is to lose that integrity. In Lao She's only satirical novel, *Cat Country*,[15] an enlightened young Martian—the story unfolds in a country on Mars populated by citizens resembling cats—named Scorpion explains the history of Cat Country's modern system of education to the first-person narrator, a visitor from Earth:

"If even our old system of education was able to foster honesty, a love of parents, and an obedience to rules, how is it that the new and improved system has failed to make a comparable showing? Everybody says—especially the educators themselves—that it is because of the dark evils of society. But whose responsibility is it to get rid of those evils? The educators know only how to blame social conditions, but have entirely forgotten that their responsibility lies precisely in making society a better place to live in. To be sure, society is black, but they have forgotten that their own personal integrity should serve as a bright star in the night sky." (Cat Country, page 180)

If we take *Cat Country* as China, and Scorpion as a spokesman for Lao She, the message is clearly a conservative one: institutional change will, in and of itself, never guarantee the well-being of the Chinese nation, for that is something that can be accomplished only through the dedication and morality of individuals.[16]

In the short stories as well, we occasionally find the bitter-sweet recognition that personal integrity, no matter how striking the heroism of the individuals involved, may not be enough. "An Old and Established Name" is a case in point. The story details the collapse of a traditional Beijing silk store, a business failure that the chief apprentice of the store, despite his indisputable integrity and heroic dedication, is powerless to prevent. At a slightly deeper level, the story can also be seen as a chronicle of the demise of traditional China. One can perhaps see traditional Chinese people as apprentices in Chinese culture, a culture that, like the Fortune Silk Store, governed the smallest details of one's daily life. The Fortune is "an old and established name" with a glorious history behind it, but, like China itself, the store proves helpless in the face of modern, rationalized business practices. The senior apprentice at the

Fortune, Xin Dezhi, watches in dismay as newer stores with no traditions or ethics prosper.

> *The Village had prospered, while the Fortune had gone downhill day after day. But why? He couldn't figure it out. It certainly couldn't be that there was an inexorable law at work that* required *a business be run completely divorced from any code of ethics before it could make money. If this were really the case, then why should stores even bother to train apprentices? Couldn't any old oaf off the street do business just as long as he was alive and kicking?* (page 20)

The answer, of course, is yes, for modernized businesses are more abstract and rationalized than traditional ones and therefore more efficient and profitable as well. In such establishments clerks *are* virtually interchangeable and "any old oaf off the street" will do just fine, thank you. Stores are no longer integral parts of an old neighborhood, where Mr. So-and-so who attended my daughter's wedding last August runs the local dry goods shop and has a reputation for "knowing his silks," but are rather retail outlets vending the mass-produced materials that come out of large and impersonal factories. Similarly people who live in modern states are citizens of this or that country rather than vehicles of "old and established cultures" that regulate every detail of one's life. There is no longer a necessity for training apprentices any more than there is a need to steep every Chinese in the traditions of the past. Like the Fortune, traditional Chinese society is slipping silently into a past where it becomes an object of study rather than the author of meaning.

From his earliest writings on, one of Lao She's favorite objects of derision is the concept of *wenming*, a term that became common coin among intellectuals and then society at large in the nineteenth century; it meant "civilized," "cultured," or even "enlightened," depending on context. It is ironic that China, which prided itself on millennia of civilization, should somehow become convinced—at least among intellectuals— that it was not *wenming*, at least in the modern sense conveyed by the term. Since virtually all modern things came from abroad, *wenming* also simply connoted "foreign."[17] In the early part of the twentieth century, spoken plays, for example, as distinguished from traditional Chinese operas, were referred to as "civilized operas" *(wenming xi);* a gentleman's "walking stick" (newly introduced from abroad) was called a "civilized stick"; and nontraditional weddings were known as "civilized weddings" *(wenming jiehun).*[18] During the time when Lao She wrote most of his fiction, *wenming* continued to mean "modernized" or "foreignized."

Lao She found thoroughly offensive the idea that modern, foreign things were considered "civilized" while traditional Chinese ones were not. We find the idea roundly criticized in "Neighbors," a story that has been discussed earlier in a different context. Young Mr. and Mrs. Yang, both teachers, have been bullied by their neighbors the Mings as well as the Ming children. Nonetheless, in his dealings with the Mings, young Mr. Yang has always been the perfect, civilized gentleman. He has become so "educated" and "civilized" that he no longer understands how to stand up for his own rights. He returns home one evening just after the Ming children, acting on their parents' orders, have utterly vandalized the Yang yard.

> He tried to collect himself so that he might objectively consider his options. . . .
> Try as he would, though, he was no longer capable of objectivity. That tiny drop of barbarian blood that was

left in him after so much education boiled up and made
dispassionate thought impossible. He tore off his coat and
gathered up an armful of bricks. Taking careful aim
across the wall at the windows in the Ming house, he
let fly. (page 143)

Could not this same story have been written in the United
States or England during the 1930s? Perhaps, but the emphasis
would have psychological rather than nationalistic overtones;
in the China of that time, rejecting "civilization" and extolling
"barbarism" (foreigners saw Chinese ways of doing things as
"barbaric") was an in-your-face reclamation of one's pride in
being Chinese. In standing up to Mr. Ming, young Mr. Yang
is indirectly standing up for China against a lackey dog of
Western imperialism, who bullies his Chinese neighbor yet
fawns before his foreign employers.

The protagonist of "Crooktails" (Waimao'er) sounds more
interested in society at large than do most of the other characters with which Lao She peoples his stories. Much like Lu
Xun's madman in "Diary of a Madman," Bai Renlu sees people
as they really are when his "sickness" is on him. In this case the
illness involved is a change in his eyes that enables him to see
through people's outer facades to what they really are—
"repulsive." When Renlu's friend, the first-person narrator,
suggests that what Renlu sees as contemptible in people is
actually only weakness, he suggests that everybody is subject
to "weaknesses, but that doesn't necessarily make them
repulsive." Bai Renlu replies:

> *"No, I'm not talking about weaknesses. A weakness can*
> *disgust you but it can also call forth your compassion and*
> *sympathy—give you the sort of feeling you have toward a*
> *friend who's an alcoholic. Actually, you can observe the*
> *sort of thing I'm talking about even without these sick eyes*

> *of mine. . . . When you look at a person, don't look at the whole face, but just the eyes, nose, and mouth—especially the eyes. For example look into the eyes of someone who's lecturing you on such grand themes as benevolence and righteousness, and if you look closely enough, you'll see vivid pornographic images flickering there. And even while that person's mouth is spouting all that righteous crap, you'll see a grin on the lips! A grin!"* (page 155)

This may well remind readers of Lu Xun of my translated passage in "Diary of a Madman" (*Diary of a Madman and Other Stories* [Honolulu: University of Hawaiʻi Press, 1990]) where the diarist reports his experience in reading history:

> *You have to* really *go into something before you can understand it. I seemed to remember, though not too clearly, that from ancient times on people have often been eaten, and so I started leafing through a history book to look it up. There were no dates in this history, but scrawled this way and that across every page were the words* BENEVOLENCE, RIGHTEOUSNESS, *and* MORALITY. *Since I couldn't get to sleep anyway, I read that history very carefully for most of the night, and finally I began to make out what was written* between *the lines; the whole volume was filled with a single phrase:* EAT PEOPLE! (page 32)

Between Lao She and Lu Xun, however, there is a significant difference. Lu Xun is interested in his characters only insofar as he can utilize them to reveal truths about Chinese society as well as themes in his own thinking; Lao She, on the other hand, is interested in Bai Renlu as an individual about whom he has an interesting and extended anecdote to tell. To be sure, there are political and nationalistic overtones, but the focus is on this particular individual.

Lao She, by his own testimony, got the idea for "Crooktails" from J. D. Beresford's "The Misanthrope," a story which so impressed him that he translated it into Chinese in 1931 as "The Hermit" (Yinzhe). He was apparently attracted to the gimmick that lies at the center of Beresford's story: the hermit protagonist sees people as they really are whenever he looks back at them over his shoulder, and what they really are is so dreadful to behold that he becomes a hermit in order to avoid the agony of seeing that way. Lao She, the craftsman, was so intrigued by the possibilities of this device that he decided to put it in a totally Chinese setting, and the result was "Crooktails." According to Lao She's lifelong friend, the noted linguist and philologist, Lo Changpei (1899–1958), the story reflects their experiences together in primary school.[19]

As is commonly known, Lu Xun's "Diary of a Madman" was inspired by Nikolai Gogol's story of the same title. Lu Xun, however, was not fascinated with the story per se, so much as he was with the possibility of using it as a means of revealing the truth about Chinese history and society as he saw it. In Lu Xun's writing, the social philosopher is predominant; with Lao She, the conerns of the fiction writer are foremost.

Few things in Lao She's fiction are either all good or all bad. However intense his nostalgia for traditional Chinese culture may have been, it did not prevent him from lambasting its shortcomings. In his very first novel, *The Philosophy of Lao Zhang*,[20] for example, there is a charming description of a kind and loving woman, Auntie Zhao, who, because of her traditional mentality, does much to contribute to the suffering of her orphaned niece, whom she sincerely loves. Illiterate and more toward the bottom of the social scale than the top, it is inconceivable to this warmhearted woman that young people ought to choose their own mates. In presenting the relationship between Auntie Zhao and her niece, Lao She inserts an authorial intrusion on the subject of love, in which he says

If people cannot have the freedom to love, all other free-
doms are phony; if people cannot enjoy love between the
two sexes, all other forms of love are meaningless.
(The Philosophy of Lao Zhang, page 84*)*

Many authors contemporary with Lao She would have presented
Auntie Zhao as a thoroughly contemptible representative of
the elder generation doing everything in her power to suppress
youth. Typically, Lao She does not. This characteristic of his
writing often lends a bittersweet flavor to his work. In Auntie
Zhao's case, he realizes that an otherwise wonderful old lady,
deluded by traditional beliefs, can be capable of contemptible
acts. Lao She condemns the act far more often than the person.

A similarly complex way of viewing people is found in "An
Old Man's Romance." In this story, it is apparent that Lao
She does not approve of his "romantic" protagonist, Old Liu.

Name one thing in which he hadn't done right by people
or in which he hadn't given it his all. Name one thing
where he had just been a tagalong or where his strategy
had been anything less than brilliant. You couldn't! And
how about politics? Name a single influential political
party he hadn't been the first to join. Or take social wel-
fare. Name one profitable work of charity that he hadn't
launched. And how about his relationships with people
in general? Was there anyone worth cultivating that he
hadn't gotten in good with? (page 88)

In the hands of Lu Xun, someone like Old Liu would prove
ever more despicable as the story unfolded, yet as Lao She's
story develops, the reader finds it increasingly difficult to
thoroughly dislike Old Liu. Why? One might argue that in
taking us inside this sixty-year-old's mind so much during the
story, Lao She commits a tactical error: it would be easier to

despise Old Liu at a third-person distance. But as in many of the stories, Lao She slips back and forth from a third-person to a first-person stance almost without our realizing it. As we increasingly see the world from Old Liu's point of view, our understanding of him deepens and—though we may still disapprove of him—it becomes difficult to dismiss him as some monster completely different from ourselves and deserving only our scorn.

On a cold, blustery Beijing winter day, Old Liu goes out to dun a debtor, Feng Er. It has occurred to him that it lies within his power to pressure Feng Er into giving his daughter in marriage to Old Liu's moronic son. Yet as he warms himself in the emotional glow of this poor man's home, his thoughts take a different tack.

> *To be sure, out there in society, he had a need to accomplish something, to overcome Fei Zichun and his ilk. But beyond that, he needed to invigorate his home life as well—even in bed. He wasn't old. He could feel the blood coursing swiftly through his veins. . . . Well, his moronic son would just have to wait! . . . It was about time that the father gave priority to his own interests for a change. Throughout an entire lifetime, no matter how he'd schemed, Old Liu had never managed to get out in front of anyone. . . .*
>
> *He looked at the Feng girl: rosy face, big eyes, shiny black hair—a tasty morsel if ever he'd seen one. Why shouldn't he take a bite for himself? Even from her point of view, it would be a good deal: he had some money. . . . And if he died first—if—why, she'd be secure for the rest of her life. Yes, in working things out, he couldn't just think of himself. No, Old Liu was a fair man. She'd be pretty well off—plump, prosperous, and happy—all thanks to Old Liu.* (pages 103–104)

The humorous "if" in Old Liu's train of thought disposes the reader to laugh with him more than at him; rather than seeing him as the somewhat selfish, dirty old man that he is, for the moment, we begin, if ever so uncomfortably, to see him more as "one of us," a part of the *zamen* that Lao She seldom escapes even in his third-person stories. This is not to say that there are no examples of totally unsympathetic characters in Lao She's works, for there are; nor is it to say that he *intended* to present Old Liu in quite this sympathetic a light, for perhaps he didn't. It is to say that he found it easier—perhaps better suited to his own personality—to understand than to condemn.

In "Hot Dumplings," Lao She affords us an appealing glimpse of puppy love as the adult first-person narrator fondly remembers a beautiful young woman he once knew during his boyhood. "Sis-in-law Qiu," as he called her, was rather sexy; her husband, Young Qiu, alas, was not, and thereon hung the entire tale. Back then, while making allowances for her on the basis of his schoolboy's crush, even the narrator had thought her a bit too "free and easy."

He once heard her justify herself to Young Qiu for having produced no children. "What do you expect with that soft thing of yours?!" Enigmatically, Sis-in-law Qiu disappears for half a year or so, and then just as mysteriously reappears— much to the delight of both Young Qiu and the boy narrator. And that's the plot. All of it! Skimpy material for a story, and yet Lao She imbues it with such charm that the reader is likely to long remember this anecdote about Young Qiu, Sis-in-law Qiu, and the narrator. In "Hot Dumplings" we also sense that nostalgia present in many of the stories for the way things were before the intrusion of Western imperialism and the modernity that came in its wake.

Humor permeates the majority of Lao She's works. He was known for it. In 1936 he published an essay on the topic in *Cosmic Wind* [23] (Yuzhou feng) in which he said:

*Above all, humor is a frame of mind. We all know people
who are overly sensitive and always approach things with
a surcharge of emotion, never willing to make allowances
for others. . . . A person with a sense of humor is not at all
like this . . . he sees the flaws in mankind and wants to
point them out to others; however, he does not stop at
merely spotting these flaws, but goes on to positively accept
them. And thus everyone has something funny about him,
the humorist himself being no exception. . . .*
("On Humor" [Tan youmo])

In the same essay he goes on to distinguish humor from satire:

Satire must *be humorous, but is more biting . . . [it]
doesn't let us laugh contentedly, but rather makes us smile
coldly, and when we have finished smiling, then—in light
of our own conduct—[it] makes us blush. . . . A humorist
is warmhearted; the heart of the satirist is cold.*

In explaining what he saw as the failure of his only sustained
attempt at satire, *Cat Country,* he intimates that by tempera-
ment he was a humorist and for that reason his failure at satire
was a foregone conclusion.

*Friends often exhort me not to be so humorous in my
writing. I appreciate their intentions, for I too realize
that because of my humor, I often slip into being
obnoxious. But after . . . failures [like* Cat Country*], I
realize that it is most difficult to change a dog into a cat.
(Old Ox)*[21]

In most of the novels as well as the short stories contained
in the present collection, Lao She keeps his humor under

control. There is one exception, and we have included it in this volume—"The Grand Opening" (Kaishi daji), a story that borders on slapstick and represents humor gone round the bend. It opens with a characteristic first-person narrator whose tone announces that we are dealing with a different level of humor than we are accustomed to in most of Lao She's stories. The narrator, Qiu, and Wang's wife have opened a small hospital:

> No matter what kind of business you undertake and no matter how few people are involved, you just have to split up into cliques and factions—otherwise it won't look as though you're taking the whole thing very seriously, right? At any rate we had the sides all figured out in advance, and if it ever got to the point where we had to work Qiu over, then—including Wang's wife on our side—we'd have the advantage on him by three to one. His father-in-law, of course, would probably help him, but he was so old that Mrs. Wang could probably clean his clock all by herself. (page 1)

There is, of course, a note of social criticism in this fictional slapstick. Nonetheless, it is soon drowned out by the antics of the narrator and the other quacks who staff the hospital so that by the end of the story, rather than viewing the narrator and his cronies with contempt, we simply find them amusing. Perhaps this is because we see everything from inside the mind of the first-person narrator, who strikes us as more entertaining than contemptible.

Even when Lao She tells a story in the third person, he is fond of shifting in and out of the minds of his characters. He does this so often that sometimes it is difficult to tell whether Lao She is addressing the reader through the perspective of this or that character or whether he has slipped back into his favorite guise of narrator and is actually expressing his own ideas directly. Stories like "An Old Man's Romance" and "Also a Triangle" are cases in point.

Even when Lao She does switch to interior monologue, the presentation is straightforward and logical. "A Man Who Doesn't Lie" (Bushuohuang de ren) provides a good illustration. The protagonist, Zhou Wenxiang, receives a letter from the Liars' Society inviting him to join. He is indignant, but his indignation is vitiated by the events of his day. His son, Xiaochun, doesn't go to school because of a stomachache. As the story unfolds, Zhou takes his son to a practitioner of Chinese medicine, suspecting that the doctor will reveal the child's dishonesty. To his astonishment the doctor actually writes a prescription for the boy.

> *Having paid the doctor's fee, Zhou Wenxiang took the prescription and thanked him. When he took Xiaochun out, he couldn't decide whether to go get the prescription right away or simply ignore it altogether. Xiaochun was, in his opinion, not sick at all. On the other hand, giving some medicine might be just the right punishment. See if he would still pretend to have a stomachache then! But if Xiaochun wasn't sick, and the doctor wrote a prescription anyway, then the* doctor *must be lying. If he went to fill this phony prescription, it would mean he believed in the lie, and he would be a victim of the doctor's ruse. Xiaochun lied, his wife lied, and the doctor lied. Only he was honest. He thought of the Liars' Society. He had to admit it—that letter did make some sense. But he himself was, after all, an exception, so he still didn't believe altogether in that letter.* (pages 181–182)

Though we are inside Zhou's mind, as is the case in his other stories as well, we follow a logical progression of thought addressed to a single issue.

There is a very noteworthy exception to this method of presenting a character's thought in the story "Ding" (Ding), in which the shift from third-person narrator to the interior monologue in the protagonist's—his name is Ding—mind occurs in the second paragraph. From then on we see the world predominantly through Ding's mind and eyes and become quickly aware that his thought is not at all a logical progression. We are rather aware of everything that impinges on Ding's consciousness and whatever associations he happens to make—logical or no. Ding is lying on the sand at Qingdao, a port city noted for its beaches and beer. By the fourth paragraph we are completely inside Ding's head.

> *The fort, a stretch of green, can't see the cannon, a green of such poetic beauty. Yes, red when it's time to kill and green when it's idle, like phlegm. Struck the chest once. Lungs too narrow. Could it be tuberculosis? Couldn't be. The sailboats look terrific. Find a woman. Both of us in swimsuits. Get on a small sailboat, and drift, drift, drift to over there by the island. That island. Looks like a fly on blue paper. Gross! On the small boat, mess around . . . bit of romance! No, better to go up on Mount Lao. There's a Western-style restaurant. Western style, everything is Western style. China's made progress!* (page 166)

So far as we know this is Lao She's only experiment with the stream-of-consciousness technique and surely one of the earliest examples of the technique in modern Chinese fiction. It is another indication of Lao She's familiarity with, and openness toward, the experiments being made in contemporary English literature. Marshall McLuhan has claimed that we find the earliest use of what later came to be known as "stream of consciousness" in Charles Dickens' *David Copperfield*. As a reader and admirer of Dickens, Lao She was perhaps first exposed to the possibility of such a technique in that novel; it is more likely, however, that the most direct influence was from James Joyce (*Ulysses,* 1922) or Virginia Woolf (*Mrs. Dalloway,* 1925, and *To the Lighthouse,* 1927), whose novels employing the technique appeared during his sojourn in England.

The breadth and depth of his knowledge of Chinese society and his familiarity with popular forms of entertainment contributed to one of the most noteworthy stories in this collection, "Rabbit" (Tu), which is remarkable in two ways: it shows us the underbelly of one of the most prestigious Beijing art forms—the opera—and touches on the topic of homosexuality. The story contains close descriptions of the milieu of the Beijing opera and gives the reader, in effect, an introduction to the sociology of the opera world. We learn that there were three stages through which an aspiring opera performer might be transformed into a professional performer: (1) such a person would begin as a hard-core aficionado, in opera circles known as a "ticket-friend" *(piaoyou);* (2) then the ticket-friend might move to a second stage in which, despite his amateur status, he would receive under-the-table compensation for a performance, a practice referred to as "dealing in improper compensation" *(shi heichu; chu* being "opera," as well as underworld slang for "money"); and finally (3) he would become a full-blown professional, popularly known as "going to sea" *(xiahai).* Lao She describes the conventions and related economic difficulties surrounding each of the stages in some detail. The decent and warmhearted first-person narrator (in the persona of loyal friend to an unrealistic opera star wannabe) is quite typical of Lao She's shorter fiction.

The association of homosexuality with the Beijing opera is

succinctly explained in Colin Mackerras' *Chinese Drama: A Historical Survey* (Beijing: New World Press, 1990). Speaking of the system of indenture that existed from the eighteenth century on, Mackerras states:

> *Entrepreneurs bought little boys from parents in the south, principally Jiangsu and Anhui, and took them . . . to Beijing. There the boys entered training-schools in the main companies and were taught the arts of the theatre. . . . These boys may have enjoyed a fairly high standard of living if they did well, but this was an extremely exploitative system all the same. The lives of the great majority were miserable, with nothing to look forward to after a brief career on the stage. Most were forced to become homosexual, and they were merely playthings for patrons who often regarded them as little better than male prostitutes.*
> (page 66)

A selfish lack of patriotism marks the protagonist of the satirical "No Distance Too Far, No Sacrifice Too Great." Upon hearing rumors that Shanhaiguan has fallen to the Japanese, Mr. Wang's only concern is a self-centered one: let me have some fun while I still can—I'll get married! Throughout the story Lao She satirizes Mr. Wang's selfish, antiheroic way of always considering his own interests at the expense of China's. However, the author presents his protagonist in such a bizarre fashion as to make the story come across more as good fun than serious satire.

> *Couldn't get a train ticket! . . . Since he had no idea as to where he was going anyway, Mr. Wang couldn't care less whether he left from the East Station or the West one. Didn't matter where he left from as long as he got out of Peiping.*

> *Now it wasn't that he was afraid of the Japanese, mind you. Only a horse's ass would be frightened by them. It was just that on the off chance he did fall into their hands, who would be left to go get married? Be it East Station or West Station, he had to get out of Peiping; ticket or no ticket, he had to get out of Peiping.* Get out of Peiping—*that was the name of the game!*
>
> *In the midst of his quandary, Mr. Wang was seized with an inspiration. Why not go to the baggage room, slap a tag on himself, and travel as luggage. Wouldn't need a ticket. Trouble was the jackasses in the baggage room refused to take luggage that came with legs attached, so poor Mr. Wang had to content himself with calling them a bunch of shit-for-brains.* (pages 29–30)

In "No Distance Too Far, No Sacrifice Too Great" our antipathy toward Mr. Wang is mitigated by humor; we have seen social criticism softened by Lao She's humor in "The Grand Opening" and "An Old Man's Romance" as well. A weakness or a strength? We leave it to our readers to decide.

Lao She had an unusually broad knowledge of contemporary Chinese society, and the themes he dealt with in the stories were correspondingly wide ranging. For example, Chinese and foreigner alike are familiar with the penchant of some people for collecting, but few authors have been sufficiently intrigued by it to use it as a theme for fiction. Lao She does so in "Attachment," a story that might just as well have been titled "The Collector." As a study of the psychology of the collector, it is one of the most arresting of his stories. In probing the psychology of his protagonist, Lao She makes it clear that Zhuang Yiya has taken up his hobby in large part to make his mark in the world. Mr. Zhuang is a government clerk and a teacher, but he will never excel in either occupation to the point where he will make a name and perhaps be remembered after he is gone. Nor does he have any children who might "raise his name to future generations." It is just possible, however, that his hobby, his collection, may assure him of some modicum of posthumous fame. Hence when the Japanese invade Jinan, capital of Shandong Province, and ask Mr. Zhuang to serve as director of education in the puppet government, he is faced with a desperate choice: if he agrees, he will be able to hang on to his collection, but if he refuses, the Japanese will confiscate it. What is he to do? Should he serve and be considered a traitor by his fellow countrymen or refuse and risk losing his precious collection—the only thing that gives his life any distinction? What would the average reader have done?

Written in an inimitable language, Lao She's remarkable stories reflect a unique period of Chinese history that is eminently worth remembering. Through his stories, Lao She shares with us, among other things, his views on human nature. He describes the cities of the period and the people who inhabited them in a prose noteworthy for its fluid Beijing flavor and distinguished throughout by humor, sympathy, and a bittersweet nostalgia for all that was passing.

William A. Lyell

Notes

1. The "Lao" in Lao She rhymes with the English word *how;* the "She" may be closely approximated by saying the English word *shun* and then dropping the *n.*

2. Some of the material in this section is taken from the introduction to William Lyell's translation of *Cat Country* (Columbus: Ohio State University Press, 1970); some from the *Lao She Modern Literature Library III* (Nanjing: Yilin Press, 1992); some from Gan Hailan, *Lao She nianpu* (A chronology of Lao She's life) (Beijing: Shumu wenxian Press, 1989); and some from papers presented at the First International Conference on Lao She held in Beijing in 1992. Other material is as noted.

3. "My Mother" by Lao She, translated by Carmen Li with D. E. Pollard in *Renditions* (autumn 1992): 63.

4. For a discussion of this novel and its significance, see C. T. Hsia, *A History of Modern Chinese Fiction 1917–1957* (New Haven: Yale University Press, 1961); for a more recent treatment see David Der-wei Wang, *Fictional Realism in Twentieth-Century China: Mao Dun, Lao She, Shen Congwen* (New York: Columbia University Press, 1992).

5. Shu Yi has done a great deal of research and publishing on his father, becoming in effect his semiofficial biographer. He is presently vice director of the Beijing Institute for Modern Chinese Literature. He visited the United States in 1994 and collected materials on his father's stay in this country between 1946 and 1949.

6. Shu Yi, "Father's Last Two Days," trans. Harriet Clompus, *Renditions* (autumn 1992): 112.

7. Ibid., 112.

8. As noted above, Lao She's family name was Shu, his given name, Qingchun. "Sheyu" is a "style" *(zi),* a name taken on reaching the age of twenty.

9. Ibid., 116.

10. The Gang of Four consisted of Jiang Qing (Mao's wife), Zhang Chunqiao, Yao Wenyuan, and Wang Hongwen. After the death of Mao Zedong on 9 September 1976, these four close associates of the chairman were taken as scapegoats, responsible for most of the

excesses of the Great Proletarian Cultural Revolution. Chairman Mao himself was never blamed. Those responsible for Lao She's death have not had to answer for their crimes.

11. Included in the appendix of this volume.

12. For an interesting, extended discussion of this story, see Leo Ou-fan Lee's "Lao She's 'Black Li and White Li'" in Theodore Huters, ed., *Reading the Modern Chinese Short Story* (Armonk, New York: M. E. Sharpe, Inc., 1990).

13. See "How I Wrote My Short Stories" in the appendix to this volume.

14. This is also true of Lao She's first novel, *The Philosophy of Lao Zhang* (Lao Zhang de zhexue).

15. See William A. Lyell, trans., *Cat Country* (Columbus: Ohio State University Press, 1970).

16. In his best-known novel, *Rickshaw* (Luotuo xiangzi), Lao She questions this point of view, though he never completely abandons it.

17. In 1903 Li Baojia wrote a satiric novel titled *A Brief History of Civilization* (Wenming xiaoshi), lampooning the modernization of traditional China.

18. There is a rather lengthy description of one such "civilized" wedding in Lao She's very first novel, *The Philosophy of Old Zhang* (Lao Zhang de zhexue).

19. See Lo Changpei, "Lao She yu wo" (Lao She and I) in *Zhongguo ren yu Zhongguo wen* (Chinese people and Chinese letters) (Hong Kong: Long Men Bookstore reprint, 1966).

20. *Lao Zhang de Zhexue* (The philosophy of Lao Zhang) in *Lao She Xiaoshuo Quanji* (Complete fictional works of Lao She), vol. 1 (Wuhan: Changjiang chubanshe, 1996).

21. Lao She, *Laoniu poche* (An old ox and a broken-down cart) (Hong Kong: Universe Bookstore, 1961), p. 43. Reprint of the 1937 edition first issued by the Human World Book Company (Renjian shuwu) in Shanghai.

Acknowledgments

William Lyell thanks his colleagues and students in the Department of Asian Languages and Literatures of Stanford University for all the questions they have answered and suggestions they have made over the years. He is particularly indebted to his cotranslator, Sarah Wei-ming Chen, for first suggesting the idea for this book. He is also grateful to the Center for East Asian Studies at Stanford for grants that facilitated the production of this collection.

Sarah Wei-ming Chen thanks her teacher and mentor William Lyell for not only supporting the idea for this book but also for sharing the work. Had he labored alone and not had to show her the ropes of translation, *Blades of Grass* would have been completed long ago. She dedicates this book to her mother, Hsiang-li Chu Chen, and to the memory of her father, Hsien-mo Chen (1924–1996).

Finally, we should both like to express our gratitude to Sharon Yamamoto of the University of Hawai'i Press for her encouragement and patience, and to Cheri Dunn for her creative and meticulous editing.

STANFORD UNIVERSITY
OCCIDENTAL COLLEGE
1998

A Note on the Translations

The stories in this collection were originally published in Chinese in the periodicals indicated below. With the sole exception of "Life Choices" (Shengmie), we have translated the stories from the books, as noted, in which the stories were later collected. "The Grand Opening" (Kaishi daji), *Maodun* 2, no. 2 (October 1933); translated from the text in Lao She, *Ganji* (Shanghai: Liangyou tushu yinshua gongsi, 1934). "An Old and Established Name" (Lao zihao), *Xin Wenxue* inaugural issue (April 1935); translated from the text in Lao She, *Gezao ji* (Shanghai: Kaiming shudian, 1936). "No Distance Too Far, No Sacrifice Too Great" (Buyuan qianli er lai), *Lunyu* 16 (May 1933); translated from the text in *Lao She youmo shiwen ji* (Hong Kong: Shiyong shuju, 1972). "Black Li and White Li" (Heibai li), *Wenxue jikan* inaugural issue (January 1934); translated from the text in Lao She, *Ganji* (Shanghai: Liangyou tushu yinshua gongsi, 1934). "Also a Triangle" (Yeshi sanjiao), *Wenyi yuekan* 5, no. 1 (January 1934); translated from the text in Lao She, *Ganji* (Shanghai: Liangyou tushu yinshua gonsi, 1934). "An Old Man's Romance" (Laonian de langman), *Wenxue* 4, no. 1 (January 1935); translated from the text in Lao She, *Yinghai ji* (Shanghai: Renjian shuwu, 1935). "Hot Dumplings" (Rebaozi), *Tianjin yishi bao* (January

1933); translated from the text in Lao She, *Ganji* (Shanghai: Liangyou tushu yinshua gongsi, 1934). "Life Choices" (Shengmie), *Wenxue* 3, no. 2 (August 1934); translated from the text in same. "Neighbors" (Linju men), *Shuixing* 2, no. 1 (April, 1935); translated from the text in Lao She, *Yinghai ji* (Shanghai: Renjian shuwu, 1935). "Crooktails" (Wai mao'er), *Wenyi yuekan* 4, no. 4; translated from the text in Lao She, *Ganji* (Shanghai: Liangyou tushu gongsi, 1934). "Ding" (Ding), *Qingdao Minbao* "Bishu luhua" 8 (September 1935); translated from the text in *Lao She xiaoshuo jiwaiji* (Beijing: Beijing chubanshe, 1982). "A Man Who Doesn't Lie" (Bushuohuang de ren), *Tianjin yishibao* (May 1936); translated from the text in *Lao She xiaoshuo jiwaiji* (Beijing: Beijing chubanshe, 1982). "Rabbit" (Tu), *Wenyi yuekan* 11, no. 1 (July 1937); translated from the text in Lao She, *Donghai bashan ji* (Shanghai: Xin feng chuban gongsi, 1946). "Attachment" (Lian), *Shi yu chao wenyi* inaugural issue (March 1943); translated from the text in Lao She, *Pinxue ji* (Chongqing: Wenjin chubanshe, 1944). "Autobiography of a Minor Character" (Xiao renwu zishu), *Fangzhou* 39 (January 1937); translated from the text in Hu Jieqing and Shu Ji, eds., *Wenniu–Lao She shenghuo zishu* (Hong Kong: Sanlian shudian, 1986). "How I Wrote My Stories" (Wo zenyang xie duanpian xiaoshuo), *Yuzhou feng,* no. 8 (January 1936); translated from *Lao She wenji,* vol. 15 (Beijing: Renmin wenxue chubanshe, 1990).